Unlikely Allies

C.C. KOEN

Unlikely Allies
Copyright © 2015 C.C. KOEN

Publisher: C.C. Koen
www.cckoen.com

Editing by:
Laurie Boris

Formatting by:
Christine Borgford, Perfectly Publishable

SPECIFIC GRAPHICS CREATED AND PROVIDED BY THE AUTHOR
Duck image attribution: Teguh Mujiono © 123RF.com
Box image attribution: provinc © 123RF.com
Tea cup image attribution: Ratchanee Chanhom © 123RF.com
Flower image attribution: 16185323 © Dreamzdesigner/Dreamstime.com

Cover Design by:
www.SelfPubBookCovers.com/Shardel

Dedications

To anyone who has been touched by the love of a child.
A child is an uncut diamond shaped by the hands of others.
~ Adapted from: Austin O'Malley ~

To my baby, you will always and forever
be my greatest accomplishment.
My soul's first embrace, cradled you with tender loving care.
My heart entwined to yours, enlivened from beat one.
My love transcends eternity, a guiding star
enlightening the darkness.
May your soul nurture.
May your heart treasure.
May your love inspire.

Mama's Rule #1:

Don't talk to strangers.

Rick strolled into the office and collapsed into the leather chair behind his desk. Piles of manila folders spread across the top, reminding him of all the work he still had to do tonight. He reached for a file, and a movement to the right of his shoulder caught his eye. A pudgy white mouse was propped on the computer keyboard a few feet away. He stared in disbelief as the rodent licked its furry arm and scrubbed its face. Where did it come from?

"Herbert, Herbert. Where are ya?"

The urgent request drew his attention to the hallway and then to his watch. Seven o'clock, no one should be here at this hour. On a Friday night, his employees always left at five.

"Herbert. Come here."

The muffled traffic noise of New York City twenty floors below didn't mask the demanding voice that got louder and closer to his doorway.

Before he could get up to investigate, a little girl with candy apple red hair shuffled into his office, peeking to the right and the left. "Herbert, ya in here?" she demanded, ducking down on her knees and searching under the sofa to the right of the entry.

Careful not to startle her, he stayed behind his desk and gently cleared his throat.

The little pixie's head popped up, and she rose from her knees, plopping a thumb in her mouth. She took a step toward his desk and then another and another, her brow pinching tighter with each move. Lips clasped around her finger, her words came out garbled. "Woo see Heverp?"

Surprised by the unexpected visitor, it took him a few seconds to recall her question and a couple more to figure out what she asked. When he did, his gaze darted to an empty computer keyboard. *Crap.*

Bent over and searching under the desk, he saw no sign of the runaway mouse. When he scooted his chair back to stand, he felt a poke on his shoulder. He turned and came face to face with dozens of freckles sprinkled across the bridge of the little girl's nose and cheeks and an overwhelming bubblegum-flavored aroma. Her huge, light green eyes stared at him.

"Woo okay?" She pulled her moist thumb out of her mouth and set it on his chin, resting her palm on his cheek.

When was the last time anyone asked him that?

"Ya look funny." She leaned forward, her knees resting against his shin, and patted him on the shoulder with her other hand. "Itta be okay." She soothed like a wise old woman, her upper gums glistening and revealing several missing teeth.

A scratch and tug along the hem of his pant leg drew his attention to the floor.

"Herbert, no," she scolded, scooping the mouse into her arms and petting the furball's back. The rodent returned the affection, rubbing its pointy nose along her cheek.

His employees brought their children to the annual company picnic, but he never thought twice about them. This child, though, intrigued him. What was she doing here? Where were her parents? About to ask her, all of a sudden a furry stomach was shoved into his nose.

2

"Ya can hold him."

He clasped the mouse's bottom and guided it downward, suspending the animal between them.

"He don't bite," she stated with utmost sincerity.

"Who are you?" he prompted as the impatient creature squirmed in his palm.

"Cecily Bryna Tyson," she announced as if she were the queen of England being presented to her constituents, back straightened and chin held high.

"Well . . ." He pressed his lips together, resisting a smirk, and offered a formal greeting in return. "It's nice to meet you. I'm Richard Maxwell Stone."

"What ya doin'?" Cecily scanned the room again, her eyes coming to rest on his computer, the Gateway Enterprises logo scrolling across the screen. "Ya got games on here?" She tucked Herbert into the front pocket of her sunflower-patterned dress and buttoned the flap enclosure. Shuffling around Rick, she wandered over to the large monitor behind him. Herbert's pink nose and arms poked out. She shoved the mouse's clutching paws back in. "Stay."

"Uh, is he going to get out?"

Cecily sighed. "Prob'ly. He don't like it in there." She punched several buttons on the keyboard. The monitor came to life, displaying an ocean desktop scene. She glanced at him. "Can I play?"

"Cece, Cece, where are you?"

They both turned toward the door.

An adult version of the pint-sized girl appeared in the doorway. This variation, though, had hair on the cherry side of auburn with twists of milk chocolate streaming through the strands. A messy ponytail slung high on top of her head, and thick, curly waves fell over her shoulder, instead of bright, reddish-orange pigtails like Cece's.

"Cece, come here." The woman's stern tone communicated there better not be any arguments. Cece marched across the

3

room. "My daughter shouldn't have run off. I'm sorry if she disturbed you."

A company logo and name written in gold script in a circular pattern above her left breast caught his attention: Westlake Security Services. His best friend, Matt, owned the firm adjacent to his office. She'd have to pass his suite to get there, yet he'd never seen her before. He inspected her uniform, a gray polo shirt and black slacks. An outfit he'd seen many times before, but it never looked that good on anyone else. The fabric, tucked in at her waist, had a cut that hugged her handful-sized breasts, and slim pants accentuated her curvy hips.

He lifted his gaze and found the woman ushering Cece out the door. "Wait."

Cece turned, beaming a huge smile at him. "I would a told ya bye." And just as fast, her little face morphed from happy to perturbed, aimed at her mother, and with her arms crossed, Cece shook her head.

Without missing a beat, and as smooth as his mother would have, the woman redirected Cece. "Say good night to Mr. . . . ."

"Stone, Rick Stone."

She set a hand on Cece's shoulder, nudging her and casting a do-what-your-mother-says stare. "I have to get back to work. Say goodbye to Mr. Stone."

"What's your name?" He couldn't let her get away that fast.

"Maggie."

"Margareta Cassidy Tyson," Cece shouted with emphasis, a pause between each distinction. "My mama works here." She pointed toward the hall. "She plays on a phone and 'puter. It got *lotsa* buttons." She shook her head, pigtails flinging back and forth over one shoulder then the other, followed by an overdrawn sigh. "She don't let me push 'em. Don't ya think I should get to push 'em? He let me push *his*." Cece looked up at her mother and shot her arm toward him, her shrugging shoulders communicating, "See, everybody can do

4

it. No big deal."

Rick chuckled and then stopped when Maggie spun around, hands set on her hips. He rubbed his palm along the back of his neck and shifted from one foot to the other as an uncomfortable silence engulfed the room. "Let me explain."

Mama's Rule #2:

Mind your Ps and Qs.

At that moment, Herbert leapt out of Cece's pocket and scurried toward his desk. Cece dove after the feisty rascal, crawling on her hands and knees.

He crouched down, his hands dangling from his bent legs and at the ready for the escapee. Cece caught Herbert by the scruff of his neck and came to a stop underneath his desk. She glanced up at him, shaking her head like an impatient mother. "He's bein' bad." She crawled closer and plopped the squirming ball of fluff on top of his hand. "Ya take him."

Before he could take hold, Cece's mother plucked the mouse away. Helping her up off the floor, he grabbed Cece's arm and pulled. As soon as she got to her feet, Cece extended her hand out to her mother.

Maggie held Herbert a foot above her daughter's reach. "I told you to leave him at home."

Cece's other hand slipped into his, her fingers warm and a little damp. Maggie's gaze dropped to their joined grasp. His did too. Cece's little fingertips peeked out between his thumb and forefinger. A light squeeze in his palm brought him out of his stupor. Cece looked at him and jerked her head toward her mother a few times, whispering to him, "Tell her, 'kay? I didn't do nothin' bad."

His shoulders stiffened as he faced Maggie, her pinched mouth and squinty eyes darting from Cece to him and back again multiple times. A look mothers perfected, causing even an adult male to cringe. He ran a billion-dollar mergers and acquisitions company, dealt with money-hungry investors, a demanding board of directors, his overbearing, power-crazy grandfather, and fifty quick-witted employees, yet one harsh stare from Maggie sent him in an unexplainable tailspin. No wonder Cece crossed one foot then the other back and forth while cowering into his side.

"Cece was looking for Herbert. He was on my keyboard, then he wasn't. After a while, we found him on the floor. She saw my computer and pushed a few buttons. That's what she was talking about." He spit out his explanation as quickly as possible under her scrutinizing glare.

Maggie's mouth fell open and shut several times. "I'm sorry. It won't happen again." She handed the mouse back to Cece. "Put him in your pocket. There's a box in my office we can put him in." She took hold of her daughter's arm and marched toward the exit.

"I'm hungry, Mama." Cece's growling stomach seemed to agree.

"I have some snacks in my bag, we'll get them when we get back to the office, okay?"

Cece spun around to him. "Ya like hot dogs?"

He smirked at her out of the blue question. "As a matter of fact I do."

"Ya wanna g—" Maggie's hand covered Cece's mouth, but the persistent wonder continued to speak, her garbled muffle asking, "eh smmm?"

The little dynamo tugged at her mother's arm and wasn't intimidated by him, yet staff who'd known him for years walked on eggshells even though he treated them well. In all the time he managed the business alongside his grandfather, replacing him after his retirement a couple years ago, none of his employees ever invited him anywhere, let alone to get something to eat.

Cece shoved Maggie's arm, knocking it away from her mouth.

"Yes," he replied before Cece could say anything else.

"No," Maggie countered. "We'll get out of your way now." She tugged on Cece's arm, but as soon as they crossed the threshold, Cece plopped down on her rear end, cementing herself to the floor.

"Mama, he says yeah." Cece twisted toward him, her lower lip extended.

Rounding the desk, he approached them, both on the opposite ends of a tug of war. Maggie pulled as Cece leaned her full body weight in the opposite direction, her back an inch above the carpet. "Maggie, it's no big deal. There's a hot dog stand at the end of the block."

In a swift maneuver executed better than any soldier in ground warfare, Cece rolled, leapfrogged, and dashed to his side again in less than two-point-five seconds. She grabbed his hand, shooting him a megawatt grin. He repeated the gesture.

Maggie threw her arms in the air, huffing out a huge breath. "I have work to do, Cece. There are plenty of snacks in my bag. That'll do for now. When it's time for my break, I'll take you to the hot dog shack."

"I know your boss, he wouldn't mind. Get your daughter what she wants."

Cece's stomach growled louder and right on cue.

"I can't leave the phones unanswered for too long. I was only supposed to take Cece to the bathroom and come right back." Maggie glanced at her watch. "We've been gone for more than fifteen minutes. I have to go. *Now.*"

"I'll get whatever she wants and bring it to you," he offered.

8

"I wanna go." Cece's green eyes pleaded with him.

"No." Maggie motioned to her daughter with a crook of her hand. "Mr. Stone is a busy man. Come on. Let me get back to work, and I'll see what I can do about getting you a hot dog."

Cece's gaze dropped to the floor, and she shuffled over to her mother. She peeked back at him and trudged out the door. The complete devastation on Cece's face made his chest hurt.

In a soft voice Maggie said, "Mr. Stone, Cece has to learn she can't have her way all the time. This is a business, and she knows I have a job to do. She had dinner, so the snacks would've been enough."

He raised his hands in surrender and nodded. Why was he getting involved in something that had nothing to do with him? He had tons of work to finish tonight, and he needed to focus on that—not them.

"You're right." He returned to his desk, flipping open a file and writing notes in the margins. What he jotted, he had no idea. He didn't even see the words on the page. The image of Maggie still standing in the doorway was stuck in his peripheral vision.

"Have a nice night, Mr. Stone."

He nodded, maybe grunted, and continued to scribble on the paper.

"Bye." Cece's disheartened farewell drifted from the hallway.

When he eventually looked up, a closed door locked him in—all alone.

Mama's Rule #3:

Always say please and thank you.

Rick waved to Paul, the evening security guard, and exited the office building. Another midnight departure. It wasn't that Rick noticed the time anymore; a fifteen-hour work day was common for him. Tonight though, he left with each task on his to-do list accomplished.

Dead tired, he focused on the parking garage across the street. At the walking signal, he jogged to the other side. Two huddled bodies in the bus stop enclosure captured his attention. "What are you doing?" He rushed toward them, stopping at the edge of the bench.

Maggie jolted and glowered at him. "You scared me half to death. I'm waiting for the bus."

Was she out of her mind? "It's not safe. You can't even defend yourself. Not with a sleeping girl in your arms."

Maggie rested her cheek on top of Cece's. "I don't have a choice."

"You could have caught a cab."

She tilted her chin up, shot him an agitated brow, and buried her face against Cece's. "It's far. It would've been too expensive."

"I'll drive you. Where do you live?"

"No," she whispered.

"It wasn't a choice, Maggie." He leaned down to scoop Cece into his arms, but Maggie put her hand up, stopping him.

"Don't." She stared, unrelenting, and her back scooted into the corner of the booth. Her tight, squared shoulders were on full alert. "How do I know *you* aren't some lunatic?"

He wanted to laugh, he really did, but her honest reaction shouldn't have surprised him. Used to getting his way, he hadn't thought twice or considered she'd protest the offer. His mouth pulled into a frown as he considered his intimidating stance towering over her. He backed up a few steps, raising his hands. Unwilling to relent, he scrolled through his cell, pressed a few buttons, and when he got an answer, he kept his focus on her. "I need you to vouch for me." His best friend's laughter on the other end ticked him off, but he wouldn't rest until he had his way. "Mention I'm a good guy." Then he eased closer to Maggie, his hand extended, urging her to accept a concession he wasn't used to making.

Her eyes flicked from him to the phone and back a few times. He wasn't sure if the blank look on her face meant she believed him or she'd scream for help. Several tense seconds later, she plucked the cell from his hands, her fingertips clipped to the top and nowhere near close to touching him. "Hello." Her quiet, reserved whisper revealed hesitancy, but her intense observation demonstrated she wouldn't surrender easily. "Maggie Tyson." After a brief pause she answered with a relieved and happy bounce in her voice, "Oh, Matt, hey." She listened and nodded, her lips curled into a quirky smile and disappeared before he could appreciate it. "Yeah. Uh, huh. Will do, bye."

After he tucked the phone in his suit pocket, his hand clenched it over and over, waiting for her to say something, anything. Tired of the long silence and her scrutinizing inspection of his eyes, nose, mouth, and grinding jaw, he rocked back and forth on his heels for the second time. "Well?"

Without any further hesitation, she stood and said, "Okay."

After all that, he got a simple yes? When he made his next move, scooping Cece into his arms, Maggie didn't resist. Groggy eyes fluttered open and a tiny smile graced Cece's lips as she cuddled her forehead into the crook of his neck and wrapped her arms around his shoulders.

Before Maggie could change her mind, he marched into the garage, pushing the up button at the elevator. Maggie came to his side, her eyes diverted to the tile floor.

"Where to?"

"Riverdale, Independence Street."

"Is that in the Bronx?"

"No, a little south of Yonkers."

They exited the elevator on the fourth floor. He shifted Cece in his arms and fumbled for the keys in his pocket. One click of the fob, and the lights and bleep of his Aston Martin greeted them. At the passenger side, Maggie placed a supportive hand on Cece's back and the other gripped his shoulder. "I can put her in."

"I got her."

Maggie surveyed him like he spoke another language.

He jutted his chin to the car. "Open the door and I'll set her in."

Maggie blinked and grabbed the handle, giving him the space he needed to buckle Cece in the backseat. He took off his suit jacket, folded and pillowed it under her head. "Do you think she'll be okay without a car seat?" The cozy bundle had her knees pulled up to her chest and a thumb in her mouth. Maggie's light touch on his arm redirected him away from her daughter.

"I'll sit with her."

He dashed over to the driver's side, started the car, and before he went anywhere, turned around to make sure they were both secure. Maggie placed a dainty kiss on Cece's temple, skimmed a thumb over her plump cheek, and set Herbert on her chest. The mouse snuggled under her chin, curled onto its side and closed its eyes. The sight lodged a lump in his throat and formed a vise around his chest. Even with a mouse nestled in her red hair, Cece looked precious, natural, as if the occurrence were the most ordinary thing in the world.

"All set?" he asked, his voice soft, careful not to startle any of them.

Maggie glanced his way. "Do you need directions?" She removed her sweater and laid it over Cece's shoulders.

"I'll figure it out or the GPS will. Without traffic it shouldn't take more than twenty-five minutes."

Maggie averted her eyes, directing them out the window.

He took that as his cue, typed in the street and town, and drove the car north toward Riverdale.

"You take the bus often?" He glanced at her in the rear-view mirror.

"My sister drives us in on her way to work, and Cece goes home with her. I take the bus after my night shift."

"What time is she done?"

"Five thirty."

"When does she start?"

"Nine."

He contemplated that awhile, his curiosity increasing. "Why do you have Cece with you? What do you both do all that time?"

"She goes to preschool downstairs."

When she didn't give him a complete answer he repeated the question. She hadn't bothered to look at him; instead her stare remained fixed out the window. Streetlights cast flickering shadows on her face, enhancing the mystery of his tight-lipped passenger.

"My sister had to go out of town." Another long pause. "I take classes."

What was with her? Usually women told him their life stories. Since he didn't typically spend more than one night with them, he didn't care about the details. But for some reason, he needed her to talk to him, tell him more. Whether it was the hint of secrecy that caught his interest, or the fact she didn't wear a ring, he didn't know. He couldn't explain his odd fascination.

"Which school do you go to?" He tapped his thumb on the steering wheel to the beat of the soft rock playing through the speakers.

She exhaled in a long, drawn-out way. "Culinary Institute."

He snapped his eyes back and forth from the road to the mirror, glancing at her several times and waiting for her to add a few more details. After an unnerving silence, he asked, "What's your specialty?"

"Ethnic cuisine."

His chuckle came out in a loud burst. She had to be the least talkative woman in the world.

"Is something funny about that?" Her clipped reply and flippant attitude challenged him and gave him a sick kind of satisfaction.

"No, not at all." His grin came slowly at first, then pulled up to his cheeks the longer she chomped on her lips. "Come on, you gotta give me more than that."

She smirked, but her eyes held steady on the passing scenery. "All kinds. I love studying different cultures, trying out recipes handed down through generations, learning about traditions, and experimenting with spices. All of it."

"So a fusion kind of thing?"

She snorted and pinned him with *the look* mothers used to warn kids to stop saying the wrong thing. "A *purist* kinda thing." Her statement came across demanding, similar to his in the boardroom during negotiations.

"Oh, that healthy, grassy, tasteless crap."

Maggie crossed her arms, more than fired up, pinning her sizzling green daggers on him. Man, she had all the signals down. And why did that turn him on so much?

"No, what I meant was, pure home cooking from a variety of countries. The kind people loved when they were growing up. There aren't restaurants that offer that. If you want ethnic you have to go to an Italian, Chinese, or Irish pub or whatever you're interested in, and even then they only serve their specialty. Someday I'll have a place where I can cook a variety of recipes from all over the world, not just one. There's nothing like that in the city or surrounding area."

She had a good point. He'd lived in Manhattan most of his adult life and worked in the heart of downtown for fifteen years. He'd never dined in a place like she described. Being a bachelor and working long hours, he didn't have time to cook. He ate out or ordered in a lot. Except on Sundays when he went to his mom's for dinner.

"When are you finished with school?"

"Not for a while yet. We've only been here a couple months."

Ah, so that's why he hadn't seen her before.

"You're not from around here then?"

"No," she whispered so low, he barely heard it over the music.

Should he ask? Oh, what the hell. "Where you from?"

Maggie didn't respond, and for some reason he didn't repeat the question. Was it him or was she purposefully being evasive?

"Get off at the next exit. At the stop sign turn right. We're a mile down on the left. Seven hundred four Independence."

The rest of the trip was silent except for the annoying GPS automated voice.

"There, the yellow Cape Cod with the white fence." Maggie's pointy finger came into his view, inches from his nose. He pulled into the driveway. After he shifted the car into park, Maggie opened the door, scooped Cece into her arms, and jumped out before he could remove his seat belt and help her.

Cece's hands dangled and bounced from Maggie's shoulders as she rushed down the sidewalk and toward the house.

He caught up with her, matching her stride. Every few steps, she would peek at him. "You have a key? I'll open the door." She shook the dangling ring looped around her finger and propped underneath Cece's leg. He tried to take them from her, but she clamped down on the swinging bundle.

"I got it." She catapulted up three steps onto a porch, thrust a key in the deadbolt, and eased the door open with a tap of her shoe. A lamp next to the entrance lit the living room, showcasing a well-loved home with toys on the floor, pictures on the wall, and comfy furniture. A stark contrast to the white, empty walls and stiff contemporary couches and chairs he had at his place.

He gripped the door to close it behind him. Maggie whirled around and grabbed the knob, jostling Cece, her other arm pinned beneath her daughter's bum. "Good night, Mr. Stone."

His chest melded to Cece's back, and her front pressed to Maggie's, connecting all of them in some way. Cece's hand slid from her mother's shoulder and rooted onto his forearm. Her half-lidded eyes looked up at him. "Thanks, Max." Her mumbled words came through crystal clear even though she said them while yawning. Her eyelids closed right after, but her position on his arm remained fixed.

His chest tightened along with his hold on the door. His eyes followed suit and clamped shut. From the time he'd been a little boy, his dad, Maximilian Connor Stone, preferred Rick's middle name, Max. No one else in the family called him that. Which made hearing it bittersweet. Thirteen years ago, a few months before his eighteenth birthday, his father had a massive heart attack. After hours in surgery and several days in ICU, he woke up long enough to tell him he loved him and made him promise to take his place in the family business. Not long after, he died.

Everything changed in that moment.

His hold loosened on the door, and he skimmed his finger down Cece's button nose.

"You have children, Mr. Stone?"

He snapped his eyes up to Maggie. "No." His response had been abrupt and gruff, a knee-jerk reaction. He couldn't imagine being a father. Ever. Maggie peered into his eyes as if she could figure out all his secrets and get him to tell the truth, challenging him, like his answer might have been a lie.

"Good night." He jogged down the steps and escaped to his car. With the door propped open, his sight gravitated to the jacket in the back seat. He collapsed behind the steering wheel, snatched the coat, and tossed it on the passenger side. An image of Cece and Herbert cuddled on it came to mind. The light from Maggie's house disappeared and left him in the darkness. He examined the white picket fence, trim lawn, flower boxes propped along the porch rail, and a wooden swing hung from the ceiling and swaying in the gentle breeze. The living room was exposed through wide-open drapes in the bay window. A faint glow from an unknown source cast a half-moon shadow along the powder-blue walls. A picture-perfect sight found on most covers of home and garden magazines.

A buzzing in the center console pulled him away from his exploration. "Stone." He didn't bother to read the number. At one in the morning, he knew who'd be calling. "Is that so? Put on the sheer black negligee. I'll be there in half an hour."

He snapped the phone shut and gunned the five hundred horsepower sports car, aiming it downtown. His new acquaintances were shoved out of his mind and a night of carnal activities replaced them. Exactly what he needed to shrug off melancholy memories: his dad, mom, him, a perfect family. Until it wasn't.

Focused and relentless he could relate to. Home and hearth—never.

Mama's Rule #4:

Don't swallow bubblegum, your stomach will explode.

Maggie flipped the palachinkis on the griddle and glanced over her shoulder. "What filling do you want?"

Her sister, Kat, asked for cottage cheese and sugar at the exact moment Cece yelled, "Jelly." Kat got both out of the refrigerator along with the fresh fruit Maggie had washed and put in a bowl before cooking their favorite breakfast. A recipe their mother, Irena, passed down, and they'd grown up eating. A family tradition she planned on including in her own restaurant someday.

Everyone had been seated at the table, and Maggie leaned across to get a crepe to put on Cece's plate, when a sugary sweet smell that had nothing to do with the food hit her. She glanced at Cece sitting next to her in a booster seat, chomping away at a mouthful of bubblegum. No matter how often she portioned out and restricted the treat, Cece always found a way to confiscate every stick in the pack and shove it in her little mouth. It didn't help that Kat kept a secret stash, dishing it out to her daughter regardless of the number of times she told her not to. The two of them would make her gray before her next birthday. Both pushed the limits and broke her rules on a daily basis.

By the time Maggie got a napkin and put it up to Cece's chin, the open-mouthed chewing had stopped. Cece sat up straight, her fingers clasped together in front of her, smiling wide and proud, as if she just saved her mama from the hazardous deed of discarding the sticky, messy clump.

Kat's giggle had her shooting a perturbed glare across the table, warning her sister to quit reinforcing and encouraging Cece's bad habits. Kat ignored her as usual, and focused on filling and rolling one crepe after another until she had four lined up along her plate, including three scoops of sliced strawberries and blueberries on top.

Ever since childhood, Kat could eat an enormous amount and not gain an ounce. No such luck for Maggie. After giving birth to Cece, her weight had been up and down, mostly up. It didn't help that she hadn't felt like exercising even though in high school she'd been on the volleyball team and remained active until pregnancy. Before she knew it, she'd gained fifty pounds. Instead of a size eight, she now wore a twelve, and at five foot six, her pear shape wasn't all that complimentary. Her gaze switched from Kat to her pride and joy, the pint-sized version of the rebel Kat had been growing up.

"Mama, all gone." Cece patted her stomach and an innocent good-angel smile appeared, displaying a gap from the missing top two front teeth.

"What did I tell you about eating gum?" she prompted while trading the napkin for a crepe filled with jelly and setting it on Cece's plate.

Instead of answering and before Maggie could cut the roll into pieces, Cece scooped it off the dish and shoved the entire thing in her mouth. Knowing her daughter, she prepared for the possibility, making several of them a little over bite-sized. Cece had an appetite that rivaled Kat's, and in no way did she take after Maggie, except in hair color and freckles. Cece's push-the-limits attitude mirrored her aunt's and unfortunately her father's too.

Maggie met Jake in high school. He'd been in and out of juvenile detention several times as a teenager, and growing up in Brady's Prairie, Texas with less than eight hundred people, many knew about his bad reputation. Even though they went to school together since kindergarten, she had nothing to do with him until her senior year, when she'd been assigned to tutor him as a condition of his probation.

It wasn't love at first sight or anything like that. In fact, Jake barely spoke to her during their after-school sessions. He'd grunt and stare her down with his arms crossed, resisting any effort she made to help him pass his classes. His indifference and willful attitude didn't change until her car broke down on her way to volleyball practice. When her Honda lost power, she pulled to the side of the road. Her dad, police officer Sean O'Brian, always worried about his daughters' welfare, and taught them the basics of car maintenance. He said his girls needed to be prepared and shouldn't have to depend on a man for simple things like checking fluid levels and air pressure or changing a tire. Even so she figured pretty quickly the problem was more than the basics when she tried to turn the ignition over multiple times, and the power flickered and died. In case something had come loose, she popped the hood to check the cable connections. At that moment, a tow truck swerved in front of her and out hopped Jake from the driver's side. He didn't acknowledge her at all. Instead, he jumped behind the wheel, tried to start it, and then after a check under the hood, hooked it up to the tow truck. All the while she stood on the curb and watched his every move in complete astonishment. The next thing she knew, he opened the passenger door of his truck and returned to his seat. When she didn't move, he honked the horn a few times, jolting her out of her trance.

After she got inside, the silence continued, and instead of taking her to the only garage in town, he swung by the school and dropped her off for practice. She got out and stood at the door. Jake had turned toward her and said, "It'll be ready tomorrow." She nodded, and after she closed the door, he took off. That was the totality of their interactions that day, and it also marked a time of change.

The next week during tutoring, Jake put forth a little more effort in completing the assignments. It wasn't a remarkable difference but a slight one that improved after a while. Their conversations also got better, beginning with her asking about his job as a mechanic and engaging him in "shop talk." If she learned a little about him, then it might help her reach him. She took her tutoring job seriously and hated seeing students struggle. Everyone had strengths, and it was a matter of finding out what they already knew, and using that knowledge to make connections to the content. The technique worked before, ever since she volunteered in the tutoring center in tenth grade.

"Mama, I want down." Cece's demand pulled Maggie back to the present. Kat had already finished eating and started clearing the table. At the sight of Cece's empty plate and the last remnants of breakfast, she felt awful for zoning out. She looked down at her own half-eaten meal and decided she couldn't stomach another bite.

"She ate five of them and all her fruit too," Kat remarked, nudging Maggie in the shoulder on her way to the sink. "You feeling okay?"

Unhooking Cece and helping her off the chair, she gathered the rest of the dishes as her eager daughter took off for the living room. She allowed her an hour of TV after breakfast on the weekends, and Cece took full advantage of every minute.

"I've got a lot on my mind." She tried to shrug off her sister's inquiry and inspecting stare by turning on the faucet and washing dishes.

"What's going on, Mags?" Kat set her hip against the

counter and picked up a towel to dry.

Maggie should have known Kat wouldn't drop the subject. Her private investigator mind never let up. Their father and Kat had the same tenacious attitude when working on cases and both earned reputations as rebels growing up. Other than that, the similarities between Maggie's sister and father ended. Kat's features were almost identical to their mother's: both five foot nine, slim with darker complexion and hair, a reflection of their mom's Greek and Russian heritage. If Kat didn't dye her hair a white-blond, it would be hard to tell them apart. The Irish side, red hair and freckles, which Maggie embodied, came from their dad. Genetics amazed her, how it mixed up characteristics and features among siblings, sprinkling a little here and there, compliments of each parent.

"Nothing. Give it a rest, will ya?" Maggie scrubbed the plate harder, even though she already removed all the stains.

"You didn't get another letter did you?" Kat prompted, and yanked the cleaned dish out of Maggie's hands.

The gushing water seemed interesting enough. Better than Kat's inquisition. Maggie dropped her chin into her chest and stared at the stream, avoiding Kat's penetrating eyes. Her sister could always tell when she was lying, a gift their dad used often.

Kat clamped down on the handle, shutting off the tap. "Mags, look at me."

Dang it. She faced her, knowing if she didn't, this conversation would never come to an end.

"He wrote you again?" Kat didn't wait for her to respond. "Let me see it."

Maggie sighed and picked up the next plate, her reflection marred by clumps of jelly and contorted by the daylight glinting off it. Their discussion would probably end up in an argument. She loved her sister and appreciated that Kat had taken them in, but she came to New York to escape the constant barrage of questions and curious stares in their hometown.

Hoping to start new, she'd moved halfway across the country to get away from the constant scrutiny. Since Maggie and Kat were only eleven months apart in age, they'd been inseparable growing up. When Kat left Texas, taking a job out of state a year ago, it crushed her. By that time, Maggie's divorce had been finalized, and she and Cece took over her and Kat's childhood bedroom. Her ex had been sentenced to three to six years in the county prison, and her life and emotions were a mess. She thought being with her mom and dad, her safety net, would provide some stability. Instead, even though her parents were supportive and never complained, something inside her felt unsettled and antsy. The fact her ex wouldn't stop tormenting her, which she refused to tell her parents about since they worried a lot already, made the environment more suffocating. If she complained to her dad and revealed what Jake kept doing, her ex would get angrier and end up in more trouble. She already felt guilty enough. Each day as the pressure increased, she thought if she went away, perhaps Jake's anger would fade. Unable to escape her sister's interrogations and in a weak moment, she told Kat about Jake's threatening letters and phone calls. Tired of the gossips and more than ready for an escape, she asked Kat several months ago if they could move in with her. Her sister welcomed them with open arms.

"I put it in a box with the others."

"So let me get this straight. Jake has his drughead brother mail you crap, and what, you just sit back and do nothing?"

"I don't want to make things worse."

"If you're talking about visitations then you have nothing to worry about. No judge in their right mind would let him within a foot of her. Besides, you have full custody. He can't touch her without going through you. Not that he would anyway."

"He's her father."

"He's a criminal. When are you gonna remove those

rose-colored glasses? This isn't high school. You're not his rescuer. He's a grown man that made his choices. Just because Daddy said over and over again meeting Mama was the best day of his life, and she saved him from going to juvie or worse, you've had this bleeding heart complex for lost causes. You always were a sucker for fairy tales, but Jake wasn't Daddy. He took bad boy to another level and reveled in it. He didn't want fixed. Nobody does. A person has to wanna change, he didn't."

Maggie tossed the plate in the sink; stoneware smashing against metal rang out like a bell at the start of a boxing match. "You don't think I know that. I'm the one that turned him in. I'm the one that testified against him. Those glasses you're talkin' about disappeared a long time ago. I'm not that altruistic girl anymore, and I can't stand you throwing it in my face."

Kat grabbed her shoulder and gave it a gentle squeeze. "I'm worried is all. He's not gonna be in jail forever. If you don't deal with him now, he could cause problems when he's out."

Maggie looked outside to the backyard. Kat had a point, but she wasn't sure what steps to take. She felt guilty for contributing to his incarceration in the first place. Their relationship had plenty of ups and downs, but he was still Cece's father. He just never fit into the role of dad. Married when they were twenty, she figured the first year had been routine: wake up, go to work, and on occasion they'd eat together. If they were both home at the same time, she'd read or do chores, and he'd offer to run errands or would mention that his brother or buddies invited him out. Not wanting to squash his independence or be too clingy, she didn't complain and often went to bed alone. Way after midnight, Jake would stumble in and collapse onto the mattress, waking her up with the scent of alcohol and smoke. Six months later when she'd told him she was pregnant, he became distant, more so the closer the due date came. No matter how hard she tried to be a good wife and get him involved with Cece, her efforts didn't work. Then, when her daughter was a year old, their world crashed down around them.

The local newspapers and television broadcasts had been running reports for months about a string of armed robberies. Since she grew up listening to a police scanner and watching the nightly news, she'd always been vigilant even though their tiny town didn't have a lot of crime. When she saw the video showing the thief on TV, wearing a black hoodie, skull mask, and green gloves, she hadn't given it much thought. While cleaning out the garage, she found duffle bags with money and a gun inside tucked behind a bunch of boxes. In a backpack nearby, she came across similar clothing described in the robberies. Instead of confronting Jake about it, she'd gone to her dad with her suspicions. Not long after, Jake was arrested. If she hadn't done that, perhaps none of this would have happened, and Jake wouldn't be lashing out.

"Mama, I want juice," Cece yelled from the adjacent room.

Maggie went over to the fridge, filled a sippy cup with organic white grape, Cece's favorite, and took it to her. "Half an hour, no more. After I'm done in the kitchen, we'll get ready and go to the zoo. Okay, sweetie?" She brushed Cece's bangs to the side and out of her eyes. She needed to give her a haircut soon.

"'Kay, Mama." Cece had already forgotten about her when Barney sang another song. Ugh, his voice grated on her nerves. The tunes lodged in her brain, replaying an insane number of times during the day and sometimes in her dreams too. Directors no doubt planned it that way, making kids' shows as annoying as possible to drive parents all over the world crazy.

As soon as she got back in the kitchen, Kat started. "What are you gonna do? And don't think I've forgotten. I wanna see the letter."

Maggie nodded while grabbing the griddle off the stove. "Let me get the rest of this cleaned up. I'll get it for you before

Cece and I leave. Just be careful. Don't say anything in front of her."

"Give me more credit than that. I'd never do anything to hurt my little bucket head."

For the first time all morning Maggie had something to laugh about. Leave it to Kat to know exactly what to say to lighten the mood. "Would you stop calling her that? The poor girl is gonna grow up with a complex."

Kat snapped a towel against Maggie's leg, giggling along with her. "I can't help it. With all those rules you have, you think you would've taught your daughter to not walk around with that damn yellow bucket on her head."

Maggie tried to punch Kat in the shoulder, but her Flash Gordon reflexes had her flying around the table and over to the refrigerator before she could get a good shot at her. "Hey, look whose talkin,' glue girl. It's a wonder you grew up with an active brain cell after all the paste and Elmer's you ate growing up."

"I'll have you know I had the highest score at the police academy, so stuff it, Magoopie."

"Oh my god, are you really pulling out that lame nickname after all these years."

The slow-paced saunter and roll of Kat's shoulders should have been Maggie's warning, but the lighter turn in the conversation had set her at ease, which gave her sister an opening for a sneak attack. Quicker than an arrow flying at a target, Kat wrapped an arm around Maggie's neck, attempting to give her a noogie. She countered by snatching Kat's wrist and struggled to hold it above her head. "You couldn't stop watching that stupid cartoon." As Kat mocked her, she got Maggie in a chokehold, gaining the advantage by threatening to cut off her air supply.

Maggie shot an elbow into her sister's ribs. Kat's hips jerked back and instead of surrendering, Kat yanked, tightening the grip even more. Wrestling like they'd done most of their life, Maggie grabbed as much skin as she could on the backs of Kat's thighs, twisting and pinching. A huge intake of air filled Maggie's lungs when Kat loosened the hold enough to give her a second wind. "If anything *you* were Mr. Magoo, and I was Cholly. He was the straight-laced sidekick, and just like me, pulled along into his counterpart's shenanigans. Cholly was the sane one, keeping Mr. Magoo out of peril."

"Did you seriously just spout off a lecture sounding like a 1950s housewife?"

Maggie head-butted Kat in the shoulder. "You're a pain in my ass, you know that?"

"Mama, ass a bad word," Cece shouted, leapfrogging up to them, her sippy cup swinging around her thumb. "More, please."

Kat swooped her niece into her arms, both laughing all the way to the fridge and back out to the living room.

Now *she* felt like the biggest ass, chastised by a four-year-old. Not like it was the first time. Cece loved pointing out her mama's faults whether they were or not. Put Kat and Cece in a room and the likelihood that a major flub up would occur increased by a hundredfold.

Yep, she'd be gray by the time she turned twenty-seven in a couple months, no doubt about it.

Mama's Rule #5:

Be careful what you wish for, you might just get it.

The honking horn could wake the dead and all of Riverdale for as long as Kat laid on it. Jeez, they weren't running that late. Maggie zipped Cece's jacket, set the backpack on her shoulders, and grabbed her hand. Her daughter liked being a big girl and wanted to carry the bag herself. "Let's go, your aunt's being impatient this morning."

Cece nodded and yanked her toward the door, all of a sudden in a rush, even though she was the reason they were behind schedule. It had been a Monday morning from hell. Maggie's alarm hadn't gone off, at least she didn't think so. Then Cece decided she didn't care for the two outfits placed on her dresser despite the fact they were her top choices the night before. To give her some independence, it was their ritual to pick out clothes after her bath and before a bedtime story. This saved a lot of time and arguing in the morning. Instead, Cece yelled something about it being yellow day, and tore through the closet, throwing anything and everything onto the floor, whether it was that color or not.

Thank goodness on Sundays Maggie prepared egg-and-cheese sandwiches, quiche, or some other breakfast item they could heat up in the microwave to eat on their drive into the city and made their lunches each evening before going to sleep. The routines helped them get out the door much faster.

After snapping Cece into the booster, no sooner had Maggie gotten in the passenger seat than Kat shifted into reverse and peeled out of the driveway. "It's about time. What the hell took so long?"

"Hey, what did I tell you? Don't swear in front of her." Maggie tilted her head toward Cece, whose brain catalogued everything.

"She can't even hear me over the insane kiddie tunes."

"God, Kat, she only listens to it on the way in. Other than that it's your choice. In fact, I remember it being *your* rule, sister dear," she said sweetly, turning the volume a tad louder for the hundred-song CD to annoy her even more.

"Ha, I have no rules. Don't be blamin' me," Kat countered.

"Mama, we gonna see Max?"

Kat's gaze darted to the passenger seat, held for several seconds, much longer than she should have since she was driving, and then back onto the road. Long enough, though, for her squinty eyes to lodge twenty questions without speaking a word.

"He in your class?" Kat turned down the music, her inquisitive brain on overdrive.

"No." Cece stretched out her response like her aunt wasn't very bright for asking such a simple question.

"Max, my new friend . . . and Mama's." Cece pointed to her. "Can we get a hot dog with him, Mama?"

Maggie cringed. Three, two, one . . .

"Who the hell—heck is Max?" Kat looked at Maggie and then up to the rearview mirror. When they were little, she hadn't minded Kat's protective nature. Now though, she didn't appreciate the hassle.

"Nobody." To avoid her sister's scrutinizing glances, she

turned toward the passenger window and read the useless bill-boards lining the highway.

"He lemme push his buttons," Cece shouted, kicking both of their seats.

Maggie inhaled, holding in a groan along with her frustration, anticipating an extensive and excruciating trip. For as long as she could remember, her control-freak sister wanted to become a private investigator. The independence suited Kat's don't-tell-me-what-to-do persona. At the first opportunity, her sister accepted an investigator position at Westlake Security, the leading personal, commercial, and entertainment protection agency in the nation. Detecting a story and sniffing out the clues were Kat's priority, and the "Max" subject wouldn't be dropped soon. Since intel came easier from a four-year-old, Kat tilted her chin up and spoke to the rearview mirror. "What buttons?"

"On his 'puter."

A punch at the top of her arm shoved Maggie into the conversation. She shifted in her seat and rubbed the aching spot. Nowhere else to go, she bit her tongue and wished they didn't have thirty minutes left in the commute. Since Kat nor Cece would let up, she figured it would be better if she got the interrogation over with.

"He works in the office next to ours."

"Huh, I have Gateway's account and do the background checks before they hire. I don't remember a Max though. He might've worked there before I got the job."

Maggie stared at her hands twisting in her lap and recalled the engraved CEO title. Mr. Stone embodied the role well. A T-shirt and jeans more her style, a man in a suit hadn't appealed to her before. Yet, when she'd entered his office, she couldn't miss him. A wall of windows with a mirrored sheen reproduced and reflected his powerful persona. A cherry wood desk provided a dividing line between the haves and have-nots. At the helm, Mr. Stone's wealth and no-nonsense demeanor exuded a halt-right-there scent, bringing her to a stop at the entrance and barring her from his elite domain.

Determined to retrieve her wandering daughter who'd cozied up to a complete stranger, she held firm and prepared for any challenge. His scrutinizing examination of her clothing wasn't missed. If she didn't have the Westlake Security emblem showing, he probably would've called them to have her removed from his office. Since her boss managed video surveillance for the entire building, she comforted in the fact Matt would have gotten a chuckle out of the comical request.

As Mr. Stone gave her the once over, she'd done the same. His crisp, white dress shirt had one sleeve rolled up to his elbow, which accentuated and exposed his prickly arm hair, and the other had come unrolled and settled an inch above his wrist, reducing him a notch from her standpoint. Disheveled dark brown hair, as if he'd been stewing over something and fisted the short strands multiple times, gave him a sloppy, casual appearance. His frustrated sexiness called out *rescue me* and appealed to her sympathetic heart.

"He nice, huh, Mama? He likes Herbert. He holded my hand. We rided in his car. Don't ya think he nice, Mama?"

Ugh. She squeezed her eyes shut and rubbed her knotted up neck. This day wasn't getting any better. A headache would make the trying morning complete. At the zoo and all weekend long, Cece asked questions about Max, the same ones over and over again. Kat had been in and out Saturday and Sunday and must not have heard Cece talking about him. Otherwise this discussion would've happened a lot earlier. Now she'd have to confront this head on, otherwise the inquisitions would just get worse.

"What the h—"

"Don't." Kat needed her potty mouth sewn shut. Maggie constantly reminded her not to cuss. It didn't help that they worked with a bunch of foul-mouthed men at the security firm. For the most part, she tuned out their raunchy discussions, but Kat fired them up and kept them going. At worst their banter bordered on sexual harassment, at best, off-color political jokes that had the majority of them laughing their butts off.

Matt had assigned her to a private workspace away from distractions and other employees. Her data-entry job involved inputting confidential and time-sensitive information into the computer system and answering service requests. On the opposite side of the office, a centralized space housed forty or so investigators and a handful of call center employees. Most of the agents were bodyguards, conducted field research, or inspected off-site locations. In her exclusive spot, she didn't see Kat or the others too often and didn't get involved with the rowdy crowd.

"That's not his name." Before Maggie could say anything else, Cece cut her off.

"Uh ah. Is too," Cece insisted, crossing her arms and aiming her squinted eyes at her mother, convinced she told her aunt the truth and nothing but the truth.

Maggie shoved her fingers through her hair and raked her nails along her scalp, blowing out a sigh of frustration. "His name's Rick." She got that far before getting interrupted again.

"Stone? Is that who you're talkin' about? When the H-E-double hockey sticks did you meet him? And why am I just findin' out about it? I heard he's smokin' hot, Mags. The ladies at Westlake gush over him, but I haven't had the pleasure. Matt raves about him too. Best bros, nobody better, and all that man-crush crap."

Drowning out her sister, Maggie turned the music up and glanced over her shoulder. Cece had already lost interest and had a library book propped in her lap. That girl loved to read and had a head start for a kid her age, recognizing basic sight words and sounding out a lot of the others she didn't know. Thank goodness, her daughter got at least one positive trait from her mother. Early on, she bought a collection of nursery rhymes, fairy tales, and other classics they enjoyed at bedtime.

"Your niece didn't listen when I told her to wait outside the bathroom stall. She ended up in his office looking for Herbert, the escape artist, who tagged along against my wishes. Go figure."

Kat flashed a grin in the mirror at her rebellious niece in training. "How'd you end up in his car?"

She picked at some nonexistent lint on her pant leg. Kat wasn't falling for her diversion technique and grabbed her flicking hand.

"Mags."

A Virginia tag with MOVEOVR became fascinating reading material as she formed an explanation. "He insisted on taking us home when he saw us at the bus stop. Even called Matt and had him tell me not to worry."

"Um hmm."

The telltale undertone ticked Maggie off. She twisted around in her seat, hot under the collar and primed for a confrontation. "What's that supposed to mean?"

Kat shrugged, picking up on the beat of the bumble bee tune, buzzing in the correct spot right along with Cece.

"Sing, Mama, sing," Cece shouted, feet pounding against the seats in rhythm with the thumping bass.

Hard to resist her daughter's cheerful request, she took the easy out. "Buzz. Buzz. Buzz."

They entered the lobby with fifteen minutes to spare, the only good thing about the morning so far. Kat planted a big smooch on Cece's cheek and broke off from them, waving on her way to the elevators.

Maggie yanked open the door to the preschool and almost

slammed face first into the center director. Cece ran for her classroom, throwing off her backpack and coat as Maggie signed her in.

"Miss Tyson, do you have a few minutes? I'd like to talk to you about Cece."

Maggie groaned, expecting unpleasant news. The first week after she enrolled Cece, the director, Miss Sally, cornered her when she came in to have lunch. Cece somehow snuck out of the house with a pack of gum, and instead of throwing it away when caught, she hid it. At some point she stuffed the pieces in her mouth and stuck the messy goo on tables, chairs, and shelves rather than her typical swallowing it. The second week, she brought Herbert in without permission, scaring teachers and kids when the rodent scrambled around the classroom. And on and on it went, one thing after another. Even with privileges revoked, as much as Maggie could take away from a four-year-old, Cece continued to break the rules. She really wasn't a bad kid, just didn't adjust well to change sometimes. The move, even though Cece got to see her aunt more, hadn't gone as smoothly as Maggie hoped. Three months in their new home, routines established and less frequent "bad" reports, she thought Cece had adjusted much better than those first few weeks. It wasn't unusual for adults to need time to ease into life changes too, so she hadn't been all that upset about the incidents and handled them in stride like she normally did.

"Sure." What else could she say?

"Let's go to my office."

Maggie nodded and followed the director across the hall. After they were seated, door closed, which also hadn't been a good sign, Miss Sally wasted no time.

"We have a new girl starting tomorrow."

Okay, that was a strange beginning. Maggie sat on the edge of her seat, waiting for the ball to drop.

"I'd like Cece to be assigned as her buddy. All the new

kids get one for a few weeks, to help with their transition."

Yeah, Sean, a cute blond boy, had taken an immediate shine to Cece. She still spoke about him even though they weren't partnered anymore.

"All right." Her response dragged out, waiting for a punch line or some other addendum. After the bumpy start, she didn't think the director liked either one of them, let alone trusted her daughter to be anyone's role model.

"There's something else you should know."

Yep, she knew there had to be bad news coming.

"The little girl is deaf."

Maggie sat up straighter, this time surprised for a different reason. "Uh . . . are you sure?"

"Well, of course I am. I met with her mother and we discussed her needs at length. I don't talk about the children with other parents, but when I told Robin's mom she'd be given a buddy, she gave me the okay to share these details with you."

"No. What I meant was, are you sure you want Cece?"

Miss Sally giggled and sat down in the chair next to Maggie. "You have a special little girl. I'm sure I don't have to tell you that." Her smile widened, and it didn't look disingenuous. "She's one of the brightest, friendliest children in the class. She'd be a great buddy. You should see her take charge and direct everyone around the room, reminding the other kids of the rules when they step out of line."

The wooden frame of the chair rammed into Maggie's spine when she fell against it. "You're kidding me, right?"

Miss Sally tilted her head, humored delight pinching her brow. "Why are you surprised?"

"Uh, you do remember she didn't get off to a great start. I'd think you'd want someone else."

"Oh, that. Goodness, that was months ago and not the worst that's happened. She's been trying her best ever since, and she loves helping people. In fact, I think you may have a future teacher on your hands."

35

Maggie's mouth fell open and shut and open again. After a few seconds, she blurted, "She doesn't follow my rules."

"A lot of kids don't. You shouldn't be concerned, that's normal. She will eventually. When they're young they try things out. The structure and limits in school, peer pressure, and a lot of other things help them conform. When they go home, kids like to let their hair down, so to speak. Don't we all need that, even as adults?"

Hmm, when she put it that way, it made sense, sort of.

"We have a specialist coming in to help the kids and teachers learn sign language. They'll be spending extra time with Robin and Cece if you don't mind."

"Sure, whatever you think will help. Is there anything I can do?"

"Since you come in sometimes for lunch, you might have the girls show you the signs. You could practice with Cece. All kids are welcome here, and I want Robin to feel accepted. Cece will be a good friend to her. Besides, the other children already follow her lead."

Jeez, she never could have predicted this morning would've turned out so positive. Well, at least she now had confirmation her daughter recognized limits and could follow rules. She'd just have to be patient and celebrate the moments when she did at home too. Use praise, lots and lots of praise, and maybe stickers. Cece loved them.

"We good?" Miss Sally got up and opened the door.

"Yep. Excellent, in fact. You just made my day."

Miss Sally's understanding and warm smile made her feel better about her parenting skills. See, rules weren't so bad after all. She returned a glorious grin, feeling it all the way to her ears.

As soon as she entered the lobby, she pumped a fist at her side. "Yes." The curious stares of the passersby at the security and information desk didn't bother her one bit. Nope. Not this time. Satisfied in her abilities as a single parent, she couldn't wait to rub the good news in Kat's face over and over again. As much as she loved one-upping her sister, she delighted in being right even more.

Mama's Rule #6:

If you can't say something nice, don't say anything at all.

Between classes at the Culinary Institute and cooking the early and late curriculum lunches at Le Gourmet as a portion of her grade, by the time Maggie arrived at Westlake for the night shift, her feet were throbbing. She couldn't wait to collapse in the ergonomic leather chair Matt had purchased for her. When the elevator opened on the twentieth floor, she attempted to take a step into the foyer, but Cece darted past her. "Stop." She reached out to snag her backpack and missed it by an inch. Cece kicked into warp speed and dashed through the double-wide glass doors of Gateway Enterprises. As she ran after her and into an open workspace with clusters of desks grouped together, employees' heads turned and tracked them as they ran past, around the corner, and down the hallway.

At Mr. Stone's closed door, Cece came to an abrupt stop, giving her a chance to catch up. God, she felt old. Since when could a four-year-old beat her in a foot race? Pitiful. Cece dropped her backpack, lifted her hand to knock, and Maggie caught it just in time. "No."

"Mama, I wanna see Max." Cece's lower lip jutted out. "I

got somefin for him."

"Can I help you?" A woman with gray hair and glasses approached them. Dressed in a pale yellow silk skirt and blouse, the professional outfit matched the surroundings, but her simple, courteous greeting came across as warm and welcoming in this intimidating environment. The lady crouched down to Cece's height and said, "Hi, what's your name, sweetie?"

"Ya know Max?" Cece's bold persistence continued to shine. "I gotta give him somefin."

"Max, hmm, well, I do. He's in a meeting right now. If you tell me your name I can let him know you stopped by."

About to redirect her daughter, Maggie reached out, but Cece spun around, threw a hand over Maggie's arm, and pounded on the door. "Max, Max."

Maggie yanked Cece's fist away and addressed the woman. "I'm so sorry."

"It's okay. I'm his secretary, Mrs. Collins." She offered her hand in greeting along with an amused smile.

The gesture returned, Maggie introduced herself and Cece, and apologized again for her daughter's behavior.

"Don't worry about it. He's not even in there. He's in the conference room." Mrs. Collins pointed to a door across the hall. Just then, two men in suits appeared in the opening.

"Max." Cece ran over to him and another man, staring at both of the giants. "I got ya somefin."

Mr. Stone's eyebrows rose and the other man chuckled, elbowing him in the arm. "You going to introduce us?" Mr. Stone's mouth opened, but nothing came out. The other guy stuck his hand out and said, "Hey, who are you, little lady?"

Again, Cece ignored the introduction and took Mr. Stone's hand, dragging him over to where she and Mrs. Collins stood. He stumbled forward, his gate at odds with Cece's tiny steps. She unzipped her backpack and pulled out a piece of yellow construction paper. "See. I made it for ya."

All of the adults were huddled around looking at the duck-shaped cut-out, green strips like grass affixed to its mouth. *Cecily* written in crooked and jagged letters across the stomach and *Max* too. In between, what could be mistaken as a plus sign or just one of Cece's scribbled letters. "I drawled it." Cece shoved the image toward Mr. Stone, almost punching him in the stomach.

Maggie grabbed Cece's shoulder and tugged, trying to get her to take a few steps back. The muscles under Maggie's hand stiffened as Cece's body became a statue and remained front and center, toe to toe with Mr. Stone. "Ya like it?"

He brushed a fingertip over his name and cleared his throat. "Yes." But it was so low, had Maggie been a foot away, she wouldn't have heard. His stare shifted from Cece and the picture to her and held there a while. His expression blank, lips set in a straight line, and not a flicker in his pinpoint, hazel eyes.

Maggie got lost in his penetrating gaze. Ringing phones in the background, murmurs of people talking, and the clacking of fingers on keyboards faded away. A strange bodily reaction took over: chills, heat, chills, heat. If she didn't know better, she'd think menopause had set in. Since that wasn't likely, she figured someone must have been messing with the temperature in the room, because changes like that weren't common for her.

"Maggie, your sister's looking for you," Matt called out,

Cece already in his arms and chatting his ear off. Her daughter adored him. A family man with three young girls, Matt doted on her from the time they met, giving her the undivided attention she craved.

A few days after moving here, Kat drove her and Cece into downtown to show off where she worked. Not long after introductions, Matt had offered her a job. She'd already been accepted at the institute, a unique chance to learn from the top chefs in the city. When she relayed that to Matt, he suggested the night shift, and it had become the perfect solution. Kat's rave reviews about her computer skills didn't hurt either. She didn't mind since she wasn't in any position to turn down work. The fact he paid five dollars more an hour than her grandparents did to cook at their Greek restaurant helped too. So far she enjoyed working for him and getting to know the ins and outs of the security industry.

Mrs. Collins handed Cece's backpack to Maggie, bumping her arm and pulling her thoughts away from her boss. "It was nice meeting you."

"Thank you, you too." Maggie returned the gracious smile Mrs. Collins offered.

After picking up a purse from her desk, Mrs. Collins said good night. The executive who'd greeted Cece excused himself from the group, mentioning he'd call Rick in a few days. Matt snuck off with Cece, heading toward his office. Maggie glanced at the duck still clasped in Mr. Stone's hand. "I can take that and put it in my purse. I'll hide it when I get home if you don't want it."

He waved the cut-out in her face. "You heard her. She made it for *me*. You're not getting it."

"I just—"

He stormed into his office. As she watched his departing back, the CEO nameplate and wood panel shut in her face. That hadn't gone well. She raised her hand to knock but withdrew it. Nope, she didn't need to explain herself.

Throwing the backpack over her shoulder, she swiped a hand through a stray hair that had fallen in her eyes and went to work.

It didn't matter. He was nobody. He didn't mean a thing to her.

Mama's Rule #7:

Look at me when I'm talking to you.

Rick reorganized the files on the conference table and stacked them to give to his secretary. A door slammed behind him.

"What the hell kind of show are you running around here?"

He didn't even have to turn around. Same tune different day. It didn't matter that the board of directors and investors lived happily off his back or that profit margins surpassed a hundred percent. None of it amounted to enough for the crotchety pain in his ass.

"You gonna continue to ignore me, boy?"

With his hands fisted on the table, he drew in a ragged breath and faced his nemesis.

"Grandfather."

"Why is it that every time I walk in this place, it's like a damn circus around here? And this . . ." He waved the papers in his clenched palm. "The latest profit reports. You need to do better."

The veins in Rick's neck throbbed, and he imagined the blood pressure coursing through them, screaming for a release. His grandfather, Horatio Stone, mentored Rick to assume the CEO role while he worked on his business and law degrees. It didn't matter how prepared Rick had become, Grandfather talked to him like he was a two-bit hoodlum. Dad and Gramps were not only business partners but shared the same philosophy: family came first. But when Dad passed away, Gramps changed, focusing every bit of his energy on his son's company and driving his grandson mad. On a daily basis Grandfather called or came by to batter him about his progress, scrutinize the bottom line, and ride him about making the business a success. The power-hungry mogul escalated the stress already associated with the high-performance risks he dealt with when companies merged or bought each other out. If it weren't for the vow he'd made to his dad, he would've taken his business and law degrees and hightailed it out of here a long time ago, getting as far away from Grandfather as he could. He wouldn't though. When he made a promise, he kept it.

"I'll look at them after my next meeting." He stacked the folders and strutted toward the door. As he took a step past his grandfather, the obstinate man clamped down on his shoulder, halting his escape.

"I'm not done with you yet."

Rick's nostrils flared, and he yanked his arm away, shooting a glare that didn't hide his animosity. "I'll go over them and be in touch." He turned his back on Grandfather and strolled out of the room.

"Dinner at Presidio, seven o'clock. Don't be late," his grandfather shouted.

His briefcase in hand, Rick exited the building for a long afternoon of off-site meetings.

"Julia, nice to see you." Rick bent down and brushed his lips against her cheek, taking the seat next to her. "Grandfather."

Rick acknowledged him with a nod.

"Your granddaddy, the sweet man he is, invited me to join you both this evening. I was just telling him I hadn't heard from you in a while. I hoped to see you at the Crystal Ball last weekend, but you weren't there." She swept her thumb along the top of his hand and squeezed it. "It's been too long, Rick. I've missed you." Her purring, seductive tone relayed the underlying message loud and clear.

His grandfather cleared his throat, and Julia fluttered her eyelashes at Horatio. "Mr. Stone, you must get Rick to take some time off. I'd love to have him go sailing on my daddy's yacht for a few weeks. We could venture down to the Caribbean just the two of us. Doesn't that sound fabulous?"

"Funny you should mention that. Grandfather was in the office today reminding me I don't work hard enough. So the answer is no. I won't have time to accompany you."

Her pout couldn't have been more disingenuous. Her plump, ruby-coated lips might delight some men, but Rick refused to encourage her. She got plenty of that from Grandfather, who'd selected her as a prime candidate and beat his ear to marry her. Another thing to dog him about, adding to the never-ending list of dos and don'ts. Sometimes though, he had no choice in spending time with her. Like tonight.

The waiter interrupted, brought drinks and took orders. Endless chatter from Julia about charity events droned on for hours. When they left the restaurant, and Rick said good night to her, it had passed ten o'clock.

"Rick." His grandfather stood with him at the valet, waiting for their vehicles. "You need to put a ring on her finger, boy."

Rick shuffled the coins in his pocket and didn't bother to respond.

"Hard-headed fool you are," Grandfather grumbled. "Someone is going to snatch her up." The old man stared at him square in the eye. "You listenin' to me?"

The fists at Rick's side clamped open and closed, and his grinding teeth kept him from saying what he really wanted to. The persistent man refused to let up or stay the hell out of his life. Rick turned thirty-one last month, yet Grandfather treated him like an eighteen-year-old still learning the ropes of business and life. Out of respect for his dad, he put up with his inane rants and battering.

"I'm not getting married. Not now, not ever. So get that through your thick head."

"Her daddy wants it. I want it, and you'll do as I say. The merger of their company with ours will take it beyond any in the world. The board and investors want the union. It's best for both sides."

"I told you before, the merger is one thing. Julia is another and isn't happening."

"You don't know what the hell you're doing. You'll destroy the business and your future, all to be a stubborn jackass."

The valet whipped Rick's car into the lot and slammed on the brakes. After setting a tip in the young man's hand, Rick leaned an arm on the hood and eyeballed his grandfather. "The business is mine and has been for some time. I haven't sunk it yet. As for the board, we're looking at all options, and decisions will be made in the best interest of the entire company. Not for one person, but for everyone. The employees are the reason it's a success. I'm not making snap judgments just because you think it'll be good for you."

Grandfather stood at the other side of the car, his arms stretched across the top, hands clasped together. "I have a huge investment and stake in it. It's my money too."

"You don't have controlling interest. Dad put me in charge for good reason, and I do it for him. It's his legacy, and I'll be sure we stay on top. I won't have you interfering in that."

"Did you look at the reports?"

Rick sat in the driver's seat and slammed the door shut. At

the click of a button, he opened the passenger side window, and his grandfather ducked his head inside.

"The margins are damn good. You need me to explain the percentages to you? Let me know. Otherwise, I'll see you at the next board meeting. Good night, Grandfather." With two fingers at his temple, he saluted him and peeled out of the parking lot.

Some people eat when they're stressed, or when they have problems to forget; others choose alcohol or drugs. Rick worked tension out of his system with sex and lots of it. He didn't normally go to a bar. He didn't have to. The women in his black book were plentiful, but he didn't want any of them tonight. Nothing familiar. He needed something or someone different, a change of pace.

The jazz music the band played helped mellow him some, but he craved more than that. A glass of whiskey warmed his throat as he took the first gulp. His fingers drummed on the glass tabletop and kept beat with the tune. He scanned the candlelit tables of the semi-crowded club. A little hole in the wall, Salsalito, north of the city and not far from home, had been a favorite of his for years. Which made it an ideal choice to relax and check out the scenery. Quite a few women, all shapes and sizes, adorned the space with their beauty. Many of them had men at their side; a few did not. Seated across the room in a corner, a blond with spiky hair cut short to the scalp glanced his way a few times, but other than that she didn't seem interested. She wouldn't be a typical choice, not that he had a type. However, she looked like what he desired tonight: a little rough around the edges. The cropped leather vest forced her tiny breasts above the lapels, and the fringe on her cut-to-the-crotch miniskirt pulled a man's eyes to her long legs.

Yeah, she'd do fine. He needed hard core and rough tonight. The repressed beast building inside him had to be forced out before he exploded, and the best way for him to do that remained locked in his sight. While he chugged the rest of his drink, he signaled the waitress to bring him another, and took the next step to remedy his situation.

"Hi." He sat in the seat across from her, extending his hand. "Rick. You are?"

"Busy." She leaned her back against the paneled wall and scanned the room like he wasn't sitting there, a few feet from her face.

"Can I buy you a drink?"

"Bug off." She still hadn't bothered to look at him.

Listed as America's most eligible bachelor, he hadn't received that title for just one reason. His success running a Fortune 500 corporation and his legendary never-give-up attitude had weighed heavily in the ranking. This woman didn't realize the king of stubborn sat right at her fingertips. If he pursued a woman, his skills melted her panties off every single time. Not one rejection. Although, since they chased after him, those charms might be a little rusty. He knew what he had to do though. It wouldn't take long before he had her right where he wanted.

The empty beer bottle in front of her gave him the opportunity he needed. He waved at the waitress who had stopped at his vacated seat, scanning the tables and searching for him. When she caught sight of him, she brought over his drink, and he ordered the silent lady another of the same brand.

"You got a hearin' problem, man?" She glared at him and jerked her chin at the waitress.

"Having a drink is all. Thought I'd share."

She snorted and surveyed the crowd again, which had gotten more congested since he arrived.

He eased his back along the adjacent wall and took a sip

from his glass. "You looking for someone? I come here a lot. Maybe I could help."

"I don't have time for BS. Why don't you hike it back to where you came from and hit on that chick two tables behind where you were sittin'? She's there all alone, and I'm sure she'd help you with what *you're* looking for."

He tilted his head back and let the laughter rip. She had him pegged damn well. When he settled himself, he shouted over the music, "What's your name?"

"Kat." Her smirk showed two dimples, and the mischievous glint in her eyes softened her appearance some, a stark contrast to the heavy black and purple makeup around them.

"Well, Kat, touché." He raised the drink as a toast and sucked down a huge gulp.

The waitress came back to the table with her beer. Kat pulled out a thin wallet, removing a twenty. His fingers clipped the bill to the table. "My treat."

She shrugged and swiped the bottle from the waitress's tray. From under his fingers, Kat slid the money out and tucked it into her billfold. A picture inside stared at him, a face he wouldn't soon forget. He snatched it from her grasp.

"Hey." She leapt across the table at the same time he lunged far right and out of her reach, his arm extended to stop her.

"Why do you have this picture?" He tapped it with his thumb.

She frowned and sat down slowly. "You know her?"

"I met her last week."

Her head tilted, and she narrowed her eyes. "You Stone?"

He chuckled at her stunned face, thin black eyebrows pitched high and mouth slackened. "Heard of me, have you?" He eased closer to the table and laid the wallet between them. She yanked it away, tucking it into a pocket.

"Unbelievable. You sure know how to make an impression, don't you?"

He smirked. *I have many tricks.*

"She hasn't stopped talking about you."

His smile vanished, and his eyes snapped to the singer. The woman's soulful voice sang about taking chances, causing his skin to tingle. All of a sudden, the air in the club thickened, and it became difficult to breathe. "How do you know her?" He didn't think she heard him since his choked question got drowned out by the crescendo finish.

"She's my niece. They live with me." Her reply mimicked his tone. He heard her loud and clear though because the tune had ended and the band took a break. What timing.

His gaze shifted to the head-banger type that couldn't be Maggie's sister. They were opposite in height, skin tone, hair color, eyes, everything. Something about Kat's attitude, though, reminded him of her niece. "Cece's quite precocious." This time he grinned a little.

"Ah, she used her subtle charm on you too, huh?"

He coughed into his hand, suppressing another laugh. "Subtle?"

She tipped her bottle up to him. "I think you might know a little about that yourself, Stone. A technique you do well."

He threw a fifty down on the table and stood, chugging the rest of his drink. "Enjoy your night." When he walked away he thought he heard her mutter, "You met your match, bud. Two of 'em."

Anger and pent-up frustration drove him to pound into the raven-haired, nameless woman. Her cheek pressed onto his glass dining room table, his fist grinding into the middle of her bare back. Eyes closed, his face pointed up at the ceiling, he filled her sex and the condom. A release that even a few seconds later, hadn't satisfied him in the least.

After he yanked his pants up, he tossed the rubber in the

trash and strode toward the door, his dress shirt flapping at his sides. He took in her seductive getting-dressed scene, a slow, methodical snap of twenty-some buttons that lined the entire front of her shimmery pink dress. Loud clanking heels sounded like thunder as she stomped across the wood floor. "That's it?" Her frown should have pained him but it didn't. Every woman he had sex with tried to use her wiles and connive her way into his heart. In most instances, they made it as far as his living room, and none were invited to his bed.

He tilted his chin toward her parked car, behind his in the driveway.

"You suck, you know that?" She rammed her shoulder into his on the way out and took off down the stairs of his brownstone.

After he slammed the door, he shoved his aching forehead against the cold steel surface. Yeah, he sucked and a whole slew of other things. The walls closing in on him, he shucked off his pants and shirt, flew up the stairs two at a time, and headed straight for the shower. Scalding hot water pounded down on his taut muscles, a dozen showerheads directed at strategic spots and hitting key points on his neck, shoulders, arms, and thighs. Almost like he had a personal masseuse behind him, driving knuckles into every nerve. His arms spread-eagle along the tile wall, he widened his legs the same distance apart, rolling his shoulders backward then forward, over and over again, trying to relieve the tension. Most days, sex made him loose, not more frustrated.

Unwanted fantasies kept him revved up, an auburn beauty stuck in his head. The black-haired siren he'd used as a replacement already forgotten. Fire flared in his stomach and other parts of his anatomy. His eyes were closed, but he didn't need to look down. His angry erection rubbed along his thigh as he shifted to the right and left, trying to get the jet stream to hit him where it hurt most, and hopefully beat the damn thing into submission.

51

Disgusted with himself, he shut off the water and toweled down in quick swipes. Semi-dry, he headed toward his bed, a bright yellow figure pulling him to the nightstand. The duck, and everything it embodied, mocked him. Yanking the drawer open, he tossed the irregular, ragged shape inside.

Out of sight, out of mind.

He rolled onto the mattress, threw the covers up to his chest, and an arm over his eyes. The darkness hadn't helped a damn bit. Flashes of his new acquaintances bounced around in his head like a riptide about to suck him into the depths of a boundless sea: Maggie, the freckle-faced bombshell; and Cece, the bubbly, rambunctious preschooler.

Caught in his torrential thoughts, he spun onto his side, punching the pillow and tossing his weary head from one bumpy spot to another in a lame attempt to settle down. Forcing his brain to count sheep, repeat algebraic equations, and the Chinese alphabet he picked up traveling overseas, through it all, his mind games betrayed him and failed miserably.

One sheep, two sheep, three sheep—duck.

$y + 9 = 13$, $2n = 12$—34, 24, 36.

诶= a, 比= b—Cecily + Max.

Mama's Rule #8:

Don't chew with your mouth open.

Two plates of smoked salmon and pistachio truffle pâté were placed on the tray. Maggie wiped the blood orange sauce off the edges, ensuring perfection before delivery. She nodded to the waiter, and he served the patrons their meals. Curriculum lunch sessions at Le Gourmet brought a huge smile to her face. A designated time for culinary students to showcase their skills. Although she had little input about what would be prepared, the instructors expected the students to create their own specialty entree or dessert. A dozen master chefs tasted the samples, and if up to their standards, added a select few to the menu for a week.

Her mother's Russian Torte made the cut as a featured dessert. When Antonio, her supervisor, told her she got the seal of approval, she about peed her pants. Even though the school focused on international cuisine, she didn't know whether the worldly experts would accept a homemade recipe. Her family had taught her everything about ethnic-inspired cooking and baking, compliments of her grandfather's Greek heritage and her grandmother's Russian background. The earliest memories she could recall were of her toddling along at her mother's side, mimicking her actions in the kitchen at home and at her grandparents' restaurant. Mama would pick up her and Kat from school, drive them into Houston to Stavros's, a four-thousand-square-foot dining establishment and catering service, and after they filled their tummies and finished homework, assumed their roles as little helpers. Kat couldn't care less and often goofed off, hunkering down behind the register building towers out of wrapped silverware or shredding menus to paper mache glasses and mugs. But Maggie delighted in the grown-up atmosphere and took her job seriously. Over the years, the complexity increased from setting orders on trays when she was in kindergarten, to dressing Greek salads throughout her primary grades, and then assisting Mama with layering nuts and fillo for baklava and other desserts at the intermediate stage, until she advanced to chef alongside Baba and Pappous. She never stopped until she left town. Those moments were some of the best of her life. She'd cherish them forever. And now that she lived so far away, she kept her mom and grandparents close in thought with every recipe she prepared, each meal she set on a plate, and every dessert she lovingly whipped up.

"Hey, Maggie, how's it going?"

With the temperature switched to medium, she added the duck breast skin side down to sear, then turned around to greet the familiar voice. Matt sat at one of the five chef's tables, a two-person marble-top bar situated alongside the students' stainless steel prep station, promising personalized attention. Designated for the apprentices whose recipes were featured, the primo spots were in high demand and often required reservations. "Well, boss man, decided to take me up on the invite, huh?"

"Oh, Mags, you know I have a weakness for that torte. When you told me it'd be on the menu, I couldn't resist." He patted his flat stomach. "It's all your fault I gained an extra five pounds too. My wife doesn't mind though. She said the extra cushioning is nice when she lays her head there."

She snorted. "Yeah, right. There isn't an ounce of fat on you. Sophia told me you're a workout fiend, running five miles a day, and she has to drag you out of your home gym every night."

He chuckled and unwrapped the bundled silverware, setting the napkin on his lap. She placed a menu in front of him, and he tilted his head to the empty stool to his left. "Can I have another of those? A business associate is joining me."

"Sure." After she set another down, she picked up the next ticket and prepared several more dishes. Matt asked her a few questions as she chopped and diced, sautéed and flipped, and plated a service for four. Wiping her brow with her sleeve, she reached up for a clean pan and almost dropped it as an exasperated male voice snapped from behind her.

"This place is packed. Why'd you pick it?"

Lodged in her brain for several weeks now, Mr. Stone's guttural tenor replayed in her daydreams and in her sleep. She inched around performing a mental countdown from ten to zero, which helped cool her off when Cece pushed her buttons, and by some miracle she hoped would work in this instance too.

A steel gray oxford, no tie, and slim-fit pants with the same sheen as his button-down vest produced an unnatural reaction. Her tongue rolled to the roof of her mouth and withheld the groan his arousing professional attire and fresh-air scent planted in her head.

"Uh . . ." Mr. Stone narrowed his eyes at Matt and clamped a hand on his shoulder. His flushed face resembled the cherry red that often tinted joggers' cheeks. "Buddy, you didn't tell me Maggie would be here. Thought you said this was a business lunch." He waved a folder and tossed it on the table.

Matt's grin flashed toward her and then to his friend. "You do realize she's cooking, right?"

Just then Mr. Stone's gaze drifted across her chest, becoming transfixed for a while on the crisscrossed fork, spoon, and knife emblem at her left breast and then darted up to her face. If possible, his skin reddened even more as he dropped onto the wooden stool, an impact that scraped the chair back a few inches, rocking him into Matt's shoulder.

"Let's order. I'm starved." An elbow shot given to his buddy, Matt knocked Mr. Stone's bent arm off the edge of the table and pointed to the menu. "Pick something, fast. I need to get to dessert before it's all gone."

Using a similar mocking tone like Matt had earlier, Mr. Stone scanned the room while he spoke. "You realize we're in a restaurant that has loads of food."

She got a chuckle out of the amusing banter. Normally, she and Kat rubbed each other the wrong way. It was good to see the ribbing happening to someone else for a change.

"No, smart ass. Maggie's extra special, sweet treat. There's a limited amount."

The menu forgotten and dropped onto the table, Mr. Stone set his chin in his hand and repositioned his arm where it had been before Matt knocked it down. In a seductive murmur he asked, "What sinful goodies do you have for me, Maggie?" Extended across the counter, his hand cupped hers from underneath and gripped it like a beggar pleading for anything and everything she could give.

She yanked her fist away, and it smacked against her thigh as she jolted back several steps to escape the heat, ramming right into Antonio. He picked up the same arm, pried her fingers apart, and inspected her uninjured palm. "You okay?" His other hand settled on her hip as he stood behind her. She hadn't answered or looked at her superior. Instead her eyes wouldn't move away from Mr. Stone's, which kept darting between her and Antonio.

"I don't see anything." Antonio brushed his thumb along a line in the center, skimming a vein on her wrist too. Tickles raced across her skin and up her arm, but the zing had nothing

56

to do with his touch. The electrical charge in the air came from Mr. Stone. As if in some out-of- body experience or mist-filled dream, she became super aware of his every move. Slow and reserved, yet full of raw energy, he eased up from his chair, rounded the counter and strutted over to them. Antonio's hold at her hip stiffened, yet he didn't let go. Instead his body pressed closer and straightened behind her, an apparent protective mode.

Veins in Mr. Stone's neck stood out as he leaned into them, coming inches from Antonio's face. Clanging dishes and silverware, shouted calls for service, and a full house of patrons talking over one another didn't disguise the whispered threat he launched. "Hands off."

Antonio raised both arms but didn't move away from her backside. "Ease up, buddy."

"Okay, okay, we're all good here." Matt threw an arm over Mr. Stone's shoulder, jerked his chin at Antonio and flicked a quick glance at her before mumbling something in his friend's ear she couldn't make out. Whatever he said did the trick, and both returned to their seats, skimming the menu as though nothing had happened.

"You have tickets piling up, Maggie. Get to them," Antonio reminded and took off for the main kitchen.

Several minutes later, she filled their orders. Matt and Mr. Stone dove into the braised short ribs she delivered to them. Her typical ease in the kitchen switched to uneven dicing, shaky cutting that almost sliced a couple fingers off, and jerky tossing, causing bits and pieces to fly out of the pan and into the flames on the gas stove. Unsettled, her upset stomach flared and heat from the oven made it feel like she had a hundred four temperature. In the middle of a busy lunch service, she tried to concentrate on each order and ignore, for the most part, the two men devouring their meals at the table over her shoulder. It wasn't common for her to be so rude. She just couldn't get what she needed done correctly if she spent one more moment with *him*. Any time those hazel eyes shot in her direction, they pierced her.

Whenever she got near him, his enticing sandalwood, lavender, and berries cologne wafted up her nose and caused her heart to thrum as if each scent pulsed through her veins, surged through the left and right ventricles, and flooded the rest of her organs.

At last, the time had come for their dessert, leaving her with no choice but to pay them a visit. She set two small plates with three pieces of Russian Torte on each in front of Matt and Mr. Stone. Instead of returning to her station, her feet remained glued to the wood floor. His opinion didn't matter. It shouldn't, she told herself. Yet she stayed and waited as Mr. Stone picked one up and inspected the layers.

"Meringue." He shot a glance her way, waiting for confirmation.

She nodded.

"The orange stuff—tangerines, peaches, what?"

"Apricots," she corrected.

"Nuts on the bottom? Please tell me they're not prunes."

Unable to contain her laughter, it rushed out, relieving some of the strain that had twisted her up earlier. "Oh, Mr. Stone, if I were a cruel person, I'd lie and tell you they're the sweetest, most delectable plums, handpicked and dried especially for you." The tease caught her by surprise. It sounded sensual in her ears and must have registered with him too, because his eyebrow rose to his hairline, challenging her.

As soon as her taunt had been uttered, his tongue darted out and slicked up the side of the four-tier, decadent morsel. "Mmm." He murmured multiple times, along with a deep rumble along his throat and Adam's apple. The side of his mouth curved up, right before he opened wide and plopped the entire thing inside. His cheek bulged from the fullness, and he hummed through each chomp. Those honey brown eyes with sparks of winter green, a shade that transformed

58

depending on the lighting, remained stuck to her as he savored each bite.

"Rick, is that you?" A svelte, dressed-to-the-nines woman rested her hand on his shoulder and ducked down, brushing a kiss on his cheek and remaining on that spot a lot longer than a simple hello.

Mr. Stone rose from his seat, his lips dropping into a frown.

Maggie glanced toward Matt, but he just continued to eat, shoving the last piece in his mouth and removing the two from his friend's plate, putting them on his own. He pressed a finger up to his lips in a silent "shh" and instead of being ashamed, he shrugged his shoulders and continued to gulp them down.

"I was wondering when we could get together again." The hussy pressed a hand onto Mr. Stone's chest, right on his heart, while the other cupped his cheek, swiping a thumb along the stubble. The fake blond bombshell stepped closer, not leaving a centimeter between them. "You sure know how to show a girl a good time. I've missed you."

Mr. Stone grabbed her wrist and pushed her arm away from his face, returning it to her side. He scooted his chair with the backs of his legs and took several steps away from her. "That's not a good idea."

"Aw, Rick, don't be like that." She leaned up and uttered something in his ear.

He dropped his neck back and stared at the ceiling, drawing in several deep breaths. Then he twisted toward Matt and squinted at the empty plates. "Let's go." Mr. Stone shoved the chair under the table so hard, water splashed out of the glasses and a fork fell toward the floor.

Maggie dove to catch it but missed, her hand brushing along Mr. Stone's thigh. "Sorry," she mumbled, embarrassed at how close her fingers had come to his zipper.

Miss High and Mighty cast a perturbed glare at her and stepped into her personal space, squaring off. "Not quick enough. He loves fast and hard. Trust me, you wouldn't be able to handle him." She crossed her arms, unwilling to back down, and not the least uncomfortable that some of the customers nearby overhead her inappropriate announcement.

Clamping his large hand around the big mouth's arm, Mr. Stone tugged, and then pushed her around tables and out the door.

"I guess I'll take care of the check then." Matt came up alongside Maggie. "Everything was fantastic. If there's any dessert left over, bring me some when you come to work later." He patted his stomach again. "I didn't get enough. Don't be so stingy next time. I want at least a dozen of those."

She heard him but didn't look his way much. Instead her eyes kept gravitating outside to the couple arguing on the sidewalk. Mr. Stone paced, then stopped to say something, and darted back and forth again. The shameless woman threw her arm out to halt him, flapping her gums and yelling whatever. Anytime the door opened from people going in and out, she could hear the remnants of the determined woman screeching.

"Catch ya later, Mags." Matt strolled in front of her and blocked the view, waving over his shoulder.

She raised her hand, mimicking him, but he didn't see her. "Bye," she called. "Thank you." Her voice rose above the noisy chatter. A peace sign shot up above his head, causing her to giggle.

After paying the check, Matt exited the restaurant just as Mr. Stone hailed a cab and assisted the woman into it. He ducked his head inside and stayed there a bit before closing the door and pounding on top. The taxi took off.

Mr. Stone's eagle eyes locked on her exact position. Shivers rolled through her. Not the bad kind, the good. Too good.

"Service, Maggie." Antonio's shout jolted her and helped get her priorities readjusted.

She rushed to her station, filling the single order remaining in the machine as service wound down. A glance over her shoulder showed both men were gone.

A red leaf salad, Charcuterie Plate, Escargot, and Le Gourmet burger kept her hands busy, while she gave herself a stiff talking to: *you have responsibilities, tons on your plate, men are trouble, you don't need another problem added to the list.*
Just forget him.

Mama's Rule #9:

Do as I say, not as I do.

"And you're supposed to be a Casanova? How the hell did you get that title after that fuck up?" Matt's jab was punctuated with a hard smack on Rick's shoulder as they walked toward the office building.

"The last time I had anything to do with Lisa was at least six months ago. Believe me, I wasn't goin' there again. She wails through her whole orgasm. It's so high pitched you'd swear a car's brakes locked up. The screeching doesn't stop until the coming ends in a head-on collision. My eardrums are thanking me. I swear they burst the last time. That got old as soon as it happened. How the hell anyone could put up with that on a regular basis I have no idea." During his rant, his story picked up pace, hoping to lay it out as quickly as possible and end the conversation once and for all.

"I wasn't talking about her, shithead. No wonder you were the college dodge ball champ four years running. You duck and run better than anybody. I don't ever remember you getting hit until now."

Ticked off, Rick reeled around and let his best friend have it. "Are you on a sugar high? Because you're talkin' stupid."

Turning his back on him, he took a few steps and then bolted around, pointing his finger at Matt's chest. "Don't get me confused with you." He got nose to nose, ensuring Matt heard his message loud and clear over the honking horns and traffic. "I'm sick and tired of everyone telling me what the hell I'm supposed to do with my life. You can take that shit you're spouting and shove it up your ass." He swung his arm in the general direction of the restaurant and snarled out his parting protest. "She's *nothing* to me." When he said it, his gaze flicked away from Matt's knowing stare while the denial escaped his mouth. "No kids. No women with kids. And definitely not a woman who is obviously running from something or *someone*. Now, take your advice and give it to somebody who gives a damn."

As Rick took off at a sprint, Matt shouted, "I'll see you Sunday. Lizbeth and Harley's birthday party."

Rick extended his hand in an acknowledging and consenting wave. Even pissed off, he would never miss such an occasion. He might not want that lifestyle for himself, but he loved Matt and his family. Regardless of the bullshit his buddy rode him about, he'd never let a few disagreements come between them. They'd pledged the same fraternity their second semester and hit it off from the start. Rooming together helped, but they were also a lot alike. As bad as Rick might be, Matt had been a hell of a lot worse when it came to one-night stands, which kept their dorm room quite active. The routine continued until the end of senior year when Matt met Sophia at a party. His partner in crime fell hard, certain he'd met "the one."

Married a year after graduation, Rick had been Matt's best man, celebrating the special occasion and each one ever since. Whenever he had a few hours to spare, he spent it with them. The twins turned six this weekend, and Grace, a pudgy little thing just a few months old, didn't do much more than sleep, eat, and vomit. A few times when he'd been burping her, she got him good, spurting disgusting, yellow slime down his back. Once, so much spit came out of her, it seeped into his pants and boxers. Yeah, if that wasn't enough to tell him kids were a pain in the ass, that event would have convinced him for sure. The best part though, when he said goodbye, he didn't have to deal with glitter being sprinkled in his hair, his nails being painted neon yellow, princess tiaras thrown on his head, and kiddie tea parties again until weeks later, or as soon as he could fit in another visit.

Nope, he didn't need any of that insanity.

Board meetings took three to four hours. A new goal of Rick's had been to keep them as brief as possible. He just set a record, finishing in under two. At least he'd done something good today.

"What the hell are you doing?" Grandfather's shout echoed in the conference room.

He peeked over his shoulder expecting to see him there. When he didn't, he walked into the hallway. Behind his secretary's desk and sitting in her chair—Cece, spinning in circles. Did anyone pay attention to where that kid went? Where the heck was Maggie?

"Quit that right now, young lady," Grandfather demanded while Cece continued to turn even faster.

By the time Rick came up behind him, Grandfather's arm had shot out to catch the whirling chair. His did too but latched onto the old man. "Leave her alone. I'll take care of this."

"Another example of why this place is falling apart. If this kind of thing goes on when I'm here, I can only imagine what happens when I'm not."

"Max," Cece repeated with each swing around until she came to a gradual stop. He could've sworn her face turned yellow then green as projectile vomit spewed out of her mouth, down his pant legs, and onto Grandfather's custom-made Italian loafers. Bent over, she held her stomach as never-ending chunk-filled, watery globs flew out.

Stunned silence, except for the retching, happened first. Then more chaos.

"Shit." Kat rushed to Cece, scooped her up and over to a trash can, ignoring the splattered mess on Cece's overalls and the gook that now stuck to Kat's Westlake shirt.

"Take that wretched little—"

Rick held up his arm, cutting Grandfather off. His glare communicated he'd better not say any more. For once the grouch listened and turned tail, shaking his left and then right shoe, grumbling on his way out about the business being in the gutter by year's end.

Before Kat could whisk her niece away, he ducked down to get a good look at Cece. He set his hand on her back, rubbing up and down. "How you feeling?" Brushing a lock of red hair out of her eyes, he swiped his thumb along her flushed cheek.

"My tummy hurts."

"Yeah? Mine would too if I spun like that."

Cece reached up, her hand coming to rest under his chin. "I take care a ya."

The stab to his heart caused the air in his lungs to gush out and blow across her face, flitting tiny, sweaty curls back and forth and clinging along her temple.

"I'd better get her in the bathroom and cleaned up." Kat walked around him, carrying Cece toward the Westlake office.

With her fingers pressed to her thumb, Cece's duck-bill-shaped goodbye and chubby-cheeked smile over Kat's shoulders kept him at his secretary's desk unable to move until she disappeared.

"Oh, my," Mrs. Collins said behind him.

He looked at the lumpy globs on the carpeted floor.

"I'll get something to clean that up," Mrs. Collins chimed, not showing the least upset about the mess sprayed around her desk.

"No, I'll take care of it."

A pat on his shoulder pulled his attention to his secretary. "I can do it. This could take a while. Besides, you have a meeting in an hour." She pointed to his pant leg. "And you need to get cleaned up too."

Since he didn't have time to rush home to change and often needed to be ready for any occasion, a walk-in closet in his office, which he'd stocked with professional and casual wear, came in handy. A bathroom with a shower in his suite also made it easy to get refreshed at the last minute.

Unwilling to have Mrs. Collins take care of something that had nothing to do with her job, he went hunting for paper towels and garbage bags stored in the break room. When he returned with his hands full, Mrs. Collins was already on her knees with gloves up to her elbows and a bucket at her side. The ammonia hit him. "Whoa, that stinks." After setting the supplies on the spotless half of her desk, he grabbed her arm, stopping her from doing any more cleanup.

"More than vomit?" she mocked, pinching his bicep. "I told you to leave it."

"When do I ever listen?" he countered, pecking her on the temple.

She dropped the rag in the pail and faced him, her eyes softening. "You're a good boy. Don't worry about your grand-father. He wants the best for you and doesn't know how to communicate it as well as your dad."

For the second time his chest constricted, in this case, a reminder of his supportive father and how he always knew the right thing to say.

He ripped the paper towels off the roll and dove in, mopping up and dumping clumps in the trash. Before he knew it the floor, chair, and desk were spotless. His sweaty shirt and pants stuck to his skin, and he reeked of sour milk and who knew what else. His lower back had stiffened from being bent over for so long. He stood and rubbed it.

"Uh, excuse me, Mr. Stone. You left this at the restaurant."

Exhausted and annoyed, he rocked back on his heels and turned toward Maggie. She set a folder on Mrs. Collins's desk and said, "Um, you don't look so good." Her unnecessary reminder pricked the hair on the back of his neck. She pinched her nose. "What happened?" Her nasally, muffled question pissed him off, and his control evaporated.

"Well, let's see." He swiped the moisture off his upper lip, needing a minute to figure out what he wanted to say. The extra time hadn't helped. It just renewed his fire, a carryover from lunch. "If you watched your kid better, you'd know." His arms crossed along his chest, and he went on, ignoring her wide green eyes and gaping mouth. "That smell is from your daughter throwing up all over the place." He whipped a hand toward his damp and smeared pant legs, her gaze drifting over them. "She was unsupervised, again." Then he swung his arm to the sparkling clean chair. "Spinning around in my secretary's seat. No one with her. Nobody, Maggie." He closed in, moving nearer to her with each account and continued to rattle off one jab after another. "What if she got lost? Hurt? What if someone took her? Do you have any clue what she does? Where she goes?"

Mother bear fangs appeared in an instant and a snarl pinched the corner of her mouth as she pounced. "How dare you? Don't tell me how to take care of my daughter. She's the one person I'd run through flames to get to, jump into rushing water to save, and give my life for a hundred, thousand, million times over to make sure she lived another day, took another breath, and had every dream come true." When she finished, tears flooded her eyes, rolled over her cheeks, between her lips and dropped off her chin. Her claims wavered from strong and determined, to deep and gut wrenching, to low and soft, then back again. He'd never seen so many emotions cross a person's face. So much heart, too much anguish, and complete devastation. But an essence poured out of her, enlivening the distance between them—glorious and awful. Even though he remained standing the entire time, the unconditional and eternal love she felt for her child rocked him to his knees.

"Mama, ya here," Cece yelled, plowing into Maggie's legs. A glowing smile her norm, when she looked up and saw her mother's face, a frown came at once.

Maggie picked Cece up and brushed a few fingers through her curls. "How you feeling, baby?"

"Ya sad?" Cece wiped the remnants of her mother's tears with her palm, smearing them over Maggie's nose, and then leaned in cheek to cheek. "Don't cry, Mama. I okay."

Maggie hugged her, rocking side to side.

"I wouldn't do that if I were you." Kat giggled, her grin disappearing when she saw her sister's blotchy face. Kat mouthed over Cece's head to Maggie, "You okay?" When Kat came up alongside him, her pincer grip snuck up from behind, pinching and twisting his waist. Without acknowledging her, he took the hit, understanding her nonverbal warning.

"Mr. Stone, your appointment's here. They're in conference room C."

"Let them know there's been a delay. I need another fifteen minutes or so," he instructed Mrs. Collins.

"Sure, no worries, I got it handled."

She always did. His dad's assistant took him under her wing from day one, ensuring everything ran smoothly. He didn't know what he'd do without her.

"If you'll excuse me. I have a shower to take." He placed a kiss above Cece's fluttering open and closed eyes. "Hope you feel better, sweet pea."

"Had fun." Cece yawned, and not a second later, her eyes shut and stayed that way.

A shove into his shoulder knocked him sideways a step as Kat removed Cece, resting her in the exact same position she had been in Maggie's arms. "Time to go. I gotta get the monster home, bathed, and in bed." Kat jerked her chin down the hall. "Aren't you gonna be late, Mags?"

Maggie and Kat exchanged several squinty-eyed volleys and head shakes, the meaning of which he didn't get. An only child, he didn't do sibling- or sister-speak. Whatever it meant though, Maggie marched down the hall after giving her sleeping daughter a goodbye kiss above her ear and whispering something in it.

Kat shifted from foot to foot like a boxer in a ring, shooting daggers at him over Cece's sleeping head. "She doesn't need your crap. Whatever you said, I'll get it out of her. I'm your worst nightmare, asshole."

"Mr. Stone, I'm sorry to interrupt, but they're waiting, sir."

He shoved a hand through his grimy, sweaty hair and nodded. Mrs. Collins to the rescue. "Believe me, it won't happen again."

"Keep it that way." Once more, Kat rammed into his shoulder and stormed past him toward the elevator.

His hands clasped behind his head, he closed his eyes and sucked in several deep breaths. Different day, more shit added to the heap.

Women were trouble—every last one of them.

Mama's Rule #10:

Say you're sorry and mean it.

Four years of high school sports and learning the ropes of running a restaurant drummed into Maggie the importance of being punctual. Plus, she just hated to be late. Therefore, they arrived at Matt's house an hour before the party started. Kat grumbled the entire drive, and Cece had been delighted at the possibility of extra play time with Harley and Lizbeth before other kids got there. Yet Maggie figured Matt and Sophia could use the extra hands to get things set up. One child kept Maggie busy enough. She could imagine how crazy their place would be with three.

Located a block from Lake Mohegan, their home had five bedrooms and must have been at least four thousand square feet. The family-friendly decor had comfortable furnishings and toys scattered about in every room. If she ended up staying in New York, she'd love to live in this neighborhood. Even though Matt paid her an hourly rate that exceeded her expectations, the real estate prices in this area would always be above her income level. But a girl could dream, and she would.

Portable tables had paper birthday hats and kazoos at each

setting. Streamers were hung on the walls and doorways, and a corner of the living room had been designated for gifts. Kids in the backyard played on the swing set, while the adults helped get the place ready with little disruption and a half hour to spare. Sophia's and Matt's parents assisted in the preparations, but for the most part, supervised the children outdoors.

"Well, I think everything's about ready. I have a few things to get out of the fridge and then we're all set," Sophia said, leading the way from the living room into the kitchen. Maggie followed and found Kat with her mouth full and a hand diving into chips and pretzels she'd been assigned to put into bowls for each table.

"What? I'm hungry," Kat replied when Maggie shot her the evil eye, embarrassed by her sister's rudeness.

"You don't have to wait. Eat what you want, that's what it's for. Pizza will be here soon. There's BBQ wings in the crock pot in the dining room, and Matt should be finished with the hamburgers and hot dogs on the grill in a few minutes. Both of you make yourselves at home. We don't stand on formality around here." Sophia ducked into the fridge and pulled out a pre-made salad and several dressings, setting them on the counter.

Kat stuck out her tongue at Maggie, tossed popcorn in the air, and caught it in her mouth.

Maggie shook her head. At least Kat hadn't dropped any on the floor. There wasn't much she could do to contain her sister. She never could. "What else can I help with? How about drinks?"

"There's juice boxes and sodas in coolers on the patio. All taken care of. I can't think of much else. We're all good. I'll put these last few things in the dining room and let's go outside for a while."

Not long after, all three of them joined the others in the backyard, which had tons of space to run and play with every outdoor toy available: slip and slide, hula hoops, any kind of

sports ball, sandbox, badminton, volleyball, a kid-sized bas-
ketball hoop, batting tee, even a tree house and an in-ground
pool with floating rafts and foam noodles.

Maggie hadn't bought anything for their yard yet, but she
hoped to get a swing set soon. With summer coming and a
warmer than usual May, she spent a lot of time outdoors and
wanted Cece to have something fun to do. The postage-stamp
sized lot at Kat's place had enough room to add a few play-
things. Her savings account had several thousand in it. Even
with school expenses, which her loans paid, she wasn't hurt-
ing for money. She just needed to choose a weekend soon and
take Cece to pick out a few things. June thirteenth was Cece's
birthday, but she didn't want to wait that long. Maybe next
Saturday. She'd have to check with Kat and see if she could
use her car.

"Uncle Ricky. Emma," Harley and Lizbeth called out,
rushing toward a side gate, Cece not far behind. The kids
ran across the yard to him and joined the brunette at his side.
At least it wasn't Miss No Manners from the restaurant. She
didn't want to relive that again.

An arm thrown over Maggie's shoulder pulled her gaze
onto her sister. "Who's the chick?" Kat said it loud enough
for Sophia to hear as she rooted through an adult cooler next
to them. Thank goodness Matt had just gone inside with the
last of the food he cooked, and no one else was around them
on the patio.

Sophia handed Maggie a wine cooler and Kat a beer.
"That's Emma."

Yeah, Maggie got that much. When the kids reached Mr.
Stone, they dove; Harley and Lizbeth grabbed onto his hips,
wrapping their arms around him from each side, jumping up
and down and screaming, "What you'd get me? Where's my
present?" Cece came to a sliding stop in her bare feet and
yanked on his T-shirt, yelling, "Piggy, up, piggy."

Knocking her head into Maggie's, Kat mumbled, "She got

that half right. A pig who's an asshole."

That remark had Sophia whipping toward them but directing her question to Kat. "You don't like Rick?" She stated it as if Kat's opinion had been a complete and utter impossibility.

Instead of giving Kat a chance to answer, Maggie called out, "Is that Grace I hear crying?" As any good mother would, Sophia took off, probably checking the portable intercom in the kitchen.

Once Sophia had gone back inside, Kat disclosed the white lie. "I didn't hear anything."

Maggie faced her sister and attempted to lay down some ground rules. "Knock it off. Let's just have a good time. Stop embarrassing me and yourself. For once, Kat, shut the hell up."

"Hell a bad word, Mama." Maggie heard Cece sigh out the reprimand behind her, but she didn't acknowledge her right away.

With a finger pressed to her tight lip, Kat tapped it, smirking from ear to ear. The witch must have seen Cece there, yet didn't say anything. One of these days, when Kat least expected it, Maggie would get revenge. Paybacks were a bitch.

Ready to face the music and fix her foul-mouth mistake, Maggie spun around. Cece had her arms thrown over Mr. Stone's shoulders and clasped under his chin, riding piggyback style. The Emma person had her hand positioned at Cece's bum, holding her in place. Emma's amused expression was similar to Kat's, except she bit her lip instead of tapping it.

Now that Maggie could see Emma up close, radiating came to mind, a wrinkle-free glow shining on her flawless complexion. Whatever makeup she used gave her rosy skin a light shimmer. A pale peach shade made her round green-brown eyes pop. The longer Maggie assessed and compared Emma's thinner frame, which was most likely a size four, against her beefier figure, a pang of envy and jealousy rushed in. The little devil on her shoulder shouted: *Why is that woman touching my child? How dare she?*

"Mama, say sorry," Cece demanded, pressed to Rick's cheek. Her brows pulled down and nose scrunched up, shooting her mother a fake mad face.

Both Emma and Kat laughed, and to drive the knife deeper, her sister heckled, "Yeah, Mags, say you're sorry and mean it."

Fire lit in her belly, and Maggie envisioned her sister's favorite NY Giants jersey in the same state—up in flames. Last week, when she moved the couch away from the wall to sweep behind it, she noticed a happy face painted under the window seal. At first she'd been shocked, then she realized who must have done it. She called Cece over and showed it to her. Instead of fessing up, Cece denied it. After giving her multiple chances to tell the truth, out of frustration, she shouted at her to apologize. The exact same phrase Kat demanded she use. As soon as they got home tonight, Kat's shirt would be history.

"You're right, honey. That's a bad word. I shouldn't have said it."

"Say sorry," Cece insisted, while concentrating on something or *someone* over Maggie's shoulder and giggling as she did.

"Let's race over to the slide. Birthday girls are waiting." Mr. Stone bounced up and down a couple times and without waiting for agreement, trotted away.

"Be careful. Don't drop her." Emma raised her voice over the whinnying he kept doing as he galloped across the yard. "You have a beautiful daughter."

"Thanks." Maggie scanned the area, watching a few more people arrive through the gate and trying to avoid any more conversation. "I better go see if Sophia needs help."

"Oh, I'll go too."

"Later, I'm goin' in." After Matt mentioned there'd be a

pool, Kat came prepared, wearing a bathing suit underneath her shirt and shorts. Undressed in record time, she tossed her clothes on a lounge chair and dove into the deep end.

Yep, that jersey would burn for sure, and maybe a few more of Kat's things.

Sliding the screen door open, Maggie entered the kitchen. Emma came too but kept on walking into the living room and then disappeared. Hmm, mighty comfortable with her surroundings. She must've been here before. Since Mr. Stone and Matt were friends, and she came with him, it made sense. Why did that thought annoy her?

Not realizing she'd zoned out, it wasn't until Sophia and Emma returned to the kitchen with Grace in her mother's arms that she felt like an idiot. Maybe she could play it off and pick something up to take into the dining room. As she scanned the empty surfaces, Sophia came over and gave her Grace. "Hold her a few minutes. I need to get a bottle warmed up."

Emma eased in next to her and brushed her thumb over Grace's tiny toes. "Babies are so adorable. Aren't they?"

Couldn't argue with that. Maggie rocked the sweetie pie with black tufts of hair sticking up like a Mohawk and dressed in a pink onesie with yellow polka dots. Unable to resist, she brushed her nose against Grace's; the baby powder scent, cottony soft skin, and look of wonder on the infant's pudgy face were so mesmerizing.

"You think you'll have more children?" Grace gripped Emma's finger and tried to pull it toward her mouth.

The pang in Maggie's heart told her yes, but she figured the likelihood of it happening would be slim to none. Since she didn't want or need another mess of a man in her life, a baby wouldn't be possible anytime soon. Maybe ever. She shifted her attention from the bundle in her arms and examined Emma closer.

Was it rude for a stranger to ask such a question? Not really, but for some reason she didn't like it coming from her.

Shoulder to shoulder in shared baby wonder, she noticed a few things she hadn't picked up on outside. Faint age lines spread from the corners of Emma's eyes. Sunshine from the large picture window behind them cast a sheen on her hair, revealing streaks of copper and red. The turquoise tank with matching cardigan and jean capris seemed casual enough for a birthday party. Compared to the loudmouth with Mr. Stone last week, Emma's soft tone and gentle manner so far had been the complete opposite. Yet still, something about the woman didn't fit right.

"My son's a great catch."

Maggie blinked several times. "Huh?"

Sophia came over with a bottle in hand, removing Grace. "I'll be in the rocking chair. If you want to round everyone up, they can come in and eat now."

Without a baby to concentrate on, Maggie's stare settled on Emma. "Son?"

"It may be presumptuous of me, but I didn't see a ring on your finger. You'll have to excuse me, I'm a little old fashioned. I realize not everyone wears rings these days. You're single, right? I thought Matt mentioned you were."

"He did. I was there," came Sophia's shouted confirmation from the living room. "And yes, she's single. Tell your son to get his butt in gear, Emma. He's gonna have to change his tactic to get someone as special as Maggie."

"Son?"

Emma nodded, her smile gradual at first, and when Maggie said "son" again, Emma pointed outside. "Rick, he told me you met several weeks ago."

Maggie rubbed her temple, a headache setting in. "How old are you?" Sophia's coughing laughter came from the living room. Maggie turned on the cold water and filled a glass, gulping it straight down. The kitchen window hid nothing. At least a dozen kids swarmed like bees and chased Mr. Stone and Matt around the backyard, kicking soccer balls from one end to the other.

"Your daughter likes him," Emma remarked as she rested her hip along the counter and looked in the same direction. Her remark narrowed in on the problem and prodded way too close for Maggie's peace of mind. "He works too much. A good woman—the right one—could give him something else to focus on. And I should know. You know why?" Without waiting for acknowledgement, Emma elaborated. "Because his dad was the same way before we met. I was a twenty-two-year-old college student working as a waitress to pay my way through school. During a dinner rush, a handsome young man not much older than me sat in my section. I didn't have a lot of time for more than a quick chit-chat and hadn't paid him much attention. On his way out, he handed me his bill, a fifty-dollar tip, and then told me some oddball joke. The kind that was so absurd you couldn't help but laugh. He came in several days a week, doing the same thing for a month. Then one night, when I went to retrieve the bill, he was already gone. Sitting on the table had been enough money to cover his bill, his normal tip, and a red rose. On the back of the receipt was his name and phone number."

During Emma's story, Maggie took a seat at the breakfast nook, and became immersed in the memory as though it were her own. Sophia also joined her, burping Grace and rocking side to side. When Emma didn't relay any more, she couldn't help but ask, "And what? Did you call him?"

Emma's cheeks turned red, and she shook her head no.

"Why not?" Maggie and Sophia said over one another.

Shrugging, Emma sighed and joined them on the bench seat. "It wasn't the right time. There was so much going on, and I didn't need the distraction."

"So how'd it happen?" Sophia prompted. "Don't leave us in suspense."

"All right, I'm starved. Let's eat. The birthday girls are screamin' for cake," Matt announced, while a parade of adults and kids followed him inside, all of them going into the dining room where the burgers, dogs, pizza, and other goodies had been set up.

Figuring she'd better go hunt down her daughter, Maggie scooted across the bench, about to get up. A second later Cece appeared, attached to Mr. Stone's legs, her fingers gripping the belt loops on his jeans. Unable to walk normally with the extra weight, he flung his leg forward with Cece on it like a pendulum, and rocked back and forth with each step. His arms latched around her back, in a protective embrace. A collective sigh from the peanut gallery next to Maggie echoed in the kitchen, and she refused to admit the sound came from her own parted lips, too. Cece's beaming smile and glowing adoration for Mr. Stone almost had her jumping out of her seat and snatching her daughter away. That single expression stabbed her in the heart, and brought a reappearance of the devil on her shoulder. *No. Not him.*

Perfect timing as usual, Kat swept in, yanked Cece off of him and declared, "Time for grubs, monster."

"No monster, sweet pea," Cece corrected.

The fact her daughter preferred Mr. Stone's nickname landed another strike, stabbing Maggie between the eyes. She face-planted in her awaiting hands, cushioning the blow— somewhat. Someone rubbed up and down her spine.

"You feelin' okay?" Sophia's concern had been appreciated but unnecessary.

"Uh, Maggie, could I talk to you? In private." Mr. Stone's voice sounded close by. *Too* close.

No, you can't. Go away.

Call it woman's intuition or whatever, she almost kissed Emma for her out of the blue save. "Let Maggie get something to eat. I heard her stomach grumbling. She must be starved."

Maggie could feel the jostle of the table as Emma and Sophia must have gotten up. Since she still had her face buried she couldn't tell, just guessed. Counting to ten, she dropped

78

her hands, expecting to be alone. No such luck.

Across from her, Mr. Stone tapped his thumb on the wooden surface, inches from her fingers. "When you're done, we need to talk. It's important."

Years of dealing with her sister's antics and handling the constant challenges that came from being a single parent, she rose as steadily as possible, more than prepared to tackle the next stumbling block. She leaned in, knuckle to knuckle, a bead of sweat rolling down her spine as she whispered, "What could you say that you haven't already?"

A faint caress tickled the hairs on her finger, dragging her away from his attentive eyes. His thumb lifted and fell on the table in a flicking, daring taunt. If she didn't get away from him right this minute, she'd smack him for a different reason.

One person after another walked by them on their way outside, tossing curious glances. Time to get a grip. She patted his shoulder and added a squeeze, clenching it a little too tight on purpose. "Well, Mr. Stone, better dive in before all the food is gone." Then she escaped, filling a paper plate and doing her best to avoid his heated gaze.

Throughout the party, Mr. Stone attempted to corner Maggie. Cake being her favorite part of birthday celebrations, she scooped up a slice of vanilla just as a strong grip caught her elbow, almost dropping the perfect piece with three pink roses on the floor. He pressed his warm lips against her ear. "Stop avoiding me. I'll be in Matt's office down the hall. Bring the cake and meet me."

As nonchalantly as possible, she licked the frosting off her fingers, pretending he hadn't said anything, and that his zipper wasn't glued to her behind. A cursory glance showed a few Westlake employees and other guests she didn't recognize gathered on couches and chairs around a flat screen TV. The open-space concept presented a clear view from the kitchen through the dining area into the living room. A NASCAR race had the attention of the males and females, chatting and snacking as they took in the action on the screen. No one paid her any mind.

After he left, she stacked another huge slice of yummy goodness on the other piece and went outside to the swing set. Stuffing her mouth full of icing, she shoveled one forkful after another between her lips and watched the kids. They glided down the slide, swayed back and forth on the seats next to her, and jumped for the o-rings, rocking back and forth like monkeys. The distraction served its purpose. She had no intention of meeting him anywhere.

Filled with her daily dose of sugar and relaxed from a soothing swing, she wandered to the pool for a dip. With her feet dangling, she closed her eyes and aimed her face toward the sun. Kids' shouts of glee made her smile and delight in their simple pleasure. Matt and Sophia knew how to throw a party. A variety of activities kept the thirty-some kids busy. The picnic tables had finger paints and art supplies. Brand new motorized Barbie jeeps drew boys and girls. Some of them were entertained by jumping on mini-trampolines, while others stood in a long line, including Cece, waiting for a pony ride. He who shall not be named had arranged the attraction as the twins' gift.

No sooner did she have the thought, she felt someone sit next to her, along with a kerplunk and a gush of water splashing her thighs. "If you stay put and act casual, no one will know you're pissed at me," Mr. Stone uttered in a monotone.

She lifted the leg closest to him and kicked. The intent, splash and drown him out. Her sucky plan drenched her T-shirt and shorts. His wind-sucking howl indicated she must have missed him by a mile. Since she refused to open her eyes, she didn't know for sure.

"Well, that was smart."

Her annoyed quip came just as quickly. "What would be smart is if you stayed away."

"Now, if I did that, I couldn't give you my secret message, Maggie." His cutesy tone aggravated her even more. Why couldn't he take a hint?

"You see, the good thing about secrets is that they're supposed to stay that way. So take it and shove it up—"

A huge hand covered her mouth, halting her whispered tirade. It didn't stop him though. "I'll tell you what. If you won't let me say it, then I'll have no choice but to write it down and send it to you."

On automatic impulse her body stiffened. Other not so pleasant letters came to mind. The most recent arrived yesterday. It had been two weeks since she received the last threat. Jake's brother, Donnie, helped him communicate from behind bars. Often Jake followed each correspondence with a call too, repeating the same message and blaming her for his conviction, even though she hadn't been the deciding factor. Fingerprints and eyewitness testimony weighed in the decision, proving he robbed over twenty convenience stores. Yet, he swore she'd pay, an eye for an eye.

"Shh, relax." Mr. Stone dropped his hand on her thigh; a sudden burning sensation, either from the sun or him, seared her skin. Seventy-degree temps gave her a chance to wear jean shorts. Now, with him touching her, she regretted having worn them. "It's okay. Just give me a couple minutes. I don't want to say what I have to around all these people."

A sudden cry had every parent jerking around left and right trying to find out who was hurt. Next to a trampoline, a little boy lying in the grass had bloody teeth showing as he screamed in pain. Several adults rushed over to him, checking his arms and legs and helping him get up.

She stood and searched for her daughter. Both Kat and Cece were in the middle of a bunch of kids waiting in line.

"Get over here, Mags. Your turn. I need a potty break."

"Yeah, Mama, come here. Ride the horsey." Jumping up and down, Cece held Kat's hand and with the other waved her over.

Grateful for the opportunity to escape, she jogged over to them. Kat walked around Maggie, ducked down, and spoke low enough that Cece didn't hear. "You know that little voice in your head, Mags, and all those rules you have. Listen to them." Then off Kat went, darting past clusters of guests.

From fifty feet away, Maggie watched as her sister careened over to Mr. Stone and stood inches apart from him. Kat's globe-sized sunglasses prohibited Maggie from getting a read on her sister's facial expressions but it didn't matter. She could just imagine Kat's words of wisdom, none of which could be repeated around impressionable children.

Now she regretted telling Kat what Mr. Stone said about her parenting skills. In return, Kat told her to "ignore the ass" and avoid him. Easier said than done since events like this made it impossible. As much as she tried to play keep away, he sought her out. It didn't help that Cece wouldn't stop hounding him either. Maggie wasn't sure how to handle him. She might not want or need a man in her own life, but that didn't mean Cece couldn't gain a lot from good men like her boss. As for Mr. Stone, she'd go with the flow and figure out how to limit Cece's access.

"My turn. Pick me up, Mama." Cece yanked her forward. The pony stomped its hoof and the guide held his hand out, prepared to catch the bouncing little girl eager to get on.

Hoisted onto the saddle, Cece grabbed the reins and watched as the elderly man showed the proper way to loop a thumb and forefinger through them. As the pony and guide moved, so did Maggie, following the designated path. Thank goodness for the restricted area, since large clumps of poop made it difficult to navigate, causing her to dart around at least ten piles. Yuck, what a mess. If she were Matt, she'd force Mr.

Stone to clean up before he left. A kick in her knee pulled her gaze away from her flip-flops to Cece's enormous grin. She forgot about everything else and took pleasure in her daughter's happiness.

That much she could provide.

There weren't many children in their neighborhood Cece's age, so when she asked to stay longer to play, Maggie had a hard time saying no. By eight o'clock though and most partygoers long gone, she went upstairs to check on the kids. Lizbeth, Harley, and Cece were asleep in beanbag chairs, *Frozen* playing on the TV. She turned it off and picked up Cece. A heavy sleeper, the jostling hadn't even woken her. She'd let Matt know about the girls when she got downstairs, since Sophia had the baby in the bath.

Headed through the hallway, she turned toward the stairs and ran right into Mr. Stone as he stepped onto the landing. With her foot midair, she lost her balance, bouncing off him. His strong arms wrapped around her waist, yanking her and Cece into his chest and backing her into the wall. Face to face, breath to breath, lips a mere centimeter apart, shivers flowed in slow motion from her toes to tingling mouth. His broadened stance and rock-hard thighs braced hers. With Cece cushioned high on her waist in between them, they were pelvis to pelvis. That thought sent pins and needles through her, causing her core to clench and eliciting another tremble.

Mr. Stone breathed, "Maggie." His lower lip slid along hers as he tugged her tighter.

Ignoring better judgment, she nipped his moist flesh and sucked him into her mouth. He groaned, and their tongues twirled and entwined, battling for control. His firm grasp cupped her behind and lifted her toward him, rubbing and stroking his hardness into the throb between her legs. Over the thumping heartbeat in her ears and a shift of weight in her arms, common sense got slapped into her when she heard a sleepy, "Max . . . Mama."

She wasn't sure which of them leapt away first. When it happened, they wore similar expressions: flushed cheeks, glossy lips, and wide alert eyes. The impromptu tryst took her by surprise too. Their heavy panting batted back and forth, off of each other. Her throat tightened and flashbacks assaulted her—Jake, his explosive desire for her in the beginning, and then Cece came along, and he couldn't stomach the sight of her or his daughter. Lust, attraction, pheromones—whatever this might be wouldn't last. Men wanted one thing—sex, a challenge. Once they had it, they moved on. Just as Jake had, cheating on her time and time again. This man wasn't any different. His one-night stand disclosed as much at the restaurant, and his reaction proved it.

Finished with the encounter and him, she concentrated on Cece instead. Her daughter's eyes were shuttered and there hadn't been another peep out of her. She grabbed the railing and dashed around him, catapulting down the stairs. No one trailed her, and she marched through the vacant first floor in search for Matt, finding him sprawled on a hammock in the backyard chatting with Kat. After letting him know the girls had to be tucked into bed, she ordered her sister out of the hot tub and hurried toward the gate for a quick escape.

Her sister's head-banger tunes did nothing to obscure her manic thoughts or drown out her brain's furious and distraught lecture during the drive home.

That was beyond stupid.
Forget he exists.
You have enough to deal with.
You need to focus on your daughter.
No matter what Emma said, he's not a family man.
He'll break your heart and your daughter's.

Whatever it takes do not let him in.
No way.
No how.
Never.
Ever.

Mama's Rule #11:

It's no use crying over spilt milk.

How did he fuck that up—again? All he wanted to do was apologize for mouthing off and embarrassing her in front of his employees. He hadn't been sorry for what he said, just how it came out. She really needed to be more careful where the little bugger kept running off to. Twenty-five floors high, their building provided a lot of nooks and crannies for Cece to hide in, let alone the worst possibility, someone *could* take her. He might not want kids of his own, but he never wanted harm to come to anyone else's children.

Given multiple chances to set things straight, he'd blown it. Not only with that, he screwed up big time by kissing her. Damn, that had been stupid. His tongue was still on fire, and the second he had Maggie in his arms, he got an instant hard-on. If they had been alone, he would have ripped off her tiny shorts and rammed into her from behind. And that thought pissed him off all over again.

Slamming his fist against the wall, he sucked in an over-whelmed breath and blew out his frustration. All he could smell were vanilla cupcakes, sprinkled with a dozen candy-coated flavors. Maggie's passion fruit center and her addictive spices clung to his taste buds and permeated every cell in his body. In an attempt to scrub her scent off, he rubbed a hand over his mouth and clasped them on top of his head, beating a path up and down the hall, cursing to high heaven and himself.

A clearing throat halted him mid-step at the twins' bedroom. When he glanced over his shoulder, he cringed at another head-on collision waiting to happen. Matt leaned against the railing, his arms crossed. "What'd you do?"

"Fuck off." He dropped his arms and bolted to the stairs. "I was gonna give the girls a kiss good night, but you can do that for me. I'm outta here." Before he made it to the second step, Matt grabbed his shoulder, stopping him.

"Why you fightin' it so hard? Just give in. Maggie would be perfect for you."

He clamped onto Matt's wrist and backed up a step, squaring off and putting them on even footing. "You must have one hell of a boring life if you can't stay out of mine. Maybe you're not gettin' enough. Is that it? Tryin' to live through me, Matt?"

An instant shot came at Rick's jaw and got blocked by his forearm before he shoved Matt off. Never one to miss out on a good fight, Matt dove in again, taking a potshot at his cheek when Sophia jumped in between them, slapping their chests.

"Knock it off."

Had Rick not been pissed, he would've gotten a good laugh out of Sophia trying to manhandle two hundred plus pounds, and the six foot two males, dwarfing her.

"You hotheads, cool it. Whatever the problem is, it isn't worth ruining your friendship." Sophia grabbed her husband's cheeks, insisting he look at her. "We all had such a good time, let's not finish it this way." Pussy whipped, Matt forgot all about him as he yanked Sophia by the hips and crashed his mouth onto hers. Then Matt lifted his gaze and shot him the middle finger.

Aiming one right back, he darted down the stairs, slamming the door on his way out.

After another jam-packed schedule, one off-site meeting after another, Rick entered the lobby at four thirty hoping Mrs. Collins didn't have a pile of messages waiting for him.

"Hi ya, Mr. Stone, how's it goin' today?" Sam, the security guard, called out.

As often as possible, Rick would stop and shoot the breeze. Grateful for the diversion, he set his briefcase on the counter, relaxing for a change. "Did you catch the fights last night?"

"Don't miss 'em." Sam swung his fist toward his own chin, mimicking an upper cut. "Mendoza KO'd Faust in the first round. How about that? You owe me a Jackson. Your loss is my gain, Mr. Stone. You keep on addin' to my retirement fund." Sam rubbed his hands together and extended his palm out.

Rick pulled the wallet from his back pocket, thumbed through the cash, and tossed a twenty on the counter. "I thought I'd beat you this time. Faust was the favorite."

"Ah, you got to look at more than the odds. Mendoza may be up 'n' coming, but he didn't get the bout with the middle-weight champ for no reason. That boy has fists of steel."

"Rick, there you are. I was just in your office and your secretary said she didn't expect you for hours."

Because Mrs. Collins knew he didn't want to see Julia, now or ever. As she drew closer, he scanned the enormous lobby, hoping for an easy escape. Even Sam ducked his head, concentrating on the video screens lining his desk, a grimace pinching his mouth. Julia Kensington got a fight-or-flight effect out of most people, since she had a bad habit of treating everybody as if they were beneath her, regardless of income level. With nowhere to go, he locked his feet in place, prepar-

88

ing for her barrage. "Was there something you needed?"

A designer white silk pantsuit added to her look-but-don't-touch persona as she sashayed, heels clicking on the marble floor. Her smile widened, and she tucked her arm through his, clamping her claws onto his wrist. "Yes, you. I want you to take me to dinner." She smoothed a hand down his lapel and repositioned the handkerchief in his breast pocket even though it didn't need it. Too close for comfort, she settled her hand on his shoulder, smothering her chest against his. "I'm tired of waiting for you, Rick. If you won't come to me, I'll have to chase you." Julia's rapid fluttering eyelashes were not at all appealing to him.

As he stepped away from her, something plowed into him from behind and wrapped around his thighs, squeezing hard. When he looked over his shoulder, Cece beamed up at him, not saying a word, unlike her normal shouted greeting. "Where's your mom?" Again, no speaking; instead she pointed behind her to the other side of the lobby. The moment he caught sight of Maggie, his chest tightened as well as other parts of his anatomy.

Engrossed in a conversation with a woman and little girl who wore identical navy blue and white striped sailor dresses and berets, Maggie glanced at him and just as quickly refocused on the matching brunettes, a mother and daughter who took stylish to an extreme.

Ducking down to Cece's height, he yanked her up from under her arms and placed her on the counter. "How are you, sweet pea?"

Cece lifted her hand, pressed two fingers together and pointed to the left, followed by sticking her pinky up. Tongue bit between her teeth, she scrunched her brows and tucked her thumb under three fingers. Then switched the arrangement to cupping her palm closed, thumb extended, and then crooked her forefinger up.

From over the counter, Sam relayed, "She said, 'Hi, Max.'"

Shocked by what he'd seen and Sam verified, Rick addressed the little wonder. "Were you signing?"

Her answer came as clapping. Cece threw both arms around Rick's neck and squeezed tight. As if it were the most natural thing in the world, he nestled her against his chest in a tender embrace. Intense pride engulfed him. Unable to resist, he told her exactly that. A faint peck on his cheek lodged a swollen lump in his throat. As he took a step back, Cece pointed across the lobby again and continued to sign. He looked across the counter for assistance.

"Robin," Sam announced.

Rick followed Cece's arm, pointing to the girl. Two plus two put together, he asked, "Is that your friend?"

Again, rapid head bobbing and a toothy Cece grin.

Adding it all up, he prompted, "Did she teach you that?"

More clapping and Cece bouncing up and down on the counter.

"Show me how to say, 'Hi, Robin.'" Cece grabbed Rick's arm and lifted one finger after another, repositioning them in sequence and demonstrating the greeting. Once again, pride and something else he resisted shouting out loud hit him in the middle of his chest. After practicing a few times, Cece confirmed with a pat on his shoulder that he'd performed it accurately. Ready to test out his new skills, he signed the salutation toward the dark-haired cutie with pigtails braided just like Cece's and received a "hi" from Robin in return.

Nails scraping up the back of his neck and through his hair had him spinning around. "Rick . . ." Julia tugged on his lapel and walked backward, whining, "Let's go. I'm hungry."

Rick remained glued at Cece's legs. Unwilling to take no for an answer, Julia stomped toward him. Done with her antics, he raised his hand, bringing her to a stuttering halt. "I've been out all day. I have calls to return and reports to finish."

Her lower lip extended into an over-exaggerated pout. If Julia knew it caused wrinkles around her mouth, he doubted she'd ever repeat the unflattering expression. Maybe he'd tell her and she'd run off in embarrassment right to her plastic surgeon. And with her bloated arrogance, she probably kept him on speed dial.

"You have to eat. I'll call Putriccios to deliver something, and we can dine in your office."

"I had a late lunch a half hour ago."

Determined to be the center of attention, Julia slid in between him and Cece. Julia brushed her hands through her blond locks, and she reshaped the strands, shifting them across each shoulder into makeshift pigtails.

Cece's fingers formed into rabbit ears and bobbed up and down above Julia's head, her other hand covering her snickers.

Swallowing the gut-wrenching laughter he wanted to let rip, he twisted toward the counter and coughed into his fist. Sam didn't have that problem; his booming howls echoed off the windows and thirty-foot ceilings.

"Time to go, sweetie." The sound of Maggie's jubilant voice snapped Rick's lax muscles into a constricted mass. Before he took on the full force of Maggie, he drew in several deep breaths, and on the edge of his toes, inched around toward her. As he did, he caught sight of Sam wiggling his bushy eyebrows. No longer in a joking mood, his lips tightened as he confronted the swarm of females, each possessing a stinger that could strike without warning.

Regardless of the angle, Maggie's natural beauty shone through, highlighted by her alabaster skin and the freckles sprinkled across her temple, the bridge of her nose, the crest of her cheeks, and the arch of her chin. From the instant they met, he ticked her off. This time wasn't any different. She darted a few glances between Julia and him, then scooped Cece into her arms and scurried past them. "Wait." He put an arm out to block her, but she stormed around it. "Please, Maggie, don't go."

Her pace slowed and came to a gradual stop near the elevators. She glanced over her shoulder and nodded. He couldn't move or stop staring at her. Snug jeans hugged her hourglass hips. Her mint-colored T-shirt brightened the green in her eyes, beckoning him to come closer. The sun spotlighted Cece's orange-red hair, which appeared in varying shades within Maggie's auburn strands.

"Dinner will be here in half an hour." Julia popped up in front of him, blocking his view.

"Enjoy it on your way home." Intent on getting to Maggie and Cece before they ran away, he grabbed his briefcase and sidestepped around Julia. A force he couldn't understand propelled him to the dynamic duo. His stride strengthened and his heart lightened, floating higher with each step as the distance between them lessened. A mere foot away, Julia shouldered past him and stood in his path. Maggie and Cece partitioned behind her.

"Don't disappoint me like that, Rick. You know your grandfather wouldn't be pleased." A reminder of another overbearing control freak didn't help her case. Julia's gradual smirk and all-knowing dig sparked a fire in his gut, renewing his determination. He opened his mouth, about to tell her where to go when her violent screeching knocked him back several steps. Julia had run her hands through her hair again, except this time, wads of gum were clumped in fistfuls of strands on each side.

Cece's snickers rolled out of her. Maggie's mouth fell open when she examined Julia's hair and pinched shut when she aimed a pierced scolding at her daughter. Red blotches appeared along Maggie's neck and across her arms. Instead of ducking tail and running, she apologized for Cece's behavior.

Julia pointed her finger at Cece's nose and shouted, "You're an awful, despicable, evil brat."

The ringing in his ears and a clenched jaw kept him from going off on her right away. It didn't matter; Maggie beat him

92

to it.

"Don't you dare speak to my daughter or anyone like that. I don't care who you are. You don't treat people that way. You ever hear karma's a bitch? I wouldn't push your luck. Never know what will come swinging your way."

"Is that a threat? I saw the way you looked at Rick. You think you found a pot at the end of the rainbow, don't you? Well, he's taken. You and your little hellion need to get lost. Find some other Neverland. Your dreams aren't coming true here."

"Enough." He grabbed Julia's arm and tugged her out the door. A row of cabs made for an easier exit. "Get in." He yanked the door open and waved her toward the seat. The prima donna hissed at him but did as he instructed. "This is your only warning. Stay away from them." He gave the driver her address and ignored her crocodile tears as she begged him to come with her.

A lone black briefcase remained in the place he left it moments ago. No Maggie or Cece. Whatever spark he felt before dashed into his vacant gut, and his hollow heart followed suit. He closed his eyes and rubbed his palms into them. Dammit. He swept the case off the floor and shuffled into the elevator. In the decade-plus he'd worked in this building, not once had he been alone on the ride to the twentieth floor. For some reason there wasn't another person or any stops. Go figure. Whether the claustrophobic walls in the cube closed in on him or the recent events were responsible for sucking the life out of him, either way, he never felt so lost or alone.

Numb, he trudged past Mrs. Collins's desk and out of the corner of his eye noticed her silent and perceptive examination. Locked inside his office, he dropped the briefcase on his desk and looked outside. The five o'clock mad dash produced streams of suits like marching ants rushing into mounds of cabs. Bumper-to-bumper traffic, horns honking in urgency all disappeared in a blur. He pressed his temple against the glass and pounded his fist against it. Countless vibrations pulsed through him, yet that wasn't what registered.

A miserable reflection stared back at him.

Beaten, hunched shoulders weakened his stance.

His confidence vaporized in bits and pieces with each heated breath until a meaningless shell remained in its place.

A fragment of the man he once knew.

Mama's Rule #12:

Never look a gift horse in the mouth.

The Gorilla playset Kat circled in a sales flyer caught Cece's eye. Not wanting to spend that much on a swing set, Maggie showed Cece several others that were much less expensive. However, two against one didn't fare well in their household, making Maggie the odd girl out and losing to the strong-willed pair. Kat kicking in fifty percent of the cost reduced her anxiety about spending close to a thousand dollars on a mega-sized toy. During the entire drive to pick it up, Maggie justified the decision, telling herself that after taking Cece away from the only home she'd known, the least Maggie could do was get her daughter something that would provide a lot of joy. Besides, the playset Kat picked out really was awesome. Over nine different apparatus, including a cedar fort with a canopy, a rock wall, slide, swings, ladder, sandpit, trapeze with o-rings, steering wheel, and a telescope. Enough to keep an active little girl busy for quite some time.

After breakfast, Maggie and Cece went shopping. Seated in the kiddie cart that resembled a race car, Cece might have been enjoying the carefree view of the warehouse-style home improvement store, but winding up and down one enormous aisle after another just made Maggie anxious to get what she needed and hightail it out of there. Steering the cart around an enormous wood display, she swung to the left and rammed right into a buggy coming down the other aisle.

"Max," Cece yelled, bouncing up and down in her seat. "Mama gettin' me a swing." Caught in his hazel eyes, Maggie didn't respond. It wouldn't have mattered; she had no idea what she wanted to say. It had been a week since the lobby scene. She'd avoided him by getting off the elevator a floor below and climbing a back stairwell to bypass his office. For several days she got away with the diversion by telling Cece they were hiding from a big, bad dragon just like in the fairy tales she read to her before bed. By Friday though, her all too inquisitive daughter wasn't buying the tall tale anymore and wanted to take their regular route. Cece said "Max missed her" since he hadn't seen her for so long.

"Funny running into you guys." Matt threw an arm over her shoulder, pulling her into his side.

"See if I bring you any more Russian Torte or any other goodies," she huffed under her breath, ramming her elbow into his ribs. He knew damned well she would be here. Yesterday when he asked about her plans for this weekend, and she told him, he kept prodding for more information about the day and time of her shopping excursion.

"I gotta show ya, Max." Cece pointed up ahead; ten-foot banners of the monstrosities hung from the ceiling above the displays.

"Which one you gettin', Mags?" Matt prompted, leaning more of his weight against her, one foot crossed in front of the other as if he had all day to shoot the breeze.

"Fort, rope, rocks," Cece screamed while pogoing out of her seat with each description, causing passersby to look in their direction, smother a smile, and go about their shopping.

Mr. Stone unlatched Cece from the race car buggy and

picked her up, strolling several feet away. "Which one?" Wide shoulders and muscled biceps bulged from the grip he had on Cece, and his firm backside tucked into well-fitting jeans had her checking out his confident stride. Since the displays were located in the same direction, she pretended her focus had been on them instead of Mr. Stone and his too-fine physique. A sigh came out of her mouth way too loudly and had her performing a quick cover up. With the list crunched in her hand, she fanned her face as if she were overwhelmed by the feat in front of her. "Why in the world did I think Kat and I could put that monster together? It'll take us a month."

She should have known Matt wouldn't fall for her diversion, since his investigative skills were well-honed. "Umm hmm. I saw you getting a good look at all those parts, Mags. Lotta work there, but well worth it in the long run." Somehow she didn't think he meant the play structure, just like she hadn't been measuring the amount of time it would take to piece it all together.

Taking a huge leap, she accepted the bait and went along with his underhanded tactic. "You think I can handle it?"

His grip tightened on her shoulder, and he declared, "You're the one, Mags. You might need a little help . . . from friends. Take in that view." He jutted his chin toward his buddy, who directed a salesperson over to the exact playset Maggie had come here to get. "Cece picked a strong piece that'll make her very happy and provide a lot of support. It can handle any obstacles that'll challenge her and you. There's a bunch of them. But give it time, you'll figure it out."

"I'm not sure. There's too much. A lot I don't know about . . . it's all so complicated."

"You trust me, Mags?" He ducked down, blocking some of the distractions by getting right in front of her. "I'll help. I promise. You can do this."

Before getting to know Matt, and his caring and supportive nature, her family made up the majority of the people she put her faith in. She could add Matt to the list. An all-around good guy, he hadn't given her any reason not to so far. Unable to verbalize a response around the lump in her throat, Matt inspected her reaction and then stepped aside. Cece and Mr. Stone examined each feature on the display—smiling, happily exploring, adorable.

Terrified and stuck in place, all she could manage in reply was a stiff, minuscule nod.

Matt gave her a swifter, more confident one in return. "All right, let's go get what you guys need." He grabbed her arm, the buggy, and led the way.

A payment in full had been made, delivery arranged for next Saturday, and after all the items on her list were loaded in the car along with Cece, she thanked Matt for helping her find everything. More than comfortable with the surroundings, he'd located the tools and any other essentials that would be helpful for the job. That left Mr. Stone. She hadn't said a thing to him. The fact Cece hadn't stopped talking to him helped cover for Maggie's lack of manners. It made for a good excuse too since she didn't want to be rude by interrupting her daughter's nonstop chatter.

Mr. Stone saved her from the uncomfortable silent stand-off. "We're done. Let's go get the stuff you need for the twins' playhouse." The first part stated matter of fact and directed toward her. The latter mentioned in an upbeat tone to Matt while Mr. Stone patted him on the back.

Her mouth flapping, she responded with a mumbled, "Uh, um . . ."

"Nope, not yet. I'll be at your place next weekend, so will Rick. Lots to do. You're gonna need the help."

A phone ringing had all three of them searching. Chills rocked her when she saw the unknown number, a common occurrence when Jake called. On a rare occasion she received a sales pitch, but other than that only family contacted her.

"Maggie?" Matt's questioning prompt didn't divert her

from the task at hand.

Over and over she jabbed the red button, silencing the chirping. It rang again as she went to toss it inside her bag. This time she turned it off and buried it under the other junk she carried around in the humongous tote.

She opened the driver's door and placed a foot inside, when a tug on her shoulder tried to halt her. Determined to get away from any more male interference, she plopped down in her seat. "Kat and I can do it." After shutting herself inside, she turned the ignition on and wound down the window. "Why do men think women can't handle things on their own?" Not waiting for a response, she clarified her point. "I know how to read. In fact, everything is crystal clear now." She tapped her temple, put the car in gear, and closed the subject. "You both have plenty to take care of in your own lives. Leave me alone to manage mine."

While navigating through the crowded parking lot, she refused to acknowledge the shadowed figures in her rearview mirror. Instead, she moved forward, checking on her main priority: Cece sleeping in the back seat and the only person she should concentrate on—from here on out.

Mama's Rule #13:

Because I said so, that's why.

"Were you able to get the dinner reservation confirmed with Mr. Shephard's secretary?" Rick stopped in front of Mrs. Collins's desk as she turned off her computer, ready to leave for the day.

"All set. Time changed from six to seven. Agnes said Mr. Shephard had several meetings run late, so it worked for him too."

"Good, messages?"

"They're on your desk already. Oh, and you had a visitor." Mrs. Collins pointed over his shoulder to his office door.

Taped to the front was a piece of white construction paper. The closer he got to it, the tighter his chest grew. He tucked a finger under the sticky tab and lifted, opening the folded sheet, which revealed a huge swing set drawn in colorful red and brown crayons. Cece at the top of a slide and sitting on Rick's lap, both of them with hands in the air and smiles stretching from ear to ear. He blinked away any remnants of emotion, refusing to admit what so plainly surfaced in that sketch. As he examined the image closer, in the far left corner at the foot of the rock wall, Maggie stood with her hands on her hips and a frown on her face. If he hadn't been so flummoxed he would've laughed at Cece's spot-on disapproving representation of her mother.

A soft touch on his shoulder hadn't pulled his sight away from the picture. "You make her happy." Mrs. Collins's voice matched her gentle hand, and then she tapped the image of Maggie. "If you're going to win her over, you have a lot more work to do. She's a harder sell."

He folded the paper in half as it had been on his door and shut out the images. "It doesn't matter. I'm not buying. Some things aren't negotiable. You've always looked out for me, but don't push me on this. I'm not a wet-behind-the-ears eighteen-year-old. I can make my own decisions and don't need anyone telling me what to do."

Mrs. Collins rubbed his back in a soothing motion like his mom often did when he'd lost his temper as a little boy and had to be calmed down. "Sometimes a person's vision can become so narrow and focused on a single-minded goal, they lose sight of the most important things. Your daddy was on that path until he met your mom. She brightened his world and opened his eyes to a whole different life. Maybe he would've come to the realization on his own, but sometimes we're offered one chance. A little window of opportunity, and if we don't look its way or consider it seriously, we'll miss out on a gift meant for us in that moment and time. If we don't take it, we'll never have that reward offered again. Something may replace it, but it will never be as sweet as the one intended for us all along." By the time Mrs. Collins finished her spiel, he was sitting behind his desk and staring off at the Manhattan skyline. Every part of her message had been heard and pounded in his brain along with an enormous headache. "Good night, Mr. Stone. I hope your dinner meeting is productive." Her professional tone replaced the motherly concern. In his peripheral vision he caught her closing the door on her way out.

He spread open the picture and traced the smiles on the two faces readying for the speedy and slippery slope. To be young, carefree, and brave—casting concern aside, no clue or reservation for mishaps that could spring up. In his world, risk didn't always equate to a large reward. Specializing in five- to hundred-million-dollar mergers and acquisitions presented a daily gamble. He conducted months of research on each account, decreasing the possibility of failure. He closed every deal he worked on since becoming CEO and increased profits each year. The complexity of negotiating sales and purchases were fraught with ups and downs. Executives and shareholders from both corporations wanted their piece of the pie before signing on the dotted line. Any distraction could put him off his game, and he couldn't let anything get in the way of accomplishing what his father had started at the young age of twenty-two. The countless stories Dad told him about his struggles, his dreams to have a father-and-son run corporation, and then on his deathbed, a final request: "Son, promise me you'll go to college and take over the business." If he let anyone keep him from making his dad's wish come true and continuing its success, he'd never forgive himself.

He set the picture inside the center drawer of his desk and with a final look slammed it shut. Snatching the keys out of his pocket, he exited the office, locking up on his way out. Constant reminders of a little redheaded sweetie pie pulled at his heartstrings. Each interaction became more dear than the last. As for Maggie, he needed a lot more control and a solution for his pent-up lust. Something like a straightjacket, cement shoes, or someone to push him off a bridge. Because any time he spent in her presence, he felt like he was falling anyway. Distraction times two and double the trouble—Cece and Maggie quadrupled the heartache.

Too bad his dual degrees didn't teach him how to enforce sanctions on himself and bar access to the distracting duo. Out of sight and out of mind should've worked in theory. He'd been somewhat relieved when he hadn't run into Maggie at all last week. When Matt insisted he go with him to pick up a playhouse for the twins, the trip put him at the wrong place at the wrong time and brought front and center what he wanted to avoid. Unable to resist pudgy-cheeked Cece, he figured if he had the bundle of joy in his arms and got away from Maggie, he could prevent getting sucked in by her seductive eyes and heavenly sweet scent. The plan worked for the most part, considering Cece kept him engaged, explaining the crafts she made in preschool and talking about all the things she and Robin liked. She even taught him a few new signs as they navigated through the aisles. But the more Cece spoke to him and Maggie didn't, it just ticked him off the longer they walked around the store and she kept ignoring him. Not a word, not even a hello, like some scum she couldn't bring herself to acknowledge. By the time the tools and supplies were packed in her car, his temper had escalated to boiling. Nothing would have made him happier than to get the heck out of there. Maggie gave him the perfect out, declaring she didn't want or need his help. Since he hadn't offered it in the first place, Matt did, he'd been more than eager to get as far away from her as possible before and even more so after her tirade.

The memory launched a fire in him and renewed his determination to forget about Maggie. He wouldn't let her or any woman sway him from his goals. After his dinner meeting, he'd call someone in his black book and take care of his problem. It had been too long since he had sex. He couldn't even recall the last time or the individual he'd been with.

Yep, that would be the key—sex.

It always helped him relax and forget.

It would work now too.

Except it didn't.

Complete opposite—blond hair, brown eyes, smelled like smoke, not flowers or cupcakes.

He sent the nameless, stacked beauty home, paying her cab fare.

And took matters into his own hands—once again.

As he read the latest budget reports for two companies planning to merge, a gold "K" embossed envelope tossed on top blocked his view. "You didn't RSVP."

He flicked it aside and continued reading. "That's because I'm not going."

"You will. Julia wants you to be her escort, and since it's her daddy's annual fundraiser, he's expecting you to be there."

Flipping to the next page, when he reached for a highlighter to mark a few sales figures, his grandfather clamped down on top of his hand. "Look at me, boy."

Rick opened his mouth to snap at him but stopped. It would only aggravate the situation. Leaning back in his chair, he crossed his arms and glared at him instead. More misguided revelations were about to be added to an already stressful day.

Seated across from him in the leather club chair, Grandfather mimicked his posture and expression. "Let me lay it out for you since you don't get it. Her daddy's company is the largest brokerage firm on the East Coast. You marry her, partner with him, you'll be able to go international. With their contacts and what they do, the expansion possibilities are enormous. You'd be able to open an office in China, Hong Kong, the Netherlands, France, anywhere. Don't you see the potential? That girl is head over heels in love with you. She'd be a dutiful wife, a beautiful trophy on your arm, and take you places you've never been. She'd introduce you to important people who'd be happy to invest their money and keep this business going for a hundred-plus years. It would grow this company larger than your pea brain could imagine. So pull your head out of your ass, put a ring on her finger, and make our shareholders happy. Pad their pockets and yours."

"You done?"

"Not unless you pull a diamond out of your pocket or go to the jewelry store and buy her one right now."

Before Rick could respond, Mrs. Collins knocked on the closed door and came in, carrying a box. "I'm sorry to interrupt, Mr. Stone. You had a delivery. It seemed important, so I thought I'd bring it to you right away." She set it down on top of the papers he'd been reading and left as quickly as she'd come in.

"Who's that from?"

A crooked bow drawn in pink crayon covered the lid. Scrolled on the front, written in blue slanted letters, the "M" printed big, the "a" tiny, and the "x" the largest of them all. Even with a pea-sized brain, it didn't take much to figure out who sent the gift. Curious, he removed the lid. A braided band of brown leather with a thin piece of red woven through the center sat on cotton balls. Cece told him they'd been practicing braiding each other's hair, but the teachers must have used that as a foundation for the craft in the box. No, not a craft, a piece of art. A beautiful, thick, masculine bracelet created by a four-year-old and an impressive piece any man would be proud to wear.

"What's that?"

Rick rolled his sleeve up and placed the band on his wrist. Velcro at the end made it easy to close and keep on.

Perfect fit.

"Whatever that is, it looks ridiculous on you."

His hands formed into fists, and Rick placed them on each side of the box as he leaned across the desk, a foot from his grandfather. "You can leave now."

"What about the invitation?"

"I'll take care of it."

"Are you going?"

"On one condition." Rick pushed his sleeve down and but-

106

toned it, then rounded the desk, closing in on the thorn in his side. He hadn't acquired the name "bulldog" from his employees for no reason. About to negotiate his way out of this mess, he clapped his grandfather on the back and walked him toward the exit. "I'll attend the fundraiser, escort Julia, and make a huge donation to her father's foundation." He opened the door and his grandfather came to a halt with a winning grin on his face. "Dad never would have wanted his business used as a reason for marriage. You know it and I know it. Don't dishonor his memory or me that way. I'm not getting married. But don't worry, my commitment is to this company and fulfilling his dream. If expansion is good for us, then with the board, we'll examine our options and figure out the next steps. It won't happen the way you want it though."

Tears filled Grandfather's eyes and his face turned ashen. He stormed off without saying another word. Good thing he didn't because the dryness in Rick's mouth glued it shut. He gripped the doorjamb, trying to stop the tremors rolling down his arm, across his chest, through his stomach, and along his legs. It didn't matter that it had been thirteen years since his father's death. Grief didn't have an end period, a limit, a stopping point. When you loved and lost someone, the pain didn't lessen. It just got pushed to a depth that let people exist from day to day. At any second, it would rear its head, as if the loss happened right then, at that moment, reliving every word, each breath, and the final goodbyes.

He collapsed into his chair and started to drop his aching head into his hands, when he caught sight of Cece's box. The lopsided *Max* brought a brief smirk to his lips as he imagined her tongue stuck between her teeth while she wrote each letter. Absurd-looking on most people, she formed the expression when concentrating, which made her even more adorable. He yanked his sleeve up, running his finger over the red strand. She'd done such a nice job. Next time he saw her, he'd let her know how much he liked her thoughtful gift.

"Mr. Stone, your six o'clock appointment's waiting in conference room A."

He put the box in his desk drawer, placing it on the picture from yesterday. With his suit coat thrown on and his tie tightened, he passed Mrs. Collins as she waved good night. In three hours he'd be able to do that too, but for now, he needed to concentrate on getting this new account. When he turned the doorknob with his left hand, the band rubbing against his shirt reminded him of the single bright light in this endless workday. A strength bolstered his step as he strode into the conference room recharged and ready to acquire this deal.

It wasn't just his dad's legacy—it was his too. That realization never registered before. Until right now.

"This came for you while you were out of the office. It's an invitation." Mrs. Collins stuck out an envelope, biting on her lip and holding back a grin.

As Rick slowed his pace, trudging closer, his temper rose. Why did he think his grandfather would give up? He should've known better. Disgusted with what he'd find inside, he dropped his briefcase next to Mrs. Collins's desk and pulled the envelope out of her hand a little too fast. The trash can at his feet would've been a good place to drop it, but he'd made a promise. He lifted the flap and yanked, expecting a card. Instead a pink cup made from construction paper came out. In the center:

108

Her name printed the best he'd seen so far.

"I cleared your calendar. Cece delivered it herself. You should have seen her. She had on the prettiest yellow dress, a smile as big as the sun. Kat was with her. Cece wanted to deliver it to you herself, but when I told her you were out of the office, she insisted I hand deliver it to you. Her exact words were, 'Ya gotta give Max my tea party card. Don't ya put it on his desk. Give it to him.'"

Mrs. Collins's high-pitched Cece imitation had been off target, but the childlike phrasing caused rumbling laughter to burst out of him. Wiping tears from his eyes, he shook his head. "So you told her I'd be there then?"

She lifted her chin high and launched her best squinty-eyed *you're in trouble, mister.* "Of course I did. You wouldn't decline and break that sweet girl's heart, would you?" Then she followed it with a pout, laying on the guilt trip. Even for a protective mother-hen type, her act had been a little much.

Since he loved the old bag and never wanted to disappoint her, or Cece, he leaned over and pecked her wrinkly cheek. "I don't think it's me you have to worry about breaking hearts, Mrs. C." He waved the invitation as he walked toward his office. "Sugar and spice and everything nice, God gave an extra strong dose to little girls, especially those with pigtails and red hair. You better be ready to rescue me when I go down in flames," he shouted over his shoulder.

"It won't be necessary. She's your saving grace," Mrs. Collins exclaimed as he shut the door.

Why did he have to hear that?

Thursday had come and gone. Off-site meetings didn't end until six o'clock, and he went home after them, which ensured he wouldn't run into Maggie.

At ten forty-five on Friday, Mrs. Collins swept into his office. "You have fifteen minutes to get downstairs. You should arrive early. It would be rude to be late."

He removed his suit coat from the chair and put it on, straightened his tie, and waited for Mrs. Collins to confirm he did it right. She gave him an approving nod as he rounded the desk and tapped his watch. "I set the alarm, so I wouldn't lose track."

Holding his elbow out for her, she tucked her arm through it and escorted him toward the foyer, giving instructions the entire way. "Now remember, ladies first. Thumb at six o'clock, index finger at twelve, and raise your pinky. Sip, don't slurp. Pick up just the cup. When you're done taking a drink, set it back on the saucer. Make sure you sit up straight, don't slump. If they're offering scones, serve Cece, and then take yours last." When they arrived at the elevators, Mrs. Collins patted his chest. "Have a good time."

"Thank you. I don't know what I'd do without all your insightful advice." The cheeriness in his voice contrasted with the ridiculousness of the lecture. He'd been attending high society functions with his parents for as long as he could remember. Granted, he'd never had tea in any of those settings, since it wasn't something he would drink. But at thirty-one, he could finesse his way through any formal event regardless of expected etiquette. He leaned over, pecking her on the temple. "I'm going to lunch after and won't be back until two. All clear till then, right?"

"You have a team meeting for the new account scheduled at three and nothing after that."

"Sounds good. An early Friday for a change." After he got in the elevator and pressed the lobby button, he saluted Mrs. Collins. "Any parting advice?"

As the doors shut, she shouted, "Smile."

So he did, along with running his fingers through his too-tight collar, adjusting his shirt cuffs, and rocking back and forth on his heels. The descent took forever as the elevator stopped on just about every floor.

Once he got downstairs, instead of going straight to the preschool, he ran outside. With five minutes to spare, he approached the corner flower cart and told the attendant what he wanted. In less than sixty seconds he reentered the lobby. As he passed the security desk, Sam prompted, "Did you forget something?"

"Nope, I'm going over there. Had to get these first." He waved the flowers in the direction of the preschool and picked up his stride, not stopping to chat. If he didn't arrive on time, Mrs. C would have his hide.

"Friendship day. Have fun, Mr. Stone. Tell Cece I said hey."

"Will do." He marched inside and up to a reception desk.

"Welcome to Little Ducklings. You here for the tea party?" A brown-haired young lady who couldn't have been more than eighteen greeted him like a bubbly cheerleader rooting for her team. After he nodded, she asked, "Your name and who invited you?" When he provided her with the information, she checked him off on a list and pressed an intercom calling for Cecily Tyson. "We have each child greet their guest and walk them back to their classroom. It helps reinforce the manners we teach." She smiled, and he did too. At least he thought he did, while scanning the pastel green and blue walls with yellow ducklings splattered all over them.

"Max," Cece called out, skipping over to him. "Ya here." Behind her stood another brunette, this one older than the other, wearing a blue pinstripe pantsuit. A name tag pinned to her lapel read "Director: Sally Morris."

He crouched down and opened his arms, welcoming Cece as she wrapped hers around his neck. "How are you, sweet pea?"

"Great," she yelled in his ear, stretching out the letters.

After their embrace, he extended the bundle of pink and

lavender petals toward her. "These are for you. They're sweet peas, and the little white things are baby's breath."

She twisted left and right, her violet, ruffled dress swishing from side to side. "Like me?"

He skimmed his thumb over her rosy cheek. "Just like you, sweet pea."

"Did ya get my present?"

He shoved his cuff up and extended his wrist out to her. "You did great. I love it."

With a beaming smile, she looped her arm around his. "Tea time."

As he passed the director she thanked him for coming, but what she and Cece didn't know—he wouldn't have missed it for a million, trillion, zillion dollars. No amount could take the place of this honor or keep him from missing out on Cece's gummy grin. Whether it was a second or an hour or whatever amount of time, she never failed to make him happy.

That he could handle—Maggie's presence, he could not.

Which produced an entirely different reaction.

Mama's Rule #14:

When you fall down, dust off your boots and get back out there.

An expected seventy-five degrees made it perfect weather to put the swing set together. The end goal being Cece's birthday a mere two weeks away, and with Memorial Day just ahead, it gave Maggie a chance to get a lot accomplished. This Saturday had been the best time to start.

Ready to tackle the enormous job and anticipating the warmer temperatures, she dressed for the occasion taking into consideration the slight chill in the morning air: cut-off jean shorts, a black tank top, her favorite "chefs are hot" hoodie, cowgirl boots, and a tool belt. When Matt put the leather organizers in her buggy, she'd tossed them back in the box they had come from. After he explained the necessity, she conceded and bought them for herself and Kat. Now that she had it on, she could see why. It contained all the essentials within easy reach. In preparation, she watched countless hours of YouTube videos about Gorilla playset construction. Confident, she walked outside with a coffee in hand and ready to jump in.

"'Bout time you got out here." Kat's perturbed remark

wouldn't deter her happy-go-lucky spirit.

"Yeah, Mama, we ready." Propped on the edge of a turtle-shaped sandbox and designated work area, Cece waved the plastic wrench in one hand and placed the other on her hip. Her huge smile showed her eagerness to dig in and act just like the big girls. Matt insisted Maggie purchase the kid set identical to their belts and the sandbox, telling her once again to trust him, because it would save her a lot of grief in the process. He might have been right.

"You could've started without me."

"Seeing as four hands won't be enough, mine alone wouldn't get it done in a million years." Kat raised her empty palms in the air.

"I thought big sisters had super powers, at least that's what you kept telling me all those years." She wandered up to Kat's side, grabbing her hand and linking their fingers together.

"My X-ray vision won't help with this, Mags."

Leaning in to Kat's ear, Maggie whispered, "If your mind wasn't always in the gutter, then you would've chosen a better power to have when we were kids. Good thing my Wonder Woman strength is here to save you, again."

The coffee got snatched out of her hand and Kat sucked down a huge gulp. "You're right, thanks for the save." Kat wiggled the cup in front of her, chuckling as she picked up the directions on top of the stacked boxes. "All right, let's do this."

"Yeah, let's get goin.'" A gruff order came from behind, causing Maggie to whirl around and confront her boss. Frozen in place, she got nothing out. Just stared as three of them strolled through the gate and into the yard. Matt, along with Alex, an investigator who worked with them, and the last person she wanted within a fifty-mile radius, Mr. Stone.

"Max." Cece jumped out of the sandbox and right into his arms. He placed a kiss on her temple, bouncing her up and down a couple times as he sauntered closer.

"What are you doing?" Maggie marched up to Matt, stopping him before he could get halfway across the yard. Alex and Mr. Stone strolled right past her, not paying her any mind or looking in her direction.

When they got within Kat's reach, she slapped Alex on the back, mumbling, "Thank goodness, I didn't think you'd come."

Alex tossed a muscled arm over Kat's shoulder and leaned into her. "I told you we would."

Ticked off her sister would go against her wishes, she turned her fury on Matt, who happened to be closer at the moment. "I told you I didn't want help."

He pulled her into a hug, yammering in her ear, "I won't pull the boss card on you, but since I know how stubborn you are, chalk it up to male ignorance or stupidity. Whatever you wanna call it. You want the swing ready for Cece's birthday, right? Grin and bear it, Mags. We're not going anywhere." A man with kids was a dangerous thing. He knew which card to whip out and throw down. She'd do anything to make Cece happy. Even put up with Mr. Stone.

"You're off my Christmas cookie list too," she grumbled while they walked side by side to join the rest of the group.

"When we're done, I'll be back on it, and you'll be adding me to your lifetime dessert a month registry." He yanked on her ponytail a little too hard, punctuating his point. She tried to hip check him, but he jogged ahead of her, taking the direction booklet out of Kat's hand and reading it aloud. Like a synchronized assembly line, each of them got in position, hands full of materials, and dove in.

Cece dug in the sand with a shovel, forming a fort Mr. Stone told her to build. "A very important job," he explained that it would help them figure out what the finished product would look like. Enraptured by anything that came out of his mouth, Cece stuck her tongue between her teeth and concentrated on "big girl work" as she called it.

Before Maggie joined the pack, she stood there, hands on her hips, taking it all in. Kat, with a tape measure and spray paint, marked the spots in the grass to set the poles. Alex and Mr. Stone dug while Matt laid out the pieces in sequence.

"Mags, get your ass over here. This was your idea, so don't think you're gonna supervise while we do all the work," Kat demanded, tossing the tape measure over to her. "Chop, chop, little sis. Put those Wonder Woman powers to good use."

That started a grand discussion and argument about super-heroes and the powers they each wanted. A tomboy and the life of the party, Kat had always been a free spirit, capturing male attention wherever she went. Opposite of Maggie who'd rather read a book or cook than socialize or run around the streets, getting in trouble like her sister. Regardless of their differences, she enjoyed every minute with Kat and hated the months they'd been apart when she and Cece still lived in Texas. This move had been the right one. Even with Jake hounding her, she liked New York. Going to school and work-ing for Matt were the highlights, but being with Kat brought a calm and settled the restlessness she'd experienced in her hometown.

Animosities dropped for the time being, she used her brain-power and flexed the few muscles she had, taking pride in what they would accomplish for the sake of her daughter. For once Kat was right—a few additional hands would be more efficient. But she'd never admit it. Even if her sister put her in a headlock and wrestled her to the ground. She wouldn't let Kat know how much she liked the bantering, the guys strain-ing muscles lifting one hefty piece after another, or their shirts flying off as the temperature rose. Oh no, she wouldn't say a damn thing. She couldn't over her cotton mouth as she exam-ined Mr. Stone's sizable chest. Suits were too much clothing for him. Professional wear gave him a refined, polished stat-ure. His shirtless, sculpted pecs, loose-fitting cargo shorts, and high-top boots displayed a rough side that kept pulling her

attention away from what she should've been doing. When he
ran his fingers through his sweaty hair, mussing it into wavy
clumps and exposing more of his abs, her heart erupted into
palpitating, arrhythmic bursts. She licked her lips and could
almost taste the saltiness dripping over the ripples and trailing
into his waistband.

How long had it been since she had sex? Four, five years?

A sudden hot flash hit her, so she unzipped the hoodie,
tossing it on the grass. Her assigned task had been to screw in
the bolts, not ogle Mr. Stone. As she attempted to concentrate
on what needed to get done, she stretched up on her tiptoes to
the end of the pole and secured the nut.

"What the hell, Maggie?"

Startled by the yelling, she dropped the wrench a centimeter from hitting her big toe. As she bent over to pick it up, Mr.
Stone shouted and made her jump all over again. "What are
you doing?" Before she stood all the way up, he shoved his
T-shirt into her face. "Put this on."

Instead of listening to his order, she swiped her hand across
her damp brow, setting it on her temple and blocking the sun.

"Christ, cover yourself up." He grabbed her other hand,
clasped it around the material, and held it closed.

Following the direction of his eyes, she glanced down.

"Forget something, Mags." Kat's ribbing hadn't helped the
situation.

Well, since she didn't know she'd be surrounded by men,
she hadn't given it a second thought when she opted out of
wearing a bra. Sometimes on the weekends, she lounged
around the house without one. On the small side, a thirty-six
B, it wasn't a big deal on those occasions. Now, with his eyes
zeroed in on her rock-hard nipples, she determined that choice
hadn't been a wise decision. Yet, instead of doing what he
said, she remained rooted in place, resisting his pull as he
tugged his shirt, and her hand up, trying to cover her. Her
libido kicked up to full blast and desire shoved her toward

him—to tease, play a little.

"Dammit, Maggie, take this. Put me out of my misery." His grumbled plea should have been undecipherable since he'd spoken it so low. The huskiness in his voice licked along her spine, and tingles followed as though his lips brushed along her skin from waist to neck.

She loosened her hold, and his hand rose, brushing a knuckle across her nipple, the exact spot he wanted to shield.

Her legs turned to Jell-O. The mushy mass below her hips wouldn't hold her up any longer. She swayed into him, grabbing hold of his waistband. Their chests beat against each other—his bare, hers begging to be, causing her nipples to harden even more. The coarse hair on his heated thighs scrubbed against her shaved, smooth ones. Her gaze kept wandering from his eyes to his tongue sliding over his bottom lip, moistening the ridges to a glistening, delectable, nibble-him morsel.

She wanted to touch him. No, she needed to. Unable to stop herself, she swept her thumb over his damp belly button, grit and sweat coating the pad of her finger. Each of their bodies called out *suck me, go ahead and taste.*

"Step back, Maggie. Get away from me, right now," he groused, his lips closing in, a breath apart from hers. At least a half foot taller, his height difference didn't matter. He sucked her in with his beautiful eyes that had so many variations of brown, green, and blue in them, she could've been gazing in a kaleidoscope. "Last chance." The warning came out as a soft growl, his lips slicking against hers as he attempted to scare her away.

"Mama, Dada on ya phone."

"Give it to me." Kat ran toward Cece sitting on the stoop by the back door. When Maggie last checked, Cece had been dropping her Barbie dolls off the top as if they were performing various stunts from a high dive. Maggie had no idea how her daughter got her phone, which had been left inside on purpose.

118

Jumping from the top step, Cece took off in a zig-zag gal-
lop, her arm with the cell held out in the opposite direction
from Kat. "He said Mama, he said Mama," she screamed over
and over.

Her daughter's high-pitched yell jolted her into gear. She
sprinted over to Cece, sweeping the jackrabbit into her arms.
By then Kat caught up to them. "Take her inside."

Kat's bug-eyes and grinding jaw communicated her disap-
proval, but she did as Maggie asked. Grabbing a kicking and
wailing Cece, tears streaming down her cheeks, Kat headed
toward the house. "I wanna talk to him," Cece kept shouting
while being carted away. The back door slammed shut. Her
screams could still be heard through the open kitchen window.

With a finger stuck in her ear, Maggie tuned out the screeching. Then did some of her own. "Jake? Jake, you there?" She
pulled the phone away and saw five reception bars, and the
time ticker still moving. "Jake."

The click came next. Dammit. She stabbed the recent calls
and searched for the number listed at the top—unknown, and
when she pressed redial, the ring went unanswered. A cold
sweat rushed over her skin, and she didn't realize her body
was trembling until someone gripped both of her shoulders,
steadying her.

"You okay?" Mr. Stone's sturdy stance pressed against
her back should've been supportive, but instead it sent a tidal
wave of fury, disgust, and pain through her.

Her eyes closed, and the tremors rolled through her again.
"Jesus, Maggie, you're shaking like crazy." He pulled her
tight, his arms wrapping around her stomach, and whispered
something she couldn't decipher. All she could register was
the dead phone call in her hand, and the sobs still choking
Cece. Whenever her daughter got that upset, she would gag
and sometimes throw up. Maggie could relate. She wanted to
do the same thing right now.

"I have to go to her. Get her calmed down."

119

"Of course." He released her.

She turned around to say something but didn't know what. "I . . . I . . . It could take me a while."

He shook his head, grabbing her shoulders again. "Don't worry about it. We'll keep going out here. We won't bother you. I promise."

Overwhelmed, she threw her hands up to her face and broke down into sobs too. No questions, chastising, or complaints, he tucked her against his chest and held her until her tears dried up. After she swiped her arm over her wet eyes and nose, he walked her to the house, opening the door and waiting until she went inside.

Cece's hiccupping whimpers hit her first. Kat registered next, arms crossed and on guard between the kitchen and the living room. It didn't matter how ticked off her sister might have been, she needed to get to her daughter. In several large strides, she shouldered past Kat and marched to the couch, where Cece had curled into a ball. She carried her upstairs to console her and when calmed down, she'd talk to her about her father, in a way a four-year-old could understand.

If only Maggie did. Because no matter how many times she tried, none of it ever made any sense to her. She loved her daughter more than life itself, and she didn't know how to make up for the fact that Jake acted like Cece didn't exist. Did she want him calling and threatening her every chance he could? No. But she would listen to it every day if it meant he would care about his daughter like she did. She'd put up with anything if Cece didn't have to experience heartbreak at such a young age. No child or adult deserved to be treated with such disregard. Jake had refused to hold her as a baby, play with her as a toddler, and barely spoke to her. What would cause a man to treat his own flesh and blood with such indifference? She just couldn't understand it. The amount of joy Cece brought into her life couldn't compare to anything else. Not even cooking, which she couldn't imagine not doing. Yet without Cece at her side, taking part in the process, it wouldn't be the same. Just as her own mom had done, she taught Cece basic cooking techniques from the time she turned two. She wouldn't have it any other way. All she wanted was for her daughter to be happy and loved. If Cece got that, then Maggie had what she needed.

As they lay in Cece's princess bed cuddled in each other's arms, she made a solemn vow to ensure her daughter always had that. No matter what.

Exhausted from the breakdown, Cece fell asleep almost as soon as her head touched the pillow. It wasn't uncommon for her after an emotional event. She'd be knocked out for the next hour or two.

About a half hour later, Maggie made her way downstairs, baby monitor in hand. The screen door slamming darted all eyes her way. The amount of progress they'd made astonished her. The fort base and climbing wall were secured, and the poles for the swing portion were stacked and ready to mount. Maybe she'd been upstairs a lot longer than she thought.

The more Matt, Alex, and Mr. Stone watched her, the more agitated she got, because she could just imagine the slew of questions on the tips of their tongues. As she trudged toward them, she ended the discussion before it began. "I don't want to talk about it."

"Oh, good, 'cause you're too late. I already gave them the run down." Kat's snide declaration had her fuming all over again.

"Have you lost your ever f-in' mind?" She charged up to her sister, shoving Kat in the chest. "What's wrong with you?"

Kat tapped her chin and mocked, "Go ahead, hit me. At least you'd be *doing* something. Maybe you'll find those guts you used to have, Mags, and stop Jake from harassing you."

As she bent over ready to wrestle Kat to the ground like they used to as kids, strong arms wrapped around her middle, hauling her off her feet. "Whoa, calm down. That won't help."

Her hands swung in the air along with the pent-up frustration and anger Maggie had building toward Jake, not her sister. It came gushing out as she growled and kicked.

"Dammit, Maggie, settle down. You're pounding the hell out of my shins," Mr. Stone demanded, twisting her further away from Kat and setting her down, but he didn't let go. His arms remained secured around her waist like a corset.

Hopping from one foot to the other, Kat jabbed her fists from side to side, taunting, "Come on. Come get me, Mags." Kat darted behind Matt, but he walked away and grabbed a pole, while Alex picked up the other end, continuing to work and ignoring the crazy sisters.

"Kat, put those hands to good use over here." Matt jerked his chin toward the far side of the fort. "Bring the bolts and socket wrench. We might get this done today if you quit messin' around." He propped the cedar plank in place and chided, "Boss's orders."

With her tongue stuck out, Kat sauntered past, keeping a foot away and out of Maggie's reach.

"You know what they say about paybacks," Maggie grumbled under her breath.

Kat patted her mouth, yawning loudly and echoing it in the process.

There must be a strand in sibling DNA that carried the stick-it-to-you gene. If Mr. Stone didn't still have a stronghold on her, she would've taken a potshot when her sister passed by. Kat knew how far to dig the knife without gutting. Just enough to agitate the hell out of her.

"Do you need a time out?" Of all the people to start badgering, he should be careful, since he had a part of his anatomy sticking into her behind that she could damage in a matter of seconds. She rested her head on his shoulder and looked up at him. It might be a good time to remind him. Since actions spoke louder than words, she did just that.

In a circular motion, she rubbed her butt cheeks against a very primed and hardened part of his shorts. Paybacks. Her grin widened and she almost laughed out loud as his eyes grew larger and his lips parted; a hitch in his breath rocked his chest into her back even more.

His grip tightened, and whether he realized it or not, loosened and drifted over her stomach, creeping south. Before he could reach whatever destination, she grabbed his hands, stopping him.

Jumping back several steps, he shoved his palms against his closed eyes, mumbling something she couldn't figure out. Then he glanced over at the playset where Matt, Alex, and Kat had the swing portion affixed and were untangling the chains, ready to hang them. None of them paid any attention to her or Mr. Stone. His eyes darted to her, then dropped to her chest. Yep, she'd forgotten to put a bra on when she'd been inside. She had other, more important things on her mind. The reminder had her dashing over to the monitor she'd dropped when she went after Kat. Cece's gibberish put a pep in her step and had her jogging toward the house. Mr. Stone paraded past her, going in the opposite direction. Focused on her target, she hadn't acknowledged him, and out of the corner of her eye, she didn't think he'd glanced her way either.

Right then, it didn't matter. She ran inside, taking care of her first priority.

A huge feast had been prepared and the table set. Maggie's precious assistant helped serve a late dinner as a thank-you for a job well done. Cece insisted "Max is hungry" after he came inside patting his stomach and said, "Feed me, sweet pea." As if the earlier catastrophe hadn't happened, Cece's dogged determination and extreme focus on getting "Max's order" had her daughter singing, "This is the way we make our food, make our food, make our food," with a huge smile as she washed vegetables, got pots and pans out of the cabinet, and put plates, silverware, and napkins out for six people.

After getting washed up in the adjacent powder room, Matt roamed around the kitchen picking up lids and peeking under covered dishes. "What'd you make me, Mags?"

She pushed him out of the way, smacking his hand as he tried to snatch a thumbprint cookie from a tiered serving platter. Since Cece could put together most of the ingredients from memory and because they were her favorite dessert, her daughter took charge and got the majority of it mixed while Maggie whipped up an oatmeal pie. An uncommon choice, but the few instances she baked one, everyone raved about it.

"You wanna eat? Take a seat, boss," she teased, shoving him toward an empty chair. Everyone else had already crammed in around their comfortable for four people, jammed for six kitchen table. She recited the menu as if she were presenting the Culinary Institute catering service to high society. Next week, she'd be doing just that, since they were contracted for a fundraiser event. She might as well practice on a non-hoity-toity audience.

"Okay, we have mild and hot Italian sausage with red and green peppers and Vidalia onions, slow cooked in my homemade tomato sauce. Secret ingredient undisclosed. You'll have to guess. An American classic, ham barbeque, sweet with a bit of tang. And in honor of my Irish father, shepherd's pie. Bon appetit." With a wave of her hand over the feast, one by one they scooped their selections onto their plates and heaped mounds of meat on the fresh-baked rolls she'd readied at breakfast. At various points throughout the building project, she ducked inside and cooked, expecting she'd have to feed the crew. Being a bulk shopper, she stored reserves for any occasion. Her usual fourteen-day menu saved her plenty of headaches in the past, and once again, came in handy. A combination of leftovers and just-cooked entrees, along with plenty of easy to put together sides, provided a variety for any appetite.

After everyone finished the main course, Maggie hoped they left space in their tummies, since Cece repeated at least a thousand times that she baked dessert "for Max." She'd share though, "'cause big girls do, right, Max?" From one week to the next, her speech changed as baby teeth fell out, leaving gaps and contorting the sounds. Seated in her booster chair next to her idol, Mr. Stone, she chattered away, providing a rundown of her preschool adventures and entertaining all of them with her witty comebacks. Alex, Matt, and Mr. Stone gave her their undivided attention, asking questions about cooking. Encouraged even more, Cece boasted about her wealth of experience and how she enjoyed teaching her mama too.

"Okay, that pie goes on my dessert of the month delivery." After three servings heaped with whipped cream, Matt wiggled his fork and his last bite, talking over the mouthful he'd just shoved in.

"You taking orders?" Alex prompted, "What else do you bake?"

"Mama and me makes good stuff." Over a cookie-filled mouth, Cece spurted crumbs of proof with her testimony. Maggie shoved a napkin over the flying bits, keeping them from landing on the crab-stuffed mushroom cap. She picked up the plate to put it on the counter, when Alex snatched the last piece, and after one chomp, swallowed it without batting an eye.

"Good stuff." He imitated Cece, his mouth clamped shut so it sounded the same as her garbled compliment.

As a round of laughter and giggling filled the kitchen, she

examined the faces of delighted family and friends, grateful for the positive end to a chaotic day.

After the huge meal, Cece insisted Max join her on the playset. Dusk had set in, and it was almost time for a bath. Maggie tried to sway her daughter from the mini-adventure by putting *Cinderella* on the DVD, but Cece didn't want anything to do with the distraction. About to offer another compromise, a puzzle, coloring, or anything else that would keep her daughter inside and easy to wrangle, Maggie didn't have to because Mr. Stone did.

He pointed to his watch, showing it to Cece. "See the big hand, right there?" After Cece nodded, he said, "When it gets to the twelve, you have to tell me." He tapped the exact number, making sure she did too.

Her brows scrunched and repeating her favorite word in the world, Cece asked, "Why?"

"Well, you wanted me to read a bedtime story. I can't do that if you don't get your bath. That means we have five minutes to play. That's when the hand is on the twelve."

Her fingers linked through his, and Cece yanked him to the back door. "We better get goin.' Ya gotta read to me."

On his way out, he glanced over his shoulder. "Thank you," she mouthed as he got dragged out the door, a smile as big as Cece's brightening his attractive face. When the screen slammed shut, his elated, *haha, I'm doing something you can't do* laughing eyes accentuated a charm he didn't often let show. She saw the serious CEO, not an at-ease, teasing boy next door.

The clean-up had started but wasn't finished. Maggie scrubbed the dishes while Matt dried. Alex and Kat took off down the hall, mentioning they had a case to discuss and needed privacy. Maggie's and Cece's bedrooms were upstairs, and Kat's on the first floor. Discrete for the most part, her sister didn't bring men home. Instead, she engaged in sexual escapades elsewhere. Any fears Maggie might've had were alleviated when Kat indicated she didn't want Cece to deal with strangers coming and going. And so far, she stayed true that practice.

Her sister's sacrifice had been appreciated but she felt bad too. If Kat and Alex were fooling around, she wouldn't mention it. Cece would be in the bath and bed in no time, and she didn't want to be a nag. They had enough arguments for one day. She'd rather end on a high note.

"If you need help with your problem, let me know. I don't want to butt into your business, but I'm here for you."

The dishes were done. She shut off the water and turned toward the dear man who'd been nothing but kind to her. "Can we talk about it at work this week? I'd appreciate some suggestions. I'd ask Kat, but you saw how well that went. Just tell me what I owe you for the consult."

Matt threw a towel on the counter and grabbed her hands. "You've been feeding me for four months, and I didn't pay you a dime. You think I'd take money from you? Don't insult me."

"I—"

"Don't argue, just nod and smile, you stubborn pain in the ass."

So she did, squishing him in a giant bear hug. "All right, give me your requests. I'll make you a dessert the first of each month from now on."

He chuckled. "Told ya I'd be back on the list. I'll have a year's worth for you on Tuesday."

Her brotherly smack hit his shoulder, and she followed it with a reward, a plate of cookies she saw him eyeing. He kissed her temple and then shoveled the day-old peanut butter tidbits into his mouth. While chewing, he mumbled, "Everything will be all right, you'll see."

"Bath time, Mama." Cece stormed into the kitchen, yanking a stumbling Mr. Stone behind her as his boot caught on the jamb.

"Slow down." She picked her up, giving him a much-needed break no doubt.

Twirling around, Cece threw her arms out to him. "Max, ya comin'?"

"Uh, um . . ."

Before Cece could launch her next attack, she interceded. "He'll be up after your bath and when you're tucked into bed. Right?" She directed the question to him, suspecting he'd agree since he already made the promise.

"Yeah, yes, I'll be up. Call me when you're ready. I'll be down here keeping the cookie monster away from your thumbprints."

Cece giggled all the way upstairs, relaying everything Max said while they were sliding, swinging, and climbing the rock wall. Throughout her bath, as she dressed in her nightgown, and when she jumped into bed, Cece recounted each activity and relayed Max's hysterical antics: pretending to be a gorilla, scratching his armpits, and chasing her around as if he were King Kong trying to capture her.

Earlier, she thought her heart had broken from her daughter's upset. She had been wrong. Cece cuddled along Mr. Stone's side, his arm propped above her pillowed head, the other holding *Guess How Much I Love You* as he read it from Cece's lap; her lips mimicking and moving with his had tears flowing along Maggie's cheeks.

Hidden in a blind spot in a corner of the hallway, her heart exploded into smithereens and every ounce of air gushed out as she smothered heaving sobs with her hand.

From behind her, someone squeezed her shoulder, and then Matt whispered, "He needs you . . . and her, Maggie."

She clutched her quivering stomach, unable to respond. She didn't need to.

A picture was worth a thousand words, and in this case, reality—a million times louder.

Mama's Rule #15:

You can't always get what you want.

The tux and his dad's monogrammed silver bar cufflinks completed Rick's tailored attire. He splashed his favorite Drakkar cologne on each shaved cheek. Appearances were everything, especially at the annual fundraiser Julia's father held at their residence. He'd attended in past years, a worthy foundation and cause that had personal ties to him and benefitted homeless teens.

Mr. John Kensington had been an honest-to-goodness rags-to-riches story. In and out of the foster system, he ended up living on the streets at sixteen. Over twenty-plus years and a hard-fought battle, he took steps to correct the situation. He earned his GED, obtained scholarships for a business degree, and worked his way through the corporate ranks. In his late forties, he launched his own brokerage firm, becoming a success almost overnight and a multimillionaire in the process.

Rick's father met the seventeen-year-old panhandler at Lexington Market. His dad gave Mr. Kensington a job at Gateway Enterprises, set him up in a permanent shelter that provided educational support, and served as his mentor. A story his father relayed a time or two, but Mr. Kensington reminded him of often. Forever indebted and grateful for what Dad had done, Mr. Kensington established the foundation in his honor. Humbled by the tribute, Rick funneled a hundred grand a year into the effort, knowing his dad would have done the same thing. Attending shouldn't have been in question. But with pressure from Grandfather to marry Julia, he delayed the RSVP and considered being a no-show. Since he'd offered a concession to get Grandfather off his back, he didn't have much choice. He'd made a promise.

At eight o'clock on the nose, Rick pulled his Aston Martin into the semicircular driveway, handed his keys to the teenage valet, and climbed the stairs one reluctant step after another. When social engagements were added to endless research, haggling executives, and browbeating shareholders, it was no wonder he didn't do much else.

Except last Saturday when Rick had plans to sleep in for once, and Matt showed up at eight in the morning demanding he get his ass up and help him. Consumed by a sleepless night of tossing and turning, he'd been in no mood for his BS. Even with the door slammed in his face, Matt wasn't deterred. Since his best friend had a key and let himself in, Rick's knee-jerk reaction hadn't been a smart choice either. It didn't matter though. At that moment, he had a goal in mind and shuffled into the kitchen.

"Well, I'm guessing your foul mood has nothing to do with a pleasurable evening with one of your lady friends. With that scowl, I'd say you struck out and you're gonna take it out on me. Right?"

After hitting the power button on the coffee maker, the scent of Columbian roast built anticipation while Rick collapsed onto a stool at the island until he could get a dose. "Go home. Don't you have another project or somethin' to do? Like putting together a toy or some other junk you keep loading your backyard with."

"Yeah, that's why I'm here." Matt's constant give-me-a-hand requests and a loss of sleep had him dropping his exhausted head into the crook of his bent arm. Weariness set in as he thought about the possibilities. The longer Matt stayed quiet, the more anxious he got. Since Matt would wait him out a lot longer, he sat up and brushed the stubble on his unshaven jaw, waiting for the pain in the ass to spit out the plans.

Picking up a mug and ducking it under the stream, Matt diverted the java from the carafe. With his back turned toward Rick, Matt sipped and ignored him. "Stop stallin.' What do you want?"

Matt mumbled, but Rick couldn't hear what he said over the brewing gurgle.

Tired of the game, Rick slapped his hand on the butcher block. The ricocheting boom hadn't produced a flinch out of the nerves-of-steel security specialist. "Matt." Since it seemed his buddy would draw this out, Rick needed reinforcements too and filled a mug.

Matt saluted him with his cup and shifted his attention to the backyard, taking slow gulps. Quiet and reserved weren't characteristics Rick would associate with his happy-go-lucky counterpart.

"What's goin' on? You okay, the kids, Sophia?"

"If I told you something was wrong, what would you do?"

The out of the blue, oddball question had his skin prickling. "Wha-what do you mean?" He dropped the mug on the counter and coffee splattered on the granite. "You know I'd do anything for you guys. Just tell me and it's done."

Matt's straight-lipped attitude changed on a dime to a shit-eating grin that disappeared just as quick. "Good, good. Then let's go."

"Where?" Rick took a step back, ready to get started and do whatever Matt needed. "Let me get changed. Give me five minutes tops."

"Go ahead, jump in the shower and get dressed."

"For what?"

"I'll explain on the way." Matt turned his back on him again and refilled his mug. "Go ahead."

Headed out of Manhattan and north on the interstate, after fifteen minutes of dead silence in Matt's truck, his buddy revealed where they were going and who needed the help. Trust between them had never been an issue before, but in that instant, Rick didn't think he'd give Matt the benefit of the doubt ever again. He had to dig deep for control and resist killing him on the spot after finding out they were on their way to Maggie's to put the playset together.

When a butler in a tux opened the doors to Kensington Manor, Rick shoved the reminders of last week out of his mind and entered the grand foyer. Twin crystal chandeliers were suspended from the twenty-foot-high ceilings. A grand staircase with a red oriental runner provided a restricted pathway to the second floor. Gold mirrors graced the walls on each side of him. A stark contrast to Maggie's home, with toys scattered everywhere and a kitchen miniature in comparison, which had family photos and preschool drawings magnetized to every available surface of the refrigerator. And yet, with the amount of money invested to make this place prim, proper, and perfect, it paled in comparison.

"Your invitation, sir?" He handed it to one of Matt's security guys. After receiving the okay, he proceeded down the crowded hall, nodding to nameless beauties clad in silks and furs and the escorts hovering next to them.

The dinner, silent auction, live music, and dancing commenced in the ballroom and wouldn't end until well after midnight. Politicians, executives, entertainers, and anyone who could afford the fifteen-hundred-dollar-a-plate donation would be in attendance. With all the glitz and glamour, no one would have known Mr. Kensington came from humble beginnings. But even with all his wealth, the man hadn't lost sight of his blessings, nor did the streetwise mogul kowtow to anyone. Mr. Kensington retained a down-to-earth outlook and became a man he respected a great deal. Because of the close tie to his father, Rick had the opportunity to watch him achieve his goals, and over time, they'd developed a close friendship. Regardless of his grandfather's prodding, attending had been the right thing.

"About time you got here. I've been waiting for you." Julia tucked her arm through his and fell into step without glancing at him. Miss America smile put on, she waved to her daddy's guests, relishing the adoration and attention. He steered her around the clusters of people, ushering her toward her parents to pawn her off.

Overcompensating like many mothers and fathers do, Mr. Kensington ensured his only child had every advantage he didn't and granted Julia's every wish regardless of cost. Since Mr. Kensington and his dad were friends, they often attended each other's family gatherings. When Julia became a teenager, even though she was five years younger than Rick, her mother, Marie, dropped not so subtle hints about them dating. Resistant to the idea and just not interested, Rick never entertained the thought. Some would find her honey blond hair, dark chocolate eyes, and plastic surgeon enhanced double-D breasts mighty attractive. But he didn't. Her almost non-existent butt and pin-straight hips did nothing for him. Even as a horny teenager, he never touched her, fantasized about her, or exhibited any feelings for her. Granted, with the close association to his family, he wished her well, but she wasn't even a blip on his radar. Besides, he didn't mix business and pleasure or intermingle family and the women he slept with.

"Mr. and Mrs. Kensington, a pleasure to see you again." He released Julia next to her father, shook his hand, and then pecked her mother on the cheek.

Mrs. Kensington's claws dug into his wrist, holding him in place before he could dash away. His intended destination, the bar, where he planned to spend considerable time this evening. "We haven't seen you in quite a while. As the guest of honor you'll be seated at our table, next to Julia of course."

If he could've gotten away with rolling his eyes, he would have, after her less than subtle matchmaking. Unable to do so, he gave a clipped nod and addressed the more sensible of the two. "Can I get you a drink, sir?"

Mr. Kensington clapped him on the shoulder and said, "I'll go with you."

About as tall and wide as Rick, Mr. Kensington had always been in good shape. As one person after another stopped them on their way to get a drink, by the time they eased up to the bar, he determined the liquid sustenance would help him get through the engagement and ordered a double scotch on the rocks for himself and a whiskey sour for Mr. Kensington.

"Thanks for coming. I know you don't like these monkey-suit events, but I appreciate it all the same."

Saluting him with his glass, Rick wanted nothing more than to chug the liquor, relishing the burn on the way down, but followed etiquette and sipped instead.

Mr. Kensington scanned the crowd, nodding to a few passersby, and then focused on him. "Everything okay? Burning the midnight oil, no doubt."

"Same old, same old. Nothing ever changes." Rick didn't complain often or allow himself the release. Yet for some reason, his reserves were depleted.

Leaning against the bar, Mr. Kensington's relaxed posture didn't match his serious, pinched brow. "I know you're set in, doing a great job running things. But have you given any thought to the future? What your plans will be?"

Rick's spine snapped straight and jaw clenched. It could have been his imagination, but the mention of future plans came too close to Grandfather's prodding. His gaze darted to the exit and he envisioned a quick escape. He'd have to bulldoze a hundred or so people blocking it.

"I respect you doing your own thing. Your dad may have

started the company, but you've done a fine job making it your own. I'm proud of you, and he would be too."

At the mention of his father, his stance shifted and his shoulders fell along with his elbow, ramming into the bar. The glass slipped out of his hand and spilled onto the marble surface. An observant bartender threw a towel on top. In seconds, a fresh replacement appeared in the cleaned spot.

Rolling his neck from the left to the back and right, Rick cracked it, releasing some of the tension, but not all of it. His knuckles produced a similar crunch as he pressed his palm into them. If this conversation continued, he'd end up drinking a lot more than he allowed himself at these events. Since he didn't want to act like an ass in public, he left the alcohol alone for now. Sometimes though, a man just needed to tie one on and this occasion might drive him to.

Mr. Kensington set his hand on his shoulder, squeezing it. "I didn't mean to upset you. I just wanted you to know. Maybe this wasn't the place or time. I'm sorry."

As sincere as Mr. Kensington might be, any conversation related to his father or the future unsettled him. While grinding his teeth together, the stubble already forming on his jaw began to itch. He scrubbed a hand over it and then through his trimmed-shorter hair. "Your opinion means a lot, thank you."

"Can we get together sometime, just the two of us? Too bad neither of us plays golf, or I'd suggest we meet on the course. You still jog in Central Park?"

Relieved by the change of subject, Rick chuckled, shaking his head. "When I have time. Otherwise, I just run on a treadmill at home."

Mr. Kensington patted him on the back. "All right, give me a call, and we'll coordinate schedules, make it happen."

"Sure you can keep up with me, old man?"

"Since you're the betting type, we might have to throw down a little wager." Mr. Kensington tucked a hand in his front pocket, jingling coins.

In the past their bets had amounted to thousands, so he doubted Mr. Kensington intended the challenge to be chump change. His mood lightened, and he picked up his drink and saluted him again. "You're on."

"The Mrs. is waving me down. I better go hit up the celebs, make sure they're emptying their pockets, or in this case, their checkbooks." After guzzling the rest of his whiskey, Mr. Kensington rubbed his hands together. "All right, enjoy your night."

"I'll place some bids at the silent auction."

"You always do. I'm sure you'll find something. Lots of good options." With a wave of his hand over his shoulder, Mr. Kensington wandered up to couples, greeting and schmoozing. Charismatic and easy to talk to, he'd increase donations with each stop.

Determined to do his share, he studied the auction descriptions that scrolled along on a movie theater sized screen. Positioned between two sets of French doors and above the stage where a ten-piece orchestra played classical and jazz music, the location and pace of each slide made the presentation easy to read. Efficient and organized, ballots were available at the tables, and teens from Kensington House, the foundation-supported youth homeless shelter and safe haven, walked around to collect them.

As the list advanced in a cycle, he took mental note of the items he wanted to bid on. One in particular caught his eye. His normal fifty-times-the-value bidding would be upped to a hundred, ensuring he got it. He picked up a donation slip and filled it in.

"What are you getting me?" Julia whispered in his ear, grabbing his writing arm and jostling it so much, he had to crumple up the card and start over.

"Don't you have enough?"

"Actually, no. I don't have you." She flicked her tongue over his earlobe, nuzzling it with her nose.

As swiftly as possible, he shrugged her off his shoulder and strolled several chairs away, as if he needed to move there to pick up another bid card.

"When are you going to stop playing hard to get."

He nailed her with a scowl. "Believe me, I'm not playing." He stated it louder than intended, emphasizing the "not."

She crossed her arms along her chest, shoving mounds of flesh above the plunging v-neckline of her glittery red gown. If she believed that move would spur a reaction out of him, she would've been wrong. Sure, he loved everything about a woman's breasts, but he'd always been more of a curvy hip and plump ass man. That brought an image of Maggie and her behind grinding into him, along with something else that popped up, an aftereffect whenever she came to mind. Thank goodness his tux jacket covered the evidence. Still, he turned around and filled in another card, losing track of the amount he'd completed so far. He didn't want Julia thinking his hardened condition had anything to do with her.

A bell ringing at the stage signified dinner would be served in five minutes. Guests shuffled about, locating their seats and readying for the four-course meal. He strolled around his assigned table, recognizing the same names he did every year. Settled in his chair, he ignored Julia brushing her thumb across the nape of his neck as she sat to the right of him.

Under her breath, she chastised, "You're being rude. You could've at least waited until I was seated."

Ever since they were kids, she'd attempted to boss him around and correct his actions or inactions. For the most part, he ignored her mightier-than-thou attitude, but her snide remark pushed his limits. Or maybe the thought of his grandfather, expected to be seated on his left, added to his agitated mood. He anticipated a whiplashing effect coming from both sides, replaying the same nightmarish tune nonstop.

Mr. and Mrs. Kensington, along with their best friends, the Shepherds, took their seats. Grandfather scooted in his chair and brushed his shoulder against him, grumbling, "Glad to see you kept your word, boy."

Rick's fists clenched next to the silverware. He drew in slow, even breaths, attempting to calm his rising temper. The pressure of being in between them for the next four or five hours soured his stomach. As usual, he'd pick through his meal, counting the minutes before he could bust the hell out of there, and instead of being relieved by the much-anticipated escape, he felt worse. The foundation not only honored his father but gave youth an opportunity to succeed. All of which Rick supported too.

Zoned out, it wasn't until he saw a bowl with green mush on his plate that he looked up and recognized a familiar face—Antonio from Le Gourmet. Shock along with chills rolled over him. Shoulder to shoulder next to the Italian Stallion poser and clad in a white chef's coat with hands tucked behind her back in a military stance—Maggie Tyson. Shit.

He had to give her credit. When they caught sight of each other at almost the same time, he expected a surprised reaction from her. Yet the only thing he noticed were her sage green eyes darting to his right, narrowing on Julia, and then flicking to the stage. Antonio whispered something in her ear. The guy might have been her instructor or supervisor or whatever, but Rick noticed the lust-filled glances directed at Maggie. Not just tonight, but the last time he saw them together. The soup spoon bit into his palm while he refused to deflect his stare-down at the asshole.

Maggie cleared her throat and presented the courses with professional flair, similar to how she'd done for Matt, Alex, and him. That time though had been much more friendly and relaxed compared to her stiff posture now. "We have a cream of asparagus soup. For the entrée, a baked shrimp scampi and lobster tail with creamed spinach and roasted rosemary potatoes, followed by a cool cucumber salad. Completing the meal will be a selection of desserts, including your choice of baklava, apple strudel, or powdered sugar beignets."

Her lips moved, spoke, yet it wasn't her words that registered. Her eyebrows, the right one pitched a tad higher as
she took a breath between each explanation. The dip in her
upper lip curled the slightest bit as she rattled on. Her pixie
nose and a nostril twitched after Julia placed her hand on his
white-knuckled fist. He slid out of her grip and picked up a
glass of ice water, taking long, drawn-out sips.

After Maggie finished, she and Antonio swung around in
unison, escaping to where they'd come from. Halfway across
the room Antonio clenched her shoulder and bent down,
speaking in her ear. What the fuck?

He threw his napkin on the forks, breaking protocol and
high-society etiquette. As he began to rise, Grandfather
clamped down on his arm. "Stay where you are. Sit down,
boy."

"Rick, is something wrong?" Mrs. Kensington prompted,
darting a glance to Julia and then over to him.

He yanked and Grandfather released his grip. "I'll be just
a minute. Excuse me."

Most guests were engrossed in their meals and paid him no
mind as he pushed his chair in. Julia executed a snatch-and-
grab maneuver attempting to alter his direction but missed
him. As he passed Grandfather though, his red-faced fury
promised retribution. Since he didn't give a damn and knew
Grandfather would never make a scene in public, he picked
up his pace.

Well acquainted with the layout of the Kensington's home,
he marched into the kitchen, scanning the restaurant-worthy
space and finding his target tucked in the corner by a walk-in
freezer. Antonio had Maggie pinned, engaged in a too-private
discussion. She scrubbed her palm against her forehead, rubbing it in circles.

The closer he got, the more his face heated. Visions of the
two of them kissing filled his head, but when he overheard

Antonio's hushed reprimand, his anger switched to protection.

"You don't want your grade docked. You'll get your head on straight."

He came up behind Antonio, speaking over him. "Is there a problem?"

Antonio turned toward him, and Maggie ducked around her teacher, mouth dropping open when he came into her view.

"What do you want?" Antonio's arm extended, blocking or holding her behind him; he wasn't sure which.

Instead of answering, he asked her, "You okay?" He didn't know what caused him to do it, but he reached out to her. And to his surprise, she took his hand, sidestepped Antonio, and strayed over to his side.

Ducking down to her height, he inspected her bloodshot eyes and smashed-together lips, brushing his thumb over her rosy cheek. "Hi. Funny running into you here." He meant it as a play on the common pick-up line yet hadn't intended it in that exact way. He just wanted to see if he could get her to smile.

"You're going to have to leave. We need to serve the entrees, and Maggie needs to get to work."

Straightened to his full height, he glared at Antonio. "Go ahead, do your thing. When I'm finished talking to her, I'll send her over."

At least twenty or thirty chefs prepped and plated while servers lined up nearby. Called to lend a hand, Antonio warned Maggie not to take long, then rushed over to a cart, grabbing an empty tray.

A squeeze on his wrist pulled his attention away from Antonio's back to Maggie. "I have to get goin.' He won't be happy if I don't."

"Is something going on with him? He almost added, "and you" but left that part off since he wasn't sure he wanted to know. It wasn't his business what she did or what guy she did it with. As another image of Maggie and Antonio in a passionate embrace entered his head, his earlier fury amped back up.

"No." But her furtive glances over his shoulder and timid response didn't instill confidence in him. After seeing her willingness to tackle Kat to the ground and challenge him, her slouched posture contradicted earlier interactions. "Mr. Stone, I should g—"

He held up his hand, not willing to let her leave yet. "Say my name." Now he had her pinned, his arms pressed to the wall, thumbs lining her neck. Her lips parted, but nothing came out. He leaned in closer, his nose inches from hers. She stared at his mouth and licked her own. "You have to use the right one, and then I'll let you go." *Maybe.*

A quick smile came and went, her eyes darting up to his. "Di—"

He thrust his fingers against her lips, chuckling at her stubbornness. His mouth inches from her ear, he said, "Maybe this will work . . . pwease." And then he felt the lightest caress above his belt, her thumb rolling in circles above his belly button.

She tilted her head a bit, her mouth brushing against his ear and exhaled, "Rick," just as a screeching cackle called for him.

"Rick, what are you doing? Dinner is being served." Julia had her nose in the air and weaved around the waiters, aiming her quick stride toward him.

"I have to go." Maggie skirted around him and rushed past Julia. As she did, Julia watched her until she returned to the counter, picking up several plates for service.

"Is that the woman whose brat put gum in my hair?"

"Shut up." Rick stormed past her, returning to his seat. Within seconds his dinner had been served, even though the others at the table already had theirs.

"I told them not to deliver yours or Julia's until you got back," Mrs. Kensington announced.

Waving a fork a few inches from Rick's nose, Grandfather

demanded, "At least apologize. What's gotten into you?"

"I'll tell you what's in him. See that woman over there, Mr. Stone." Julia pointed at Maggie following servers to the teenage volunteers' table. "Your grandson was in the kitchen with her. Do you know who she is?"

"Julia, sit down." Most of the time the princess could do no wrong, but Mr. Kensington was no fool. His stern demand insisted she better not argue.

More than aware of who provided her lavish lifestyle, particularly since she didn't have a job, Julia eased into her seat. "Yes, Daddy." Fake smile cued up and cast to everyone except for him. She had another act in mind. Her hand drifted across his thigh, slid between his parted legs, and her fingernails ran along the inseam.

He dropped his fork onto the floor and when he leaned over to pick it up, shoved her hand onto her lap. On his way back up with the silverware in his grip, he placed his mouth next to her ear. "Don't push me. You won't like the results." He waited until her eyes shifted from her plate to him. When it did, he added a final warning. "Leave her out of this."

From wide-eyed wonder to narrowed scrutiny, Julia flipped the topic on its head. "You—you're in love with her, aren't you?"

His heart skipped a beat, then pulsed in spurts with the blood rushing to his head. He slammed his eyes closed, wincing from the stabbing pain or her declaration; he didn't know which.

"You two better eat your food, it's bound to be cold." A scolding by most standards, but Mrs. Kensington's smile widened as she examined their foreheads and shoulders pressed together.

Twice in one night, he excused himself from the table, this time, using an acceptable reason. Once he entered the bathroom, he headed straight to the sink and splashed ice-cold water onto his face. He bent over and cupped his palms under the stream, drinking several gulps, hoping it would cool off his overheated body.

He wasn't sure how long he stared at the gushing water. It pooled in the glass bowl. Someone knocked at the door and asked if anyone was in there. That got him moving.

After the valet handed him the keys, he gunned the engine. The streetlights flashed across his dash like the events flickering in his head. A reminder of the evening's bright and gloomy moments.

His cell phone rang and rang. He clicked it off. It was an interruption and interference he didn't need. He'd pay the price later. For now, he couldn't talk to anyone.

Nope, he had a specific purpose—tying one on.

Mama's Rule #16:

I'm doing this for your own good.

The height of the early lunch crowd didn't give Maggie a minute to think about anything else except pan-seared branzino, octopus tandoori, and saffron fettuccini with Prince Edward Island mussels. She ignored the growl of her empty stomach while she prepared one delectable dish after another. During any down time and prep though, her mind wandered. This morning after dropping Cece off at preschool and while walking to class, she got a call from Jake. She ducked into an alley, shielding herself from the street noise, and listened as he carried on, warning paybacks were a bitch and so was she. As usual, his tirade took less than a minute, but the aftereffect had long-lasting impact. Did she need to answer? No, but she did. A glutton for punishment, she had a twisted belief that no matter what he'd done, he was still Cece's father. The Jake she knew in high school, when they dated, and their first year of marriage hadn't been a bad guy. Lost yes, misguided sure, cruel no. That came later. She fell for the bad boy. Kat believed she was a hopeless romantic, and maybe her sister's complaint had merit. Her role models, her mother and father, had married young too and were proof of the power of love.

Now though, after analyzing her and Jake's relationship to death, she realized divorce would've been inevitable. His belief that children were a burden would have always contradicted with hers: they were a blessing. Stars in her eyes and caught up in the excitement of her first and only lover, she needled Jake about marriage. He wanted to live together, but she didn't, not without a ring on her finger and papers in her hand. Besides, she knew her parents would be disappointed, and their opinion meant a great deal to her.

So maybe their failed relationship had been her fault too. In some awful way, perhaps she pushed Jake into returning to his criminal past, even though she thought he'd put it behind him. He had a steady job working as a mechanic until his arrest. Afterward she visited him in jail and pleaded with him to explain why he'd done it, but instead of defending himself, he told her to go home and not come back. She tried talking to him again before the trial and he refused. He gave her no details, no excuse, nothing. When she filed for divorce, he hadn't even fought it, just signed the papers, agreeing to the settlement.

Last week she gave Matt details, including a breakdown of the events that transpired between her and Jake from the time she discovered the money in their garage to present day. He asked lots of questions, took notes, and promised he'd do what he could to protect her and Cece. He cautioned her to restrict contact, to not accept any more calls, and if she received additional letters, she needed to turn them in.

"Hi, Maggie."

Not recognizing the voice over the buzz of the customers' chatter and the crackle of heat when she tossed a handful of mushrooms into the olive oil, she peeked over her shoulder to see who had called out. "Oh, Emma, hi. How are you?" Maggie turned the flame down, wiped her hands on a towel, and stepped over to the counter as Emma took a seat.

"Good, real good. How about you?"

A simple question, but after repressing her tumultuous emotions all morning, she chomped on her inner cheek, not responding right away. Bending under the counter, she reached for a menu, giving herself a few more seconds to push the anxiety into her empty gut before answering. "Matt tell you about this place?" She placed the lunch options in front of Emma and extended a quick smile.

"Actually, Rick did."

She nodded, and not wanting to discuss that topic, told his mother she needed to return to the stove before the food burned.

Back in the swing, she picked up where she left off, getting plates prepared and ready for service. When finished, she approached Emma again. After all, the Le Gourmet experience centered on the individual attention given to customers seated at the chef's tables. Used to multi-tasking, she didn't have a problem managing the back and forth demand since her grandparents' restaurant existed on a similar belief. Before customers left, either she, Pappous, Baba, or Mama would visit the patrons to make sure everything had been to their satisfaction. That personal touch had contributed to the success of their Greek restaurant and made it the place to go in Houston.

"So Emma, what will you have?"

"What do you recommend?"

Tapping her finger on her chin, Maggie smirked and prodded, "How adventurous are you? The octopus is good but not everybody's up for that."

Emma closed the menu, pushing it aside. "I'll take it. I've never had it before, but I trust your recommendation."

"Good. I'll get it started then."

"Before you do, can I ask you a question?"

"Sure."

"I had another reason for coming here today."

Maggie remained motionless as she asked with caution in her voice, "Oh, what's that?" Not interested in any more surprises, she held her breath, waiting as her stomach flipped from empty to nervous clenching.

"Well, I have a release party coming up. The caterer I hired backed out, and I need a replacement. I was wondering if you'd do it."

"What do you mean release?"

"Oh, it's for my novel."

Being an avid reader, she leaned an elbow on the counter, eager to hear more. "You're a writer?"

"Yes, mysteries."

As soon as Emma mentioned the genre, she realized she might be in the presence of her all-time favorite author. "Oh my god, are you E.M. Stone?" Excitement made her bounce up and down on her tiptoes. She clasped her hands together as giddiness caused the nerves in her stomach to jump even more.

A blush lit Emma's cheeks. "Yes."

"Oh my god, oh my god, I can't believe this. Why didn't you say something at the birthday party?" Her voice rose at least an octave, causing customers to rubberneck her way.

Emma shrugged, picking up a fork and setting it back down and repeating the action. "I don't talk about it unless someone asks."

"Seriously? Jeez, I'd be shouting it from the rooftops. That is so awesome. Will you sign my copy of *Midnight Hour*? Please, please, please." She thrust her hands into prayer formation, adding a pout on top of her pitiful begging.

Emma's chuckles made her feel a lot better. "Of course."

"Yes." She bounced up and down, clapping.

"You got orders up," Antonio yelled from behind her, making her jump again, except this time it wasn't the good kind. Looking over her shoulder, she nodded, acknowledging him. "I better get back to work before I get in trouble. Listen, when I have some down time and while you're eating, can we talk about the catering thing?"

"Sure, sure, go ahead. I'm sorry. I didn't mean to distract you."

"It's okay. I just need to pay attention."

"I understand. If we can't talk here, would it be okay to call you?"

"Yeah, that would be fine."

"Now, Maggie." Antonio stood next to her, jerking his chin toward the oven.

"Yes, sir." An embarrassed smile offered to Emma, she pulled the order tape from the machine and returned to cooking.

Meals served, patrons happy, and Antonio off her back, she touched base with Emma here and there when she could, gathering as many details as possible. The timeline would be tight with just two weeks to plan. Since she didn't have anything scheduled that Saturday, she told Emma she could do it. Good thing it wasn't this weekend because it would have fallen on Cece's birthday, and she wouldn't have agreed.

When her classes and shift were finished, she gathered her jacket and umbrella and exited the restaurant. A torrential downpour and powerful winds bent her umbrella inside out, swinging it left to right and making it challenging to walk the seven blocks to Westlake. If she got there late, then Kat would pick up Cece, a plan they put in place early on.

As the rain came down even heavier, she stepped up the pace and jogged the last block, tucking the useless umbrella under her arm. Her hood provided some relief. After she ran into the building, instead of picking up Cece right away, she darted into the ladies' room. Unzipping her drenched jacket and setting it on the counter, she yanked some paper towels out of the dispenser and dried off her face, neck, and hair. There wasn't much she could do about her drowned rat appearance. She pulled the ponytail band out and ran a comb through the clumpy mess, twirling it into a bun on top. Wet and sleek, it didn't look awful, just manageable.

While drying off, Kat called, telling her they were waiting upstairs. Since she wanted to see Cece before they went home, she rushed out of the bathroom, waving at Sam as she passed the security counter. The woman talking to him glanced up. "You, wait. You, I want to talk to you." Not wanting to speak to her, she kept on walking to the elevator. "I said, wait." The rapid clicking of heels picked up speed. When she punched the up button on the wall, the woman yanked on her shoulder. "I know you heard me."

Ignorance could be bliss, but in this case, it didn't help. When the determined woman tugged on her shoulder again, she had no choice and faced her. "What?"

"Don't take that tone with me, missy."

Maggie snorted and crossed her arms, repeating, "What?"

"I said, I want to talk to you."

Stabbing the up button several more times, Maggie snapped, "So talk."

"I have a proposition for you." The blond monster from the previous lobby altercation and the fundraiser unbuckled the leather band on her designer bag and reached inside. The initials on the purse looked familiar, but she didn't know who created it. Even if she could afford it, she'd never spend her hard-earned money on a useless extravagance.

The woman pulled a checkbook out and started writing. "I have something to give you." Not having a clue and not caring to find out, Maggie scanned the corridor for an escape. The one she'd been waiting for still hadn't arrived. Ready to head for the stairs, a stronghold on her arm kept her stuck in place. "Here, take this."

The check had Julia Kensington embossed in gold script at the top. As Maggie's eyes drifted from left to right, she noticed the "to" line had been left blank, but the amount had been filled in to the tune of ten thousand dollars. "Here." Ms. Kensington lowered the monogrammed parchment paper, picked up Maggie's hand, and shoved it into her palm.

The check fell onto the marble floor when Maggie dropped her arm to her side. "I don't know what you're trying to pull, but whatever it is, I'm not interested."

Ms. Kensington tapped a pen on her cheek and remained silent, her keen brown eyes piercing her target. "I think you will be. You see, I bet you'd love to give your daughter anything she wanted. That will do it."

"Are you on crack?" Maggie spun away from the lunatic and hurried to the stairwell. If she had to climb twenty floors, so be it. She'd heard enough and lunged up the steps, ignoring the heels hobbling behind her.

"Listen, if that's not enough, I'll give you twenty."

On the landing between the first and second floor, fury bursting from her gut, Maggie grabbed the handrail and swung around. Hot on her tail, Ms. Money Bag's chin rammed into her shoulder when she stopped. "What is wrong with you?"

Ms. Kensington backed up a step and lifted her nose high in the air. The frown she'd been sporting flipped to an awful imitation of sweet and charming. Staring straight in Maggie's eyes and with a dead serious, unrepentant tone she said, "I'm giving you and your daughter a wonderful gift. You should be thanking me."

Unable to control herself any longer, instead of screaming at the idiot, Maggie's outburst came in the form of laughter. "Let me get this straight. You, who I do not know, want to give me and my daughter twenty thousand dollars."

"Exactly," Ms. Kensington responded as if it were no big deal, and she did this kind of thing every day.

Yeah, if she believed it to be a true offer for one second, rather than the malarkey she knew it for, she would've thought she hit the lottery. But that wasn't her kind of luck. Out of patience and all funniness gone, she got within spitting distance and demanded a final time, "What do you want?"

The beauty queen must've had enough too, because she stopped mincing words. "Stay away from Rick."

Rick? This BS had to do with him? As Maggie shook her head, a chuckle rolled out of her, but she swallowed it fast when she realized what the money meant. "Unbelievable." She stomped up the stairs. "Don't follow me. If you do, I can guarantee you won't make it out of here without a black eye or two." As she rounded the next landing, she glanced down between the stairwells and saw Ms. Kensington still on the step where she'd left her. Bent over the rail she yelled, "Don't you ever, *ever,* try bribing me again. You're a piece of work, you know that? You're disgusting. Stay away from me, or you'll be very sorry."

Tired of climbing or just being in the same space as filth, she yanked the door to the third floor open and entered the elevator that appeared in the nick of time. After stabbing the button for her floor, she scooted between two guys and collapsed against the paneled wall. She leaned her head back and pressed her fingertips to her temple, rubbing clockwise and then counterclockwise. This day sucked. When the bad outweighed the good, she guessed the rest of the night had a higher probability of disaster too. The ride to her floor happened in no time. Furious, she hightailed it down the hall not paying any mind to her surroundings. She fumed and grumbled the entire route: *I have a proposition for you. I'm giving you and your daughter a wonderful gift. You should be thanking me.*

As she came around the corner, she ran right into the individual who'd caused this entire fiasco. "Get away from me." Shoving Rick in his chest, she sidestepped around him. Before she could kick up her pace, he grabbed her upper arm.

"Whoa, hold it just a second. What the hell is your problem?"

She yanked out of his grip and charged on.

"Maggie, what's going on?" His voice trailed behind her, coming closer.

She quick-stepped into Westlake's lobby, waved at Alice the receptionist, and dashed into her office. The location to the right of the entry made for an easy escape. She locked the door and plopped onto the leather chair behind her desk. Then waited and waited and waited, staring at the wood panel, expecting knocking to follow. She checked the digital clock on her desk and noticed five minutes had passed. Even though her reluctance to see him kept her in her seat, she realized there wasn't much choice. She still needed to see her daughter. Easing the door open, she peeked into the reception area.

"Look who I found."

"Mama." Rick held Cece in his arms. Their beaming smiles increased when they saw her.

She should have figured the bastard would use a down and dirty trick. Her daughter's hands stretched out, and Cece almost leapt out of his hold and into hers. She kissed Cece on the temple and each cheek, and gave her a big smooch on the lips, while squeezing her tight and swaying side to side. "Hi, pumpkin. I missed you." Maggie closed her eyes and breathed in Cece's baby powder mixed with glue and crayon scent, almost breaking down into tears. Stress overwhelmed her and clogged her throat. "I love you so much, sweetie. So very much." The whispered testament strained over a swelling lump, which grew larger as she spoke. She opened her eyes to a hazel examination that scrutinized each tic and twitch on her face.

As if coaxing a terrified kitten, he asked, "Are you okay?" Concern creased his brow, and he reached out to her but then dropped his hand to his side.

Cece grabbed her cheeks and smashed them together, puckering her lips. "Ya gotta make cupcakes."

"When?" Her question came out muffled, constricted by her fish mouth.

"Tomorrow." Cece punctuated the announcement with a peck on her lips, releasing the strong hold on her face.

As though Maggie hadn't heard right, she repeated, "Tomorrow, tomorrow."

Bobbing her head up and down, Cece confirmed, "Yep-pers, Mama."

Groaning, she ignored Rick's smirk and marched toward the investigators' cubicles. "Kat." Her sister's head popped up over the partition. Alex's had already been visible since he had a habit of sitting on Kat's desk, gossiping. Which he did better than any old lady.

"Did you check Cece's backpack? Is there a note about cupcakes tomorrow?"

"Yes." Cece answered for her, shrieking the response and dragging it out like a train whistle.

Kat shrugged, glanced left and right, and then picked up the glittery pink tulle bag. Undoing the drawstring, she pulled the take-home folder out and flipped it open. "Uh, yeah, there is."

"Told ya." Cece repeated the phrase three times, a very annoying parroting habit, relishing in the fact she'd been right and the adults were wrong.

Maggie snatched the paper out of her sister's hand and read the reminder. "Fifty? Who are they feeding, an army?"

"What kind you makin,' Mags? Save me some," Alex requested, high-fiving Kat and then Cece.

"Oh, I'll get right on that, while I'm answering phones and inputting your months of travel receipts in the computer. I'll hop on over to the break room, whip them up, and pop 'em in the microwave just for you."

"Cool." Alex's sarcastic reply and "yummy" added to it while he patted his stomach had not been appreciated.

Instead of taking her wrath out on him, she aimed a glower at her sister. After she handed Cece over to Kat, she ordered, "You two have to do it. Cece knows where the recipe is. She can make them with her eyes closed."

"Yeah." Cece bounced up and down, clapping her hands. "Go, Kitty, go."

No matter how often Maggie heard Cece blurt her aunt's

pet name, she couldn't resist giggling. Kat hated it and knowing that fact delighted Maggie even more. After the piss-poor day she had, she'd take pleasure wherever she could get it.

"I can't bake, kid, so I'll supervise. You do all the work. Deal?"

"Yippee." Cece wrapped her arms around her aunt's shoulders, pressed her mouth to Kat's cheek, and blew raspberries on it.

"Ew, gross." With the back of her hand, Kat swiped away the slobber and planted one in the crook of Cece's neck, tickling her in the process.

"I want chocolate with fudge frosting." Alex didn't know when to let up.

"Ya betcha. Max, ya want some?" Cece shouted.

Figuring he would've been long gone by now, Maggie whipped around to find him resting an arm along the metal-trimmed partition. How long he'd been there she had no idea.

"Yes, sweet pea. Whatever you make."

"All right, monster, let's go home. Give your mama another kiss and we need to go."

After another round of hugs and smooches, including "Max too," Cece waved both of her hands over Kat's shoulders while being carried out.

Seated behind her desk, she jabbed at the keyboard, pretending to work. A bad attempt to ignore Rick, who stood in her doorway with his shoulder leaning against the jamb. "We need to talk."

"No, we don't." His requests and her denials fired back and forth for the next ten seconds or so, and the longer it went on, she considered flinging pencils at him from the decorated cup, which had Cece's photo and "Happy Mother's Day" on it. She might not be a good shot, but she'd hit something, since his oversized male ego and broad shoulders took up the entire space, blocking the exit.

"What was that about? And don't say you don't know."

"If I tell you, will you go away?"

"Yes." He agreed, but she wasn't sure he meant it. Regardless, she had tons to do, and if she didn't fess up, he'd never leave.

"Fine."

"Finally," he huffed, shutting the door and pulling a chair up right next to her. There wasn't a lot of room in the eight by eight square, and with both of them using their chairs' armrests, sitting elbow to elbow, arm to arm, it felt even tighter. Of course he didn't bother to budge even with a good foot or two on the other side of him.

She picked up a piece of paper and waved it back and forth, fanning her face, neck, and chest. "Is it hot in here? Are you hot?" Once she blurted the second question, she realized how it sounded. The jackass laughed at her expense and had the nerve to grab her wrist, redirecting the air onto him.

"I think I am." He eased his shoulder along hers, inching his hazel eyes, suckable lips, and everything closer.

"Stop that." She yanked and his grip loosened, giving her a chance to scoot her chair several inches away. His deep, guttural chuckles echoed in the overheated, shrinking box.

"Quit stalling, Maggie. What's going on?" His demeanor changed from jovial to serious and professional in an instant. All joking aside, he sat back in the chair with his hands clasped, resting them on his buttoned-up suit and flat stomach. "Out with it."

"Don't you have a meeting to go to?"

He leaned forward, gripping the edge of the armrests like he might jump out of his seat at any moment. "Knock it off. I'm serious. Why are you so pissed?" His voice got gruffer, if possible, when he asked, "Does this have to do with Antonio?"

"Antonio?" Absolute absurdity bubbled up and over, and her hilarious uproar howled in his face. "You're kidding."

"No. You going to tell me there isn't something going on between you two."

"Oh that's rich." She shoved her chair back, banging it against the wall hard enough to leave a mark, and rounded her desk. When she flung the door open, she thrust her arm toward the reception area. "Get out."

"No." He relaxed into his chair again, lips firm and eyes determined. He'd get his way or else. The master negotiator was in his element. He had her on the defensive and at a supreme disadvantage.

"You're gonna get me fired," she pleaded, a whiny grovel her next play, and exaggerated with a sniffle. She needed to work on her acting skills, because without an ounce of sympathy, he tilted his head toward the ceiling, rolled his eyes, and released a tired exhale.

For a brief instant, she wished she could be four years old again: get away with stomping her feet, throwing herself on the carpet, and screaming and kicking her way out of this with a temper tantrum. About to turn twenty-seven next month, she figured she couldn't. All that maneuver would get her would be a straightjacket and a speedy trip to the psych ward.

With his thumbs rapping on his stomach, he stared and waited. He thought he had the advantage since he was bigger and more powerful, or he'd just wait her out and she'd give up. He was right.

She shoved the door closed and plopped into her seat. As she gathered her thoughts, he stretched his hand across the divide, grabbed onto her chair, and wheeled her into the exact position she'd been before. Except now, his arm was laying across hers on the rest, holding her in place. "Talk." He linked his fingers with hers and squeezed them. His expression turned to tender and supportive. The hardened negotiator long gone, replaced by sincere compassion.

In no way could a woman resist him when he wore such emotions on his face and sleeve, tugging at her heart. Everything that happened earlier vanished, and instead of anger, she melted and got lost in *him*. He really was gorgeous. His ash brown hair had streaks of golden beige, shimmering black, and a single silvery whisker in a sideburn. His finger-tousled strands—longer and thicker on top, buzzed at the sides, cropped short at the nape—didn't resemble any executives' style she saw. No, the sexy, natural cowlick and curl that darted toward his left eye gave his face a hint of boyish charm. His dimpled chin had a five o'clock shadow and extended from his sideburns, along the ridge of his angular jaw and above his upper lip, emphasizing his caveman side and screamed: *scrub me, lick me, bite me.*

She swore she could still taste his salty, tangy tongue on hers from the too short of a sample a month ago. He'd sucked her in, lips clashing and tongue swapping, gifting her with the best French kiss she experienced in her life. Oh, the twirling, twisting motions he did with that muscle had left her with erotic images for weeks now. Her lusty dreams woke her up in the middle of the night. In order to go back to sleep, a temporary, disappointing relief came about from pleasuring herself. Yet "pleasure" didn't equate to satisfaction in the least. The only way to achieve that miracle would be to throw off his pinstripe suit jacket, rip open his white dress shirt, and slowly loosen the red-and-black paisley tie he had laced in a professional knot at the hollow of his neck. She'd pull and clutch it in small clumps, flicking the tip against her taut nipples as she straddled him. Her core would rub against his erection, a sizable offering he didn't have a problem providing before.

"Whatever you're thinking, Maggie, you need to stop right now." His down in the gutter, Adam's-apple-bobbing order revved her up even more. It didn't help that his arm held hers down, producing a whole slew of images: his hairy thighs pressed against her smooth ones, his hands clasped to hers above her head, his naked chest smashed against hers in an embrace so tight, neither of them would be able to breathe.

He lifted their joined hands from the armrest, pressed their forefingers together, and sucked them into his mouth. Seducing, tempting, luring—he massaged them along the crease of her lips and teased the divide.

Her legs scrunched together and hips bobbed—up—down—and as she squirmed her panties dampened more and more. The stiff seam of her pants provided a rigid hardness she craved. His gaze narrowed on her clenched thighs, and their fingers began a descent: over her tingling chin, along her begging neck, across her shirt to a pleading nipple, swirling around and around. His thumb used as leverage, he pinched and pulled the puckered tip, then drew their linked hands down the center of her chest and stomach, catching on the button of her pants and flicking it open. He pulled down the zipper, widening and separating the material. His knuckles tickled her flesh and increased her breathing. With his head bent, watching, heated air blew against her stomach, sending prickles along her skin. Together, their fingers coasted over her sheer peach panties, revealing her shaved mound.

Sensual—no.

Provocative—not even close.

Sizzling—warmer, but still far, far off.

"Oh shit. Fuck. Damn. Uh, sorry." Matt's outburst and quick retreat got a similar result from them.

As Rick stormed out of her office, his departing claim promised, "This isn't over. Not by a long shot."

She realized he might be right—this time.

Mama's Rule #17:

Stop crying or I'll give you something to cry about.

There wasn't any reason to stick around because Rick's appointments were finished for the day. Besides a certain freckle-faced, drive-him-insane Irish cook, whose gingersnap cookie, apple blossom, lemon drop, ever-evolving fragrance wouldn't let him concentrate on anything else but her. He had to clear his head and ran toward the emergency exit. His cantering descent down twenty flights of stairs did nothing to vanquish the demons chasing him.

Arriving home before six thirty, a rarity for him, he stripped away the suit that smelled like Maggie and threw on shorts and a T-shirt. The intent: exercise the hell out of his unresolved lust, mind-blowing confusion, and rid himself of the growing-exponentially-by-the-second affection.

When the doorbell rang an hour later, he jabbed the off button on the treadmill and lumbered his tired ass toward the entry of his brownstone.

"Mr. Stone, delivery for you." A messenger extended a Kensington Foundation embossed envelope toward him. "Can you sign, sir?"

After initialing the pad, he tossed the package on the sideboard. "Hold on, I need to get you a tip." He turned around to run upstairs for his wallet.

"I got it." The next to the last person he wanted to see called out from behind him. Matt shuffled inside once he paid the messenger and leaned against the closed door.

"I'm in the middle of a run. See ya. Don't come back." He charged toward his gym, ignoring Matt hot on his tail.

"Too bad. I got a lot to say."

Resetting the digital reader for the two-mile indicator, Rick picked up where he left off, at a steady pace, but his tightening gut told him otherwise.

Matt whipped off his T-shirt, lay on the bench, and lifted the two-hundred-pound weights on the bar. The massive bulk he hefted didn't deter his mouth muscles though. "I'd like to say I'm happy you got your head out of your ass and took my advice, but I'd be lying." A few raises later he added, "You got the wrong message, bud. Maggie isn't one of your bimbos, and I don't appreciate you treating her that way."

"When exhaustion sets in from your 'I know better than you' attitude, and the weight crashes and strangles you, don't look at me for any help after that bullshit remark. Your ass can stay stuck on that bench for all I care, and I might throw on another hundred pounds or two." He'd amped up the incline to mountain trekking mode; sweat poured down his back and rage rolled over his skin with it.

The muscles in Matt's arms twitched as his hands clasped and unclasped between his parted knees. Matt shook his head. "How'd you get so fucked up? There's a difference between hot and heavy one-night stands, and you'll regret it if you fuck it up, mind-numbing, throw me down, tie me up, do whatever the fuck you *please* love. In case you haven't figured it out, Maggie deserves the please-me type. I thought you had that in you, but now I'm not so sure. Maybe you're just a minute man."

Rick dove off the treadmill, tackling Matt. Fists swung at jaws, cheeks, and ribs. Rage ripped through him, and each shot landed released his pent-up frustration, which should have empowered him. Instead, it exhausted him. They both collapsed at almost the same time, lying on their backs with their arms stretched across the carpet, neither admitting defeat. They were too old for this shit.

"So what are you gonna do?" Matt's question stuttered between his prolonged inhales and exhales.

Battered and bone-weary, Rick slung an arm across his sweaty brow, and his stammered reply mimicked Matt's. "I don't have a fucking clue."

"I could've told you that."

"I believe you already did, a few times now." They chuckled as Rick rolled onto his side and propped his chin in his hand. After several unraveling breaths, he admitted, "How am I supposed to make any sense out of this?"

Matt looked him in the eyes; pissed-off tension disappeared and sympathy replaced it. "You don't. You go with the flow. One day at a time, buddy. She swings, you duck. She says jump, just do it, don't bother asking how high. She wants a rabbit pulled out of a hat, don't stop until you find it and give her everything she wants. Because I'll tell you, her rewards will be so damn sweet. You won't be able to crave anybody else. Your body won't want to see, smell, or taste anyone but her."

Overwhelmed by that insight, Rick's mind whirled, and he collapsed onto the carpet. He covered his eyes with his arms, while a sour taste flooded his stomach and bile surged through his throat. "Dammit."

"I know, buddy. Believe me, I feel your pain."

"Fuck."

"Mm hmm. That's the good part though."

Unable to contain his laughter, Rick let it roll. "You know that security app you installed on my cell? The panic button I

161

told you I'd never use in a million years."

"Yep."

"You better answer when I do."

Matt's humored reply came in a split second. "I have your back, bud. Never doubt it."

With his workout complete and fatigue setting in, Rick consumed a half gallon of water in the time it took him to walk Matt from the gym to the front door. On the way out, Matt glanced at the sideboard. "How'd the fundraiser go?"

"Oh, yeah. Hold on a sec." Rick grabbed the envelope and tore it open, flashing the tickets. "I got these for us. For the twenty-first. You up for it? Treat Lizbeth and Harley."

Matt removed *The Lion King* stubs from his hand, reading them. When he looked up, he asked, "Sure, but there's five. What are you doin' with the other one?"

Rick rubbed his hand along the back of his neck, his nerves hopping all over again. He wanted to buy time and think through his plans. Since he brought up the subject, he couldn't stall and ended up spitting his thoughts out. "I wanna take Cece."

A gradual smile appeared and Matt waved the tickets. "That's what I'm talkin' about. You're teachable after all."

"Shut up." The girls' surprise got stuffed into the envelope, and he set it on the table, running his thumb along the edge. "I just think she'd like it, that's all."

"You realize what day that is, right?"

Rick glanced toward the envelope again, checking his mental calendar. Nothing coming to mind, he asked, "What?"

Matt squeezed Rick's shoulder and smashed his lips together, repressing a smirk. "Oh, buddy, you are goin' down the *hard* way."

"Come on, knock it off." He laughed at Matt's ridiculous prodding and keen ability to point out when he screwed up. "What did I do wrong now?" He considered for a brief second the possibility of groveling, but he'd never give him that advantage. It went against his belief: never let them see you sweat.

Taking a deep breath, Matt burst out on an exhale, "Father's Day."

Rick stared and stared, waiting for him to change the answer. Since Mighty Matt couldn't do that, he took his exhausted ass over to the couch and collapsed instead. Damn. He forgot. Thirteen years since he'd been able to spend that special time with his dad. Four thousand, seven hundred and forty-eight days and counting since they'd gone fishing. Their customary Father's Day outing.

"Hey, I'm sorry, man. I can be a shit sometimes." Seated in a chair next to him, Matt flicked his gaze to the bookshelf and TV stand, where photographs of him and his dad were lined up, a remembrance of the good times.

"Just sometimes?" he reminded.

"Yeah, I have an off day every decade or so."

Rick appreciated the attempt at humor, but he wasn't in the mood. "You think Maggie will let me take her?" The change of subject might help distract him.

"You've got a good excuse at least."

Not sure what Matt meant, he thought about it while picking up a couple pillows and propping them behind his head. After he got somewhat comfortable on his rock-hard sofa, he asked, "What's that?"

Matt leaned forward, hands clasped between his knees. "It's Cece's birthday this weekend, on the thirteenth." He shrugged, relaxing back into his seat. "You could tell Maggie it's her gift. What mom would refuse a present for her daughter? Besides, dude, it's *Lion King*. Cece would love Simba."

"Damn, that's right. I lost track of the dates." Unable to relax, Rick sat up.

"Well, I'm outta here. Sophia's probably wondering where the heck I am." At the door, Matt turned around. "However you spring it on her, don't screw it up."

163

"Gee, thanks for the vote of confidence."

"Hey, that's what I'm here for. I'd rather point out your faults since I'm so damn perfect."

Rick whipped a pillow toward Matt. Good aim, but horrible timing.

Matt ducked outside and slammed the door before Rick could get another shot at him. He peeked his head back inside. "So damn sad. You need to work on your technique, my man." Then slammed the door again, his roaring laughter heard through solid steel.

"That's not my problem," he grumbled to the empty room. Grimy and sticky, he needed a shower and leapt upstairs two steps at a time. Maybe he'd come up with some ingenuity while washing the dried sweat off his body.

The goal: get Maggie to allow Cece to go with him.

He should've anticipated his condition and what arose. Any time he showered and had Maggie on his mind, his situation never turned out satisfactory. Stripped bare and hot water on full blast, pounding against him, he envisioned Maggie sprawled in her office chair, nipples he hadn't licked yet, her legs spread wide, pants unzipped, and peach panties he wanted to bite off. He would've slicked his tongue along her smooth mound, dipping between the folds, sucking, tasting, and savoring every bit of her sweetness.

Since that strategy failed along with several attempts to have sex with random hook-ups weeks ago, it left him with one choice—another hand job. Which deserved its own honorary title since it worked long hours and so damn hard.

"I brought coffee. Wanted to talk before you left," Grandfather greeted him first thing in the morning on the front stoop of his home. Rick had opened the door with his briefcase in hand to find the grump with his knuckles poised, ready to knock him in the head. His arrival a surprise, but his hard-hitting position not unexpected.

"This isn't a good time." Rick stood in the doorway, blocking his entry.

"It's important. I don't want to discuss this at Gateway."

Well, Rick didn't want to either, here or there. Left with few choices, he stepped back and let him in. Better to have it out here than in front of his employees. No telling what his grandfather thought important enough to come by at seven a.m.

Seated in opposing chairs, a coffee table between them, Rick situated himself on the edge of his chair, another uncomfortable place to be. Since he flat-out despised wasting his time in stores, he furnished his house through online purchases. The only task in his life that could be accomplished by a simple click of a computer mouse, a virtual finger snap. But the problem with taking short cuts and hedging his bets on the images alone, his choices were a lot like gambling. He lost more than fifty percent of the time. Unable to test out the furniture in advance, he got stuck with cement encased in overpriced leather.

"So what's up?" Rick sipped his coffee, taking the offensive, figuring the sooner he got this meet and greet started, the quicker he could leave it behind him and get to work.

Grandfather tossed a folder onto the table. As an active member of and contributor to numerous charity organizations, the senior got his rocks off on sticking his nose in other people's business and often carried around files. It slid toward him, but he didn't touch it. "What's that?"

"I think you should read it." Grandfather leaned his back along the cushions, but his stiff posture didn't look relaxed.

Rick pulled the folder toward him and flicked it open. He got halfway down the page and figured out his grandfather's intentions. Flipping the cover shut, he sat back too, masking his face. He needed to shore up his defense. The muscles in his thighs bunched, and he squeezed the armrests so hard, he could've been an astronaut preparing for blastoff. He stared into space at the bare white walls, a mental countdown ticking. After several calculated breaths, he launched, "So?"

"What do you mean so?" Grandfather countered, a scowl and disdain emanating from his ramrod posture. His bushy eyebrows pulled down, and the wrinkles on his worn, seventy-two-year-old expression multiplied.

"What did you think you'd accomplish by doing that?"

Grandfather tilted his head to the side, using a dead man's stare to intimidate him.

A hard-nosed negotiator and patient man himself, Rick knew the strategy well and used it during business too. Unwilling to reveal his hot under the collar sweating, he waited him out. The silence dredged on as Grandfather no doubt calculated risks and profits, determining his next maneuver. Rick happened to be doing the exact same thing.

"She has an ex in prison, a bratty kid, and is nothing more than a food-stamp-carrying taxpayers' burden."

Without disclosing the explosive eruptions inside of him, Rick wandered to the fireplace and flipped on the switch. The flames provided a perfect place to throw the garbage. As he watched the orange and red flickers, Grandfather dug the knife deeper. "You're the one who said you're never getting married and don't want kids. What's your intention then? You keep telling me you want nothing to do with Julia, yet you're willing to play around and jump in the fire with a welfare gold digger? What? So everything you've worked hard for can end up in the gutter? I'll protect you until I can't anymore, and even when I'm taking my dying breath, I'll still be looking out for you. You're all I have left now, and I won't let anyone take away something that means a great deal to you."

All the cards laid out on the proverbial table, Rick's own arguments came back to bite him. His grip tightened on the mantle, and he used every mental trick he knew to stop his nervous twitches and quiet his labored breathing. Out of the corner of his eye, he could see Grandfather, still propped up on his superior, all-knowing throne.

In that moment, Rick came to a realization. He'd been stuck all along. Not between a rock and a hard place. Nope— only one way out.

Mama's Rule #18:

When you have children someday you'll understand.

A dozen helium balloons were gathered in her hand. Maggie went out to the front yard to tie them on the porch railing and mailbox. Wanting to help too, Cece had three of her own. "I five now. A big girl."

Her daughter had been raring to go from the time she woke up. Two hours before any of the preschoolers were expected to arrive, Cece put on the party dress purchased for the special occasion. They'd gotten the hundred-dollar gown from the Princess Pea, a girls' only clothing store located a few blocks between Westlake and Le Gourmet. The kelly green, sleeveless sequined top and tulle tiered skirt with a satin bow at the waist resembled New Year's Eve wear. She tried to talk Cece out of the selection, but no matter how many sensible and cheaper choices she had Cece try instead, that was the "pretty one," according to her everything-has-to-sparkle-like-a-princess daughter. She found it difficult to deny her and caved in. Now that Cece had it on, sunlight streaming along flaming orange curls, her heart clenched and her stomach flopped. With Cece's Irish side shining through, she had a sudden flash of teenage boys chasing after her daughter. A painful eventuality she didn't look forward to. As quick as time went, thirteen would spring up before she knew it.

"Mama, I can't tie 'em." At the bottom of the stairs, Cece had the strings of the three balloons twirled at least twenty times around the railing. Her fingertips pinched the itty bitty scraps at the tail end.

"Here, hold these." Maggie handed her dozen to Cece and began unwinding the twisted and knotted threads.

"Max." Cece's shout sounded farther away than right over Maggie's shoulder, where she'd been a second ago. In an instant, Maggie jumped up from her knees and sprinted after her daughter galloping toward the street, and as Cece reached out to grab Rick, the balloons floated into the air.

Parked on the other side of the road, Rick jogged across, yelling, "Stop," at the same time Maggie did. All three of them came to a standstill at the curb. He swooped Cece into the safety of his protective arms before her feet touched the pavement. Maggie wrapped her arms around her daughter's waist and caught a piece of his T-shirt too. Smashed together, one of his hands loosened from Cece's back and captured the hollow of Maggie's in a stranglehold. The cars passing by and her startled, heavy breathing faded away as she got lost in their heart-pounding embrace. A squeeze on her hip pulled her head off Cece's shoulder and up to Rick's enlarged and a little freaked-out eyes.

"It's my birfday." Cece grabbed both of his cheeks, smashing them together as her megawatt-level announcement ensured everyone within five blocks understood the significance of the all-about-me occasion.

"That's why I'm here, sweet pea." He placed an endearing kiss on Cece's temple, resting there for quite a while.

Unaware of the potential tragedy or that she'd done something wrong, Cece asked, "Whatcha get me?"

The happy-go-lucky responses he used when talking to

Cece hadn't made an appearance yet. Instead, his serious business tone remained. "What do you see behind me, Cece?"

Her eyebrows scrunched together, and Cece shrugged, not understanding. But Maggie caught on. Curious how he might handle the matter, she let him take the lead. After the party, she'd take her turn at the lecture, which she'd given before.

"See the cars? See how fast they're going?"

Cece ducked around his shoulder, bobbing her head as a mini-van and sedan passed by. Situated in a circular cul-de-sac, their neighborhood had a twenty-five-mile speed limit and didn't have highway traffic. Regardless, Cece should have realized the possibility of being hit existed.

"What would happen if you went out there and a car didn't see you or couldn't stop?"

Her head tucked against his shoulder and face flushed as Cece whispered against his neck, "I get a booboo."

He pressed his mouth to Cece's ear and said with tears pooled in his eyes, "If you got a booboo, I'd be so sad. It would break my heart."

Unable to contain her own waterworks, one after another trickled over Maggie's cheeks and dripped off her quivering chin. She fell in love with him right then and there, nestled in his arms, emotions exploding all over the place. The seriousness of what might have happened and reeling from her overwhelming discovery, the realizations should've dropped her to her knees. Yet his firm hold steadied her and kept her on her feet.

"Do I have to do all the damn work again?" Kat's screaming broke the intimate moment.

Maggie kissed Cece on the cheek after Rick did and got caught in his sympathetic gaze. He swept his thumb under her eyes and dried her tears.

Cece popped her head up from his shoulder and hollered a pitiful-ol'-me response. "Kitty, I gotta booboo."

Mouth-gaping concern replaced Kat's stern look. She

jumped down the four steps from the top of the porch and ran toward them. "What happened? Where you hurt?"

With her arms stretched out, Cece pointed to a nonexistent spot on the inside of her wrist, in the crease of her elbow, and on her heart, repeating a grumbly variation of "here" each time. Kat's eyes tracked Cece's movements, no doubt expecting to see blood after her dire report. "Where? What happened?" Kat examined her non-injured hand and sequined chest.

"Gimme a Band-Aid," Cece continued with her pitiful pleas. "A bunch of 'em."

Worn out from the draining events, Maggie put Kat out of her misery. "She's fine. Not a scratch on her."

"Uh, ah." Cece twisted around, pleading to Rick. "Tell 'em. Cars gimme booboos."

Kat shot Maggie a glare instead of at the messenger. "What the hell?"

Maggie rolled her eyes and placed Cece on the sidewalk, gripping her make-believe injured hand. "Save your yelling for later. We have too much to get done." She glanced at her watch and made a mental note that they had an hour and a half before the guests arrived. "Did you get the tables set up?"

Willing to do anything for her niece, Kat zipped her lip for once and stormed toward the backyard. But not before shooting Maggie the evil eye. With lots to accomplish on the to-do list, Maggie ignored Kat and dragged Cece toward the porch. Behind her, Rick's shuffling footsteps and khaki slacks rubbing together made her hypersensitive to his every move. Cece jabbered away, telling him all about her princess party, which would be held in the courtyard: her fort decorated with streamers and pillars constructed from painted gray boxes to resemble a castle, a chair covered in glittery red fabric for a makeshift throne, and her subjects who would be seated at two tables covered in gold velvet.

About ten children were expected. Maggie sucked up the

panic and put on her happy face, prepared to provide the best birthday party possible. Her daughter deserved it. Cece might be impulsive, quick to react, and resistant to rules, but she was also lovable, affectionate, and a sweetheart too.

After they got inside, Maggie went straight to the DVD player to keep Cece preoccupied and away from any more catastrophes. She popped in *The Lion King,* another of her daughter's favorite movies, and pressed play. As Rick and Cece settled down on the couch, she scooted toward the kitchen, giving him time with the princess of honor.

"Maggie, can you hold up a sec?"

She stopped in the archway between the living room and kitchen. From his back pocket, he pulled out a slender box and a flat package, both decorated in Barbie paper. His glances flicked from her to Cece. "Is it okay if she opens these now?" After Maggie nodded, Cece climbed into his lap, bouncing up and down, clapping with excitement.

"I have two gifts for you," he explained, setting the thinner of the two in Cece's outstretched hand. Without waiting, Cece ripped half the paper off in a second. Relaxing his back along the cushions, he chuckled at her enthusiasm.

"Mama, Simba," Cece shouted, waving a rectangular slip with that character on it.

"It's for the musical next Sunday. Matt and I wanna treat the girls."

Well damn, how in the world could she deny her daughter that? Bad enough that Cece already rattled off a thousand and one questions about the ticket, and what it meant. Unwilling to crush her daughter's spirit, she nodded okay.

After Cece ran out of things to ask, she must have remembered the surprises weren't done yet. "I got two, Mama." She picked up the next one, waving it like an air traffic controller wand, almost smacking Rick in the nose a couple times. Again, Cece threw more wrapping paper on the floor, but instead of doing the same with the box lid, her erratic move-

172

ments came to an abrupt stop. Maggie observed Rick, who'd been watching Cece's overexcited craziness with a beaming smile. "When's ya birfday?"

He blinked a few times, not answering at first. "March twentieth." The first day of spring and the same date Maggie's mom was born.

Her nose scrunched, and Cece looked up at the ceiling, and then toward Rick. "Next monf, like Mama?"

"Uh, no, my birthday's a long time away. It's past already."

"I gotta get ya a present."

"You gave me one." He pulled his arm away from Cece's back, touching a braided band on his wrist. "Remember? You made this for me."

When he put the playset together Maggie saw the bracelet on him but didn't know Cece had given it to him. It looked fantastic on him then. Now she loved it even more. That thought made her smile and sent a pang to her heart.

A frown tugged at Cece's mouth, and she collapsed, dropping her head on his shoulder. "Here." She lifted the box and set it in his hand.

"What's wrong, sweet pea? That's for you."

"I gotta get ya two first."

Maggie gasped, pressing a hand over her mouth to cover her reaction as much as possible. In her ear, Kat whispered, "You and your damn rules, Mags. God, the kid can't even enjoy her birthday. 'It's better to give than receive, don't take more than you give' BS ruined this for her."

Under her breath, Maggie grumbled, "Shut up. When you have kids someday you'll understand."

Kat snorted, pinching her waist. "Ha, not a chance."

"Well, sweet pea, how about this? Next week when you're at school you make me something. Besides, you invited me to the friendship tea, and that was a gift."

Cece's head popped up, frowns and sadness all gone. "'Kay." He placed the box in her lap, and she removed the lid. "Pretty. See, Mama?" She displayed a silver link necklace with a shamrock pendant that matched the shimmery green sparkles of her dress.

"Want to put it on?" After Cece's confirming head bob, he put the chain around her neck and secured the clasp. He cuddled her in his arms and in a soft timbre said, "Once upon a time there was a leprechaun, a fairy, who lived all alone. He didn't have any friends or family and nobody to love him. The more time that went by, he got sadder and sadder, lonelier and lonelier. One day when he was walking through the forest, he heard a noise. Above him, hanging from a tree branch, was a little girl stuck in a net. She didn't scream, she didn't cry, but she was afraid. You see, she got lost when she went walking in the woods. The leprechaun knew what it felt like to be scared. He didn't like living by himself. And he hated seeing her stuck there because he knew the trap was set to capture him. But did you know that leprechauns are magic?" Cece shook her head no.

"If they get caught, then they can use their powers to get free. But they can't use their magic on humans, so he couldn't help her that way. Since he didn't live far from there, he promised the girl he would be right back. At his house he had tons of tools because he's a shoemaker. When he returned, he took out the ones he needed, put them in his pockets, and climbed the tree. Cutting a hole in the net, he helped the little girl get out. Together they climbed down the branches, holding on to each other until they reached the ground. The girl was so happy, but the leprechaun was not. He knew that she would go away like many others, leaving him all alone again. Grateful the leprechaun saved her, she wanted to give him a gift. She removed her necklace, kissing each of the three petals before putting it on the leprechaun." Rick picked up the pendant and showed it to Cece.

"A shamrock, just like yours. These petals mean something." He tapped the first one on the left. "This one stands for hope. The little girl, Rachael was her name, told the leprechaun she hoped all his wishes would come true." He pointed to the middle leaf. "This one is love. She wished the leprechaun would find love and happiness." He touched the last petal. "This one is faith. She held the leprechaun's hands in hers and told him she'd be his friend for life and to have faith in that promise. And that is what I wish for you, sweet pea."

Kat sniffled behind her, and once again, tears drenched Maggie's cheeks, and Rick's and Cece's too as they hugged each other.

Not long after, he gave Cece a final embrace and quietly said, "I'll pick her up next Sunday at noon." Then left before the first guest arrived. Too stunned for words, Maggie nodded and waved as he walked out the door. Cece hit replay on *The Lion King* video, preparing for her chance to "meet Simba." And Kat volunteered to tie some balloons on the mailbox.

In the past, cooking kept her mind preoccupied and helped calm her. Now though, nothing could keep her mind off Rick's gloomy frown, slouched shoulders, and shuffled departure.

Maggie and Kat carried the food, while Cece stood on her tiptoes and rang the doorbell way too many times.

When the barn style, paneled entrance swung open, Emma jumped in too, removing one of the three bags Maggie had clutched to her chest. "Oh my, I would have come out to help."

Cece dashed around Emma, into the foyer and down a hallway, exploring the new surroundings. Maggie yelled, "Stop," and for once her daughter listened.

They followed Emma past a cozy family room with a fireplace and dining room with an antique oblong table in the center, into a massive kitchen with snow-white cabinets. Casement windows and French doors comprised an entire wall, offering a crystal clear view of the picturesque backyard. The lush lawn and floral gardens were even more magnificent, surrounding a pond big enough to fish in. Cece entertained as usual, chatting in hyper-speed mode, telling Emma about her "big girl, I five" princess party. The topic of discussion for a week now. More than polite, Emma asked questions and oohed and aahed, giving Cece the attention she adored.

After numerous trips to the car and the essentials piled on the butcher-block island, the eight-foot-wide countertop disappeared. Kat and Cece said their goodbyes, making a quick exit before Maggie could suck them into helping with the enormous job. The only things on their minds were *The Penguins of Madagascar* movie, a visit to Build-a-Bear, and the Brooklyn aquarium.

Emma had no problem, though, unpacking the bags along with her.

"I didn't realize how much it would take to feed fifty people."

Maggie was used to preparing for any type of event at her grandparents' restaurant, which had an additional thousand square feet for catering weddings, class reunions, or corporate functions. This party wouldn't be much different. She put the contents in the double-wide refrigerator, lined up the items for the first recipe on an empty counter near the windows, and fell into the comforting motions that were old hat to her. "The menu you chose has a nice selection. Your guests will have plenty of options. We'll start with hors d'oeuvres at four. Where would you like that set up?"

"Between the living and dining room. The doors slide open. We'll put tables there."

Maggie nodded, noticing that feature too. The vintage panels suspended on tracks would expand the space, providing ample room for fifty. "Your home is beautiful. How long have you lived here?"

Emma's whimsical smile appeared and vanished with a

tinge of sadness. "My husband, Max, had it built for me not long after we married."

Maggie's pounding heart beat into her ears. Cece's insightful knack for choosing nicknames hit her full force.

"He passed away over a decade ago, but it still feels like yesterday."

Reaching across the island, Maggie's tingling hand took hold of Emma's.

"He was such an amazing man just like Rick. The two of them were inseparable. Max worked long hours, but he always dropped everything for his son. Nothing got in the way of their time together. It didn't matter my husband was still getting his company off the ground. What mattered most to him was family."

"You mentioned how you met, but you never told me the rest." She'd always been fascinated how couples ended up together. As bittersweet as the story would be, she hoped Emma decided to share.

The grin that appeared contrasted with Emma's previous one and remained as she revealed the past. "He was like a bulldog, relentless in his pursuit. When I didn't call him, he stayed away for a month or so, and after that time, returned every day for lunch or dinner, depending on when I was working. I found out later he didn't come back on purpose. It had been part of his strategy. He told me sometimes you don't realize life's true gifts until there's a risk, and you're confronted with losing it forever." Tears pooled in Emma's eyes, but they didn't fall. She drew in several deep breaths, sucking them back and replacing them with renewed concentration. The perseverance and determination Emma admired in her husband were embodied in her too.

"I fell in love with him a little more every visit. He was such an easy person to talk to. As our conversations evolved, they got deeper. He buttered me up by bringing a different flower each time." Emma pointed to her backyard. "Every one of them, he planted for me too." A tear rolled down Emma's cheek. Maggie squeezed Emma's hand, holding back her own.

"There aren't many men that compassionate," Maggie mumbled, envisioning Emma's husband on his knees, digging in the dirt, leaving his mark and beauty on his sweetheart's life.

"Rick is. He just needs the right woman."

Maggie looked toward the pond, turning her back on Emma's momma-knows-best inspection. She refused to discuss that hot topic. Grabbing the nearest bag, she pulled out the homemade bread and pastry shells, placing them on a cutting board by the windows. Emma paid her no mind though and kept talking.

"He's had a hard time since his father's death. He worries so much about making his company a success, he doesn't give love a chance. It breaks my heart to see the business take over his life. His dad never would've wanted that. Yeah, Max had grand plans to work with his son. But as much as he wanted that, he would've sold it all if he knew it would hurt Rick like it has. Max believed in family first and work later. More than anything, he wanted his son to find love and happiness, get married and have kids. He always said that's what brought him the most joy. He wished the same for Rick."

During Emma's hard-to-tune-out plea, she imagined Rick at various stages, toddling along the grass, his father close behind in case he stumbled, and sitting on the dock, his dad with a fishing pole in hand, teaching his son how to cast and reel. Just like her dad had done at their favorite watering hole. "Is he okay?" Caught in the melancholy spirit, her concern for Rick grew. She moved around the island and sat on a stool next to Emma. "I mean, he came by our place last week to give Cece her birthday gifts. But he seemed worried, depressed, I don't know. I didn't ask." Disgusted by her childish behavior, she avoided him all week by taking the stairwell instead of going by his suite. "I should have."

"He puts on a good show most of the time. But just bundles everything up and refuses to talk about his problems. He thinks I'll be disappointed if he says anything negative about work. He worries so much about my feelings. I've told him a thousand times I'm proud of him no matter what he does. He just pretends everything's hunky dory. I even told him to sell the company. You would've thought I asked him to cut off his head as pale as he got. But he sucked it up. Instead of screaming or yelling at me, or even telling me hell no, he pretended I hadn't said anything." Emma's sighs exposed the agony and concern for her only child. Something Maggie could relate to. A phone rang and Emma hopped up from her seat, running out of the kitchen.

Instead of jumping into preparations, Maggie opened the French doors and walked to the pond, gazing into the ripples. Tomorrow he'd pick Cece up for *The Lion King*. Maybe she could talk to him. She didn't know what she'd say. Hopefully, she'd figure it out by then. One thing for certain, she wouldn't tell him she was in love with him. That would open up a whole other mess she couldn't handle. Being the first to admit her feelings hadn't turned out so well before. She pushed Jake to marry her and didn't want to be in that situation again. Besides, he might love Cece, but what man could take on Maggie's "idiot-syncrasies" as Kat called them. Just as Emma admitted, he focused on business. No doubt Rick would be opposed to a woman plus one and repelled by an insta-family.

Well, at least being a mother taught her a valuable lesson—sacrifice.

It wouldn't be the first time she went without.

And it won't be the last.

Mama's Rule #19:

Sometimes reality isn't all it's cracked up to be.

Better late than never. Twenty novels ago, arriving a half hour past the start of the release party might've been an issue. Now though, Rick's mother had become accustomed to his tardiness. As much as he took pride in her accomplishments, the crowd, almost all women, drained him. Another social function where he'd have to chat up strangers, make nice, and talk about one useless topic after another. Besides, it never failed that a female writer, editor, or some other guest whose name he couldn't remember came on to him. The number of diversions he'd have to come up with was exhausting.

"Honey, I'm so glad you made it." Mother radar on high alert, she noticed as soon as he entered the family room.

"Congratulations. May you write a hundred more. No offense, but I think this is your best yet." He pulled her into a hug, whispering the last part in her ear.

She pinched his cheek, replacing the sting with a kiss. "It's easy when you love what you do."

Sensing an underlying message, he tucked his arm around her, leading her to the food and hoping she'd find something else to focus on. He picked up a mushroom cap resembling Maggie's and popped it into his mouth. Tasted like hers too. "Mmm, very good, Mom. Your caterer didn't make these before. They're excellent." He ate three more, careful to maintain decorum, even though he wanted to scarf down the whole tray. They were that good.

"Thank you, sweetie. I used a different caterer this time. That's why."

He moved on to the next tray, sampling a bacon-wrapped something on a skewer. "Oh my God. What is that? It's phenomenal." He spoke with a mouthful. Not waiting for her response, he ate another.

She giggled and said, "You wouldn't believe what those are called, angels on horseback. They're an English specialty with oysters inside." Pointing to each selection she rattled off the rest, all of which he planned on diving into after he ate at least ten more of heaven in bacon first. "Bavarian meatballs, Chinese pot stickers with veggies and pork, Greek grape leaves stuffed with rice and lamb, falafel, it's a Middle Eastern fried chickpea patty, and I can't have a party without my favorite, German deviled eggs."

"Well, you've got at least half a dozen countries represented. Nothing like traveling the globe for your release. When do you go on the book tour?" He walked around the tables, picking and sampling.

"Oh, in a few weeks. I love traveling. Which city are you going to meet me in this time?"

"Since you haven't given me your itinerary, I have no idea. Tell me where and when, and I'll be there." As soon as he got that remark out, his mom's publicist crept up to him, snagging and squeezing his arm. "I'll make sure you get that on Monday."

He pulled out of her grip, filling both of his hands with an appetizer. Reading him like a book, his mother smirked at his evasive maneuver. "How about run in the kitchen for me, sweetie, and ask the chef when dinner will be served?"

Grateful for the escape, he took it.

The closer he got, blaring music registered first, then a somewhat out of tune, high-pitched chanting hit him next. He came to a halt in the archway the instant he caught sight of Maggie. Every ounce of oxygen vanished from the atmosphere and his breathing ceased, immobilizing him.

Beyoncé's "Naughty Girl" played to perfection from her cell phone, but the version Maggie sang resembled a pirated, flawed copy at best. Hips swinging left to right along with the intense beat, she waved a whisk in the air and then shoved it up to her mouth, using it as a microphone. The hacked up lyrics and lip-syncing came across like an amplified megaphone that kept screeching and cutting out. He would have laughed his ass off any other day, but he couldn't move.

This would be how he remembered her—forever. Right here, right now. At her best: happy, carefree. Her throw me down, tie me up, please me—love me state.

Tossed in a bun with curlycue twists at the edge of her hairline, loose strands stuck out of the messy clump on top and wisps caressed her ears. He loved when she wore her mass of auburn pulled back from her beautiful freckled face. Every inch of her neck exposed, he memorized the slope and the two dimples at the bottom. She had earrings in today, gold hoops. No chef's coat and her bare arms were exposed by a white tank top with a scripted warning: Back up! Hot stuff coming through.

Mesmerized, he made it through that song and the next, "When a Man Loves a Woman," the sentiments taunting him. It wasn't until "Sexual Healing" came on that he caved—surrendered to her—and their isolated circumstance.

He eased up behind her and gripped her curvy hips. She jumped and tried to turn around but relaxed when he spoke. "Shh, don't say anything. Feel me . . . you . . . us." As his pelvis rocked to the sensual beat, hers glided along. He removed her hands from the counter and linked their fingers together. Their arms crossed over her stomach, he tucked his chin and lips into the crook of her neck and sang the passionate lyrics. His tenor dipped an octave or two as the sensations of having her alone and in his arms took control. Ripped from his heart and soul, he deepened his tone and relayed all the longing and desire he felt for her and always would—craving, wanting no other.

The final stanza came with an overpowering tagline.

"What the hell is going on in here?" his grandfather yelled.

Maggie tried to turn around, but he squeezed her middle, steadying her.

"Horatio, stop it. Leave him be."

"I will do no such thing."

That cue prompted Rick to react, pressing his lips to the hollow of Maggie's throat, chin, cheek, and temple in ever-lasting kisses. A final one meant to last a lifetime, positioned on top of her left hand, third finger.

Then he walked out through the French doors—silence following him.

"What the hell? It's two in the morning."

Rick stared, stumbled over the threshold, and fell against Matt.

"Oh, shit. Fuck." Matt grabbed him under the armpits, but he slid to his knees anyway and his spinning, heavy head collapsed onto Matt's thigh.

"Is everything okay?"

"Go back to sleep, Soph."

"Oh my god. Let me help you."

"Wait a sec. Let me get a better hold on him." Matt's vise grip wrapped around his back and pulled. "Up you go, buddy." On his wobbly legs, his stomach rolled, causing him to belch in Matt's face.

"Oh god, what happened?"

"You can't smell the brewery?"

"Matt, please, let me help."

"I got him. Move back, babe. I'm dumping him in the guest room." His dead weight pressed to Matt's chest, Rick had no idea how Matt performed the twist and turn he did, propping him along his hip. Hobbled stutter steps commenced until Rick's view changed from wood floors to a mattress.

"I'll get some water, wet cloths, and aspirin," Sophia called out.

"Thanks, babe. Okay, down you go, buddy."

He face-planted onto the cushy pillow and rolled onto his side. "Ahhh."

"Please tell me you didn't drive here."

"Tax. . . . tax. . . . i," he stammered into the feathered softness.

"Okay, okay. Don't worry about it. Just lay there and sleep it off."

"Ca . . . can't."

"Uh, yeah, I think you can. You're half zonked already."

"Can't . . . do . . . it."

"Come on, buddy. Let's get your shoes and clothes off."

Rick kept his eyes shut, rolled onto his back, and willed the gurgles in his stomach to stop. Matt tugged his loafers off and grabbed the bottom of his T-shirt. "Oh, Christ. Did you throw up?"

"Do you need a bucket?"

"Yeah, babe, get the one from the bathroom, would ya?"

"Okay. Oh, Matt, I hate seeing him like that."

"I know, babe. I know."

Rick mumbled, "Can't . . . do it . . . anymore."

"Matt, what's he talking about?"

"I don't know, babe. It could be anything. Lord knows,

he's got tons of shit piled on him."

He opened his mouth to say something, tell Matt to shut the fuck up, but the words wouldn't come out.

"What can I do?"

Bile crept up his throat, and he swallowed and swallowed, but it didn't help.

"Hurry up, get the bucket, he's hackin.'"

"Okay, okay, here."

"Upsy daisy, bud." Matt yanked on him again and the motion, along with his gagging, left him with no choice. He slumped over Matt's knee, expelling the contents of his stomach in the plastic pail, acid burning his throat and tongue, making his eyes water.

"Shit, that's foul. You haven't been like this in a long time. This is fuckin' nuts."

"Can't . . . do . . . it."

"Don't talk when you're hurlin,' man. Soph, where'd you put the water and towels?"

"On the nightstand next to you."

"Okay, okay."

"Done. Lay down." Rick spit out the order instead of vomit and wiped his mouth with the towel Matt shoved in his face.

"Shirt off first." Unable to get his limbs to work, Matt saved him again, pulling the damp, sweaty fabric over his head. "Lay back."

Rick dropped his head on a cushioned, soft surface and his eyes closed again. A cover got laid over his shoulders and on an exhausted breath he muttered, "Tired."

"Yeah, I bet."

"Lost," he mumbled.

"Yeah, that too."

"He shouldn't sleep in those pants. They might be a mess. Take 'em off him, Matt."

"Sleep," Rick answered.

"He'll be out in a second. Leave him alone."

"Lone . . . nobody," he grumbled.

"Oh god, Matt. He's breaking my heart."

"Welcome to the club, babe. Fucked up for a long time."

"He doesn't deserve this."

"No, he doesn't. Best damn man I ever met. Come on, let him sleep it off. I'll talk to him in the morning."

"You have to help him."

"I'm trying, Soph. I really am."

"Have you asked Emma? She might have some ideas."

"She's on board already."

"Good. Between the two of you and me, we should be able to figure something out."

"Yeah, I'm hopin.' Goodnight, buddy."

"Night," he murmured, his eyes popping open when he felt a kiss on his temple. When it wasn't the person he hoped, he slammed them shut. The squeeze pinched and amplified the stabbing and ramming in his head.

"Sweet dreams," Sophia said on his forehead.

"Dreams," he whispered, and on his next breath, "Maggie."

A freezing rush of air washed over Rick's bare chest. He threw an arm over his pounding head and the other across his aching stomach.

"Let's go. Get up. We got stuff to do."

His right eye opened, but the other wouldn't cooperate. Rick glanced at Matt, hands on his hips, dressed and raring to go. Rolling onto his side, he stuffed a hand under the feather-soft pillow and attempted to tune him out.

"There's sweats on the dresser. Get a shower. Don't bother going back to sleep. I swear if you do, you'll be covered in an ice bath like we used to give pledges at the frat house."

Rick mumbled, telling Matt exactly what he could do with that BS technique.

"Okay, fine. I'll call Maggie and tell Cece you're not coming. Go ahead and break her heart. But see if I ever talk to you again. Don't call, don't write, don't fucking come near me."

Regardless of how bad things got, Rick never reneged on a promise. He propped his arms on the mattress, muscles straining under his unsteady weight and a truckload of other burdens crushing him, yet he somehow staggered to his feet.

Ignoring Matt's you're-dead sideways glares, Rick shouldered past him, snatched the clothes from the dresser, and slammed the bathroom door, grateful for the peace and quiet. Too bad his spinning and pounding head didn't agree.

"When you're done having a pity party, you'll find me in the kitchen making your hangover breakfast. Then I'll take you home to change."

With the hot water turned on full blast, he tried to drown Matt out.

It didn't work.

"All right, I'll wait in the car with my girls, you go get yours."

Rick fixed Matt with a narrowed scowl. The underlying prod hadn't been appreciated, but he wouldn't bother to argue with him. They already had it out when he exited the bathroom, dressed in Matt's sweats, and found him sitting on a bare mattress, sheets and covers piled on the carpet. If he hadn't known Matt for over ten years and better than the back of his own hand, he would've taken offense with the fucked-up insults to his manhood and spit-flying brutal attacks to his wounded and already battered frame of mind. When all was said and done though, Matt pulled him into a man hug, pounding him on the back. "Time for a strategic move, buddy.

Face the writing on the wall. Read what it says, process it, and don't ignore the save-your-sorry-ass message."

"Max," Cece chanted his name over and over like a cheerleader yelling for the star quarterback. Rick leapt out of the car and swept her into his arms. Maggie came up not far behind, the momma bear focused on her straying-again cub. "Ya came."

Setting Cece on her feet, he got down on a knee and clasped her hands in his. "Of course I did, sweet pea. I said I'd pick you up at noon." He showed her his watch, positioned above her leather bracelet, and pointed to the big hand. "See that. It's on the nine, not twelve. It's eleven forty-five. I'm early. And since I am, you need to plant one right here." He pointed to his cheek, waiting for his reward.

Cece giggled, threw her arms around his neck, and smothered him with a slobbery kiss.

"You look beautiful, princess. Is that a new dress?" Different from the fancy attire worn on her birthday, but no less frilly, the purple layered tutu and shimmery camisole would be something found on a ballerina.

"Yeppers." Her arms stretched wide, she twirled in a circle, beaming at his compliment. Her smile brightened her chubby red cheeks. The sunshine highlighted them and made the garment glisten as if she were front and center on stage under the spotlights.

"She's never been to a musical before. I tried to explain, but she's stuck on the ballet since I've taken her a few times."

"Hmm." He stood, deciding on a tactic. More than excited about the opportunity to spend the day with her, he didn't want her disappointed when she got there and found out it wasn't what she thought. On the sidewalk, in front of Maggie and the entire neighborhood, radiating through his heart, he sang, "Love Will Find a Way." A musical rendition he recalled from *The Lion King II* and enhanced by motions that went along with the lyrics. He extended his hand out to her, and as graceful as a prima ballerina, she spun and twirled in a circle along with him as he held them above her head, providing the support as a premier danseur noble male lead would for his partner.

Each of his verses resulted in a different move, facial expression, and emotion: covering his eyes to represent darkness, clutching his arms and shivering to show fear, pointing from his eyes to Cece's demonstrating enlightenment shining through, and the grand finale, jogging over to the porch, where Kat laughed in hysterics, but he didn't care. With a firm hold on the railing, a leg and arm suspended midair, he sang about love, home, and togetherness from the top of his lungs.

When he finished, the standing ovation came from Matt, Lizbeth, and Harley who had jumped out of the car at the beginning of his performance. Maggie and Cece whooped cheers and clapped in a roundabout fashion from the top of their heads, down to their waists, and back again in a circular motion. His affection for them clogged his throat. And Kat, with a forefinger and pinky thrust between her lips, whistled like a sailor. His bow completed the once in a lifetime show. He swooped a hyena-laughing Cece into his arms, and after she gave Maggie and Kat goodbye kisses and hugs, he secured her in the booster chair in the back of the SUV. Lizbeth and Harley climbed in and buckled their belts too, while he made his grand exit, collapsing into the passenger seat.

In the side-view mirror, Rick caught sight of Maggie being held in Kat's arms, heard hiccupping whimpers through his open window, while Matt shifted into reverse, retreating out of their driveway. Oblivious to her mother's affected appearance, Cece's exuberant chatter about meeting Simba and singing the same song "like Max" consumed their excursion.

As best as he could, he pretended his own internal, gaping wounds weren't visible. After his less than stellar performance last night, Matt wasn't buying his stoic expression. His hunched posture, trembling hands, and vacant stare intensi-

189

fied the longer Matt drove. Numbness crept through his limbs, replacing the blood that used to pulse through them, a zombie-like replacement sitting in his seat.

When he turned thirteen, excited about becoming a man, he couldn't wait to be a grown up. He'd been wrong—it sucked.

It didn't take long for them to arrive at West Forty-Second Street due to the low traffic on a Sunday. A half hour before the performance started, Rick watched the girls pick through the hundred or so souvenirs. Matt bowed out, stating he'd be right back. He returned with a bottle of Five Hour Energy, demanding Rick chug it. "Since you had enough of the stuff that didn't work last night, this and the aspirin you took should help." Not wanting to guzzle anything in front of the kids, Rick waited until after Matt took the girls into the auditorium, and went into the bathroom, doing what he ordered for once.

Their seats in the front row were located on the left side of the orchestra pit and stage. They got situated in a particular order: Matt on the end cap, then him, Cece, Lizbeth, and Harley. The girls had coloring books out and dove in, using the crayons to shade Simba and the other Disney characters.

While Rick flipped through the pamphlet, reading the cast bios, scene descriptions, and highlights, Cece climbed over the armrest and into his lap, crushing the brochure and his hands underneath her. "I gotta ask ya somefin, Max."

"What's that, sweet pea?"

"Ya gotta dada?"

A hot iron seared his gut and dried up his unblinking eyes. Not sure how long it took for a reply, at some point, he muttered, "Yeah, he's in heaven."

Her eyebrows scrunched up and bottom lip turned into a pout. He darted a wide-eyed plea to Matt, but his supposed savior just tilted his head and shrugged an out-of-the-mouth-of-babes non-answer.

"Like my frog?"

Snatched out of the heat by Cece's question, he blurted, "I didn't know you had a frog."

She patted his cheek. "'Cause he's in heaven, silly." On the flipside, she asked, "Ya gotta sissy or brofer?"

"No."

Scooted onto her knees and sitting back on her bent legs, she faced him. He gripped her upper arms so she didn't fall while she assumed her new position. "I don't got none of 'em eifer."

His mouth dropped open, closed, and opened again. All he could manage was wheezing short gasps. He had no idea what to say.

The orchestra cueing the first song saved him, triggering Cece to leap across the armrest and into her chair. Excitement bubbling, her behind bounced up and down in her seat. As the costumed characters appeared, breaking out in song, Cece, Lizbeth, and Harley hopped to their feet. Their bodies shifted into girly swaying while they joined hands and crooned along, becoming more and more captivated by the musical adventure. For Lizbeth and Harley this hadn't been the first time he and Matt brought them to a Broadway show. Often invited along for many of their father-daughter activities, since he enjoyed hanging out with them, he hadn't given much consideration to their time together. But now, as he processed what Cece called attention to and observed her joyful delight, she brought to mind a lifetime of memories of father and son outings: fishing in the backyard pond, his dad holding on to the back rim of his two-wheeler when the training wheels were removed, showing him how to hold and toss a football, painting and constructing model cars, and so many other precious moments.

Although Cece's representation hadn't been accurate, she

had a daddy. Still, in her young mind, maybe it felt like she didn't. Any gaps in his knowledge about Maggie and Jake's history had been filled in by Kat and added to by hyper-alert Matt. None of which he asked for. It didn't take him long to wish he had a minute alone with Cece's dad though. He wanted to beat the shit out of Jake. Every child deserved to be loved, wanted, and have a safe home. His dad showed him in every way he cared. His mother did the same.

"Sing, Max, sing," Cece shouted over the music.

He did, noting she already sang much better than her mother. That thought had him smiling along with Cece. Her happiness and thrilled energy wrenched him from his depressing thoughts. The bundle of joy, swinging his hand, bouncing on her tiptoes, deserved many more experiences like it.

And he didn't need the title "father" to make it happen either.

Mama's Rule #20:

Don't make faces or it will freeze that way.

Maggie didn't mind the night shift since fewer than a handful of employees were on the schedule at this hour. The peace and quiet after a fast-paced restaurant atmosphere provided a calm end to her hectic day. Time away from Cece wasn't pleasant though. When they lived in Texas, the shifts she worked at her grandparents' place varied. Three nights a week she supplemented her salary with a part-time data entry position at a customer support center. The extra pay contributed to her personal go-to-culinary-school-someday fund, with half set aside for Cece's college savings.

When she and Jake married, he insisted their finances remain separate. He already had his own savings and checking account and so did she, setting it up when she turned thirteen to deposit a small salary she received for hosting and handling the register for her grandparents. The request wasn't out of the ordinary because her mama mentioned she and Daddy had done the same thing.

During their four years of marriage, they lived in a rented house and didn't have many bills. She had the Honda Civic her parents bought her when she turned sixteen, and Jake had a motorcycle, which he paid off. Once a month they divvied up expenses, but he refused to contribute any money for Cece's care: clothes, diapers, formula, baby food, everything. He said since he didn't want kids, and she did, she'd pay for it.

It—he used that reference for his own daughter, not once or twice but too many times to count.

She argued with him, but her pleas hadn't mattered. His complete indifference made no sense. Who would act that way? Why? Yes, he had a horrible upbringing. An alcoholic father who had nothing to do with him and a mother who took off, abandoning him when he was six months old. The replacements: a revolving door of women who kept his dad entertained. Even so, she wasn't anything like them. She loved Jake and did her best to show him. But he still didn't want Cece or her.

Jake's tough exterior and wounded spirit tugged at her heartstrings. Another of her "idiot-syncracies" as Kat reminded her over and over again. Her sister tried to talk her out of marrying him, but she didn't listen. For as long as she could remember, she wanted to have kids and a husband. Her dad didn't like Jake, and her mama worried but allowed her make her own decisions. Maybe she had a little rebel in her too because Jake had been the only time she'd gone against her family's wishes. And look how that turned out. As a parent, up to her neck in hindsight, she understood now.

"Excuse me. Ms. Tyson, right?"

She jumped in her chair, and her head whipped from the computer screen to the opened office door. The clock above it showed nine p.m. The receptionist locked up on the way out at six thirty, so she had no idea how the elderly gentleman had gotten in. She stood and moved closer to the phone at the corner of her desk. "We—we aren't open. I—I mean, you have to come back between nine and five if you need something." Her nerves were rattled and she stammered through the unprofessional explanation. In the four months she worked here, no one had been let in after business hours.

"I know Mr. Westlake personally." His refined posture, suit and tie, and calm demeanor didn't put her at ease.

She looked over his shoulder to see if the glass entry doors were closed, but she couldn't tell from her position. All she could see was the corner of the receptionist's desk and an empty seat.

"Maybe I should have introduced myself first. I'm Horatio Stone, Rick's grandfather."

Now she recognized him, somewhat. For a brief second in Emma's kitchen, by the time she finished staring at Rick's hasty retreat and turned around, all she saw was the back of a gray-haired man wearing a business suit, and Emma chastising him as they left. Her concern for Rick and reeling from their intimate dance together, she hadn't paid the man and his strange outbursts any mind.

Collapsing into her chair, she attempted to relax by resting her shaky hand on her rapidly beating heart and chuckled at her silliness. "I'm sorry. I guess I'm just a little on edge. Visitors and clients don't come by at this hour."

"Yes, I know."

That comment along with Mr. Stone closing the door and taking a seat at the front of her desk launched sirens and alarm bells in her ears. She sat up as ramrod stiff as he had in his seat, her hands clenched on a Westlake Security calendar pad.

"What's going on? Is Rick okay? Emma?"

"I'm glad you asked. As a matter of fact, there is a problem."

Concerned, she prompted, "Did something happen?"

Quiet for several nerve-racking heartbeats, he stared as she shifted to the edge of her chair. Calm, cool, and collected, his lack of clarification should have alerted her.

"I'm a businessman, Ms. Tyson. I don't mince words. I'll be frank with you."

His don't-mess-with-me professional tone became her defensive position too. "By all means, you won't leave until you do. So say what you came here to."

"My grandson may be savvy in business, but he's stupid when it comes to his personal life." She opened her mouth to deny she had anything to do with that, but when he held his hand up, she paused. Not because of his silence-imbecile action though. Her internal battle and warring emotions kept her from speaking. "You've been offered money to stay away, and since you haven't, that makes you a fool too."

She bit and clipped the side of her tongue, blood pooling under it. Over the sting and the lump in her throat, she swallowed the acidy-salty fluid into the pit of her sunken stomach, along with her infuriated, clamped-down response.

"When at first you don't succeed . . . I'm sure you've heard that saying before, Ms. Tyson. In the corporate world we learn tenacity, perseverance, and how to overcome adversity. Otherwise, we fail. I study my opponent, do my research, and change strategies. I always get what I want. *You*—I do not want for my grandson. You and your brat are welfare-laden expenditures, expecting a handout, and an inconvenience—an expense my grandson does not deserve. So, I'll appeal to your parental side, and the affections you may have . . . *created* for my multimillionaire grandson."

As he belittled her and Cece, the best, most precious gift she'd ever received, tears streamed down her cheeks and over the shaky hands covering her gaping mouth, repressing her screams, but not her whimpers.

He leaned forward, hands clasped on the edge of the desk, ready to launch his closing attack. "You—are to stay away from my grandson. You—are not to pursue him any longer. You—are not to bring that bastard child anywhere near him. If you do, Ms. Tyson, you will lose. I didn't get to where I am today without meeting plenty of influential people. One call, that's all it would take to destroy you. You think your husband was bad. You have no idea what evil is until it comes knocking. Or in this case—faces you, head on." Mr. Horatio Stone stood and slammed the door on his way out, expecting his solemn vow to be followed without haste.

The one and only time—he'd been right.

Mama's Rule # 21:

Don't judge a book by its cover.

Thirteen days, three hundred and twelve hours, and eighteen thousand seven hundred twenty seconds passed since Rick saw Maggie or Cece. Several months of intense negotiations had culminated in two weeks of hell, leaving him with little sleep and not much time to do anything but work. He'd even slept in his office a few nights. A sign-on-the-dotted-line critical moment, his Thursday had been spent visiting both corporations to ensure the owners and CEOs had their wishes finalized. His success depended on preventing any last-minute catastrophes, especially before the three o'clock powwow in his conference room. When he entered the office at one, Mrs. Collins racing up to him didn't decrease the incredible tension.

"Mr. Stone, I'm sorry, sir, but you need to go to boardroom right away." Her flushed face, hurried marching, and frantic plea put him on instant alert. In all the years he'd known her, he'd seen her that way one other time—the day his dad had a massive heart attack.

Taking her lead, he picked up his pace, a rapid stride matching hers. "Catch me up before I go in there. What's going on?" If a person could turn stark white, he could've sworn she did. Her wide eyes caused him to stop and grab her arms in case she passed out. "What is it?"

"Your grandfather, he, he—"

Not waiting, he cut her off. "Causing trouble?"

She gave a jerky nod. "The board members are there too. An unannounced meeting. I'm sorry, sir. I didn't know. When I came back from lunch, I found them in there and then you arrived. I didn't have a chance to call and warn you."

Grandfather's impeccable timing as usual. Shit.

He took several calming breaths. If he went in there half-cocked, visibly upset, his grandfather would pounce. A few seconds would make no difference. Whatever Grandfather planned wouldn't change in a blink anyway. Every reserve he could muster sucked up, he entered the boardroom as if he expected the last-minute meeting. Yet, deep down, it would take every semblance of calm, cool, and collected executive power developed over the years to get through the inevitable disaster about to happen.

"Grandfather, gentleman, it seems you forgot a member. Sorry to crash the party, but as CEO, I should be aware of and in attendance at all meetings. Who's going to catch me up and disclose what's going on?"

Of course his grandfather stepped up, his wheeling and dealing grin in place. "I've convinced the board we need to head in a new direction."

Before his grandfather could elaborate, Rick moved in, forcing himself to stroll with confidence toward the table where all twelve were gathered. Except his grandfather—he stood front and center at the helm. "And which would that be?"

"The merger with Kensington Securities." Grandfather rested on the edge of the oval-shaped table and crossed his arms. How it didn't crash and burn from his enormous ego and inflaming plans he had no idea.

Mentors were valuable assets at any stage of life. There-

199

fore, having had several, first his father, then his grandfather, and for a considerable portion of time, Mr. Kensington, he learned strategizing from the best. The critical key: maintain a poker face and know when to bluff.

"Well, there's a problem with that." He paused for effect. His grandfather quirked his brow but showed no other visible signs or cause for concern. Besides, just as he didn't like to reveal his hand too quickly, neither did Grandfather. Horatio Stone would wait him out. "John and I were jogging in Central Park the other day, and he mentioned he had other plans that didn't include us. So . . ."

He and John hadn't gone running yet, but he bargained on the fact they didn't know that. Buying time, he shoved his sleeve up and glanced at his watch, discovering he'd wasted a good thirty minutes on this craziness. The fact he still had tons of things to get ready before three didn't help alleviate his incensed but still under control temper. He directed a don't-mess-with-me stare at each member, including his grandfather. As casually as possible, he said, "Unless you've spoken to him in the last twenty-four hours, you might want to check on that. You know, get confirmation before bothering busy board members with more of *your* plans."

In that instant, the board members launched a slew of battering questions but not at Rick. They were directed at his grandfather.

"Mr. Stone." Mrs. Collins rushed in and silence came over the room. "This message came for you."

"Can it wait?"

"No, sir. It's . . . important." She marched over to him, handing him a slip of paper.

He opened it and read the writing three times. His vision blurred with each glance. He'd been proud of his ability to keep control through this shitstorm, but it wasn't until he had the handwritten note in his possession that he truly lost it.

As shaken and frayed as his nerves were, his single-minded concentration had one target. "I have to go." He turned his back on the stunned, open-mouthed members, and directed Mrs. Collins. "Get Sherman and Shultz and K Corp execs on the phone. Cancel."

"Where the hell are you going, boy?"

He spun around, stomped up to his grandfather, and blasted him with thirteen years of pent-up fury. "You want this? You're going to get it. But it won't be with me." His arms extended out to his side, he yelled, "Take it all. You want to be CEO? Fine, you're it. You want to merge? Do it, I won't stand in your way. 'Cause you know what? I. Won't. Be. Here. I'm done. Finished. Take it, take it all!"

And he stormed out—straight to the emergency room.

He'd been in the waiting area for almost an hour without word. Nurses and receptionists hounded every few minutes produced nothing. His executive powers had no value here.

"Any word?" Matt appeared out of nowhere, plopping into the hard plastic chair next to him. After a couple pats on Rick's back, he said, "I got here as fast as I could. It's been a hell of day. I had a ton of fires to put out before I could get here. Mrs. Collins got my message to you I see."

"Thank you. Remind me someday what I owe you."

"I'll tell you what, we'll be even on your wedding day."

Rick sat up from staring at the floor and collapsed his back against the wall. He shoved his palms into his closed eyes and chuckled, sucking in a breath or two to stop the tears. "Man, I can't find out anything. Please help me." He wiped his wet cheeks with the backs of his hands and bent over, laying his arms on his legs. "You talk about pullin' a rabbit out of a hat. How about doin' that now?"

Another slap landed on Rick's back, and Matt stood.

"Done." And off his best friend went, dogged determination directed at the same receptionist Rick had asked at least forty times to tell him something.

When Matt strutted over to the hard as nails, female version of Attila the Hun, Rick glanced at the clock on the wall and in less than two and a half minutes his buddy returned, sitting next to him again. "Okay, the doctors examined her. She's been taken to surgery."

"What?" he yelled, pacing and sounding off at the same time. "What happened? Where's Maggie? How'd you find out? Can I go back there?"

"Whoa, calm down. You're freakin' me out a little and that's hard to do." Matt gripped Rick's shoulders and shook him once. "Cece has appendicitis. They caught it before it burst, but they're takin' it out. Maggie's in the operating waiting room with Kat. It's gonna be at least two or three hours. They just took her to the OR."

Rick collapsed into a seat and shoved his hands through his hair. He squeezed his scalp over and over again, trying to massage the tension out of his head. Then moved on to his neck and kneaded it too. "Fuck." He looked at Matt and asked, "How'd you get that out of Ms. Prune Face? What'd you have to threaten her with? I wanna know, because I tried a hell of a lot of 'em and got nowhere."

Shaking his head, Matt patted him on the back again. "If I didn't feel so bad about the condition you're in, I'd tease the fuck out of you. But let's just say you catch more flies with honey. Were you absent during that lesson?"

Rick blew out a breath and dropped his head against the wall, so fast and hard that the loud, dull thump sounded like someone threw a chair against it. He rubbed the ache that started at the crest of his skull. "I have no clue, except her condition sounds serious. Anything involving surgery does." His pleading eyes willed the answer he wanted to hear. "Is she gonna be okay?"

"You didn't let me finish. You were freaking out so much you forgot to get the answer to one of your questions."

Rick paused a minute, thinking, but he couldn't remember a damn thing right now. "What?"

With his finger tapping his chin, Matt said, "Hmm, no, I believe it started with can . . ."

"Quit fuckin' around. Can't you see I'm about to puke all over you?"

Matt's chuckling didn't alleviate the pressure at all, just built it higher. "All right, all right, I'll tell you. The answer is yes."

Rick blew out another breath and followed it with a shake of his head. "Remind me why I'm your friend again, because I've forgotten you are. I'm gonna prove it when I go sit in the corner. Far away from you."

"Well that's gonna be impossible, buddy, because your ass is supposed be in the OR waiting room with Maggie and Kat right now."

"What?" He bolted out of his seat and threw his hands in the air, slapping them against his hips. "Why the hell didn't you tell me that first?" He turned to get to the swinging doors that led to Cece, but Matt grabbed onto his shoulder, stopping him.

"Calm your ass down, that's why. You're not gonna help Maggie like that. I wanted you settled down before you got back there. You're at your best when you have all the details, or in this case, as many as I could get. So take a couple breaths and get it together. But don't get all fired up like you're in a boardroom. Or like you did with that poor receptionist."

"Poor rec—"

"Do you want to go back there or not?"

Rick narrowed a glare at Matt but did as he said. Several breaths later they both walked toward the entrance to the "private" barred section Rick had been trying to get entrance to for the last hour. Ms. Prune shot him a scowl and flipped in an instant to an all toothy smile for Matt.

"Oh, by the way." Matt threw an arm over his shoulder, whispering in his ear while they entered the first corridor and were directed to follow the blue footprints to the waiting room. "Congratulations, you're now engaged. That's how I got you in. Say thank you." He relayed the last portion in a high-pitched sing-song.

In a sideways glance shot Matt's way, he offered him a brief smile—his first one all day. "Thank you."

"Any time, buddy. When all this is over, and Cece's good to go, I expect payment. And I'm not talkin' about money, my man."

He knew Matt wasn't either and hoped he'd be able to produce. From the time they met, Matt always had his best interest at heart. After he made sure his girls were okay, then he'd figure out where Maggie's heart was.

And he hoped to find it—in sync with his.

Mama's Rule #22:

When the going gets tough, the tough get going.

"Quit biting your nails. They're bleedin,' and it's a disgusting habit."

Kat tugged Maggie's hand away from her mouth, squeezed her wrist, and shoved it onto her lap. "I know, I know. I haven't done it since high school. But I'm freaking out if you haven't noticed. My baby's in surgery and they're cuttin' her open. So excuse me if I'm out of control, okay?" She yanked her arm away, shooting her sister a squinty-eyed glare.

"Look, the doctors said she's gonna be fine. She was so keyed up about gettin' a ride in the 'amblance' she forgot all about the pain in her tummy. I held her hand the entire trip while she chatted up the EMTs, asking them a thousand questions. So your baby is gonna be a-okay and rarin' to go, bossin' us around in no time. Just like her pain in the ass mama."

Dropping her head onto Kat's shoulder, she hugged and squeezed her sister's waist extra hard. Tears filled Maggie's eyes as she whispered, "If something happened to her, I'd never survive."

Kat brushed a hand along her hair, murmuring with calm

assurance, "She'll be okay, all fixed up, just one less part." Maggie snorted, pinching Kat's ribs. "I'll tell you when you need to worry. When she turns thirteen, goes on her first date at sixteen . . . then you're allowed to freak out. But now, she's gonna need a thousand hugs from you and a million kisses from her kick-ass aunt Kitty. That's what you should focus on."

"She's not datin' until she's thirty."

Now Kat was the one who snorted. "Honey, I'm sorry to tell you this, but there's not a chance in hell boys are gonna stay away from her that long. Just be glad she's got a gun-toting aunt who'll be guardin' her ass 'til then."

"And me, I got guns."

Her head popped up from Kat's shoulder when Matt strolled into the waiting room with Rick following close behind. Her spine snapped straight, and the nerves Kat had lessened somewhat were jacked up all over again. She swallowed several times to keep the rising bile down. Sick to her stomach before, now she'd need to be thrown on a gurney and wheeled into the OR. Because the enormous pain pulsing through her at the sight of Rick made her chest ache and the frantic, erratic beats might mean she was in the midst of a massive heart attack. Unable to speak from the numbness setting into her arms and legs, she sat there motionless, staring.

Kat bolted out of her chair, giving Matt a hug and then Rick. "Thank you for coming. She's in surgery, appendicitis, but she'll be okay."

"Yeah, I got some details in the emergency room." Matt plopped into a chair next to her and pulled one of her tingling hands into his, squeezing it and recirculating the blood. "How you doin,' momma?"

Still frozen, Kat answered for her. "She's messed up. Freakin' out. I wouldn't touch that hand if I were you."

Matt turned it over, inspecting the damage. "Nervous habit?"

She nodded. Once they entered the room, she diverted her attention to the square tiles, counting the endless gray flecks.

"A year ago, Harley jumped out of the treehouse and broke her arm. Growing up, I think I fractured at least twenty bones and didn't blink, but when it's your baby it hurts like hell. I guess I don't need to tell you that though."

She shook her head no, still counting the specks on the floor, and tried to overlook Rick's shiny black loafers, toe to toe with her ratty old sneakers. Matt stood and disappeared, but she didn't know where he went, because she refused to pick her head up. When Rick crouched down, taking her stinging hands into his and ignoring the blood, her eyes squeezed shut.

"Maggie, can you look at me?"

Again, she shook her head.

"Please?"

Not sure how many minutes or seconds ticked by, she counted her staggered breaths, willing him to go away and not to. "Please . . ." On an inhale and through her smashed together teeth, she said, "Go home. Thank you for coming. But please leave me alone."

Instead of Rick yelling at her, Kat did. "What the hell? Have you lost your ever-freakin' mind? That is ruder than shit."

She heard what sounded like a scuffle, feet dragging. Matt telling Kat to calm her ass down and then absolute quiet. Her eyes were still closed, and she couldn't decipher a thing except Rick's firm, sure grip on her hands, his thumbs stroking along her knuckles.

"Whatever you need ask, I'll do it. Except that. I'm staying. Cece's your concern, I understand. Your heart has to be pounding a mile a minute, I know mine is. As soon as I heard, I rushed over. I've been in the emergency room trying to find out what was going on. I'm sorry I wasn't here for you."

She didn't say anything; she couldn't. Her heart was crying out to him, and at the same time, terrified of the ramifications.

"Come here, let me hold you."

Her eyes flew open, head shaking like a spastic person possessed by evil spirits. "No."

"Yes." He sat next to her and wrapped an arm around her shoulder, the other around her waist, and cuddled her within a strong embrace. "I need to hold you as much as you need someone to. So please, give me this. Let me be there for you . . . for Cece." The longer his pleas carried on, the more she succumbed to his caresses along her upper arm, his head pressed to hers, his hot breath and body heat warming her from outside in, along with his gentle, soothing voice. She closed her eyes again, memorizing the way it felt to be supported by him since it would be the last. After today, she'd never see him again. She couldn't.

There in an OR waiting room, in the midst of complete agony, she fell in love with him all over again as he hummed the same tune he had sung to Cece when he came to pick her up for the musical. She remembered most of the lyrics, having heard them on a DVD Cece kept playing, but they resonated even more so because of the affection he showed while singing them that day. She'd never forget it or him. Ever. If she could go back in time, choose a daddy for Cece, she'd pick him. A million, trillion times over.

Dreams aren't called that for no reason—they're farfetched and vanish in an instant—with eyes wide open.

"I gotta booboo," Cece announced at least a hundred times since waking up. After two hours of aggravating silence, the doctors had notified them the procedure had gone well. Maggie went to the recovery room, and Cece's first groggy declaration had been all about her wound. And much later, after the effects of the anesthesia wore off, she broadcast that her "acitis" had been good luck. The doctors told her that the appendix resembled a wishbone, and they had to take it out so she could make a wish, and someday soon it would come true. And of course she believed them. When Maggie heard that, she considered asking them to take hers out too. She might not believe in fairy tales anymore, but she could use some good luck right about now. Because Rick refused to leave her or Cece's side since he'd arrived.

While Maggie had been in the recovery room, he'd gone to the gift shop and purchased a care package for Cece, including several Dr. Seuss books, a stuffed "get well soon" panda bear, and three packs of Bubblicious, her favorite gum. After Cece had been transferred to a room in the pediatric section, the doctors indicated she'd stay overnight for monitoring and perhaps another two or three days depending on her progress.

When Cece saw Rick, and he gave her the stash of goodies, as his reward, she treated him to her undivided attention. "Max, I thirsty. Max, read to me. Max, sit with me. Max, hold my hand." On and on she made one demand after another, and he sucked it up, doing anything and everything she requested. Maggie, Kat, and Matt got reduced to mere wallpaper as Rick became the person of honor.

An hour later after Cece fell asleep, Matt went home, and Kat went to the cafeteria to grab a bite to eat, leaving her alone with Rick.

"You don't have to stay, you know. I'm sure you have lots of other things to do." She tried to test the waters again, see if she could push him far away this time.

Releasing a sleeping Cece's hand, Rick rounded the bed, and came to where she leaned against the wall closest to the door. He gazed into her eyes for the longest time, and then brushed his thumb across her cheek, resting it along her neck. Her pulse beat like crazy with him so close. The bright overhead lighting, combined with the sunset coming through the picture window, made his eyes appear fluorescent green, and the honey-brown rays spreading from his pupils with tiny golden speckles on the tips added to the brilliance. She wanted him so much, yet at the same time needed him to go. Her warring emotions, the yin and yang along with the ups and downs due to Cece's condition, had her stomach flip-flopping, her head spinning, and her heart and mind duking it out. The imminent doom ticking in her head the longer he spent in her presence didn't help her distressed state.

"You've been trying to get rid of me since I arrived. Did I do something wrong, upset you?"

His cell rang, giving her a chance to take a breath, but when he silenced it, the panic continued.

"Maybe you should answer it. You've been here a long time."

His grip stiffened on her neck the slightest bit, her pulse thumping hard against it. "What's going on, Maggie? I know I haven't seen you in two weeks. I'm sorry. I should have called, come by. I have a lot to say, talk to you about."

His cell rang, and again he reached into his pants pocket, silencing the tone.

The sting from picking at the tender skin around her fingernails hadn't reduced her anxiety. If she could get them past his arms, which were positioned at her shoulders, holding her in place against the wall, she'd have the sore cuticles and flesh in between her teeth, chomping on them. Since she couldn't, her saving grace came when his phone vibrated.

This time he pulled it out, glanced at the screen, and frowned. He looked at her, and as it continued to buzz, he said, "I'll be in the hall, not far away. This isn't over." He pushed a button on the cell, and as he walked out the door he said, "Mom, you okay?"

She heard his mumbles but couldn't make out more. Cece rolled onto her side, murmuring, and sucked a thumb into her mouth. She dashed over and rubbed Cece's back up and down like her daughter loved. Even as an infant when Cece would wake up in the middle of the night, she'd lull her back to sleep that way. As a newbie mother, she'd been hypervigilant, a worrier, checking on her baby several times a night. It never ceased to amaze her when Cece started off at twelve o'clock in the crib and would rotate to the three, six, and ten position. The odd movements concerned her at first, but the ultrasound images in a frame, showing Cece at various circular rotational states, right-side up, horizontal, and upside down, alleviated her fears.

"Maggie." Rick's clipped call-out had her flinching and spinning around. Kat ducked around him, carrying a Styrofoam container she asked her to bring. She'd had nothing to eat yet and wasn't sure she could swallow something now either. "I have to go."

She nodded, sucking in several shaky breaths, realizing this would be goodbye. Forever.

"My grandfather . . ." He paused, and her body froze at the reminder. On an exhale he revealed, "He had a heart attack. They just brought him into the emergency room. I have to get down there."

As much as she despised that man, she'd never wish a tragedy on anyone. She rushed over to him, offering the same support he gave her earlier, wrapping her arms around his waist. In his ear she whispered, "I'll keep you both in my prayers." She wanted to add "if you need anything just ask" but she couldn't. Regardless of the fact Mr. Horatio Stone might be out of commission, she wouldn't bank on the fact he wouldn't make good on his threats when he got better. She couldn't afford that risk. At this point, caution her middle name, she delivered a quick peck to his cheek. Not close to the kiss she wanted to give and insufficient for a final farewell, but all she could manage with the stinging reality overwhelming her. After another hug, squeezing his shoulders as hard as possible, she released him and began her backward retreat. One step at a time, she shuffled closer to her family: Cece's bed and her sister, situated over Maggie's shoulder. Inspector Kat O'Brian examined her face and scrutinized each of her actions as if she were some odd piece of evidence under a microscope.

Kat moved in, giving what Maggie couldn't. "If you need anything, call, okay?" Removing the phone still in his hand, Kat punched a few buttons and handed it to him. He nodded and glanced at Maggie. His mouth opened, and he took a breath as if he wanted to say something, but stopped. His eyebrows pinched together, and he shoved a hand through his hair while walking around Kat to Cece's bed. "Sweet dreams, sweet pea," he murmured, his mouth pressed against her temple, a heartbreaking, tender kiss.

Twenty, twenty-one, twenty-two flecks counted on the tiles so far, Maggie had no idea if he paid her any mind. His silence when he trudged out the door told her everything she needed to know.

Nothing.

And her response had been the same.

Mama's Rule #23:

When life hands you lemons, make lemonade.

More doctors, nurses, and waiting while Rick spent an entire evening in the emergency room accompanied by his mom. The next morning and afternoon the hours ticked by in the OR area and then CCU, where his grandfather had been moved. In between visiting hours, he dragged his exhausted body to the fourth floor to check on Cece before he got kicked out of there too.

"Max, gimme a kiss." At least Cece's greeting felt wanted and positive. Maggie turned her back toward him and looked through the windows at the downpour.

He gave Cece a peck on her cheek. "How you doin,' sweet pea?"

"I gotta booboo." She tilted her head and added a pout, tugging at his heart.

He picked up *Green Eggs and Ham.* "You want me to read to you? It might help you feel better."

"Ya got gum?"

He chuckled for the first time in what seemed like forever, glancing at the empty wrappers on the rolling cart by her bedside. "You ate them all already?"

Kat entered the room, confirming what he suspected. "Ate is the word of the day. How's your grandfather?" She set a hand on his shoulder, concern evident in her softening tone and eyes.

A crack of thunder and a lightning flash drew his attention to the window and Maggie, her hands clutched to her stomach. As he watched both he answered her sister. "He's in the cardiac care unit. They did surgery, a triple bypass this morning."

"If there's anything we can do . . ." Kat pulled him into a hug, whispering, "Let us know." She released him and sat in a chair next to where Maggie stood.

He glanced at Cece, her brows pinched together. She laid her tiny hand on top of his on the railing. "Ya papa has a boo-boo too?"

Her innocent and sincere distress sent a stabbing pain to his heart, filling his eyes with tears. "Yes," he managed to choke out, his anxiety growing to greater heights. Flashbacks from thirteen years ago surfaced after he'd been fighting and pushing the painful memories to the back of his mind ever since his mom's urgent call. Just like he found out about his dad.

"Mama, I gotta go."

Maggie came to her daughter's bedside and still hadn't acknowledged his presence. "Go where, sweetie?"

"See Papa."

Maggie's eyebrows scrunched too. "You talked to him this morning."

"No, Max's papa," Cece insisted, throwing the covers off.

"Whoa, stop right there, young lady." Maggie placed a hand on Cece's shoulder, settling her against the cushion as Cece sat up. "You're not going anywhere."

"The nurses said she needs to walk around. She could go see him, Mags," Kat chimed in.

Maggie spun around, slicing a finger across her throat. "No, she can't."

"I gotta, Mama."

Maggie faced her determined daughter. "You can't. He's not allowed to have visitors."

Cece squeezed his hand, sorrowful eyes pleading at him. "Max, can I see Papa?"

Maggie's gasp rolled out swifter than the bursts of thunder outside. Before she could shut down Cece again, he got his two cents in. Bent over the railing, he swept his thumb over her rosy cheek and spoke gently, unlike Maggie's frantic and pissed replies. "He's real sick, sweet pea. I can only see him a few times and not for long. He's not in a room like yours where visitors stay."

"But I gotta. I wanna give him my wish." Cece tugged on his hand, sitting up slowly, but ready to go right now.

How could he deny her? She wasn't just the sweetest little girl he'd ever met, but her desire to help his grandfather in whatever way she thought she could made him love her that much more. If that were even possible. It dawned on him right then; he'd been a goner from the moment he met her. His gaze drifted from Cece to Maggie, and he waited for recognition, hoping her hostility would disappear after hearing her daughter's profound appeal. If it affected him as much as it did, it had to have a greater impact on her as Cece's mother. At least he thought so.

Yet again, Maggie's reaction shocked him. She stormed out of the room, leaving all of them in stunned silence. The rain battering the window resembled the turmoil inside him. He had no idea what just happened, or what could have contributed to the cold shoulder.

Kat bolted out of her seat. "I'll knock some sense into her." Before she could leave, he grabbed her arm. "Wait. Let me talk to her. Do you mind?"

She shook her head and went over to the cart, picked up

a book, and began to read aloud. He told Cece he'd be back soon and went into the hallway in hot pursuit. Long overdue, he needed to find Maggie and get whatever bothered her out of her system. He couldn't stand the tension.

Instead of hunting all over the place, he asked the nurses sitting behind a counter outside Cece's room if they'd seen an auburn-haired, green-eyed woman about this high, placing his hand below his chin. One of them pointed to a lounge at the end of the hall.

He entered the room and all the oxygen in his lungs seized. Hunched over, Maggie's forearms lying on top of a vent, air blew wisps of hair around her bowed head. He thought he had the weight of the world on his shoulders. The sight of her slouched, depressed state sent a wave of panic and protection through him. All he could imagine would have that impact on her might be Jake. And even though he'd seen that reaction before, this somehow seemed a hundred, no, a thousand times worse. Instead of taking her into his arms, he sat in a chair in the corner, within throwing but not hitting distance. With her volatility, he didn't want to push his luck, since things hadn't been going in his favor.

Several nerve-racking seconds later, she tilted her head the slightest bit toward him. Clumps of hair blocked her right eye; the other one, though, focused on him. "You should be with your family. They need you."

He leaned over, held his weary head in his hands, and massaged his aching temples. Directed to the floor, he said, "What did I do, Maggie? Tell me. 'Cause I have no fucking clue." When he glanced up, his hands clenched between his legs, he asked her and her behind, which he wasn't enjoying for once, "The last time I saw you we were in each other's arms, dancing. Now you can't seem to get far enough away from me. No, I take that back. You want *me* to disappear. Under the circumstances, I wish we weren't having this discussion right now, but this can't wait. So I'll ask again. Does your attitude have something to do with me, or did something happen with Jake?"

She whipped around and threw her hands onto her hips. "Don't act like you know anything about me. You don't. So what? The two of us dancing gives you liberty to make assumptions about me. What did you think it meant? What? What?" Her face turned beet red, and her arms flapped up and down, and as she finished they spread out wide, slapping her hips when she spouted the last question.

Never in his entire life could he recall any person going off on him like she just did. Sure there were plenty of tense and heated moments during negotiations, but never complete and utter disdain. Even though his grandfather could be cruel and often misguided, Rick knew he cared. Maggie not only didn't give a shit, she couldn't stand him. Wow, he never could have misread or been more wrong about a woman ever. He wanted to beat the ever-livin' shit out of someone, and he knew who that would be. Unfortunately, his way-off-the-mark best friend wasn't anywhere in sight.

The enormity of what this meant hit him. If devastated described what he experienced when his dad died, this moment, the discovery that he loved Maggie and she didn't—shattered him. A thirty-one-year-old grown man for the first time knew what it felt like to have his heart broken—wrecked, demolished, smashed to smithereens. Slumped over, he stared at the frayed threads in the carpet and couldn't figure out what to say. When he picked up his head, he didn't need to. Maggie was gone.

"Mr. Stone." Rick glanced toward the entrance of his grandfather's room. The nurse smiled at Rick. "There's someone here to see you." She pointed down the hall toward the CCU entry.

"They're waiting out there. Said it was important."

He got up, curious who it could be. His mom left a few minutes ago, so it wouldn't be her. When he opened the door and saw Kat and Cece, he almost fell over. After Maggie walked out on him, he hadn't returned. He needed space, time to think. Now, seeing Cece in a wheelchair, overcoming her situation wearing a big smile, made him feel like a total ass. He should've been man enough to at least kiss her bye. He knelt down, taking her hands in his. "I'm sorry I didn't say good night."

"I gotta see ya papa."

He looked up at Kat. "Does Maggie know you're here?"

"The munchkin needed to go for a stroll. My sister doesn't need to know where we go or what we do." Kat grinned, slapping Cece high five. When he tapped the armrest on the wheelchair, Kat beat him to his remark. "She walked out of the room, but we confiscated a chair. I wasn't gonna have her on her feet all the way up here. Besides, I thought it might get her some sympathy points."

His legs were getting stiff from his crouched position, and he stood while asking, "And why would she need that?"

Kat pointed over his shoulder. He glanced there too, reading the sign that indicated no one under twelve years old could enter.

"I wanna see ya papa."

He rubbed his thumb along Cece's hand, soothing and trying to let her down gently. "He's sleeping, sweet pea. Besides, the sign says you have to be twelve."

"Nuh-uh, the nurse said I could."

Kat slapped him on the shoulder. "Told ya the chair would work. Plus, who could resist the munchkin." She leaned over and kissed the top of her niece's head. "Besides, I told the nurse she'd stay just a minute or two."

"Pwease." Under normal conditions Cece could be irresistible. Now though, not only wouldn't she be denied, but her kind gesture made him grieve the loss of Maggie and even more—the family they could've had together.

He walked around her chair and grabbed the hand holds. "Ready?"

Cece nodded, and Kat backed up, leaning against the wall. "I'll wait here." She slapped the handicapped button and the doors opened.

As he entered, the same nurse came up to them. "Just a few minutes, okay?" She patted Cece's hand and said, "Your grandpa will be fine, sweetheart. Don't worry." Cece sniffled and tucked her chin into her chest. "Your daughter's beautiful, Mr. Stone."

Before he could correct her, Cece looked up at him and with a shaky stutter asked, "C-can I s-see Papa now, Dada?"

For the second or maybe third time, he lost count now, his heart crashed and burned. The wind got knocked out of him, not from agony, but the euphoric high that overcame him when she called him dada. Whether she was play acting or not, it didn't matter. He wanted her to be his daughter. His eyes filled with tears for a whole different reason. Bent over, he placed a kiss above her ear. "I love you, sweet pea." Cece set her hand on his cheek, hugging and bonding him to her.

"Oh, you two are going to make me cry. You better get in there. Visiting hours are over in five minutes."

Somehow he found the strength to move, wheeling Cece next to the bed. "He got lotsa booboos."

He knelt next to her, worry taking over as he examined the wires attached to Grandfather's chest, an IV, and monitors beeping. Although her request meant well, he hadn't considered how his grandfather's condition might scare her. Lowering his tone and as gently as possible he said, "He's got one right here." He pointed to the middle of his own chest, his heart. "The doctors said he'll be fine. He even got up and walked a little like you."

Cece laid her hand on his grandfather's, tucking her fingers under his palm, and pulled it to her lips. She kissed his knuckles and with her lips pressed on that spot whispered, "Wish ya all better." Then she returned his arm to the same place without waking him. She turned toward Rick and patted his cheek. "Itta be okay."

"You know what, sweet pea? I think you're right." He grinned the slightest bit, and she gave him one too. "You're a good girl."

Pure innocence didn't describe the look she beamed up at him when she asked, "Can ya get gum now?"

He shook his head, chuckling as they met up with Kat. "Only the rugrat can make ya laugh when you feel like shit."

Now he knew where Cece got her snarky side from, because it sure wasn't from Maggie. As they walked toward the elevators, he added a quip of his own. "How 'bout give your mama some of that."

Cece sighed and bent an arm over her shoulder, patting his fingers as he pushed the chair. "She gotta get a booboo first."

Her witty comeback thrust lighthearted amusement onto his otherwise crappy day. Too bad he wasn't a kid again. He could just jump off his bike, scrape his knees a bit, and all would be better.

If life were only that simple.

"Look who I found?" His mom had a cup of coffee in one hand, and in her other she held Cece's. Instead of a hospital gown, Cece had on sweatpants and a T-shirt.

"My booboo better. I goin' home," Cece said quietly as her gaze darted back and forth from him to his grandfather while she crept closer to Rick's chair.

"Is your mama with you?"

Cece shook her head. "Kitty," she whispered as she scooted onto his lap, pecking him on the cheek, and along with it, a strong whiff of Bubblicious lingered. Her observant eyes landed on his grandfather, and she stared at his chest. "Ya heart broke?"

Silence except for the vent blowing tepid air and the monitors beeping. Cece slid off his legs and shuffled a few steps to Grandfather's chair. The nurses had him up first thing this morning, and since Rick arrived a half hour ago, his grandfather had been sitting there eating his breakfast. The tray and cart had been moved to the other side of the room, giving Cece open access. She pointed to the tape on top of Grandfather's hand and touched the edge. "It hurts." She held her hand out showing him the sticky tape marks on her own, a tinge of red evidence of her IV. Then she pushed her shirt above her belly button, tapping her stitches and repeated the painful claim. Covering back up, she dug into the front pocket of her sweatpants and pulled out a pack of gum that had one piece left. "Ya can have it. I better." She set it down on Grandfather's gowned lap and patted his knee. "I gived ya my wish. Ya better too, Papa."

Closed-off, buttoned-up Horatio Stone must not have known what to make of whirlwind Cece and her simplistic view of his condition, because his reaction from the time she entered had been just one; mouth opening and closing, he hadn't spoken a word. In fact, Grandfather had little to say since he woke up in recovery three days ago. The totality of their exchanges involved Rick asking: "Do you need anything? Are you in pain? Can I help you?" And Grandfather's replies: no, yes, no.

Cece turned and wound her arms around his neck. "Max, I gotta tell ya somefin." His mom gasped and grabbed the bed railing, where she'd been watching Cece with an amused grin until now. "I love you," she whispered, but the one thing about Cece, her voice carried like a megaphone regardless. Wrapped in each other's arms, he held on tight, because he didn't know when or where he'd see her again. He just knew no matter what, he had to find a way to spend time with her, stay a part of her life.

Pressed together cheek to cheek, he reminded her how he felt. "I love you too, sweet pea, so, so much."

Kat knocked on the door, popping her head in. "Time to go, munchkin."

Cece walked across the room, fingers scrunched into her palm, waving first at his grandfather, then at him, and at his mother, leaving them all in her wake.

After she disappeared, his mom closed the door. "She calls you Max?"

He leaned back in his chair and threaded his fingers through his hair, pushing it out of his eyes. "From the day I met her, Mom. She introduced herself as Cecily Bryna Tyson, so I used my full name too. She's called me Max ever since."

Covering her mouth with a hand, his mom spoke through her fingers. "Your daddy . . ." All she got out before a tear rolled down her cheek.

He knew how she felt. The name floored him the first time Cece said it too. Now, he didn't want to hear anything else.

"You love her."

Grandfather's gruff statement swept his gaze toward him. Rick wasn't prepared for an exhausting battle and didn't want to get in an argument. He nodded, confirmation enough.

"The girl, the mother too?"

Rick scrubbed a hand over his face, across the three-day stubble he hadn't bothered to shave. Not ready to talk about Maggie with anyone, his wound-tight nerves had him bolting out of his seat and staring at the swaying trees in the windy rain. His chin slumped into his chest as he rested his arms on the vent and let the burst of air cool him off. "It doesn't matter. She doesn't care."

His grandfather's snort had him shooting a glare at the sick man. The pain twisting in his chest and gut forced him to ignore that fact at the moment. "Don't start."

"I didn't say anything." Grandfather smirked, and after a long pause, tilted his head and asked, "You ever been in love, boy?"

Grandfather's dig cut deep, causing him to hang his head again. "Drop it. I'm not talkin' to you about it."

"She already has you wound around her finger, doesn't she?"

He snapped, confronting him at the worst possible time. "Nothing ever changes. You're not happy unless you're ridin' me about something. From the minute I turned eighteen you've dictated every move, and you can't stand I can manage without you, can you?"

"Rick, that's enough." His mom closed in, grabbing his arm. "Don't talk to your grandfather that way. Not now or ever."

His eyes shifted back and forth between them, a dumbfounded chuckle rolling through him as he attempted to set them straight. "You both realize I'm not a kid anymore, right? I've had it up to here," he stretched his arm above his head as far as he could reach, "with him butting into my life, telling me who I should be with, who to get married to, and how to run my company."

"According to you, the company isn't yours anymore." Grandfather must be all better, because he hadn't spoken this much since their confrontation in the office. Miracle cure. Too bad Cece couldn't fix his grumpiness and foul attitude.

"What's he talking about, Rick?" Mom yanked on his arm. "What's going on?"

"Nothing, Mom, don't worry about it."

"Horatio, what happened?" She assumed a mother-means-business stance, hands on hips, lips pinched. "What have you been up to now?"

"Ah, don't be getting your panties in a bunch, Emma. Your boy's just pissed because he's having girlfriend troubles."

"Girlfriend tr—" Rick argued.

Another knock on the door interrupted their heated discussion. A nurse came in rolling a blood pressure gauge and thermometer. "I have to check your vitals. Visiting hours are over. You can come again at one."

He nodded, and as he walked out, Grandfather called for him. "Don't come back. You've been out long enough. The business won't run itself. I bet they robbed you blind by now."

While shaking his head, Rick blew out his frustration, but it didn't alleviate the tension. "What are you saying? What do you want?"

Grandfather stared at him quite a while before answering. The nurse recorded his blood pressure, and when she put the thermometer up to his ear, he held his hand up, halting her. "You want me out?"

"Do we have to talk about this now? You need to focus on your recovery, not work."

"That's what I'm doing. Answer the question."

He rubbed the back of his neck and nodded.

"All right. It's yours. It always has been."

Nothing left to say, Rick turned around ready to do as Grandfather said and return to his office. As always his grandfather had to have the final word. "I won't interfere anymore."

Whether it was a concession or not, he didn't care. For once, he escaped a round against him. This time, though, Rick couldn't hold back a smile.

Mama's Rule #24:

If you keep doing the same
thing, you'll keep getting
the same results.

The half dozen buttermilk pancakes that Maggie cooked were light and fluffy and waiting for someone other than her to eat them. She put them in the oven to keep warm as Kat strolled in ready for work.

"Munchie not awake?"

"She had a hard time falling asleep, so I put her in bed with me. She didn't move an inch when I got up." Exhausted from a sleepless night herself, Maggie pulled out a chair from under the kitchen table and collapsed.

Kat filled a travel cup and dug a blueberry muffin out of the tin that Maggie baked a few minutes ago. While Kat spoke with a full mouth, crumbs spat out. "She's got the rest of the week to chill, you too. Enjoy the time off. I'll do all the work and bring home the bacon while you sit on your ass."

Maggie shook her head as she refilled her mug and went over to the screen door. Lavender tulips, yellow and white daffodils, and rainbow colored impatiens she'd planted along the fence line on both sides of the backyard were in full bloom, and the rocks Cece painted eight different shades provided a vibrant border. The crisp, morning air filled her lungs while she stared at the cloudless, pale blue sky. "I left a message for Jake."

"You what?" Kat tugged on her arm. "What the hell's the matter with you?" Squeezed together in the narrow doorway, Kat's shoulder wedged in next to her, filling up the teeny space and in full-blown intimidation mode.

Not wanting to begin her day with a heated argument, Maggie spoke matter of fact. "He had a right to know she was in the hospital."

"What part of no contact didn't you understand when Matt told you. All you're gonna do is piss Jake off more. He never wanted her in the first place. So, what, you think time away will make him change? Heart grows fonder bullshit. What planet are you living on?"

Fury burst inside Maggie. More than ready for a catfight, she faced her sister. "Don't make me out to be a lunatic. He's her father. I was letting him know, that's all. I don't expect or want anything."

"Want anything? How about him stayin' the fuck out of your life? How about that, Mags? Or do you think I'm stupid and didn't see you stuffin' a letter in your pocket yesterday? Did he call you?"

Maggie glanced outside and watched the swings sway in the gentle breeze, and after a while shook her head.

"No what? Letter or call, quit hidin' shit."

"Could you stop swearing?"

Nudging a shoulder into Maggie's, Kat wrapped an arm around her waist, pinching it. "You aren't helping the situation. If you won't listen to Matt, please hear what I'm tellin' you. Make copies of all the letters, every one of them. Put 'em in an envelope and send them to the district attorney. I checked the Vine system a few weeks ago and there's no change in his status. But that doesn't mean there won't be.

The prisons are overcrowded, and most cons don't serve full sentences. You need to take his threats seriously. And yeah, I know there's more than what you're showin' me. What I read was bad enough. I can imagine what the others say. He's pissed, and even if he doesn't take it out on you later, you have to protect Cece. Remember what you told me in the hospital?"

Without waiting for a response, Kat continued with her scare tactics. "If anything happened to her . . . that's what you need to keep in mind. Every time he's around and even when he's not, he hurts her. He might not have abused her in the physical sense, but he's cruel in other ways. Kids sense a hell of a lot more than we give 'em credit for. She might put on a brave face, but she learned to stay away. She doesn't trust him, and I don't think she ever will. You don't think kids can figure out they're not wanted?" Maggie opened her mouth to tell her sister she loved Cece and wanted her, but Kat cut her off. "You've been both mommy and daddy and believe me she knows that."

"Has she said something?" Her concern elevated to panic level.

"I'm not betraying her trust that way, but believe me, she knows he doesn't love her."

"But—"

"No buts, Mags. You can't fix him or change the way he feels." Kat squeezed Maggie's shoulder, her frown turned into a smirk and disappeared just as fast. "But you can give the munchkin something she really wants."

"What?" She grabbed Kat's hand, willing to accept her sister's insight if it would make Cece happier.

"Hmm . . ." Kat tapped her chin with her finger, drawing out the anticipation and making Maggie crazy. "I'll give you a hint . . . six-pack, thirty-something . . ."

Before Kat finished, Maggie slammed open the screen door and rushed down the steps, stomping across the overgrown lawn. She didn't want to hear any more. Taking her advice would be like jumping out of a frying pan and into the fire. She hadn't told Kat about the elder Mr. Stone's threats, and she didn't plan to either.

"What's wrong with you?" Kat stormed after her, raring to go again.

Maggie plopped down in a swing and kicked the grass, swaying back and forth. "I thought you didn't like Rick."

There were three other slings to choose from, and of course Kat picked the seat next to her. Kat's legs pumped really fast as she tried to kick the leaves hanging from a low branch Maggie meant to cut down. "I got over it, you should too."

"I don't need to get over anything."

Kat snorted, and on a downward pass, snagged the chain at Maggie's shoulder and yanked, almost knocking her off the seat as it twisted side to side and tipped forward. Maggie clasped onto the metal links above her head, threw her legs straight out, and planted her sneakers in the grass so she didn't fall. "I have enough man troubles, don't you think? Isn't that what you were warning me about two seconds ago?"

"Oh, honey, Rick Stone kinda trouble, you definitely want." Kat's growl took on a whole different tone, deep and seductive followed by heavy panting like a dog left out in hundred-degree heat.

Unable to hold it in, Maggie burst out laughing as Kat flicked her tongue along her forefinger and sucked it into her mouth, imitating a sex act. "You're a sick, demented individual, you know that, right?"

At least five feet in the air, in an upswing, Kat leapt off her seat and planted both legs on the ground, tossing her hands above her head as if she were a gymnast performing a full vault. She swung around and took a bow, saluting Maggie while walking toward the kitchen. "I gotta get to work. Do me a favor, Mags."

Since Maggie had the rest of the week off she figured Kat would assign some chore or maybe even impart more of her

sage advice. Because they ended their discussion on a somewhat positive note, she decided not to ignore her. "What's
that?"

"Get laid."

Another load of laundry in the machine, a basket of Kat's
clothes folded and ready to put away, Maggie scratched off
each chore listed on a notepad next to her cell phone on the
counter. The entire house swept, upstairs and down, she turned
the hot tap on in the kitchen and set the bucket underneath,
ready to scrub the shelves in the fridge and the interior of the
oven. The busier she kept herself, the less time she'd have to
think. Even after Kat's warnings, her brain refused to focus
on Jake. Instead it taunted her with sexy images of Rick. After
planting the "get laid" seed, he'd been all she could think
about.

Six pack, twelve, she hadn't counted. The part that kept
popping up in her mind, the rigid length he'd pressed into the
crease of her behind on numerous occasions. She wondered
how big he was. By the evidence, she guessed at least seven,
eight inches. No idea what size a typical guy might be, she
knew he wasn't average in any way. If she traced his expan-
sive shoulders and narrow waist with her tongue, his outline
would form a perfect triangle. The tip pointing to the grand
prize hidden behind his form-fitting dress pants that cupped
his butt, and the treasure she couldn't seem to stop obsessing
about, front and center, below his belt.

His scent, like a wild berry pie baked over an apple wood
fire, conjured up a different kind of emotion. Fond memories
of family and camping. For as long as she could remember,
their summer vacations were spent in the Colorado Mountains, roughing it in a tent and fishing from Dad's rowboat.

They were some of her happiest moments, and the kind she wanted Cece to experience too. An image of Rick roasting marshmallows over a campfire made her smile. She couldn't picture Mr. Executive enjoying something so primitive. What she envisioned, though, was Rick standing next to the flickering and dancing flames, unbuttoning his crisp white dress shirt in a slow striptease just for her.

As she sat back on her legs, removing a casserole dish and a bag of fresh veggies from the bottom shelf of the fridge, her mind wandered to his strong hands, which didn't belong to someone in corporate America. His thick-veined grip could be a construction worker's, more apt to lift steel beams and operate a jackhammer than shuffle papers. Whenever he yanked her against him, she got a tingling rush. To be manhandled by him, yeah, she'd love that. He'd shove her pants down, drop to his knees, and spread her legs wide. His long fingers and tongue would ram into her core. She sighed. Yep, rough sex would definitely be his style.

He reminded her of an untamed mustang. Both had a compact and natural muscular appearance that moved with commanding, swift elegance—an unrestrained wildness. Between his confident strut, determined attitude, and the force of his unyielding grip, the similarities couldn't be denied. Ever since they met, she had the hottest, most orgasmic fantasies about him. As much as she needed to forget him, she couldn't. It would take time. Lots and lots of time, but she'd get over him. She had no choice.

After the way she acted, he'd stay away for sure. The mockery she'd made of their intimacy twisted her up inside so much, she had to get out of that lounge as quick as possible. She'd been beating herself up ever since. If he said those things to her, she would have crumpled into a heap. Since she'd fallen madly in love with him. As awful as she'd been, at least she knew he couldn't feel the same. He never showed any interest other than lust and wanting to get her into bed. Although, now that she thought about it, he never implied he'd take her there either.

The doorbell rang and she slammed the fridge shut, stumbling into a jog. "Don't open it." As if in a stampede her daughter ran in the same direction. She scooped Cece into her arms and held the squirming bundle in position to look through the peephole. One of her favorite things to do.

"Who is it?"

Cece clapped and shouted, "Miss Em, Miss Em."

What the heck? Sure enough, on the porch stood Rick's mother. She had a pink bucket with books sticking out of it pressed to her chest.

"Hi, um, hi," Maggie sputtered.

"Surprise." Emma came in as Maggie took a step back.

Cece leaned over. "Let me see." With her nose stuck in the bucket, she yanked a coloring book and crayons out, shoving them in Maggie's face.

"Whoa, young lady. That is very rude. Put them back."

Both of the items were dropped into Cece's lap. She pouted and turned around to return them. "Sorry."

"It's okay, sweetie. They're for you anyway. Do you mind? Can I set it down?" Emma pointed her thumb toward the coffee table in the living room.

"Sure, sure, go ahead." After putting Cece on the wooden floor, she prodded, "What do you say to Miss Emma?"

"Thank ya." Cece hopped onto the couch next to their guest, folding her legs under her bum, the coloring book already open on her lap and crayons dumped onto the cushions.

Emma brushed a hand down Cece's arm. "I wanted to check on you. How you feeling, sweetie?"

"'Kay." Once Cece had something new to play with, little could distract her. She'd keep herself occupied for the next hour at least.

Maggie shuffled closer and perched a leg on the arm of the sofa near Emma. "I guess Rick told you."

When Emma turned toward Maggie, her brows scrunched. "Uh, yeah, he did." She patted Cece on the knee. "She came to see us in CCU. Didn't you, sweetie."

Cece's head popped up from the princess dress she'd been shading in turquoise, shaking her head side to side, eyes bugging out. Oh, Maggie knew that caught-with-her-hand-in-the-cookie-jar-and-deny-it expression well. In this case, what Cece and her idiot sister had done was far worse than sneaking sweets. Their actions thrust her into damage control mode, racking her brain with the potential repercussions. "How is your father-in-law?" She didn't give a damn about his recovery. Her concern had to do with how soon he'd strike.

"He's in step down, getting better. Strong as an ox, that man. Shocked us when he had a heart attack." Emma squeezed her hand. "Thanks for asking, that's so nice of you."

Shame rushed through Maggie for deceiving the kind woman, and she jumped up from the arm of the couch. "Can I get you some tea?" She already made it halfway to the kitchen before Emma confirmed she did. The soapy suds in a metal pail reminded her about the person she'd been thinking of while doing chores, causing her cheeks and neck to warm. Bent over, she shoved the casserole and veggies into the fridge and moved the bucket out of the way. As she turned to put it on the counter, she rammed an elbow into Emma's stomach and the water sloshed over the side, dampening her white blouse. "Oh my god, I didn't know you were behind me. I'm so sorry." Swiping a stack of napkins from a basket on top of the microwave near the fridge, she patted the wet spot, apologizing over and over.

"It's okay. Just water, no big deal." Emma sat down in a chair and laughed as she brushed a curly brown lock out of her eyes.

Maggie set a roll of paper towels on the table in front of Emma. "Here. These might do a better job."

Unraveling several sheets and folding them in a pile,

Emma tucked the bundle under her shirt and patted the tiny bump. "All good. It'll dry while you make tea."

"Oh, yeah." Maggie filled the kettle with tap water and placed it on the stove. The wooden tea box sat on the counter. She propped open the top and asked, "What would you like?"

"Hmm . . . so many choices." Emma picked up three packets in different rows before deciding on wild orange wulong oolong.

"That's a good one." Maggie selected a couple mugs from the stand next to the stove and placed them on the Formica counter. "I'll have some too." Full of nervous energy, imagining Emma could read her previous thoughts, she leaned against the counter, hands twisting. "Can I get you something to eat?" Good old hospitality and preparing food would help settle her down. She'd seen Emma a little over a week ago and even though the catering went well, she didn't expect a visit. Being on her own turf didn't reduce the jitters. Neither did Emma's scrutinizing glances, like she had something to say but wasn't ready to reveal it yet.

"I um, I can uh, make you a sandwich if you like." She grabbed a Tupperware container off the table, removing the lid. "Homemade biscotti. Would you like some?"

Emma leaned over, placing her hand on Maggie's arm. "That would be fine. Nothing else though, thank you." She tilted her head to a chair next to her. "Would you mind sitting, relax a little?"

The sweet and hopeful tone in Emma's voice had her doing as asked, but Maggie sat in silence, concentrating on her thumbnail rubbing along the rim on the plastic container.

Emma cleared her throat. "I thought maybe I could sign that book while I'm here."

More at ease, Maggie looked up and smiled. "I'd love that. I'll get it before you go."

Nodding, Emma's gaze drifted over to the fridge, scanning the photos. "You have a beautiful family."

"So do you . . ." She couldn't believe that came out. "I, uh, um, I . . ."

A smirk tilted up one side of Emma's lips. "It's okay. I agree. I always wished I had more children."

"Why didn't you?" Her hand thrown over her mouth, she couldn't understand why she'd blurted the question. "Oh god, jeez, just ignore me," she mumbled through her fingers.

Emma laughed. "It's okay." She shrugged and glanced at the pictures again, but her eyes seemed unfocused, reminiscent. "I was twenty-five when Max and I got married. A year later, I had Rick. I was a stay-at-home mom and took full advantage, writing several manuscripts. He was five when I got my first publishing contract. That's when the rat race began. Part of the agreement was traveling to conventions, doing book tours. I didn't mind. I wanted to connect with readers. Before I knew it, four or five novels a year, raising Rick, and jet-setting across the country, time got by me."

When the kettle whistled Maggie hopped up again, filled both mugs, and set them on the table. "Would you like sugar, cream?"

"You have honey?"

Maggie grinned; she liked her tea that way too. A natural sweetener. After they had their drinks fixed, she took a sip and sighed. While she dunked the biscotti and munched away, she gulped small mouthfuls to wash it down.

"I was wondering . . . about you and Rick."

Spewed tea with chunky bits flew onto the table and on Emma's thumb looped through the cup handle. Her choking gasps had Emma leaping from the seat and rubbing her back. Maggie covered her mouth with a clump of paper towels, muffling the gagging and crumbs that lodged in her throat. From the living room, she heard Cece shout, "Hands up, Mama." Which had always been her advice when Cece had a similar experience. After several swallows and deep breaths, the gag reflex stopped, and she took a swig of tea. Her eyes were watery, and she swiped them with the backs of her hands.

Emma returned to her chair and propped her chin in her palm. Using a gentle approach, she asked, "You okay?" Maggie ripped the paper towel to shreds. Quiet a long while, Emma watched and waited, her mother's X-ray vision switched on. Even so, Emma took considerable time in her examination, no doubt figuring out the real reason for Maggie's frantically beating heart.

The all-knowing stare got to Maggie. She closed her eyes and squeezed them tight.

In a soft and soothing tone, a technique Maggie often used when Cece had a nightmare, Emma spoke with comfort and understanding. "He has his faults . . ."

A sudden smirk tugged at Maggie's mouth and in order to hold in a giggle, she clenched her teeth and pinched her lips.

"He's stubborn."

Maggie's eyes popped open, and she snickered a little. She couldn't believe Emma would say something bad about her pride and joy.

A warm and placating smile flashed across Emma's lips. "Has to control things, dots every *i,* crosses each *t* a thousand times over, driving everyone insane." Reaching across the table, Emma took hold of Maggie's hand, which came to rest when the scraps were too small to tear apart anymore. "Max . . ." Emma paused. The mention of her husband brought a faraway look for a second, and after a glance out the back door and an inhale, she continued. "Was a devoted father. Doted on Rick from the time he was born. Even though he was a busy executive, he put Rick first, providing the love and support essential to a young boy and man. Like you do for Cece."

Maggie's heart leapt for a different reason. She took pride in raising her daughter, and even though she didn't need someone else's praise, she appreciated the recognition. Especially after her gloomy conversation with Kat. She nodded, squeezing Emma's fingers, a gesture that had been returned.

"For reasons I don't understand, Rick doesn't think he'd make a good father."

Her mouth fell open, and Maggie attempted to correct his mother, but she wasn't sure how to verbalize it. It didn't matter. Emma had more to divulge.

"When his father passed away, instead of withdrawing or becoming depressed, he went full steam ahead. His dad's company was his driving force. He put everything into his studies and gained experience so he could take over. That's all he's done since." Emma looked over her shoulder toward the living room and spoke while Cece rifled through the bucket and then dumped the contents on the couch. "I've seen him with your daughter a few times now." When she turned toward Maggie, Emma had tears in her eyes. "He loves her very much."

Maggie didn't need Emma to tell her that, but all the same, hearing it lodged an enormous lump in her throat. For so long, she hoped Jake would feel that way, yet Rick, a total stranger, had instead. No, she couldn't call him that. He hadn't been an outsider since the day they met. She could admit that now.

"And when he's with you . . ." While Emma took several sips from her cup, she scrutinized Maggie's face again.

The phone lying next to the chore list rang. She snagged the cell and smiled at the number displayed. "Daddy, hi." She could breathe easier now. His cheery and loving voice always calmed her. "What?" But that feeling was short lived. "When?" She paced to the door and stove, over and over. This time, chills rushed through her as she listened to him relay news that Jake had been released today. Overcrowding and good behavior, blah, blah, blah. The buzzing in her ears blocked out everything else he said. She pressed her forehead against the doorjamb, sniffling as her nose ran. He kept asking if she heard him, was she okay, but she couldn't talk.

A hand on her shoulder caused her to whip around as if

Jake had snuck up behind her. Fear slammed into her, freezing her in place. Emma's eyes searched hers, and the longer she did, the pinched frown at Emma's mouth grew.

Her dad, yelling her name, jolted her out of her trance and into action. She dashed around Emma and over to the notepad, tearing off the top sheet. "What's his parole officer's name?" Jotting it down, she asked, "Do you have his number?" After he provided both, she closed her eyes and dropped her throbbing head into her chest. Several deep breaths later, her trembles lessened. Her dad launched one question after another, but she refused to answer. The pencil snapping in half in her hand and shards flying across the counter had her examining the mess along with the scattered fragments of her past and present choices. God, why hadn't she listened, done something?

"Dad, can I call you back? I can't talk right now." His police officer alertness had been replaced by fatherly concern. If she didn't call him back in fifteen minutes, he'd be on a plane and at her front door by dinner. She hadn't doubted him for a second and reassured him she would. After she hung up and blew her nose, she looked toward the living room. Cece had stretched out on the cushions and fallen asleep. Her watch showed one fifteen, a little after nap time. Before Emma arrived Cece had lunch, so she wasn't sleeping on an empty stomach. At least Maggie did one thing right today.

Emma came up behind her again, grabbing her shoulder. "What's going on?"

Maggie shook her head. No way would she get into something so personal with her. "I'm sorry, but I have calls to make. I'll see you out." Not giving Emma any choice, she walked straight to the front door, holding it open.

Before Emma stepped onto the porch, she faced Maggie. No anger displayed after the rude request, just a mother's concern. "If there's anything I can do, you have my number. Call me anytime, Maggie, day or night, it wouldn't matter."

Touched by her kind offer, she gave Emma a hug, thanking her for Cece's gift and for coming by. As soon as Emma got in her car and Maggie waved goodbye, she began damage control.

First, her dad. She explained her reaction away as shock and didn't get into any details about the threats. Simple yes and no replies kept her off his radar, for now at least.

Next, Kat, who yelled to high heaven about her stupidity, using every swear word known to mankind.

Last, the parole officer. No answer, just voice mail. Figured as much.

With age came wisdom, or in her case, more mistakes.

Mama's Rule #25:

If you love something set it free. If it comes back it was meant to be.

Routine and structure were good. Four days in and Rick almost caught up with the mound of paperwork left for him. He never missed any time before. His vacations were nonexistent. Most people looked forward to things like that. He didn't. There wasn't anywhere he wanted to go, and keeping his eyes on the prize all along made the company thrive.

Besides, traveling never felt the same without his dad. Throughout the year, his father reserved several weeks for vacations and established a tradition early on by having them each choose a place to visit. Since Mom toured often, she chose to stay closer to home. Their log cabin in the Catskill Mountains included seventy-five acres of pure heaven on earth and had become her preference. It had a private pond big enough for large- and small-mouth bass, a bunch of crappy, and bluegill, making it their favorite place to fish in Dad's rowboat. Rick hadn't gone there since Dad died, but Mom did. She wrote her latest novel there. She tried to get him to take time off and go for a weekend, relax. But he couldn't bring himself to do it.

A big outdoorsman, Dad always chose a campground with a huge lake. His goal had been to see as many places as he could throughout the US. Since Rick's birth, and even though he couldn't remember the earliest years, they visited eighteen different states. His father said since he spent most days in an office, he wanted to be outdoors as much as possible.

Once Rick had been old enough, around four, he chose Disney World. What kid wouldn't? Each year after that, he selected a different amusement park, and even though he'd been too young and short to ride roller coasters, his obsession with them grew regardless. He'd never forget the day his dad took him on the first "real" one: The Prowler in Kansas City when he reached the critical height of forty-eight inches. The breakneck speed and thrill of the first huge drop followed by the wild twists and turns gave him a rush like no other. Except maybe hot and heavy sex.

Ugh, he didn't need to think about that now. In a dry spell and sick of jacking off, he wanted to kick his own ass for his obsession—Maggie.

"I thought I'd find you here."

Quick to assess a situation, Matt would key in to his fucked-up head in seconds and strike fast. Instead of confronting him, Rick kept staring at the people rushing along the sidewalks and taxis lined up along the street. For the past half hour or so he'd zoned out, unable to work.

"I came bearing gifts."

He already figured as much. His nose could never mistake O'Reilly's Pub's infamous hamburgers. The best on Staten Island and in New York, they had an amazing sweet pretzel bun, a pound of ground fresh sirloin and filet blend, topped with cheese, toasted onion strips, and a thick slab of hickory-smoked bacon under the patty. At least he had a different reason for salivating other than stripped nude images of Maggie. He hadn't even seen her naked, yet his brain didn't seem to give a damn, and conjured up one fantasy after another. Her tossing off a tank top, whipping down jean shorts, revealing no undergarments, bare breasts, and a shaved mound. Another of her in nothing but a lace bra and matching thong, in different colors and styles. The dreams appeared throughout the day and night, frequent enough to drive him insane and classify them as an obsession. He'd never been in a position where he didn't get what he wanted, or anyone he desired, ever. And he didn't like the jittery and anxious feeling it gave him either. He wasn't the compulsive type, but this predicament left him out of sorts, and uncertain how to address it or her. Should he leave her alone or try to push? Do something, anything, other than what he'd done—nothing.

"You gonna let these beauties get cold or are you eatin' with me? Mmm . . . you're missin' out, buddy."

On cue Rick's stomach growled, ready to devour and feed his ravenousness in another way. When he took the first bite, his low growl and eyes rolling into the back of his head made Matt bust a gut. He hadn't eaten a burger in months. The fresh-cut fries he'd dumped onto the foil wrapper became his next target, and he shoveled a handful into his mouth.

"Jeez, if I'd known you were that hungry I would have bought you more than two. Damn, man, did you have anything to eat today? I haven't seen you suck down food like that since college."

Rick shrugged and took another huge bite of the stacked and sinful beef.

"How's your grandfather?"

After Rick had a chance to swallow enough to talk, he shared the good news. "Doctors said if he keeps improving, he'll be transferred to a regular room in a few more days. When I stop by, he bitches and kicks me out after a half hour. Says not to worry about him, that I need to be working and makin' him money."

Matt shook his head, wiping ketchup off his chin with a wad of napkins. "He's a trip. Unbelievable. Good to hear he hasn't lost his bite."

Rick snorted. Fat chance of that happening. Grandfather might've mentioned staying out of his life, and their recent conversations had stuck to safer topics such as politics, world events, and Mom's book tour. So far, so good, but he wouldn't hold his breath. More stubborn than a donkey, Horatio Stone wouldn't change his spots overnight. Grandfather hadn't mentioned a thing about Kensington Securities since their falling out. Airing on the side of caution, he contacted John and went jogging yesterday. That gave him a chance to feel John out, and lucky for Rick, the owner had no interest in partnering or merging.

"Thanks for checking in on the girls while I was out of town. Soph said you came for dinner every night. I heard Harley and Lizbeth painted your toenails." Matt's smile widened. "At least I'm not the only one sufferin' through girly primping."

Rick jerked his chin up and kept chewing, then sucked down a huge gulp of the sweet tea. Matt pretended he minded the girls' froufrou play, but the doting daddy would've been right next to him watching sports and drinking beer as the twins threw boas on them, painted their faces, and anything else they dreamt up. Since Rick would do anything for them, their happiness outweighed his temporary pain. Besides, his part of the deal involved them removing the paint before he left. Since they enjoyed taking it off as much as putting it on, he lucked out. "I was outnumbered," he grumbled over another mouthful of fries. "How was the convention?"

"Aw, man, you should've seen all the new tech gadgets. As much as I hate being away from my girls, I can't resist going and tryin' them out. Besides, our booth drums up at least a dozen accounts, and I get to hunt out new recruits too."

"You hiring?" He swallowed the last bite and started on the next burger.

Matt nodded, not bothering to talk while he chewed.

"We're swamped. I need about five or six more investiga-tors and at least three bodyguards. Business is hoppin,' my friend." Finished with his fries, Matt reached across the table and snatched his.

"Hey." Rick folded the foil halfway over the top, covering the three or four left. "Hands off."

"You owe me. I came to collect." Matt leaned back in the leather chair, patting his stomach. "So how you gonna do it?"

Lowering his head, Rick concentrated on the half-eaten burger, refusing to make eye contact. He figured Matt would call in the favor he asked for in the emergency room. He just didn't expect it now. When he could talk, he asked, "Do what?"

Matt stretched his arms across the table, hands clasped in the center, like he might be sitting on the edge of his seat. "Propose."

On an inhale, a clump of bun and beef got lodged in Rick's throat, making him hack. He covered his mouth with a napkin in case it came flying out. Once his airway cleared, he yelled, "What the hell is wrong with you?"

Matt rolled his eyes, unaffected by the possibility that he could've choked to death. Rick took a few sips of tea, wash-ing any remnants of food down. He swept his hand across his watery eyes and collapsed into his chair. He wasn't hungry anymore. Good thing he just had a bite left.

A lengthy silence ensued. Matt crossed his arms along his chest, his muscles flexing through his Westlake Security T-shirt as he leaned into his seat. "Did we or did we not have this conversation before? Don't bother telling me you don't remember."

"Then why are you askin'?"

A loud sigh blew out between Matt's vibrating lips as he scrubbed his jaw, staring at him. "You've seen Maggie and Cece since the hospital, right?"

A lump lodged in Rick's throat and he swallowed, shifting

his attention to the painting of the Catskill Mountains over Matt's head. His dad bought it from a roadside antique stand when he was a little boy. He remembered the exact moment like it had been yesterday. Since he couldn't bring himself to speak, he just shook his head.

"I go away for a few days and what? You lose sight of the prize. How'd that happen?"

A crumpled napkin hit Rick in the middle of his chest and pulled his gaze downward. Picking the clump off his lap, he flicked the wad of paper into the empty food bag. "Let's just say that our feelings aren't the same in that department."

"Are you insane?" Matt chuckled into his fist. "The two of you are like magnets that seek each other out whenever you're in the same space. What makes you think that?"

The bits and pieces of Rick's lunch became more fascinating. He used a fork to flick a leftover fry across the wrapper and stabbed a chunk of bun that fell off the patty. "She just doesn't." He wouldn't relay the embarrassing altercation in the lounge. It took everything to drown out her brush-off, which kept replaying in his head ever since.

As if Rick were a complete idiot and wouldn't understand the message unless it had been delivered one clipped word at a time, Matt's deep growl sounded like it came through clenched teeth. "Did you ask her?" Matt paused and pulled in a breath before continuing his investigation. "Did you say, 'Maggie, I'm fucking crazy about you? I want you to have my babies. Marry me.'"

Sick of the interrogation, Rick jumped up, shoving the chair so hard with the backs of his legs, it fell over. He paced along the windows, resuming his steadfast fascination with taxis and people coming and going.

"I'm gonna take your non-answer as a no."

Maybe he should just beat Matt's ass, since his buddy dredged up the disappointment and defeat that crushed him, smothering his heart all over again. It sure would make him feel a hell of a lot better. He wanted to do the same thing after the fiasco in the hospital anyway. Matt's advice put him in this predicament. He came to an abrupt stop, pivoted on his heel, and marched toward him.

Matt held up his hands in surrender. "I'm not fightin' you. So don't waste your energy." As he drew closer, Matt threw his arm out, pushing him in the chest. "Hitting me isn't going to fix things with Maggie." Matt squeezed his shoulder and asked with a gentler tone, "Did you tell her you love her?"

His eyes slammed closed, and Rick replayed the whole scene in his head. Did he? No. He never did. In fact, in all the time he'd known her, he hadn't done anything except maul her, grinding his damn pecker into her ass. Not once did he discuss his growing affection. Why? Because he'd been fighting it. He rubbed his palms on his forehead, trying to stop the ache that started. "Shit." He dropped his hands to his sides, ready to kick his own ass for being so fucking stupid. "I didn't."

"Okay." Matt nodded. "You can fix that. Since it's Saturday, she might be home. Why don't you go over? If Kat's there, maybe she'll watch Cece. You could take Maggie out. Talk to her."

He glanced at the messy wrappers and then at Matt. "I'll think of something."

"Good." Matt picked up the empty bag and cleared the table in a matter of seconds. "Go ahead, I'm not leavin' yet. I still need to go to my office."

Nervous and out of sorts, he waited as Matt dumped the trash into the garbage can and walked with him down the hallway. "Any parting advice?"

Instead of joking or laughing at him, Matt threw an arm over Rick's shoulder and with a slow and steady stride, led him toward the exit. "Tell her a story."

Rick stopped walking. After that off-the-wall suggestion, he had serious doubts about entrusting Matt. "What?"

A carefree grin perked up Matt's pace as he tugged him

back in step. "About her and you. The first time you saw her. When she made you smile. A time she ticked you off. And the moment you started to fall for her, and when you did. Women love the sappy stuff and wanna know you recognize it and remember. Why do you think they're so good at recalling every date, each present, and all the other garbage they catalog and bring up at the worst possible minute?"

Rick chuckled and jabbed Matt in the ribs with an elbow. "That's supposed to make me feel better?"

After pushing the elevator button on the wall, Matt faced him. "You got this, man. Just speak from the heart. That's what matters." Matt reached out and sucker punched him in the shoulder. "That's for luck. But you don't need it. I've seen it in her eyes. She feels the same way."

He hoped so, because he didn't know how he'd take another battering. His heart wouldn't recover. Not after revealing to Maggie he loved her. The only woman he'd ever say those words to. If she didn't return those feelings, he didn't know what he'd do. All of this felt so nerve-rackingly foreign, yet invigorating too. A crash and burn would destroy him, again.

After he shifted the car into drive, he glanced at the time on the radio panel. One o'clock, traffic should be light. He'd be able to make it there in about twenty-five minutes. While driving, he beat his thumb on the steering wheel, recalling everything Matt said. He rehearsed various ways he could remind her of their brief, yet precious moments together. Hopeful that by the time he arrived, he'd have a rough idea.

Even though he wasn't a praying man, he said one just in case. He needed all the help he could get.

The sun's warmth and brightness calmed his nerves a bit. He swung his car into the same parking space, across the street, as he had on Cece's birthday. It seemed like a lifetime ago but had been a mere three weeks. So much had changed since then. The fact Kat's car wasn't in the driveway already didn't work in his favor. A worst-case scenario would be that they weren't home, and he'd have to find the courage to return. He'd rather hope for the best though, and envisioned Maggie alone, giving him a prime opportunity to deliver the big reveal in private.

When he got to the curb, a blast and a scream had him sprinting toward her house. As he got closer, the curtains in the bay window were yanked closed. In that instant a voice in his head that sounded a lot like Matt's launched him into preservation mode. He removed his cell from his back pocket and sprinted down the sidewalk, swiping the screen and pushing the app he never thought he'd use. Then he jammed the phone into his jeans.

As he leapt up the porch steps two at a time, he prayed the door had been left unlocked. Loud sobs propelled him to the knob, and he rushed into a situation he couldn't have predicted.

A bald-headed man with his legs spread wide in a prepared-to-shoot stance swung a gun from Maggie to him. "Don't move."

Oh, he wasn't. Unable to pull his concentration off of Maggie rocking back and forth, her arms clutched around her stomach, he scanned her head to toe, checking whether she'd been shot. Not seeing any blood, he released a small breath, locking his eyes on her enlarged and terrified ones.

"Hands out, spread 'em," the thug with tattooed sleeves ordered from across the living room, positioned on guard next to the kitchen entrance.

He did as asked, wishing he had his best friend's bodyguard training.

"Step back, real slow, shut the door."

"Jake, please," Maggie shouted.

"Shut the fuck up, bitch." The semiautomatic pointed to her chest.

Sometimes being Matt's friend had advantages. Rick went to the shooting range with him enough times to recognize the weapon. The name Maggie used registered, and the only person he knew with it, her ex.

"You, shut the door. Now."

Rick shuffled backward, one leg moving and then the other. His left hand snagged the steel edge and followed the directive. As he eased it closer toward the jamb, he stopped and didn't latch it.

"All the way, asshole. You think I'm stupid?"

Since he didn't think Jake wanted to hear what he thought of him, he kicked the door with his heel and when it latched, the click had an eerie resemblance to a cocking gun.

"Please, let him go."

"You asking, Maggie, is just gonna get him shot."

"No." She jumped up from the couch and scrambled toward Rick, arms reaching out like she could block a bullet.

"Stop," both he and Jake yelled, one over the other, yet Rick doubted the warnings carried the same meaning. His brain told him *keep Maggie safe*. Jake's weapon pointed at her—didn't.

"Sit the fuck down. You take another step toward him, I'll shoot you where you stand."

"Maggie," Rick called out. Her gaze whipped from Jake to him, and while Rick had her undivided attention, he jerked his chin in the direction he wanted her to go. She stumbled and reached behind her, feeling for the arm of the couch as she inched toward it. When her legs hit a cushion, she plopped onto the edge.

"This is fucking great. I get two for one." Jake sidestepped along the wall, then limped closer to Maggie, coming to a stop in the middle of the room, a small coffee table between them. "He mean somethin' to you?"

248

Maggie didn't answer. She hadn't looked at Jake again after she sat down.

"Answer the fucking question."

In all the scenarios that ran through his head, Rick never imagined the exchange would happen quite this way. Stressed the entire drive, he tried to figure out how to express everything in his heart, and now, considering the circumstances, he might not get to.

Timing was everything, and by his calculations, it took forty-five minutes on the busier than usual highway. If Matt received the alert, it could be an hour before he got out of the building and arrived in Riverdale.

If Matt hadn't gone home or somewhere else.

If the damn app even worked.

If Jake didn't shoot to kill before Matt arrived.

If . . .

"H-he's . . . a . . . f-friend." Maggie's faint, stuttering whisper almost couldn't be heard, even in the silence. The hum of the refrigerator and dull thuds, he guessed cubes dropping into the plastic bin from an ice maker thirty feet away, came across like a battering ram against the door behind him. Too bad it wasn't the rescue he hoped for, just a distraction, and one that pummeled his heart when she friend-zoned him.

"Of Kat's," she said louder, steadier, shoulders pulled up straight, firmer. Her eyes widened and pleaded with Rick, then darted toward the kitchen and back to him. She repeated the move. At first he thought she might be telling him something about Jake, but she lifted her hand, formed a fist, and placed a thumb under her chin. She rubbed a knuckle along her nostril as she opened and closed her fingers the slightest bit while scratching her nose.

"You're lying. That's all you do, I should know." Jake trudged within a foot of Maggie, which pulled Rick's focus away from her and onto him. The barrel inches from her temple, Jake bent over and with spit flying out of his mouth, veins popping in his neck, screamed, "Tell the truth for once in your life." Then Jake swung the gun toward Rick, aiming at his head. Maggie leapt to her feet, but Jake's other hand surged out, latching onto her throat. She grabbed Jake's wrists and tugged.

Jake stared at Rick, probably waiting for him to do something stupid and a reason to shoot. Not that Jake needed one. Sweat dotting her brow and upper lip, cheeks flushed, Maggie released her grip and moved a hand below her breast. Without moving his eyes too much, Rick concentrated on her and figured out what she'd signaled before and signed again—letters.

His control slipped. He dropped his chin into his chest and rubbed his fingers on his forehead, pretending the events taking place were overwhelming him.

"Looks like you crushed the man, Maggie. Exactly what you did to me, you fucking liar."

With a slight tilt of his head, Rick had the angle he needed. His hand covered his face enough as he searched the tiny kitchen, under the table, the open back door, the screen displaying an empty backyard, and then the far side of the fridge, revealing the tiptoe of a sneaker. Oh, fuck. Christ, hell no. His eyes slammed shut, and he sucked in a life-affirming breath, refusing to let the tears fall. God, please help. Please, Dad, God, whoever might be listening to his silent prayers, save Maggie and Cece. If he could fall to his knees and beg he would, but he needed to keep his wits about him. He couldn't let on. For Christ's sake, where the hell was Kat?

Jake must not know, or this entire clusterfuck would be much different. Privy to their sordid history and Jake's lack of affection toward his daughter, this just went from a nightmare to torture at the stake, dangling over a bomb fire, descending into hell in a blink.

Figuring out how to protect Maggie had been bad enough. Now he had the other half of his heart, no doubt scared, and more than her five-year-old brain could process.

His memories didn't appear in a quick flash as news reports wanted people to think when confronted by a life and death situation. The images—Maggie—Cece—him, came as a never-ending cycle. Before them, he hadn't pictured himself as a family man. Now, he might never get the chance to ask Maggie to be his wife, become Cece's daddy, have more children, live in blissful, challenge-him-every-day, pull-a-rabbit-out-of-a-hat love together.

"This is gonna be funner than I thought. The game just got a lot more interesting."

Rick's head popped up as Jake shoved Maggie onto the couch and reached behind his back, pulling out another weapon. A revolver.

Shit. Rick took a step closer to Maggie and hadn't realized he did until Jake ordered, "Stay there." The semiautomatic pointed at Rick, the pistol at Maggie. Jake shuffled to the far side of the coffee table again and set the revolver he'd aimed at her on it. "There's one bullet in it. Even though you're a lying bitch, I was gonna give you a chance to live . . . maybe. But now, I got a better idea."

"Jake, please."

"Stop whining, Maggie. All it does is piss me off. I had to listen to it for years, and what did I get but a fucking brat and three years in lockup. As if living with you wasn't bad enough, you had to get knocked up even when I told you I didn't want a kid."

Jake tilted the gun in his hand toward the table. "You're gonna pick that up, Maggie."

From the corner of his eye, Rick saw a flash of a red braided pigtail and Cece's face peek out, then return to her hiding spot. Dammit. *Okay, think how to sign a message to her.* The pantry behind the back door would be a safer place for her to hide. Fuck. How was he going to do that? What would he say? Cece could read and spell basic words. Maybe he could sign pantry, but would she know what it meant? Should he try

251

closet? Shit. His heart pounding in his ears and chest made it impossible to think straight.

"But first, you're gonna tell this sucker how you ruined my life. The lies you told, bitch."

All right, he'd go with the first rather than the latter. She might get confused and think he wanted her to come to the coat closet beside him. He couldn't send her into the yard either, even though escaping would be ideal. Between the broken spring in the hinge that caused the screen door to slam shut, and the possibility Jake might find her, he couldn't call attention to that area. Besides, at her age he doubted she'd know where to go, or which neighbor to ask for help. The chance she'd be outside wandering around wasn't the best option.

Inching the slightest bit to the right, Rick got in position toward the action—Maggie and Jake. With his left hand tucked behind his thigh, closest to Cece's view, he spelled P-A-N-T-R-Y several times. At this angle he didn't have a straight-on view of the kitchen anymore without turning his head. He wouldn't do that, not with Jake focused on him, an evil smile stretching across his pockmarked cheeks.

Shit, did he know? See him?

"Tell him, Maggie, how you lied on the stand. That way he'll know what kind of psycho you are."

Maggie flinched, her hands twisting in her lap. "I don't know what you're talking about."

Jake's boisterous, hysterical laughing polluted the tense air with a guttural and sinister howl that made Rick's eardrums buzz.

P-A-N-T-R-Y D-O-O-R H-I-D-E

He tried again and again as Jake's sight remained on Maggie.

Through clenched teeth, Jake shouted, "I didn't do it, you lunatic. Don't give me that open-mouthed shit, Maggie, because my trigger finger is getting itchy. Act like you're surprised, yeah, right. Instead of asking me, what'd you do? You cried to your fucking daddy? Didn't trust me. And worse yet, you testified against me, your *husband*. Who does that shit but a vindictive, crazy woman?"

"I asked, but you wouldn't tell me."

"After, Maggie, after. It was too fucking late then. They hauled my ass to jail. When you found the bags in the garage, you should have come to me. If you had, I would have told you the truth."

Maggie stood, her hands clenched around her stomach. "What happened?"

Jake took a few steps back, closer to the wall, farther away from Maggie, but the semiautomatic remained steady and aimed at her. "It was Donnie."

Her eyebrows scrunched together and lips pursed. Maggie lifted her hand and shifted it into her hair, squeezing, tugging. "Why didn't you tell the police your brother did it? You didn't mention him, not even at the trial."

As Maggie probed further, her statement got drowned out. Jake yanked a photo frame with a picture of her, Cece, and Kat off the wall and flung it across the room and over her shoulder, knocking a dent in the plaster before it shattered on the wood floor between her and Rick. Glass splintered and flew onto the coffee table, the sofa, and a piece hit Rick in the leg.

"I wasn't gonna turn my brother in. But you'd know nothin' about protecting flesh and blood, or someone you love, would you? At the first chance, you betrayed me."

The diversion gave Rick a chance to move, twist to the left so he could get a quick look into the kitchen while glancing down to the long, triangular shard of glass lying on top of his shoe. As he bent over to pick it up, Jake snapped, "Leave it."

Each of his moves were orchestrated to a *t*. Rick's fingers were a hair's length above the seam of his pant leg, and he angled his head just right, giving him the proper position to search for Cece. The maneuver seemed like he wanted the slivered shank off his foot, but he could give a shit about that, except the possibility of using the spear as a weapon.

No tiny sneaker, nothing. Did she figure it out, or had she tucked into a tighter ball?

"Get up."

Slow, but not steady, Rick straightened. His gut told him this ordeal might get worse. Jake bringing up such a touchy subject would escalate the situation and set off an already erratic temper. Although, he guessed it had been the intention all along. Otherwise her ex wouldn't have paid her this unexpected visit.

Shit. How long had he been here? In all this time, he hadn't looked at his watch. An inward cringe sunk into the pit of his stomach when he did. Thirty minutes. He could've sworn an hour or two had gone by.

In the personal protection lectures Matt gave him, at the top of the list: remain calm. Another, don't be a superhero. Unfortunately for him, Matt hadn't said anything about two guns, which remained an unpredictable variable, and the revolver still sat on the coffee table a foot from Jake, and at least ten from Rick.

"Pick up the gun."

Maggie shook her head, remaining in place at the edge of the couch. "No."

Jake shifted his glare to him. "She's not worth it." In a matter of seconds, Jake picked up the revolver and tucked it into the front of his waistband, rounded the table, and before Rick got halfway to Maggie, latched onto her arm and shoved the semiautomatic into her neck. "I'm gonna save you the misery." A cockeyed, evil grin in place, Jake dragged her struggling body toward the kitchen.

"Please . . . stop . . . don't . . . do . . . this." Maggie's whimpers and heaving sobs made her strained pleas almost incoherent.

Intent on keeping Jake out of that part of the house and saving Maggie, Rick advanced. In a split-second, Jake switched directions, hobbling toward him. All of them at a standstill in the middle of the living room.

"Shut up. You mean nothing. All you are is dead."

Twice the width and a head taller than Maggie, Jake peered over her shoulder. His black pupils enlarged to the point that only the outer rim displayed a murky brown. The semiautomatic pressed to Maggie's right temple and Jake's hardened stare sent chills down Rick's spine. Methodically, the grip Jake had on her upper arm slid down and clasped her hand. His beefy fingers crushed Maggie's onto the handle of the revolver and forced her to aim—at Rick's chest. His thumb pulled on the hammer, and Jake held the trigger, ready to fire.

Paler than Rick had ever seen her, Maggie's freckles shown redder than usual. Sweat dripping from her brow and through her blinking lashes cast a glowing sheen on her beautiful face. He swallowed the sour taste in his mouth. More than an arm's length away, if he lunged at Jake, the guns would go off before he could disarm him. This would be it. He failed. Hadn't done anything to rescue her or Cece. He memorized Maggie's amazing mint-green eyes. If he died, she did; he wanted her to be his last breath and remembrance into the afterlife. To carry her with him for an eternity.

Jake tainted the moment, standing guard, waiting, watching.

"I love you." Rick's vow echoed from the depths of his soul. "Forever. Always," he whispered over the tears coating their cheeks, rolling off their chins. He wouldn't die knowing he hadn't told her.

Jake pressed his mouth to Maggie's ear. "You ruined my life. Now I'm gonna do the same for you." A click came from the revolver they pointed at his chest, knocking Rick back a step after the misfire. Maggie's whimpers and trembles increased. With a sinister chuckle, Jake promised, "There's a bullet in there somewhere. Which one will it be, Maggie? I planned on saving that little surprise for you, but lover boy gets it."

Two blasts exploded.

Jake crumpled and Maggie propelled backward, dragged down with him. Three hundred pounds crashed onto solid wood; Maggie's shoulder and hip smacked against it. The blow and boom that followed resembled a bomb detonated.

And all hell broke loose.

Falling onto his knees, Rick swept Maggie into his arms as Matt crushed a boot onto Jake's wrist and snatched the semiautomatic. Kat scrambled and yanked away the revolver, kicking Jake in the ribs. "Bastard." Another swift boot in the same spot. "Fucking pig." Jake groaned and rolled onto his side, pulling his knees up into a fetal position. The next blow hit him in the nose. "Asshole."

Rick wanted to do the same thing and a whole hell of a lot more, but he had other priorities—his girls. He hurried into the kitchen, placed Maggie on a chair, and scanned her head, chest, and legs making sure all parts were intact, and thankful she hadn't been shot too. Her face drained of all color. Her eyes were bloodshot and stared over his shoulder into space. Her hands were crossed and clutched to her arms, and she rocked back and forth. "Maggie?" he called softly several times, hoping she understood him over the shouting in the other room. Fear rising, he refused to concentrate on that and decided on a different tactic. "We have to find Cece. Do you hear me, honey?" He stood and glanced at the pantry door. As he took a step toward it, a hand snatched his. Maggie got up and parroted, "Cece, Cece, Cece." Dazed confusion and pinched ridges marred her forehead. He cupped her cheeks, inspecting her dilated pupils, stretched in wide-eyed alarm. "I'll find her. I promise." His head and heart throbbed and worry for both of them consumed him.

Maybe if she saw her daughter she'd snap out of her trance. He wrapped his arms around her, pulling her toward the storeroom, and yanked on the knob. "Oh, god." The shelves were stocked with cans and dry goods, but Cece wasn't inside.

Sirens grew louder and closer. Rick twisted around and examined the living room. Most of the view blocked by Matt, he sidestepped to the right, and got a look. Slumped against a wall with his arms behind his back, Jake's bruised and swollen eyelids were closed and blood smeared like painted-on scars lined his cheek and jaw. Matt's .44 magnum trained on the asshole's chest, ready for any possibility. In that slouched and battered condition, Jake wouldn't be going anywhere except prison.

His brain turned fuzzy, and he had no idea where the piece of shit got shot. The details came in spurts, two blasts he thought but wasn't sure now. Maybe he was experiencing shock too. He shook his head, not allowing himself to get distracted. He had to stay focused.

"Matt."

Without turning around, his best friend, who he would never complain about again, responded as if nothing were the matter. "Yo."

"Have you seen Cece?"

"Cece," Maggie muttered. Her trembles vibrated along his ribs and across his stomach as he tucked her closer.

"Backyard, Kat has her."

Once the first part had come out of Matt's mouth, he propelled Maggie toward the screen, slamming it open, and rushed down the steps. In the fort, Kat had Cece wrapped in her arms, her niece's head lying on her shoulder as Kat swayed side to side.

Maggie screamed a garbled combination of her daughter's name and "Oh, god" as she ran across the lawn. In a leap, she climbed the first few ladder rungs and extended her hands out to her sister. "My baby, give me my baby."

"Come all the way up."

Maggie grabbed the holds on the cedar trim and pulled

herself into the fort. Once on solid footing, Kat handed Cece to Maggie, and all three of them hugged and cried on each other's shoulders.

All the oxygen vanished. Bent over with his fingers locked to his knees, he attempted to inhale and exhale without hyperventilating. Crackling microphones and more voices came from inside. He realized the sirens had come to a stop. The screen door opened and slammed shut behind him, but he didn't move from his ready-to-throw-up position. A hand placed between his shoulder blades and Matt's boots didn't force him out of his hunched-over pose either.

"The police are here, want statements."

Rick nodded and concentrated on his breathing. After a huge inhale, he pulled up to his full height and dove at Matt, capturing him in a man hug. "Thank you, thank you so damn much."

Matt pounded him on the back. "Anytime, my friend, anytime."

Holding on to Matt's shoulders, he pushed away and filled in the blanks. "I was afraid you wouldn't come."

An embarrassed red tinge covered Matt's cheeks. "I almost didn't."

"What?"

"When I got the alert, I thought it was a joke."

His heavy, strained arms dropped to his sides. The realization set in at just how close he had come to dying. "What do you mean?"

Matt shrugged as if his claim hadn't been a big deal. "You were freakin' out. After my little pep talk, I thought you were just foolin' around, pullin' a prank."

Rick threw his hands up, scrubbing them through his hair and yanking out his frustration. Unable to stand in place now, he paced to the white picket fence surrounding the yard, which should've provided a pleasant picture of hearth and home, but the chronic spasms in his stressed muscles almost had him collapsing against it and destroying the perfect frame.

"I'm sorry, man."

Maggie climbed down, Cece still in her arms, and Kat jumped from the ledge onto the grass at least five feet below. He jogged past Matt and almost tackled Maggie and Cece, pulling them into his chest in a tight embrace. He kissed Cece and Maggie on top of their heads, murmuring against them, "I love you."

"We need all of you inside," an unfamiliar female voice ordered.

Clustered together, Maggie joined at Rick's hip, Cece safe and sound asleep in her mother's arms, they shuffled in synchronized formation from the playset toward the kitchen where the officer waited and Matt held the screen door open. Kat trudged along, bringing up the rear.

After they were seated in the living room, and Cece tucked into bed, the officers questioned each of them separately about the incident. From what he could figure, Kat got there sometime between him signing to Cece and discovering she disappeared. Kat had been on assignment, working on a case. When she arrived home and stepped on the porch, she overheard Jake's shouting and laughter. Since she couldn't see in the window, she crept into the backyard for a sneak attack. Cece and Maggie had been playing there earlier. Maggie ran inside to get a couple bottles of water. Her cell rang, and when she went to pick it up in the living room, Jake surprised her, capturing her in a chokehold and dragging her to the couch.

Rick stormed in not long after.

And fortunately for all of them, Kat caught sight of Cece by the fridge and coaxed her outside, hiding her in the fort. That was when Kat saw Matt's SUV pull up next to the curb. They snuck in through the kitchen just as Jake's twisted Russian roulette almost killed him. Matt's shot hit Jake in the back. Kat struck his thigh, taking him down. Their keen timing saved Rick and Maggie. The paramedics checked them out and left after they refused further medical treatment.

Hours passed before the police took off. Since Matt and Kat discharged their weapons, they'd have to report to the station tomorrow for additional questioning. Both relinquished their firearms until permits could be verified. Justifiable in their action, neither would face charges for the time being, but the investigation would continue and there would be follow-up. A district attorney had to review the reports and reach a conclusion. The deputy indicated if everything checked out, none of them should have anything to worry about.

Jake had been transported to the hospital, officers accompanying him. If stable, he'd be extradited to Texas. As a convicted criminal on parole, he had a slew of charges pending against him, regardless of his claims of innocence. He couldn't declare that now, not with a room full of witnesses.

Out front, Matt stood on the porch waiting for Rick as he said good night to Maggie. He cupped her beautiful face and kissed her temple. "I'm so glad you and Cece are safe." He wrapped his arms around her and pressed his cheek to hers. They both shed a life's worth of sweat today. He doubted he smelled great. Regardless, he needed to be closer to her. He pulled her tighter and set his nose in the crook of her neck. Her skin reminded him of strawberries and vanilla. He placed his mouth there too and spoke from the heart. "I love you." As if he were praying, he repeated the affectionate pledge in her ear and at last on her lips.

When he took a step back, he clued in to her vacant green eyes, non-smiling mouth, and stiff arms at her sides. "Maggie?"

Her mouth opened, closed, and opened. Her head shook as she said, "I'm sorry."

"What?" Without air in his lungs he thought the question would be a whisper, but over the buzzing in his ears, he shouted it.

Her eyes closed, and she inhaled, repeating louder. "I'm

sorry. I can't."

His body jolted, slamming his shoulder into the doorjamb. "You can't what?" he growled, anger rather than concern for her mental state fueling him.

"Do this," she said faintly.

"This?" He grabbed her upper arms, her eyes wide open now. "Did you hear me? I love you. I love Cece. I want us to be a family. Does any of that register?"

She shook her head again.

He swung around and punched his fist into the plaster; stabbing, furious pain shot up his arm, across his chest, and into his throat. His jaw clenched so hard, he could've sworn he cracked a few molars. A hesitant, light touch settled in the middle of his back. He cringed and slammed the front door open, running down the steps and sidewalk toward his car.

Now he couldn't do *this*. Whatever the fuck it was.

When he sprinted across the road and noticed Matt's silhouette in the passenger seat, it didn't help his dark mood at all. He sure hoped his best friend prepared for an earful, because if Matt wanted a ride home, he'd get a hell of a lot more than that.

"I thought you drove," Rick grumbled, throwing the stick shift into gear and taking off.

"I gave Kat the keys. She'll pick me up on the way to the station tomorrow."

At least sports cars were good for something, and he pushed it to eighty on the highway. Matt's silence was deafening. Fine with him. He had other plans when he dropped Matt off at home. For the entire thirty-minute drive, he formulated the ass whooping which would commence on arrival.

And after Matt's shit advice, the pummeling would be long overdue.

261

Mama's Rule # 26:

This is going to hurt me a lot more than it'll hurt you.

"Hey, can I come in?" Kat poked her head into Maggie's room.

Hours earlier, Maggie had tucked Cece into her king-sized bed because she didn't want to sleep without her baby tonight. The two of them were gathered in a cozy bundle in the middle of the mattress. "Sure."

Lifting the covers, Kat crawled in behind them, threw an arm around Maggie and Cece's waist, and rested her head on the same pillow. "Mind if I stay with you guys?"

Maggie glanced over her shoulder and at Kat's watery eyes. "I never thanked you."

Kat nestled her forehead into the crook of Maggie's neck, pulling her tighter. Her damp lashes trickled tears that fell underneath Maggie's nightshirt and down her back. "If we'd been a split-second later." As if reliving the horrific events all over again, their bodies trembled.

Silent for a long time, Kat said, "Can I ask you something?" The out of the blue question caused Maggie to flinch from a half-awake doze.

While yawning, Maggie mumbled, "Yeah."

"Don't get mad, okay?"

Exhaustion wanted to pull Maggie into dreamland. But curiosity got the better of her, and she resisted. She thought they'd hashed everything out already. "Besides Cece, you're my second favorite person in the world. After everything you've done and we've been through, nothing you could say would make me angry."

From behind her, Kat's fingers brushed through the bangs on Maggie's forehead over and over, relaxing her. They always shared a room growing up. One of their favorite things to do at night had been to push their twin beds together and chit-chat and gossip for hours. During difficult times, whether friend or boy troubles, Kat would massage Maggie's temples or drift a hand through her hair until she fell asleep. She couldn't remember the last time her sister did that, and the fond gesture warmed her from inside out, replacing some of the awful memories she had trouble erasing.

"Why did you treat Rick that way?"

Wide awake now, Maggie tensed from her shoulders to tiptoes.

"More than anyone, you should know that kind of love doesn't come around every day. I know you've been through a lot, and I'm sorry for bringing it up now, but you broke his heart."

Her lips crushed together. It took all of Maggie's willpower to resist telling Kat the truth.

"I shouldn't have eavesdropped, but I couldn't resist." Kat's caresses stopped and were replaced by her fingers weaving through Maggie's, squeezing them. "What I don't understand is . . ." Kat's thumb tossed Maggie's up and down, wrestled from the top to the bottom like they used to when they were little girls. "He's nothing like shithead Jake . . ."

A groan gurgled in Maggie's throat. She opened her mouth to tell Kat to never say his name again, but she didn't get a chance since her determined sister motored on.

"Even after the asshole's threats, you didn't report him. Yet Rick, who's crazy about you and our little bucket head, you didn't just push him away, you destroyed him. Why? Make me understand, because I sure the hell don't. It's not like you. It doesn't make any sense. You give everyone a chance to right wrongs, but when it comes to a man who's perfect for you and head over heels, you tell him to get lost. If I didn't think you felt the same way, I wouldn't push, but you're gonna have tell me you don't."

Uncontrollable sniffles and jerky spasms hit Maggie. Yanking a clump of tissues out of the box, she blew her nose, wiping away the tears streaming down her cheeks. After a long while and many deep breathing exercises, which didn't work, she snuffled and stuttered through an answer. "B-because I l-love him, I have to l-let h-him g-go."

Kat bolted up, her hand crushing the pillow and causing Maggie's head to roll onto it. Given no choice, she had to face Kat's frown. "What aren't you telling me?"

Since they knew each other too well, Maggie had never been able to pull a fast one over Kat. Stressed to the max, her overwrought brain tried to think of a quick excuse.

"I can see the wheels spinning, Mags. Don't lie to me."

A doozy of reason came to her, and Maggie hated herself for using it. "Today was horrible, I'm so tired." And then she added a pout and whined, "Please, sissy." When she'd been a little girl, her pitiful pleas worked in an instant. Now though, it would be a wait and see game. Kat narrowed her inspector eyes, examining every inch of her face.

"For the record, I'm not fallin' for your 'poor little me' act. I'm pooped too, so I'll let you off the hook. *Tonight.*" Kat turned the light off on the nightstand and snuggled up to her and Cece again. All of them settled in the darkness, a knocked-down, dust-their-boots-off and get- back-up family unit.

"I love ya, Magoopie."

She lifted Kat's arm off her ribs and blew a loud raspberry and smooch on her sister's hand. "Back at ya, Cholly."

Kat's rumbling laughter helped her fall asleep with a smile on her face. And when her eyes closed, no nightmares came.

Instead, the next morning when Maggie got up at the crack of dawn, the person who haunted her dreams—Richard Maxwell Stone, the one man she'd never, ever forget, and would love until she took her final breath.

And beyond.

"You look like shit," Kat murmured in Maggie's ear before taking a huge chomp out of a slice of spinach and sausage quiche from a pie pan on top of the stove.

At four a.m. Cece got up wide awake after almost eleven hours of sleep. Still dark out, her daughter acted as if it were midday, and if she didn't get going, she'd miss out on playtime. Unable to get Cece to stay in bed, and worried she would wake Kat, Maggie threw on a robe and they came downstairs.

Maggie leaned her hip against the counter and sipped her coffee. Cece shoveled a heaping spoonful of oatmeal into her mouth. Mama's little helper prepared the large bowl, covering it with two boxes of raisins, brown sugar, and a tablespoon of heated milk. Something warm and comforting on a rainy day should be filling her empty tummy too, yet she couldn't stomach much of anything. From the minute she woke up, it had been flip-flopping. Dreams of Rick wouldn't stop replaying in her head. The thought of never seeing him again, or worse, not telling him she loved him too, had her so upset, she broke out in a rash all over her neck and the backs of her arms. The last time that happened had been after Cece's birth, when Jake hadn't come to the hospital. Thank goodness for family. Her mom and dad and grandparents provided support and were excited for the new arrival. Her sidekick had been there, serving as a coach, and the best big sister in the world.

As she took in the sight of Kat and Cece, sitting side by side at the kitchen table, teasing each other, cracking jokes, their smiles and lighthearted banter made it seem like yesterday never happened. Yet the bruises covering her hip and ribs told her otherwise. It would take a while for the soreness to subside. Not to mention the amount of time to wipe out the horrific images of a gun pointed at Rick's heart. To think he might not have escaped just increased her agony. Yes, she could have died too, and the possibility that Cece wouldn't have her mother when she already didn't have a father ripped her to shreds. She didn't know how her daughter would overcome the tragic events. Cece hadn't brought it up yet, but at some point they would have to. Cooking, computers, reading, being a mommy, she could handle. Trying to explain to a five-year-old why her father tried to kill her mama and Rick, she didn't know how to address that. What would she say? Caught up in her musings, when the doorbell rang, she jumped out of her skin, bumping her unbruised hip into the counter.

"I'll get it." Kat bolted out of her seat and dashed into the living room.

"Mama, I done. Down, please." Maggie unlatched Cece from the booster chair, and as soon as she set her on her feet, Cece ran into the other room, yelling, "Kitty, let me."

Curious who'd visit on a Sunday, she refilled her mug and followed the trail of raisins that must have fallen from Cece's lap. She'd have to get the broom and dustpan out later. A blond woman dressed in a smoky gray blouse and black slacks, briefcase in one hand, the other extended to Cece, crouched down to her height. "Hi," her lullaby-singing voice said, "I'm Cassie."

When Maggie came to her sister's side, Kat slipped her a business card: Cassandra Sullivan, Psychologist, Ph.D., Family and Child Counseling Center.

"Cecily Bryna Tyson," her daughter blared at an overexcited megaphone level. Cece shook the woman's hand a dozen times. The doctor bit down on her lip, a smile tugging at the corners.

Worried social services might be involved, she placed a protective hold on Cece's shoulder and stepped in front of her. "I'm her mother, Maggie."

"Margareta Cassidy Tyson," Cece shouted again. "Mama." Darting around the leg Maggie used to block her, Cece looked up with a sweet, angelic face. "She got ya name." Then tucked her hand into Dr. Sullivan's and tugged the stumbling woman toward the couch. "I gotta read ya somefin."

"Do you mind?" Dr. Sullivan asked over her shoulder while following in Cece's direction.

Not seeing she had much of a choice, Maggie nodded and shuffled along, taking a seat in the club chair a few feet away. Her ever-protective sister did the same, sitting on guard next to her elbow on the armrest.

After throwing several books off the shelf until Cece found what she wanted, she plopped down next to the doctor, reciting the *Mother Goose Nursery Rhymes* from a hundred-page anthology, a favorite book and collector's edition Kat bought for her first birthday.

As Cece read, Dr. Sullivan chimed in, pointing at different pictures, discussing specific phrases and events. The casual conversation the doctor used pinpointed horrific and tragic parts in the rhymes Maggie hadn't given much consideration to before. The laid-back, pleasing discussion didn't come across with an intention to cause alarm. No, the psychologist put her at ease and established a non-threatening rapport and dialogue with a five-year-old, debating the choices characters made and what Cece thought about them. At particular instances, a probing question related to yesterday's situation got woven in without being a direct reference: How was Cece feeling? Was she sad or afraid? Did she see or hear anything that upset her? It amazed Maggie how the conversation unfolded. She never would have believed it had she not witnessed Dr. Sullivan's calming assurances herself. An overwhelming amount of gratitude engulfed her. She glanced at Kat, realizing they experienced a similar awestruck reaction. They could use the same approach with Cece, even when the psychologist wasn't there to provide guidance.

The doctor stayed about an hour. A pack of crayons were spread out across the coffee table, and she drew several pictures with Cece, chatting away. They leaned against the sofa, legs crossed, in a comfortable and relaxed slouch.

The weather had cleared and Kat took Cece to the neighborhood park a few blocks away. Maggie rocked on the porch swing waiting for Dr. Sullivan to take a seat in the padded wicker chair and deliver a report. Glasses of sweet tea on a matching table provided a dividing line between them. "Your daughter's not only beautiful, but a bright and intuitive little girl." The doctor took several sips of her drink before continuing. "I envy you, and should probably add a warning."

Maggie stomped her foot down onto the floorboard and the swaying came to a stop. Already worried for her daughter's welfare, that type of announcement didn't help and snapped her into an upright position.

Dr. Sullivan placed the glass on the table. Her forearms resting along her thighs, hands clasped between her legs, she cautioned, "I counsel tons of teenage boys. When she's their age, you'll never have a sound night of sleep again." She reached out and gripped Maggie's arm. "Cece's lucky to have you and your sister. You make a fierce trio. I could see that the second I came into your house."

The compliment should've reassured Maggie, but she couldn't help worrying that more might be at play here. She'd fight tooth and nail if social services tried to take Cece away from her. It wouldn't happen. She wouldn't let them. "Who sent you?" Distress brought her blood to a boil. Her question hadn't contained any of the compassion or grace the doctor exhibited.

Dr. Sullivan reclined in her seat and drummed her fingers on the armrest. "I'm not here to hurt anyone."

A deafening pause had Maggie fidgeting along the wooden slats of the bench, unease still agitating her regardless of the psychologist's assurances. "Who sent you?" Her demand came out in clipped spurts. She didn't appreciate the fact her question remained unanswered.

Dr. Sullivan lifted her hand and twisted and twirled a heart-shaped locket hanging around her neck. Her calm and collected demeanor switched to a far-off gaze, aimed across the street at a tree or the neighbor's home. Maggie couldn't tell which captured her attention, if any.

The non-answer made Maggie antsy. She jumped up from the swing so fast, it rocked back and slammed into her calves. Her arms crossed, and she blocked the doctor's view. Her worry flipped to pissed off in an instant. "You're not taking my daughter from me. Get that straight right now." She shoved the sleeves of her cardigan up to her elbows, ready to duke it out if she had to.

"Ri—Mr. Stone called, told me what happened, asked me to come by."

Maggie hadn't missed the slip, the familiarity, covered by the formal surname. There was no reason to ask why. Rick's concern for Cece's welfare made her love him that much more. After her bitchy attitude, he still cared, looked out for them. The constant reminders and his thoughtfulness would make it impossible to forget him. She wished she could reach out to him, do something as generous and considerate. But she couldn't, not without risking his grandfather's finding out. It had been bad enough her deranged ex almost killed him. The repercussions were bound to be severe once the old man recovered and got out of the hospital. More so than the bruises burning along her left side. The stress agitated her rash, and she scratched the itchy splotches on each arm and her neck, hoping for some relief.

"Eczema?"

Uncomfortable with the doctor's professional and sincere kindness, she returned to the previous subject. "How do you know Rick?" She wasn't sure if it was jealousy or curiosity, or a whole lot of both compelling her to ask. Either way, she wanted to know how close they were. As if she could do anything about it.

Again, Dr. Sullivan fingered the locket, running it along the silver linked chain. "We went to college together."

Crap, the fondness in her voice made Maggie cringe. History, she couldn't compete with that. Ha! What was wrong with her? She couldn't do jack about it anyway. Which depressed her more than the doctor's unexpected visit. "You're in love with him." As soon as the rude accusation got blurted out, she covered her mouth with both hands, embarrassed, yet not at all sorry for saying it. She wanted to know the answer that much.

The doctor burst into hysterical laughter. After she got control of herself, she picked up the glass of tea and gulped. "Oh, lord no. Wouldn't touch that ever. It took just three of my hundred and twenty psych credits to figure out he'd be a horrible bet. There's nothing or no one that could get past the impenetrable shell Rick built around himself. Believe me, in the four years we went to school together, not one of the hundreds of women who tried could get very far. He wouldn't let anyone get close enough, except Matt. Oh, don't get me wrong, he was the cock of the walk, had a female on his arm most of the time. But he never went past one night. That wasn't my style. I'm the monogamous, marriage type. That man most definitely is not."

Throughout the blabbing, Maggie's jaw dropped wide open and remained there even when the doctor finished. A sting in her fingers pulled her focus off the over-informative visitor to her picked-raw skin around her nails, blood smeared across the cuticles and coating her thumb. Oh, dammit. Between her rash and that gross habit, she could be a case study herself. Jeez, she wondered what the insightful doctor would say about her. The detailed analysis of Rick Stone had been bad enough. She hadn't realized she'd covered her face with her yucky hands until she felt them being tugged away.

Dr. Sullivan stood there, examining, observing, her pinky tapping her lip. "So . . . I thought I caught some emotion in his voice this morning. But I never anticipated this." She set her hand on Maggie's shoulder and rubbed her thumb along it in a circular, soothing motion. Her head tilted, and a brilliant, toothy smile came gradually at first and then bloomed. "Well, I'll be damned. You're the one." The doctor chuckled but composed herself quickly. All of a sudden her eyes darted over Maggie's shoulder.

"Mama, I gotta bunch a bugs. Kitty let me put 'em in a tissue."

Dr. Sullivan's sharp-witted inspection flicked to Maggie. "You're both what he needs. Why didn't I see it earlier? My intuition is slipping."

Oh, no, Maggie wouldn't agree. The woman had a good grasp and read on people.

"Look, Mama." Both hands were over Cece's head as she showcased six dead beetles, some squished with gut juice oozing on the Kleenex.

Yuck.

"A gift for ya, Mama."

Oh, wonderful.

Kat crouched next to Cece, both beaming up at her. "Say thank you, Mags."

Dr. Sullivan took a step closer to Cece and Kat like she'd chosen a side, her lower lip pinched between her teeth.

All righty then, on the outside again. Using her fingertips and thumb, Maggie picked up two corners of the Kleenex and pulled them toward the center, clasping the corpses inside so she didn't have to look at them anymore. Ugh, she hated insects of any kind. Kat no doubt egged Cece on, daring her to bring them to her mama. They were partners in crime many times before, so she didn't doubt it one bit. She bent over, kissing Cece on the head. "Thank you, sweetie. Kitty loves mud pies. You should go out back and make her one."

"Yeah." Cece ran inside, slamming the door and screaming "mud kitties" over and over, then another loud bang came as the back screen shut.

That spring really needed to be fixed.

"Well, I better get going before your daughter decides to bring me some." Dr. Sullivan shook her hand, then Kat's. "You have my contact information. I recommend counseling for all of you. It's better to deal with traumatic events head on than bury them. It'll just make it harder to overcome and put behind you." While going down the porch steps, she glanced over her shoulder. "If CYS comes by, give them a card I left on the table. I can talk to them if you like. Give them my professional opinion."

Beating Maggie to the punch, Kat leaned over the railing, a white-knuckled grip on the post. "Which is?"

A clump of her sister's shirt clutched in her hand, Maggie hoped the fabric would break her fall if she collapsed after the doctor's account.

"Miss Cecily Bryna Tyson is living in a safe home, with a devoted, compassionate aunt, and an affectionate, dedicated mother, who both provide a supportive, loving environment." With a wave over her shoulder, the doctor got in a Dodge Dart and drove away.

"Kitty, I got ya a pie."

Both of them spun around to the door and thank goodness Dr. Sullivan had left already. Covered in mud, head to toe, there wasn't a piece of skin showing. Cece's T-shirt, shorts, and tennis shoes were coated in grimy gook. How in the heck did Cece manage that mess in such a short time?

"I useded a hose," Cece announced, her white teeth, orange eyelashes, and green eyes the only shining, untouched spots.

Groaning, Maggie became sick to her stomach as Cece tracked muck-coated footprints along the floorboards, carrying a clump of soaked dirt piled up like elephant dung in her outstretched hands.

"Give that to your mama. I gotta pick up Matt." Dangling a set of keys in her fingers, Kat shook them over her head while jogging to the SUV, laughing at the quick escape.

"Here, Mama." Cece pushed the gooey mess up to her face. Little squishing hands forced clump after clump over the sides, plopping onto Maggie's flip-flops and toes.

Great, just great.

The sight should've infuriated her, but after what they survived, Maggie couldn't bring herself to take a minute for granted or get upset over the little stuff anymore. So . . .

Maggie slapped her hands down onto the icky, lumpy sludge and with a wild hair, screamed, "You're it." Then skipped around to the side of the house.

Her daughter's jubilant giggling filled her with pure joy as Cece chased her into the backyard, shouting, "I gonna get ya."

The hose still gushing water on full blast, a mush pit swamped the entire mulch pile along the rear fence, at least ten foot wide and growing. As soon as Maggie turned off the spigot, Cece tackled her from behind, and both of them fell into the muck.

"Ya it."

Scooping her daughter into a hug, she held Cece tight and rolled back and forth, delirious and beyond grateful for the precious gift in her arms. No matter how messy things got, Cece had always been the best part of her. She'd never take her blessings for granted again.

Ever.

Mama's Rule #27:

Don't speak out of both sides
of your mouth. Do what you
say and say what you mean.

"Three with the works, two bags of chips, and a couple bottles of sweet tea." Rick dropped a fifty on the stainless steel cart and waited for his dinner.

"Max, look what I got." Cece plowed into the backs of his legs, a square slip stuck between her pinched fingers and waved over her head. Kat pulled up from the rear. He looked over her shoulder but didn't see anyone else. Disappointment packed a swift and miserable punch at the lost opportunity to catch a glimpse of Maggie. But when Cece gathered him in an embrace, her arms wrapped around his neck, and gave him a lip-smacking kiss, it helped lift his spirits a whole hell of a lot.

"Hi, sweet pea. How you doin'?"

"Look." Cece hung on to his shoulder with one hand; the other whipped around, displaying a gold star sticker. "I gotta prize. I cleaned up first."

"Mm hmm, I'm not surprised. You're a very good girl."

"Ya get me a dog?"

At first he thought she meant a real one, then Kat came up

beside him and placed an order too. "Give me four wienies. Two bare, no bun, the others, slather me up with everything you got, sweet cheeks."

The teenage boy behind the hot dog cart blushed, and like most hormone-fueled youngsters his age, scanned Kat's photogenic face and ogled her almost non-existent chest, exposed by her propped open Westlake Security jersey.

"Stone, how you hangin'?" Kat announced, causing the boy to choke on saliva that no doubt pooled in his mouth the minute she flirted with him, and had the kid coughing spit into his fist. "You're gonna put new gloves on after that lung hacking jack off, right?"

Jeez, Rick smashed his lips between his teeth, barely holding back his own gut-busting chuckles. This chick cracked him the hell up. It amazed him how opposite Kat and Maggie were. Maggie would swallow her tongue if a lewd thought even tainted it. As hot as Maggie was, he predicted, though, from the tempting, suggestive quotes on her sweatshirts, aprons, and other clothing, she had a spicy side simmering below the surface. Which just made him want her all the more. She would have to let it go somewhere, and he guessed she'd do that in bed, setting her wild, natural curly hair free in a place her daughter could never see. Damn, he didn't need to be thinking about that with Cece bouncing in his arms.

"Put the sticky on, Max."

He peeled the gold star off the waxy slip. About to place it on Cece's arm, she shouted, "No, on you." She snatched it from his hand and stuck it on his cheek, her fingers running over it, making sure it would stay on. "Good boy."

Kat's boisterous laughter and slaps on his back confirmed she agreed, but then she added a racy suggestion. "Hmm, I wonder what else would look good rubbed on you."

He narrowed a warning glare at her, jerking his chin toward Cece.

"Orders up."

Grateful for the reprieve, but not ready to relinquish Cece to her out-of-control aunt, he formulated a proposal of his own. "You guys headed home, right?"

"Yeppers," Cece answered for her aunt, who'd been too busy winking at the teen and blowing him a kiss as she removed the bag from his hand.

While they walked side by side and closer to the curb, his prize possession in his arms, he asked, "Would you mind if I brought Cece home later?"

Kat's stride halted. His muscles bunched, tensing and growing more impatient throughout her prolonged and silent examination. "And why would I let you do that?"

He couldn't resist shooting her a charming smile and added a lot of sugary sweetness to his quip. "Because I'm a good boy."

Cece giggled as she smashed his cheeks between her hands. Her proud green eyes looked at him like he'd used the right password. It gave him a brief flash into her future and jolted him back a few steps. Her allure and mesmerizing charm blinked at him and red-orange lashes batted, just like he imagined she would aim at little boys and young men. The poor schmucks would drop to their knees, ready to give her anything she conjured up in her wildest dreams. Irresistible, and exactly what Maggie had done to him the moment they met. The males in Cece's future didn't stand a chance.

"What'd you have in mind, my man?" Kat brought him into the present. His aim focused on her, determined to get what he wanted.

"I don't know yet." He glanced at Cece. "What would you like to do, sweet pea? You pick."

"Dance." Cece shouted again, clapping her hands.

Confused, he quirked an eyebrow at Kat, hoping she'd clue him in.

"She wants ballet lessons."

"Yeah." Cece threw her hands over her head, and twisted

side to side. Her legs dangled and smacked him in the knees like she'd already taken center stage and had become the prima ballerina. The only thing holding her back, his grip tightening with each of her jerky movements, afraid he'd drop her.

The pride Kat had for her niece in training was evident in her softening gaze as she observed Cece fling around in his arms.

"Is there somewhere I could take her for that?"

No sooner had he finished asking, Kat's demeanor contorted into a glare. Her stance shifted as she probed, tested. "You'd do that? Tonight? Right now?" While she questioned him, her brown eyes heated, challenged, as if he might have been lying or tricking her. A fist formed at her waist. After the experiences Kat and Maggie had with Jake, not to mention Cece's, he wasn't surprised, nor had he been offended.

"I don't make offers I don't plan on following through with. If I say something, I mean it."

Cece kept watch, bobbing her head between Kat and him, bouncing with anticipation, as if all her dreams hinged on her aunt's response.

On guard and still in a state of disbelief, Kat's voice cracked with emotion as she quizzed again. "She needs tights, leg warmers, and a leotard. Sansha's dancewear is at Eighth and Fifty-Third." Her arms crossed, and she scanned him head to toe, assessing whether he could handle the job.

Consumed by billion-dollar accounts and haggling on a daily basis, he wanted to take her aside and school her on the ins and outs of CEO life. If she thought he'd be intimidated by girly shopping, she needed a lesson or two, since he'd been doing such things from the time Matt's girls were born. Anyway, he didn't want to get into that explanation now.

Cece's patience had been pushed to the brink after their silent standoff, and the little imp choreographed her finale well. She dropped her head on his shoulder and aimed at her aunt a cute-as-a-kitten gaze and a pouty whimper. "Pwease."

Without a doubt Cece knew he wasn't the person who had to be sold on the idea. From the minute they met, he had been twisted around her little finger. Kat, the tougher nut to crack, required convincing.

If the warning Kat whispered in his ear before agreeing was any indication of her menacing promise, he didn't need to be told twice that she meant the threat. "A man is nothing without his prized jewels. There won't be anything left if something happens to her. You get me, Stone?"

Then she gave her niece a big smooch, patted him a little too hard on his gold-starred cheek, and after she tucked Cece's foil-wrapped hot dogs in his bag said, "No later than ten or an Amber Alert is gonna be the least of your worries. Have fun, guys." Her sinister howl followed her across the street to the parking garage.

He hugged Cece and then set her on her feet, securing her hand in his. "First, we eat. Then we shop. Last, we check my phone and find a place to sign you up for dance." His gate matched her short stride, ambling down the sidewalk toward the lobby of his office building to have dinner. It wasn't the most ideal place, but it would serve the purpose.

Cece tugged on his hand and came to a stop. Busy New Yorkers dashed around them while they blocked the center of the walkway. "I gotta ask ya somefin." He crouched down, prepared for the worst, thinking she might have doubts about spending time with him. Almost crawling into his lap, she moved in between his legs and pressed her mouth to his ear. "Will ya be my dada?"

His control shattered—he wrapped his arms around her and held on for dear life. His face buried in the crook of her neck, it came as trickles from the corner of his eyes, then tears streamed when flashes of *his* future hit him head on and obliterated him.

He wanted Cece, Maggie, a forever in their embrace, at their side.

278

Over blaring horns, people shouting for taxis in a rush to get home, he heard, as if his dad had whispered in his ear, "Don't give up, Max." He had no clue if the message was his father's spirit or Cece's soothing murmurs. Either way, he believed in him and her. A calm came over him and helped him gain control. Regardless of who provided the encouragement, he intended to follow the best advice he'd been given in thirteen years.

The discharge papers were issued. Rick picked up his grandfather from the hospital after a two-week stay and drove him home. The stubborn old coot refused to inconvenience his grandson and live with him while he regained his strength.

Rick shuffled behind him into the living room, his open hand pressed to Grandfather's lower back, ready to grab hold in case he tripped on the oriental rug on his way to the power recliner. It had become Grandfather's preferred spot to read the *Wall Street Journal,* James Patterson novels, and solve crossword puzzles.

"Thank you for picking me up. You didn't have to take off. I could've called a taxi."

Rick rolled his eyes and didn't bother to comment on that ridiculous statement. Not a chance in hell he'd have the old man jostled around in an uncomfortable cab that whipped in and out of traffic, horns blaring when cars and people didn't move out of its path fast enough. "If you didn't bitch at Mom about cancelling flights again, insisting she get off her ass and go sell some books, she would've been here too."

As soon as Grandfather sat down, he depressed a button on the remote and the leg rest climbed higher. He sighed in relief, and the wrinkles on his forehead and around his mouth relaxed. "It's so nice to be home." The tuckered out seventy-two-year-old closed his eyes and settled in for a nap. "Men grumble, women nag," a testament Grandfather made over a jostled snore and a quick glance in Rick's direction after he sprawled out along the matching plaid couch. Prepared to tend to Grandfather's needs for as long as it would take, he got comfortable too.

Rick propped an arm behind a throw pillow and observed the mighty and powerful man who intimidated most. The debilitating health scare knocked his grandfather down a few pegs and resulted in a deteriorated version he didn't recognize: slumped frame, the normal pink blush drained from his taut cheekbones, and his usual clenched jawline sagged and drooped into a double chin.

A nurse started tomorrow, scheduled a few hours each day throughout the convalescing until Grandfather regained his strength and could manage on his own. It gave Rick peace of mind knowing he'd have support. The old fart insisted his grandson not miss any more work, yapping Rick's ear off the entire drive about being a role model for employees and not playing hooky. It didn't matter that in the decade plus he'd worked there he hadn't taken a vacation, and in most instances, didn't finish reviewing files, researching, and preparing contracts until midnight. The diehard retiree never let up and wouldn't change. No matter how often he wished it.

As he started to doze off too, his cell rang. He didn't bother to look at it, just pushed the talk button he could locate blind, and propped it on his ear. "Stone," he mumbled from his looming REM, numb state.

"Max, I gotta tell ya somefin." The booming, cheery command snapped him to attention and in an upright position.

"What's the matter, sweet pea?"

"What ya doin'?"

The out of the blue call and question gave him pause. His fuzzy, half-asleep brain not caught up yet. "Uh, um . . ." he swallowed a yawn and asked, "Where are you?"

"Home."

He glanced at his watch—one in the afternoon. "Why aren't you at school?" He scrubbed a hand through his hair, scratching his scalp and getting antsier as he listened to her steady breathing and non-answer.

"I gotta tummy ache."

All wound up by the news, he bolted off the cushion, pacing to the windows and sofa while he probed for more details. "Did you eat? Do you have a temperature? Is your mother there?"

Her giggles, which produced an instant smile from him under normal conditions, got replaced with worry and a frown that stretched his nerves to the brink. He pressed the phone harder against his ear as if he could be transported through it and hold her close, wiping away the pain.

"Mama's here. I okay."

Well if Cece had been, there wouldn't be a reason for her to not go to school, and Maggie wouldn't have taken off. "How long have you been sick?" Since her emergency surgery, he couldn't help panicking. "Where does it hurt? Did you go to the doctor?"

He heard a banging sound and a few seconds later Maggie muttered, "Get in here, young lady. If you're too sick to go to school, you're not well enough to play. Move it inside, right now." A shuffling, rustling movement, then momma bear's growls got louder. "Is that my phone? Who are you talking to? Give me that."

Rambunctious giggles, more scuffles, and rapid panting as if Cece were running. "Ya it."

"You're in big trouble, missy. I am not playing with you, I mean it. You have three seconds . . . one . . . two . . ."

Another slam and scramble and Cece's huffing and drawn out, "Maaax," and a click. Disconnected.

What the hell was going on?

Less than twelve hours ago he dropped Cece off, a half

hour after her third ballet lesson, and she'd been fine then. It hadn't taken longer than several taps on his cell phone, and the time it took to skim a few of the five-star reviews, to choose Madame Rousseau's dance studio. No more than four foot five on an exaggerated day, the commanding spitfire, owner, and instructor welcomed them with open arms.

Caution should be Kat's middle name, because she accompanied them the next day after he found the place, checking it out with a critical eye. During Cece's introductory warm-up and stretching routine, he settled on the designated padded chairs, shoulder to shoulder next to inspector Kat and a swarm of other female spectators. Tucked into a corner in the warehouse-sized studio, he inquired about how Kat would handle Maggie when she found out. Her eagle eyes remained trained on her niece as Cece's leg flexed on a bar fixed to the mirrored wall while she threw out a response. "What she doesn't know won't hurt her. I already told the rugrat mum's the word. She won't say peep."

Five-year-olds weren't known for their restraint, and he doubted the secret would stay under wraps for long, so he pushed her a little more. "Your sister doesn't want anything to do with me. Why are you doing this?"

Kat's critical, scrutinizing response came swiftly and targeted at him. "You love my sister?"

His chest started to spasm and his winded gasps kept him from responding. The woman had no filter, just blurted out anything at any time. The high-pitched and amplified level had every female head in the room spinning and gawking at him as if they were all waiting with bated breath. Classical music consumed the space, and the ladies nearby shifted their chairs closer. All eyes were on him. They darted peeks between him and the brash woman tapping her finger against her lip like a time bomb ticking off and nearing detonation if he didn't answer her in the next ten seconds.

As he often did in tense situations, he examined the sides,

constructed a perspective, and then responded. Since he had to do that before Kat hauled off and slapped him silly, he reached out to her. He took her hand in his and settled them on his lap. Then he used a gentle and mellow tone to relay his dream. "I never pictured myself as a family man." Kat tried to pull her palm out of his, but he tightened his grip and quieted her with a shake of his head. "But when a woman like Maggie seeps into your soul, you can't picture anything else." Kat's clenched jaw eased and lips parted. "Her simmering sexiness attracted me. She's not the flashy, whiny, needy type. Her independence is off-putting, and her temper fires a guy up enough to drive him crazy." He glanced at Kat's hand, his thumb brushing against it, and envisioned the little things that made Maggie special, endearing. "She has this cute little pockmark right here." He pointed to the ridge of his jaw, under his chin.

Kat murmured, "Chickenpox scar."

He nodded, confirming, but hadn't known the origin. "She smothers her smile, doesn't let it show the cute, teeny gap between her front teeth. Self-conscious?"

"Yes." Kat didn't hold hers back though, showcasing a pearly white, narrow, and straight grin. "She's done that since kindergarten. Kids teased her."

He grunted at that fact. "Her soulful, jazzy rasp makes a man salivate, yet she can't carry a tune, and her momma bear growl thrusts a guy to his knees, begging her to rough him up." Kat snickered and the female peanut gallery cackled around him, adding fuel to the flame. "When we put Cece's swing set together, I about had a heart attack when she peeled off her sweatshirt and didn't have a bra on." Hilarious claps, high fives, and chants buzzed in his ears: "That a girl," "Free them babies," "God, I wish I could do that."

"And none of that scratches the surface and begins to express the natural beauty that Maggie has, and there's no way to explain how truly, deeply, madly in love I am with her."

Sniffles and twittering ensued: "Oh my," "Holy shit," "Do you have a brother?" echoed in a round-about fashion.

Kat leaned in and pecked him on the cheek. "That's why." She winked and crossed her arms along her chest, watching her niece perform a plié.

Cece's joyous, illuminating glow shined through after the flawless execution of her first ballet maneuver. At least he thought so, and shuffled in his seat, growing anxious to jump out of it and clap at her brilliance. Since he didn't want to embarrass her, he waved and smiled instead, and she had too. His heart filled with pride and happiness from an extraordinary chance to experience this with her. After that, Kat's approval came from a couple pounds on his back, permitting him to take Cece the rest of the week without a chaperone.

"Who was that?" Rick thought Grandfather had fallen asleep. His attentive eyes showed otherwise.

"Huh?"

Grandfather jerked his chin toward the phone still clenched in Rick's hand. "Who's sick?"

"Oh." Staring at Maggie's number, Rick plopped down on the cushion, wondering if he should call back. "Cece."

"The little girl from the hospital?"

"Yeah." Depression or exhaustion, Rick didn't know which, had him sprawling into the position he'd been before, legs stretched out, and an arm under the pillow. "She has a tummy ache."

"Probably playing hooky like you."

He rolled onto his side and shot a squinty be-quiet glare across the room. "She's a good girl. She wouldn't do that."

A belly rumble rolled out of Grandfather, a rarity and unlike his stuffy reserve. "Kids are schemers. You were."

"Hey, I was a good kid." He repositioned the pillow a little higher to get more comfortable.

Grandfather snatched a folded newspaper and flung it at him, hitting the tip of his loafer. "You were a snot."

Rick shrugged and antagonized the old man. *"Were."* And shot him a cheesy grin thinking that would shut him up.

"Now you're a pain in the ass."

Sick or not, Rick would never get a leg up from the elder Stone. They'd played this same tune since Dad died. Before that, Horatio Stone had been a doting grandpa and his grandson could do no wrong.

"Is she okay?" Grandfather's kindhearted and gentle question had Rick's drooping eyes popping open.

"I don't know. It sounded like she went outside and ran around. Her mom chased her and yelled at her to come inside."

"Told you, schemer." But for once there wasn't a bite in his retort. Grandfather's crooked grin displayed considerate affection. "Tell me about her."

Whether it had been Rick's weakened, at-odd-ends state, or Grandfather's, he wasn't sure. Either way, he succumbed to the request and revealed everything, from the time he met Maggie and Cece, until today's phone call. At times his story sped up from excitement; he couldn't relay the recollections fast enough. Cece's bubblegum chomping, red pigtails stumbling into his office in search of Herbert. Maggie showing up with her wild Irish temper flaring because her daughter brought along the mouse, and then again when Cece insisted he join her for a hot dog. And how attractive he found Maggie's fire-breathing spirit.

Spurred on, he relayed the joy and pride that came from the unique opportunity to accompany Cece to ballet lessons. Then altered the pace of his tale to slow and sensual. The passion consumed him as he recalled stolen moments with Maggie: in Matt's hallway—their first sensual kiss; in her backyard—a titillating embrace; and in his mom's kitchen—an erotic dance.

Through some of the more painful memories, Rick halted numerous times, his monotone, grim report catching in his throat. Jake pointing a gun at Maggie and the possibility of losing her forever. How Cece's father never wanted anything to do with her, and how Rick saw her as nothing but a blessing and would be so grateful to be her daddy. And the fact that Maggie didn't want anything to do with him and continued to push him away.

When he finished spilling his heart out, Grandfather's re-clined and relaxed state didn't correspond to the gruff reac-tion. Over the wisp of shifting gears, the power chair inclin-ing, Horatio Stone demanded, "I have something to tell you, Rick. Don't interrupt, just listen."

His sports car came in handy once again. Rick rammed his foot onto the accelerator, and the highway flashed by in a blur. In under a half hour he arrived at his destination, fired up and fit to be tied. His fist hammering on the front door reflected his mood. The booming bangs rattled the solid wood. When Kat answered, she threw her hand out, restraining him in the middle of his chest.

"What the hell, Stone?"

"Your sister home?" His commanding question didn't keep Kat from standing aside and giving him entry.

"Out back, making a mess in the garden."

"Cece?" His expanding temper fueled his trotting gate. Kat stepped up her pace and remained on his heels.

"Aw, can I watch?"

"VIP section," he quipped while he threw open the screen. The broken hinge and door crashed into the metal stair rail, announcing his arrival with a bang.

"Max, I gotta show ya somefin."

His arms opened wide. Cece skipped across the lawn and into them. A Ziploc baggie got smashed to his nose as she shouted, "I plantin' pum'kin seeds." Way to go Maggie, so much for her daughter staying inside. He'd have to store that in his reserves and pull it out later when he needed an advantage. Through the clear plastic he caught Maggie's silhouette, hands on her hips, pink polka-dot gloves covering her fists. A skimpy, neon-yellow tank top, cut-off and frayed at her midriff, outlined the swell of her braless breasts. He tipped his chin up and peeked over top of the zipped bag, examining every square inch of her. His brain charted a course, planning and marking the exact spot he'd bite and lick first.

He whispered a secret in Cece's ear and set her on her feet. Hair prickling on the back of his neck, he could picture Kat behind him, arms crossed, tapping her foot, awaiting the action. Every nerve under his skin was primed and readied as he honed in on his target. He anticipated his reward, but it wouldn't come without a lot of pain. Maggie would not surrender easily, and he wouldn't have it any other way. Cece dashed around his legs, her murmurs and giggles joining her aunt's.

"Maggie, you've been a bad girl."

More giggling, snorts, and huffs coming from the onlookers over his shoulder.

Maggie kicked out her right leg, tapping her bare foot along the grass.

"You ready?"

"For what?" she sputtered, puckered lips showing her dissatisfaction.

"Your punishment." Before his warning, he'd already taken off, sprinting in a football-charging pose, and driving into her. She didn't have a chance to dash away. He scooped her legs out from under her and tossed her over his shoulder. As he spun around, he smacked her once, hard, on her gorgeous ass, exposed by her slack nylon shorts.

The first of many she deserved.

"Hey, put me down right now." Her snarls went unanswered.

Kat threw her arm out in a bowing wave, twirling it toward her toes and announcing, "After you, my king."

"Traitors," Maggie grumbled.

Cece's clapping and jumping up and down in frog leaps tracked his path to the side gate and front yard as Maggie continued her protests and bucking wiggles. All his willpower waned. Her butt eye level and pelvis rubbing along his pounding chest turned him on that much more. He couldn't wait to put a blush on that bottom. She spewed several foreign phrases he guessed weren't encouragement and were most likely rude suggestions that relayed paybacks momma bear would unleash soon.

Bring it on, Maggie. Bring it on.

In a blink, he had her pinned in the passenger seat of his car, squirming and fighting the seat belt he used to contain her fury. He silenced and drained out her protests with a deep, penetrating kiss that left both of them huffing and puffing. Her sparking, dilated pupils and flaming green eyes met his unrepentant stare.

"I love you," he announced, bold and unequivocal.

He nipped at her gaping lower lip. "My grandfather told me everything. I'm more than ticked off at you for not telling me, but we'll deal with that later." On edge and reeling from that fact, his request came out louder than he intended, but then softened as hope and anticipation consumed him. "Take a chance, Maggie." He held his hand out to her, waiting to see if she'd leap and overcome whatever reservations held her back before. "You can trust me. I won't hurt you or Cece ever."

The family-crammed neighborhood could almost be mistaken for a serene countryside from the deafening silence. Birds didn't chirp, cars didn't pass by, and no one other than Cece and Kat were outside. The longer Maggie remained quiet, the harder it became to resist the nerves of defeat that started inside of him.

Instead of her hand taking his, she placed it below his chin, brushing her thumb along the stubble. Her lips kissed his jaw and drifted to his cheek, pecked his temple, and then dragged down the center of his nose, coming to rest at his mouth. Beautiful green eyes and a hundred freckles took him back to their first encounter, a brief flash and memory of her standing in his doorway. Determination and apprehension evident in her expression then and now.

"You got me?" she whispered, her underlying message loud and clear. A firm statement, but communicated she needed assurances.

This would be a whole new territory for him. Relationships weren't his strong suit. If it weren't for Matt's guidance, he wasn't sure he would've gotten this far. He'd make mistakes along the way, but he'd learn and adapt, as he'd been doing all along. As if his mind and heart already knew what to do, he knelt down on the cement, and gave her what he thought she needed. "I'm gonna screw up." Her lip twitched up on one side, replaced by a smothered laugh. "I've never been in love before." Her repressed grin and smirking gaze softened. She leaned against the seat, tilting her head and brushing her hand through the floppy cowlick on his forehead. A gesture he recognized, and she often used to soothe and encourage Cece. "You got me, Maggie? Because I need you." He glanced behind him at the little pigtailed girl who had stolen his heart too. Cece's support came from her toothy and chubby-cheeked smile. Kat's expression identical to her niece's.

Maggie threaded her fingers through his, their hands joined, resting on her thigh. She stared at them for several too-quiet seconds, and then squeezed them tight. "You can depend on me . . . to tell you what to do and not." Her teasing, happy-go-lucky response released the tension and vise grip around his chest so he could finally breathe a little.

He leaned into her, leaving just a scant inch between them. Using his confident boardroom tone, he said, "Where, when, how, it wouldn't matter, just say yes . . ." He pulled their hands up to his lips and kissed her knuckles. His eyes never left hers while his voice grew soft and tender. "You want me?" Now he was the one who needed reassurances.

"Always," she admitted, right before grabbing hold of his neck and sucking him into a knock-him-down-on-his-knees kiss. Good thing he'd already been in that position, because as she'd done from the start, he fell hard for her all over again.

And he'd gladly remain there if he could have her in his arms forever.

Mama's Rule # 28:

Make peace with your past, so it
doesn't screw up the present.

You're the only one in
charge of your happiness.

Together, Maggie and Rick stood on the stoop of his
grandfather's porch. Rick's confidence bolstered and calmed
the jumping jacks in her stomach a little. He swung the door
open, and she put her best foot forward, entering the domain
of her nemesis. Even though Rick assured her multiple times
there would be nothing to fear, she couldn't suppress her
growing anxiety. The only way out of this nightmare would
be to get it over with. Avoidance had been her tactic with Jake,
and that didn't fare well. She wouldn't back down any longer.
Fear or not, she'd face challenges that came her way, head on.
No more ducking, hoping her problems would just go away.
That wasn't realistic. Better to deal with them than let things
get out of hand. She wouldn't exist in a protective shell any
longer.

If she'd envisioned anything about the domain of the stern

and cold Horatio Stone, the surroundings didn't match her previous interactions with him. On every wall and shelf were framed images of a loving and adored family. A mothball aroma, crocheted afghans folded neatly atop an antique settee, and lace doilies on coffee and side tables weren't what she would have expected. A woman's touch evident in every nook and cranny, she barely recognized or noticed the fragile man rising from a recliner. He didn't approach her, and she hadn't gone to him. Instead, she felt an overwhelming, internal tug of war that pulled her around the living room. Black-and-white photographs to color provided a visual history and shrine of Mr. Stone, Rick, and his father's life. A devotion to family she could understand and relate to. And in that moment she realized maybe they weren't as different as she thought. A sense of calm came over her as she examined baby pictures to adulthood, learning a little more about the man she loved and a grandfather who would protect him at all costs. She sensed someone come up behind her, followed by a wrinkled, age-spotted hand, pointing to a wedding photo. "My wife, Olivia." His finger caressed the face in the picture, and his endearing, sad tone crushed her heart. "I miss her so much."

With tears in her eyes, she asked, "How did you meet her?" How couples came together always intrigued and fascinated her. No two stories were quite the same.

"She was a nurse, and I was a soldier in Vietnam. During a skirmish, I was wounded, shot in my hip and thigh. I had surgery and developed an infection. I'd been unconscious several days, and when I woke up, there she was, reading D.H. Lawrence. There was no way she could have known I had the same book in my footlocker at base camp. I'd never seen her before."

Small similarities and connections linking two strangers, a commonality she'd heard before. Brief encounters and windows of opportunity that had longstanding effects. Fate? Destiny? She wasn't sure how or why love happened when it did, but there was always some unique event, timing, location that brought a couple together. So perplexing, yet beautiful, no matter the situation.

Softly, as if unsure whether he might offend her, he claimed, "A woman was made from a man's ribs for a precise reason." Once again, he surprised her, a spiritual admission she hadn't thought possible from the man who'd threatened her welfare. "They're protectors, providing a foundation for a man's entire being, shielding vital organs, yet flexible and yielding. Without her, he's nothing but loose flesh, wandering existence alone. God ensured the idiot males of the world would recognize what was made from him."

She giggled as he laughed at himself and his gender. Another contrast, Mr. Stone had a sense of humor. Who knew?

He placed a framed photo of a baby boy in front of her, one she noticed on a side table nearby. "My boy, Max. The second happiest day of my life was when Olivia told me she was pregnant. No parent should outlive his own child."

A gasp caught in her throat, and she placed her hand on top of his in a comforting gesture. She glanced up at him, and he gripped her shoulder. "I'm sorry for what I said to you. I'll make no excuses, except to say that my family means everything. I didn't know you or care to. All I wanted was to protect my grandson and what little I had left. I forgot what it was like to fall in love. Olivia passed away in her sleep twenty-five years ago, and I've been going through the motions. Then when Max died, I . . ."

She squeezed his arm and shook her head. "I want you to know something, Mr. Stone."

"Horatio," he insisted, gently.

"There's nothing I wouldn't do to protect my family. As much as I hate to admit this, I can understand why you did it. But please know that I love Rick. I have no intention of harming him."

"Oh, I realize that now. My grandson told me how you

met, and how much he cares for you and your daughter. I hope you'll give me a chance too. I'm not such a bad person, once you get to know me."

"I don't hold grudges, Mr.—" When he scrunched his bushy eyebrows and shook his head, she corrected herself. "Horatio, I'd like that very much. I miss my grandparents and so does Cece. After you spend time with us though, you might take back your invitation. We're a rowdy bunch."

His grip on her shoulder tightened a bit. "Olivia didn't let me get away with anything, and her daredevil attitude kept me on my toes. After what I've been through, I need a zing to get me out of the rut I've been living in. I'm ready for a change, a breath of fresh air."

She tucked her arm around his waist and pulled him into a hug. Leaning up on her tippy toes, she pecked his cheek. "I'm warning you." He tilted his head, a tender expression she never envisioned he'd aim at her. "For the record, 'I told you so' now."

He laughed and walked her around, telling her all about his adorable wife, son, and grandson. Every tale full of affection and fondness. She'd never forget that moment and the effort he made to welcome her into his home, setting her at ease by establishing a connection they could both relate to.

A turning point for all of them.

Lucky for her she worked in the same building as Rick. They fell into a routine that seemed so natural and comfortable, she had to pinch herself to make sure she wasn't walking around in a dream state. After classes she stopped by his office before going to Westlake, sometimes with Cece and other times alone, depending on how late she arrived. Any breaks throughout the evening were spent with him, since he adjusted his schedule.

He came in later in the afternoon when possible and stayed till midnight so he could drive her home. "No more bus," he insisted. In most instances she'd protest at such pushiness, but she hadn't because of the sweet way he requested the change, and the fact he diverted the spotlight onto him by admitting, "I need to see you before I close my eyes every night, Maggie." What woman could argue with that?

Around nine o'clock, excited about their rendezvous, she skipped past the empty desks. When she approached his doorway and heard a female voice she recognized, her blood pressure spiked and teeth clamped down. Good manners be damned. Instead of knocking, she stormed into his office. Both Rick's and Julia's conversation came to an abrupt halt.

"Well, look what the garbage man forgot to pick up."

"Leave, Julia, now," he barked, but it didn't matter. The prima donna hadn't moved an inch from her shoulder-to-shoulder position.

The sight of them ticked Maggie off, and her mental countdown began. By the time she reached zero, she'd reined in her temper. During their twenty-question sessions while driving home, he'd told her nothing ever happened between them. Even so, she didn't like the witch within a mile of *her* man. Possessive much? She didn't care. No way she'd allow anyone to cause friction between them again. They had something great going, and she'd fight if she had to.

"Julia, I guess you couldn't use your daddy's money to buy him off either, like you tried to do with me. Ya know, the twenty thousand you offered me to stay away from Rick."

The man in the middle shot Maggie a pointed look, indicating there would be a long discussion about that detail, and the story she hadn't told him about yet. Heck, it had been just a week since their relationship became official, and she didn't want to taint their getting to know each other with something so negative. Besides, since she hadn't heard from or seen Julia since that encounter, she figured the matter over and vanquished the spoiled brat from her mind.

As she exposed Julia's devious plan, she advanced on them too and didn't stop until she eased herself in between Julia and Rick. His hands took hold of Maggie's hips, but he remained silent behind her.

Julia's glare dropped to his possessive grip, and her mouth fell open.

It would've been easy to bash her, but Maggie took a different tactic. "Have you ever been in love, Julia?" She felt the question a safe one, interpreting Julia's bribery as desperation and an established bad habit of using her father's riches to get her way without any regard given to whether the object or person sought was something Julia really wanted or not. Cold and indifferent were accurate classifications for Julia as her stare flicked over Maggie's shoulder. The longer Julia didn't answer, though, the more Maggie saw the hairline emotional fractures: a hitch and sag in her shoulders, and rapid blinking.

When Julia shifted from leaning on one foot and readjusted to two, threw her shoulders back, and aimed a hardened stare at Maggie, she recognized the recoup-your-pride act. And it motivated Maggie to make a heartfelt attempt. "*Two* people who share a bond and affection for one another. It's not something you can buy, and you can't force someone to love you." Experience taught her that, along with Kat's advice piercing her eardrums. Yeah, big sisters knew a lot after all. "If you do, it'll be doomed from the start." Swallowing her dignity, she admitted, "I should know."

Julia turned tail and left without a word. The drawn paleness of her face and quick retreat might have been an indication that the message registered somewhere in her conscience. Time would tell. Either way, Maggie would be ready.

"You're amazing."

Appreciation filled Maggie's heart and a small smile tugged at the corner of her mouth. That expression vanished the instant she spun around and grasped his broad shoulders.

"No." She flung his admission back at him. "I'm gonna screw up. Sorry I didn't tell you about her before. I wanted to forget the past and focus on us, the positive stuff. I promise, I won't hide anything from you again." His thumb rubbed along her neck, making it difficult to concentrate. She understood the importance of honesty in a relationship. Little white lies and stonewalling added up and eventually came out. She never wanted to be blindsided again and wouldn't do that to him anymore.

"I trust you, Maggie. I realize you can handle a lot on your own and don't need me, but I have your back. No matter what, we'll deal with whatever comes our way. Together, okay?"

Overwhelmed by his support, she rested her head on his shoulder, tugging him into a bear hug. Yep, she got it—they were a team. A unified one.

The Jalfrezi Maggie bit into, a hot and tangy Indian lamb dish dressed in paprika, tomatoes, and coriander, was delicious. As a special treat for her twenty-seventh birthday, Rick took her to Masala Wala, which offered an amazing blend of traditional and hip South Asian street food. His attention to detail and concentrated effort to get to know everything about her, from childhood to present, resulted in them spending every non-working minute together. They started this morning by taking Cece to ballet lessons. The sneaky arrangement now out of the bag, it hadn't surprised her that Kat had gone behind her back. Even though Maggie had wanted to sign up Cece, and Rick's involvement might've had good intentions, the maneuver still lit her fuse anyway. He pleaded his case, pulling out all the stops: puppy-dog eyes and an exaggerated fat-lip pout, which changed to kisses along her neck. Then he sucked on her earlobe and whispered he'd ask from now on, melting her like goo. A smart negotiator for sure.

In the late afternoon after playing in the park, they had lunch and cake. Kat and Cece gave her their gifts. Her sister bought her a spa day and whispered in her ear about another sexy item she couldn't give her with Cece around. Her daughter gave her a matching braided band "like Max's" but hers had red as the dominant color with a thin brown strip in the center. The opposite to his, but complementary. Cece's constant chanting of "Max and Mama sittin' in a tree" had lost its cuteness after the first week. A month later and the mantra became as appealing as the Barney songs she wouldn't stop repeating. Whether it grated on her nerves or not, the elation and excitement Cece showed wouldn't be something she'd squelch. Kat took care of that part though, redirecting her niece whenever possible.

Rick grabbed her wrist and brought the fork to his mouth, stealing her next bite. "Mmm, excellent." His eclectic palate delighted her, and he soon replaced Matt as her personal taste tester, encouraging her to use him to experiment. Even though he meant with food, there had been an underlying sensual message attached to the open invitation. She expected he'd lure her into his bed right away, but that didn't happen. He'd been dropping hints all day about a special surprise this evening. She hoped instead of Rabri Ras Malai for dessert, she'd be licking and savoring his gorgeous body. He was a hard man to resist. She didn't know how much longer she could wait.

"Open up, Maggie, taste mine," he teased, suspending Malai Tiger Shrimp from his fork.

She flicked her tongue along the tip first, capturing the sour cream and sesame oil sauce before sucking the prawn into her mouth. As seductively as possible, she twirled the tail between her fingers and mouth before biting off the end. A moan accompanied her slow chewing, and her fixed gaze and arched eyebrow taunted him, attempting to appeal to his baser instincts.

A smirk crooked up in the corner of Rick's mouth and disappeared in a blink. His thumb swept across her bottom lip. He raised the plump digit to his mouth, clamped it between his teeth, and dragged it out. "Mmm, you taste so much better."

Holy smokes, she might have just experienced a cosmic orgasm, transcending space, since he hadn't even touched her there. She swallowed, barely able to force the food down.

"Maggie, Maggie, Maggie . . ." He leaned back in his chair, rubbed his jaw, and tapped his lower lip, ensuring she'd look right there. "You have no idea what you do to me, do you?" Before she could say anything he cautioned, "I'll give you fair warning. I'm taking you to my place after dinner, and I plan on stripping you bare, laying you on my bed, and enjoying every part of you. So if you don't want that, you need to speak up now. I've tried to be as patient as possible, since I let my hormones do the talking before." He took a ragged breath, grabbed both of her hands twisting in the middle of the table, and kissed one then the other. "I'm hanging by a thread . . ." Nipping on her knuckles, his heated hazel eyes captivated her as he whispered against them, "And I'm ready to clear this table and take you right here."

That little devil popped up on her shoulder, stabbing her in the neck with a pitchfork demanding: *Yes!* Years of being a good girl and common decency kept her mouth shut. Deep down though, her inner rebel took charge.

She kicked off a shoe and slid her toes up his pant leg, scraping her nails along the hair on his shin. He sprang across the table, gripping her neck and thrusting his tongue into her in a penetrating kiss. Unable to look away, they gazed in each other's eyes. Her fingers drifted through his hair as she sucked on him harder—he groaned. His warm, heavy exhales brushed along her face, soothing, comforting. They tilted their heads left and right for the perfect angle—more of him, her. His stubble scraped her chin as he licked and savored; sweet spearmint, saltiness, and a tinge of pepper fired up her taste buds.

She didn't know how long they'd been that way. It wasn't until she heard a throat clearing that her eyes flew open, catching the waiter dropping the bill on their table and vanishing.

"You ready for me?" His question spoken softly against her lips came through loud and clear.

"Always."

Just a few bites remaining, they agreed in silence that neither were interested in food any longer. After the bill had been paid, they ran out of there and got to his home in warp speed. The frenzy and rush came to a screeching halt after he kissed her all the way up the stairs and into his bedroom and stood her at the foot of the mattress.

"Maggie." Love and tenderness came through, but so did an underlying hint of promises to come. The tiny wrinkles around his eyes softened as he scanned her face, drifting downward to her neck, chest, waist, and blush-pink painted toes. She'd selected a red nylon wrap dress with a deep v-slit down the front and a higher, gaping one along her left thigh. Some designers thought redheads shouldn't wear the same color as their hair. They were wrong. By the way he strolled toward her with confident strides, mentally undressing her, he must have agreed. His eyes shouted—*mine.*

He slid his finger, whisper light, along her collarbone. Unblinking he said, "I've waited a long time for you." Her hands captured in his, he pulled them up, placing them on his lapels. "I'm yours," he murmured, then moistened his lips and added a dare: "Take me."

The devil and inner rebel didn't need to make an appearance. She'd take the challenge and a lot more.

As if her previous fantasies came true, her mind replayed all of her dreams while she performed a dual striptease.

She threw his suit jacket off and loosened his tie, letting it hang around his neck. With purpose she undid his shirt buttons, flicking one, followed by a kiss, then the other, another peck, and marked him all the way to his waistband. She yanked the fabric out of his charcoal-gray pants.

"This . . ." She drifted two fingers up and down the center of his chest. "Is mine." He smiled and she smirked too.

"Yes," his gruff confirmation spurred her on.

Licking him from waist to neck, her tongue dipped between each ridge of his abs—a six-pack. She tucked her nose under the edge of his shirt and caught his nipple between her teeth, flicking it with her tongue over and over. He grabbed the back of her head and held her there. "Mmm . . . lower, Maggie, much lower."

Giggling, she nipped a puckered tip, reminding him she was the boss here.

When she stepped to the side and walked around him, she kept her eyes on the prize from front to back. He tried to turn with her, but she grabbed his shoulder and held him in place. "Don't move." From behind him, she slipped her hands around his waist, unbuckling his belt and drawing the zipper down. Pressed into his back, she crushed her chest into him. "This . . ." She cupped him between his legs and brushed her thumb along his hardened, twitching length several times. "Whose is it?"

"Fuck," he whispered. His shaky inhale and exhale beat against her. The thrumming of his rapid heartbeat in sync and pounding with hers.

"I'm almost there," she teased.

His head dropped back, and he looked at the ceiling. His hands fisted closed and open, again and again along her thighs. "You keep this up, Maggie, I'm not gonna last long."

"Oh, but I'm getting to the *good* part . . ." she said in his ear, "*you* and . . ." she bit the back of his neck, "the *bad,* very, very bad."

His growls rumbled along her from waist to cheek. But there weren't any protests in them, just impatience.

She followed those claims by removing his belt and tossing it onto the bed. "For later," she hinted, promised.

"Fuck me," he mumbled under his breath.

Not denying him but still prolonging the foreplay, she slipped her fingers through the slit in his boxers, grabbed his shaft, and rubbed up and down, first slow then fast. "Like that?"

Before he could answer, she stroked the tip, producing more of his groans as his strong grasp held on to the backs of her knees. His butt rotated against her. Friction *she* needed and didn't deny herself.

"Please, Maggie." She didn't know if his strangled desire did her in or if she couldn't take frustrating herself any more either. She whipped his boxers and pants down his legs and took charge again.

As she walked around him, she drifted her hand along his butt cheek and gave it a squeeze: firm, muscled, clenching. When their eyes met again, she stood where she'd been before, at the foot of his bed, a few feet away from him. At her hip, she tugged on the string belt. The bow tied there slipped free, and her dress parted wide open. Exactly why she had bought this outfit. More red, a demi-cup balconette, no padding, just lace so thin and sheer it hid nothing.

He brushed his thumbs along each breast at the same time. "Mine." Her nipples stiffened and greeted him, answering for her. She reached behind and unsnapped the clasp. The silk straps on her shoulders fell forward and onto his wrists.

"You're killing me, Maggie. I have to taste you."

Not giving him the chance, his striped black-and-gray tie became her next target. She pulled the tip forward and flicked it up and down across her chest. It must have pushed him over the edge. He tossed the silk fabric aside and took over. He cupped her thirty-six Bs and held them out for his eager lips. He latched on and twirled, suckled. From one to the other, he repeated the same tugging and nibbling actions, making sure each received their fair share.

His long cowlick covered his left eye, but she could still make out his determined expression. And even though his head was bent down, focused, he somehow still caught sight of her hand inching lower toward her lace bikinis, wanting, needing just a little relief.

Swifter than a lion on prey, he latched on to her hand, but instead of stopping her, he joined their fingers like that day in her office. He slipped them inside and all the way to her slick center, rotating them in a soft, erotic motion on her nub. Panties gone. Her head fell back and her eyes closed. She let him take her—from his knees. His mouth a bit of heaven on earth.

To steady her wobbly legs, she held on to his broad shoulders and registered every tingle, each lave, and the penetrating friction of his jaw rubbing along her folds as his tongue licked and flittered side to side. How she managed to stand, she didn't know. It didn't take long for her to fall onto the bed. When she spread her legs wide, he dove—consumed—owned.

Mine, all mine repeated in her head, but she could have sworn he chanted it too as he brought her to the top-of-the-charts-inspiring orgasm.

There, in Rick's bed, and in each minute, hour, day spent with him, she discovered what love truly meant.

"The one" didn't come close. Wasn't even accurate.

A love unlike any other, inscribed onto her heart—*for all eternity.*

And the right, clear message came through.

The only—his and hers—the way it had been intended from the start, at creation.

Bonus Material

Life's short. Break the rules.

Dear Readers,
This section provides a special glimpse into Maggie's, Rick's, and Cece's future.
Enjoy!

One year later . . .

Rick couldn't take his eyes off Maggie. Under the sparkly, bright lights above the altar, her strapless and braless lace gown stole the show.

Among a hundred-plus attendees, many of Rick's employees, family, and friends, the anticipation of this day and of making Maggie his finally came to fruition. His greatest achievement yet—Mr. and Mrs. Rick and Maggie Stone.

Riches graced and blessed him, but it had nothing to do with money. Anyone who believed an answer came from how much a person made, how hard an individual worked, or how much stuff someone accumulated couldn't be more wrong.

Family. That mattered. His mom and dad had it right all along. There wasn't any greater fulfillment. Nothing came close. Being surrounded by them on this day brought an enormous amount of joy.

Rick's exuberant mom sat in the front row, and Sophia and the girls next to her.

With a clean bill of health and as ornery as ever, Grandfather joined his side, serving as his dual best man next to Matt. Rick wouldn't have prevailed and reached this momentous occasion without them.

Maggie's mom, dad, aunts, uncles, grandparents, and cousins filled half the church. And of course, Kat, who positioned herself at her sister's hip as the maid of honor.

Cecily Bryna Stone—the name change and adoption finalized this morning before the ceremony produced a radiant glow on her face. A stunning flower girl, her wispy red curls flowed over her earlobes, the majority of the thick strands pinned on top in a fluffy, bouncing bun. She trotted giddily down the aisle, tossing red rose petals over each shoulder until she joined her mama and daddy-in-training at the altar.

Their trio all together, he slid his hand across Cece's shoulders and onto the hollow of Maggie's back. With his heart standing less than a foot in front of him, Maggie's love overwhelmed him and at the same time, humbled him.

First he recited the heartfelt vows of everlasting love and commitment to his wife, revealing the blessings bestowed upon him from the moment he met the auburn beauties. Then he crouched down, cupped Cece's chubby cheek, and relayed his promises intended just for her.

He picked up the shamrock necklace resting along her collarbone and reminded her of his wishes. From right to left, he pointed to one petal then the next.

Faith—"I, Richard Maxwell Stone, will be by your side,

whenever and wherever you need me. Have faith that I will *always* come when you call."

Love—"My love . . ." His finger tapped his heart and he did the same to Cece's. "Never, ever doubt it. You and your mama," he smiled at Maggie who had tears in her eyes, "will always be with me." He pointed to his temple and the middle of his chest. "And me with you."

Hope—"Every dream you have, Cece, I will help make true. Your hopes are mine."

He picked up a beaming Cece and pulled Maggie into the embrace. He placed a kiss on Maggie's cheek then Cece's. "I devote my life to both of you. Forever and ever."

Margareta Cassidy Stone, a photogenic, dazzling knock-out, graced local and national newspapers. Society pages carried their story, sensationalized the millionaire marrying a Texas born and raised, middle-class chef. It didn't matter. Nothing could diminish Maggie's glorious smile, the teeny gap in full view, gracing him with an expression of affection and devotion. The look remained on her beautiful face as she greeted him at the altar, when she recited her vows, and throughout the get-down-and-boogie-till-midnight reception. They danced into the wee hours, unable to keep their eyes or hands off each other. Their sensual touches displayed their eagerness and yearning for one another, and at other times, sly, tender assurances of more to come when they could sneak away from the celebratory crowd.

One year later . . .

There were no words to describe the sight. Maggie stared at her husband sprawled on the double-wide, feathertop sofa he insisted they purchase after a minor squabble in front of the salesman. Lucky for her, he adored her Irish temper and always rewarded her with fabulous make-up sex. Twelve weeks old, the twins took up their preferred spot on their daddy's chest. Maximilian cradled under his left arm, and Katarina's cheek nestled below his chin. His other pride and joy, Cece nestled along his thigh, head pillowed on his stomach. Her hand draped on top of his and sat protectively on her sister's back. All of them sound asleep, sneaking their customary, lazy Saturday afternoon nap.

From behind Maggie, Kat rested a chin on her shoulder, pulled her into hug, and stated in a hushed tone, "Told ya he was right for you."

God, Maggie adored her sister. Since Kat lived with them, in a private oasis and suite constructed in their enormous basement, Maggie couldn't get away from her. Not that she wanted to. They'd always been like conjoined twins. Permanently affixed.

"Giving you any ideas?" Maggie prodded.

Kat's snort came out loud and with a ton of protest. "You know me better than that, Magoopie." And added a pinch to her ribs. "I'll just sit back and let you do the work for a change."

Maggie grinned up to her ears. "You might be missing something." Her implication related to marriage, but she didn't want to let her oversexed sister one-up her. So she spread her hands eight inches apart, in reference to her husband's length.

"Now you're just braggin.'"

"My point exactly. You can't get the goods while hiding behind me. And I'm not just talking about sex. What's with you and Alex anyway?" Oh, that remark clamped her sister's lips shut. She faced Kat and crossed her arms, prepared to take on a battle if necessary. "Friends with benefits isn't enough for you. It shouldn't be."

Spinning on her heels, Kat scuttled into the kitchen, ducking her head into the fridge.

After Maggie got situated on a stool at the butcher block island, she dropped her chin in her palm and watched her sister rifle through one shelf after another, indecision evident in her stiff shoulders and pinched, thinking-too-much brow. When Kat opened the freezer and stared, Maggie said, "I guess I can turn down the A/C since you've frozen me out and all of Alaska."

From on top of Cece's rainbow Popsicles box, Kat snatched a Snickers bar and hopped onto a chair. She bit a small piece of chocolate off the tip. As she chewed, Kat's pointed look dared Maggie to back off. Ha! Those days were long gone.

"You like him?" A stupid question but Maggie had to start somewhere.

Kat shrugged.

"He's obviously into you since he practically lives here."

Her eyes rolled, and Kat stuffed half the log into her mouth, hacking off a chunk. How in the world Kat did that without cracking her teeth, she couldn't figure.

Tapping her lip, Maggie glanced through the windows similar to the fifteen-foot view in Emma's kitchen and watched the ripples on the water. It took them forever to find a home that had a pond. It wasn't common in most communities. Their three-thousand-square-foot house, located a few blocks from Matt's, hadn't been for sale when they started searching a month after their engagement. They were about to settle on something neither of them really wanted, but their real estate agent contacted them right before this property went on the market and they lucked out. Tricks of the trade she'd learned realtors hid. Homes in high-demand areas were often contracted in advance and listed as a formality.

"He wants more, right? Than . . ." Maggie didn't finish. Her savvy sister could interpret the sexual insinuation.

Another shrug and caramel-coated-peanut crunching.

"Do you?"

308

Glares and a snarl were all Maggie got in return. Hmm...she must be getting closer to the heart of the matter. Should she play devil's advocate, or stick with her blood-oath-sisterhood-supportive side?

"Dump him."

Holy smokes. If steam could have burst through Kat's ears, it would've. Her brown eyes blew open, and her gaping mouth displayed grotesque evidence of the smooshed remnants of a gooey center coated on her tongue. Yuck.

"Really?" Kat's high-pitched voice quipped none too pleasantly.

Maggie's shoulders moved up and down, as if it were an easy-breezy decision. "Sure, if he wants more and you don't, why stick around?"

"Is that so?" Kat's fist hit the butcher block. The candy she held in it splattered crumbles in the space between them, a tiny morsel catapulting onto Maggie's knuckle.

Ignoring her sister's pissy attitude, Maggie slurped the sliver into her mouth. "Mmm . . . very good." Then she leapt across, grabbed Kat's wrist, and bit off a huge chunk from the Snickers bar. "Yummy." She patted her stomach, like Cece often did, and Alex too. He'd joined them for dinner almost every night, and after each meal never failed to tell Maggie that exact thing, rubbing his stuffed-to-the-gills midsection. The man always cleared his plate and consumed at least three servings.

To dig the knife deeper, Maggie's cheek-popping smile aimed at Kat's scowl proved that with a little more shoving she might get Kat off her ass and moving in another direction.

The babies' crying didn't give Maggie a chance to push the subject further. She left Kat to stew on those thoughts and jogged into the living room. Her repressed giggles were stuck behind her teeth as she chomped on her lower lip.

If Maggie said the sky was blue, Kat would deny it and call it black.

When Maggie turned right, Kat went left.

Just as her sister knew which buttons to push, Maggie did too.

As much as Kat gave the impression she didn't want more, there wasn't any denying the wondering gaze Maggie caught in her sister's expression while Kat rocked the babies to sleep, dressed up in various costumes and role-played with Cece, and the wistful glances from under Kat's lashes when Rick danced with Maggie anywhere and everywhere.

Somehow she'd crack that shell Kat hid behind. *Romance-shmomance,* Kat mocked often and got Cece to parrot the phrase too, adding their own version of loud smooching onto the backs of their hands and cackling like hyenas.

No matter the opposition, her sister wanted a monogamous relationship and commitment. Too bad she wouldn't admit it. A tough cookie to crack, not many guys could handle Kat's overpowering attitude.

But Alex could. After Maggie asked him a few probing questions, she sensed he wanted to take the next step with Kat. And if she could do anything to push her sister along, she would. After all, as happy as Kat seemed, Maggie knew her sister desired more and for some reason couldn't take the leap. Marriage didn't appear in Kat's dictionary. A whole lot of other foul-mouthed terms did when Maggie brought up the subject, but not that particular one. At some point she'd get Kat to realize what she was missing. Even if she had to use a pitchfork to get her going.

There wasn't anything better than the relationship she and Rick had. No matter how many times she watched him with Maximilian, Katarina, and Cece, her heart swooned.

The twins were wide awake. Rick had one tucked in each arm. Their big sister skipped happily toward the kitchen to warm their bottles. "Her job," as Cece liked to remind them. Every day Maggie's baby grew up, craving not attention, but responsibility. Her take-charge attitude on full display, Cece's confidence shined through in her constant smile and tenacity, taking on any challenge and activity without batting a reserved eye. Ballet had been her first accomplishment. A blue belt in jujitsu another. She was well on her way toward her goal of the pinnacle red belt. And her most recent interest had become softball. Close by her side, her daddy displayed his obvious pride through loud clapping and whooping cheers. His positive reinforcement was never overdone though. It came from the heart—sincere and authentic.

As she plucked a squirming Maximilian from his arm, Rick pecked her cheek and whispered his naughty promises for later. In a thousand lifetimes she never could have imagined being married to such a man. Fairy tales had been vanquished from her mind long ago. Her amazing, compassionate husband was so much better than anything she dreamed up in her youth. Richard Maxwell Stone ensured her wishes were his command. As much as she wanted to give him everything in return, he always seemed a step ahead, putting her and the kids first. He leapt into the role of daddy and supportive partner as efficiently as he accomplished anything else.

So she had to get creative and find other ways to please him. A fantasy wrapped in reality, she enjoyed his luscious body first thing in the morning, anytime in the afternoon, at bedtime when the kids were asleep, or whenever she wanted. He was always primed and ready. With her active imagination, she had fun experimenting and driving him crazy. Since she'd always been a dedicated and hard-working student, he scored a lot. For her performance, she earned straight As, which her husband hand-delivered and recorded on every square inch of her body.

Love didn't seem an adequate or sufficient description for her all-consuming feelings. She had more blessings than she ever could've imagined.

Their family and life together was as close to heaven as she could visualize.

Five years later . . .

"The place looks great. Everything will be fine. Stop fidgeting." Kat grabbed her trembling hands, holding them firm and steady.

Maggie examined the twelve-thousand-square-foot restaurant in trendy NoMad Manhattan. One hundred fifty tables, a lounge that seated sixty, a tavern that accommodated thirty, and three private event rooms on the second floor ranged from a table of twelve to larger groups up to fifty. Her menu included international flavors from around the globe, providing service for lunch and dinner, and Sunday brunch. The grand opening tonight, a dream actualized. *Seven* originated from a free-for-all naming spree.

Emma had come over that night with her laptop and searched each title, making sure there weren't any others in the city or surrounding area with the same name. Rick's grandfather, a devoted and spoil-the-kids-rotten papa, lounged in a recliner and rocked four-year-old Maximilian and Katarina in each arm, reading fairy tales and ignoring the brouhaha. Once Cece called him Papa, he didn't want to hear anything else. Another person succumbing to her charms.

After dozens of names were yelled out, Cece took charge and wrote them on a white board. The rowdy crowd argued and crossed out each one except *Seven*. As soon as the dynamic duo, Rick and Cece, suggested it, they had all agreed on the winner. It was a perfect representation of the wonders of the world, international flavors, and the number of countries that would be featured on the menu each week.

"I'm gonna get a drink in your honor." Kat saluted, humming a carefree tune and bee-lining her buzzing butt to the bar.

Her wits frayed, Maggie escaped to her office for a few solitary minutes to calm down before booked-solid reservations forced her into the kitchen in less than an hour. Bent over her desk, she rolled her shoulders forward and backward, trying to relieve the stress. She'd been puttering around her grandparents' restaurant from the time she could walk. This should be old hat. Still, the pressure of owning her own business and taking on responsibility for forty-plus employees scared her to death.

Large hands tugged at her hips, and Rick's chest molded to her spine. Even with her chin tucked in, eyes closed, she'd recognize him anywhere. "There's somethin' I want to show you."

A messy bun on top of her head provided easy access to her neck. He took full advantage, scraping his stubble along it, shivers washing over her. Greedy, she tilted her head and laid it on his shoulder, exposing more flesh. He rewarded her by nibbling at the hollow, sucking along the ridge, and taking a nip at her chin. "Mmm."

Always on the hunt, he found a gap in her chef's coat, shoved her lace bra down and propped her breast up to his feasting mouth. His scruffy, scraggly hair bobbed below her chin. Her nipple caught between his teeth, he circled and flicked his tongue over the tip. "Very good, Mr. Stone."

"I can do better." He unbuttoned the flap from her shoulder to breast, revealing more skin. His fingers brushed along her collarbone as his eyes mapped and charted a course. "How much time do I have?"

"Hmm." She couldn't think, didn't want to.

His rumbling chuckles belted out an erotic melody, melting her in his arms wrapped around her stomach. His erection delved into the crease of her behind. She gripped the backs of his thighs, letting him take charge while she reaped the benefits.

Better than any meditation, her personal, magic stress reliever swept an arm over her desk, sending paper, pencils, and a tissue box flying to the floor. He ripped her jacket open and had her khakis undone and off her legs in ten seconds flat. He propped her bare butt on the metal surface. His broad shoulders shoved her legs apart as he dropped to his knees. He blew a heated breath over her slit and swiped his thumb through the slick center. Then he devoured her, a combination of sucking lips, nipping teeth, and thrusting fingers, stirring and fueling her orgasm. His eyes locked on hers, he adjusted his technique in response to her jolts and shutters until she flew over the edge.

He rose, licking her from pubic bone to chin and melting every brain cell she had left. Mouth to mouth he mumbled, "That was your appetizer. Call me when you're ready for the next course. I'll be at the bar stuffing myself with your treats in the meantime."

Unable to talk, mush on the inside and out, she let him take control again. He tugged her sprawled body off the desk and on to her wobbly feet. Unwound and on cloud nine, she let him dress her for the grand entrance. When he snapped the last clasp at her waist, she pulled him into a thankful embrace, breathing in his refreshing scent and invigorating spirit. "I love you, Mr. Stone." She batted her eyes and nipped his upper lip, glossing it with a lick. His wink and sweet-as-pie grin blessed the occasion, a reflection of her own happiness and fond appreciation for all they accomplished together.

"I aim to please, Mrs. Stone."

Oh, he did. No doubt about it, Richard Maxwell Stone had no problems satisfying his wife—over and over and over again.

Five years later . . .

Before entering her bedroom, Rick stood in the doorway and watched her primp. A dusting of pink shadow brushed over her eyes, a hint of rose on her cheekbones, and bubblegum-flavored gloss swiped across her lips. His heart lodged in his throat, anxiety clenched his gut, and a throbbing ache in his head told him he wasn't handling this situation well.

Cece tossed the makeup into a zippered clutch, glanced in the mirror and blotted a tissue between her lips, catching his watchful gaze. "Daddy, you okay?"

Whatever he looked like on the outside couldn't come close to how he felt on the inside. He'd been practicing a never-let-them-see-you-sweat face for a long time. Yet, in the twenty-plus years he'd been CEO nothing came close to the fire in his belly now.

Cece got up from the bench seat, greeting him at the door by grabbing his cheeks between her hands as she'd been doing from the moment they met. "It's just a date, Daddy. No big deal."

Not so. He knew what seventeen-year-old boys obsessed about. He pulled her into a tight hug and held her close, his chest pounding against hers. He rocked her side to side in a silent dance, her head tucked under his chin, wishing he could freeze time and she wouldn't grow up.

"You're my baby, you know that, right?"

She squeezed his back and pinched his ribs. "You're my daddy, the only one I ever had. Ya know that, right?"

Their strangled chuckles lightened the pressure some, but the fond memories left them both teary-eyed. He swept a thumb along the corner of her eyes, the green in them darker and bolder than the four-year-old version that captured his heart.

"Mama went over the rules: no kissing on the first date and only hold hands. And Kitty told me not to go past first base."

Pounding a fist on his chest, he hacked up the spit that clogged his airway after Cece's nonchalant presentation of her evil aunt's instructions. If it were up to him, his daughter wouldn't glance at boys or go out with men until she turned fifty. Outnumbered in his domain, the females of the house voted against him, ensuring he lost that battle.

After several long and drawn-out breaths, he pulled himself together and sucked up the inevitable. At some point it would happen. He might as well get it over with now. Besides, the doorbell ringing almost guaranteed the "date" hadn't ditched his daughter.

Wonderful.

Cece patted him on the cheek and reminded him of another time. "Itta be okay." Then she kissed his chin, leaving him alone to stew on that thought, taking him back to simpler, less traumatic moments.

Determined she wouldn't step foot out of the house before he got his hands on the boy toy and dispensed his do-and-die message, he raced down the stairs and into the living room. Hyped up on adrenaline, his grin came easily at the sight of a room full of reinforcements.

His evil-looking enforcers, Matt and Alex, stood behind the couch with their arms crossed over their bulky chests. The boy of the hour, a blond, pimple-faced geek with wire-rim glasses, eyeballed him just as Rick did. Adam's apple bobbing, his daughter's date sat squished between Gramps and Kat.

Rick marched forward in attack mode as he rubbed his palms together and warmed up by cracking his knuckles.

"Mr. St-Stone. Nice to meet you, sir." The stutterer got up and extended his hand. "Robert Stanford." Grandpa's snort and Kat's clucking had Robert's firm grip turning damp before Rick released it.

"Where you going? Who's driving?"

Shoulders firm and square, Robert looked him right in the

eye and gave him a straightforward answer. "The movies, sir. I have a Mustang my dad got me last year for my birthday."

Matt chimed in. "I already checked. No tickets."

Robert's chin whipped over his shoulder, aiming his reply at Matt. "I don't speed."

"Don't blow smoke, kid. You got a car built for zero to sixty in five seconds. You're not foolin' anyone." In a relaxed state with his arms bent and leaning on the back of the sofa, Alex's intense stare dared the kid to snap and challenge him, so he could strike swift and hard.

Robert pushed his glasses up the bridge of his nose. "Mr. Stone, you have my word. I won't go over the limit."

Just what Rick wanted to hear and opened the door for the next stage of his assault. He grabbed the boy's shoulders, squeezing them as he laid down the law. "Bring her home no later than ten. No R-rated movies. You touch anything but her hand, I break yours." The kid's eyes almost popped out of his head. "Anywhere else, I smash that part on you. Got me?"

Robert nodded, slowly.

"Any questions?"

More than Robert's head shook this time; the quakes under Rick's pinching grip indicated he understood.

"Good. Treat my daughter with respect at all times." His ominous message delivered, Rick wandered into the kitchen where Maggie kept Cece entertained. Their plan formulated in advance, his wife supported his need to protect his daughter. Maggie hadn't questioned his defensive approach, much.

"Is he still breathing?" Cece asked, knowing her dad too well.

Rick cuddled up from behind Maggie and stroked her swelling stomach. "He'll live." He tucked his chin into the crook of her neck and breathed in the new peach and honey almond scent he'd slathered on her skin this morning.

Cece rolled her eyes just like her aunt did about a hundred times a day and pecked her mama and him on the cheek. "I love you." After they returned the sentiment, she left them to commiserate with one another, tossing a casual see-ya-later wave over her head, but an eager little hop and skip relayed her enthusiasm to get going. As he watched his sweet pea take gigantic steps into adulthood, the only thing that quelled his displeasure was the fact that there might not be much remaining of Robert once she reached him.

Matt and Alex worshipped Cece as if she were their own daughter. Horatio Stone would lay down his own life for his precious princess. And Kat would hack off pieces one by one from anyone who hurt her bucket head. Once they all took their hits at Robert, Cece would have to accept whatever fragment or cell still had life. This event might just make it into the record books as the shortest dating experience in history.

Maggie kissed him under the chin and swayed along with him to the funky rap song playing from her cell phone. Her eclectic tastes in music were on whenever she cooked, took a shower, or planted vegetables and herbs in her garden.

He rubbed his thumb along her belly button and sucked on the birthmark at the base of her neck. "How's the baby?"

"Hmm, jumpy. He likes music too." She rested her head on his shoulder, relaxing into his chest while he felt her up. The bundle rotating and kicking in his hand.

"Maybe *she* just has the same taste and cravings as her mama?"

Maggie spun around and slung her arms over his neck. "You just jinxed yourself. Can you handle another girl? Because I hate to tell you this, your daughter gave you a C on the first date test. She cut you a break and didn't fail you for poor performance."

The thumping bass picked up and so did they, rocking their hips and gyrating against each other. "That's excellent. Maybe her mama should provide private tutoring. I have a lot of lessons in mind." He emphasized his need by rubbing his length over the seam of her shorts, his finger tracing the stitching and offering a hint at objective number one. "What a ya say, Mrs. Stone? Got any room for me?" He tucked his hand under the hem of her nylon shorts and slipped beneath her panties, marking the moist starting point with a stroking introduction.

"Mmm, I think I can find time on my schedule. But you're gonna have to give up something real good to convince me since I'm extremely tight."

The clench around his fingers, dipping in and out of her, confirmed he needed to squeeze in a couple incentives to get what he wanted. "What if I'm real, real bad and need extra special attention. You know, to perform just right."

Maggie nibbled along his bottom lip, humming in agreement.

He unzipped his jeans and lined up his erection. A gap appeared when he removed his fingers. "It looks like you're wide open right now." Ending any further discussion, he devoured her mouth, their tongues dueling each other. As an overeager and committed student, he braced for a hard and long ride. His legs spread wide, he palmed her butt and dove in head first.

School—now in session.

Since bad boys had tons of needs, he required Mrs. Stone's individualized attention to complete hours of homework before, during, and after instruction.

Under Mrs. Stone's guidance, he earned an A+++.

A perfect score.

Five years later . . .

"Mrs. C, where's that hammer?" Rick shouted, propping the framed Ansel Adams photograph of lower Yosemite Falls against the pine green wall. They had camped there last summer and since the park had been Cece's favorite, he figured she'd appreciate the addition.

"Are you looking for this?"

Not expecting her to arrive this early, the question caught him by surprise, causing him to lose his balance on the padded chair. He threw his hand out to the wall to steady his footing and glanced over his shoulder. A few inches shorter than his six-two, Cece leaned against the doorjamb, a hammer waving in her left hand. Her asymmetrical, shaggy haircut would take some getting used to. For so long she wore it hip length, often in pigtails or a ponytail until she turned ten, then she let the abundant, bouncy curls flow free. Over the weekend, she cut them all off, showing up for Sunday dinner with the hacked, uneven strands, shorter in the back, longer in the front, like sideburns jutting an inch below her jaw. If the cherry-red strands were dyed blond, she'd end up looking like her crazy aunt's twin. He didn't know whether it had been a rite of passage, Cece's coming of age, twenty-one-year-old thing to do, but the cutting-edge style made him cringe. The punk rock, grunge, head-banger combination represented an anti-executive stance. Since Cece always marched to the beat of her own drum, he shouldn't have been shocked in the least bit. Other than that though, she embraced every bit of the corporate powerhouse persona and suited attire.

"Daddy, you don't have to do that. I can put it up."

Once he got on solid footing again, he placed the frame on her desk and pulled her into a crushing bear hug. "I wanted your first day to be a good one. I got all the other pictures up. You're early."

Cece pulled her head off his shoulder and looked at him. Her are-you-crazy smile pulled up the left side of her mouth. "Daddy . . ." She pecked him on the chin, then swiped her thumb across his jaw, wiping off her lipstick. "I'm not a newbie. I can handle decorating my office."

Yeah, when Cece turned sixteen she started an internship

with him, attended board meetings, and trained for an associate's position. After graduating with a business management degree last week, he'd offered her a partnership, and she'd accepted.

He brushed his thumb along her cheek, his heart pinching at how fast his sweet pea had grown up. The city had been a huge draw. Cece moved into a Manhattan apartment a month after her acceptance letter to Columbia College arrived. He couldn't believe four years had gone by, and his baby would be embarking into the next stage of adulthood, an executive at Gateway Enterprises. His dad may have had grand visions of his son working at his side, but Rick never encouraged his daughter to become involved. He didn't want that type of pressure on a child, not the kind he'd put on himself anyway. Even so, the legacy had been achieved, and the company was at the top. In the process he'd learned about the necessity of balance. He hadn't let the job rule him after Maggie and Cece became his. Life was too short. He wanted to enjoy his blessings, and he had every reason to. With Maximilian and Katarina just finishing ninth grade and River in preschool, he kept slowing down more and more, took weekends off, and two months scattered throughout the year for family vacations—a renewed tradition that included his parents' cabin in the Catskills, amusement parks, and camping. As well as any other place or activity Maggie and the kids dreamed up. He became their enthusiastic cheerleader and participated right along with them. Just as his dad had done and brought him full circle. His mom said his father always wanted him to get married and have children. To focus on family, not work. But he hadn't needed Mom to open his eyes. He figured it out. Finally.

Now he had to move on to the next phase, handing over the reins. He hadn't anticipated Cece would jump in and take over. She approached him about learning the ropes, and even though he tried many times to talk her out of it, as usual, her persistence wore him down. And here they were, in her office, adjacent to his. But she wouldn't be doing it alone. He hired a dozen top business graduates the past month, many of them were homeless teens who lived in the Kensington shelter and interned at Gateway alongside Cece. His philanthropic daughter had become an active volunteer and contributor to the youth home. She obtained a seat on their board at eighteen and hit the pavement running, using her charms to schmooze wealthy execs and celebs, netting millions in donations. John took her under his wing, mentored her, and developed a fond affection for her during their jogging fests, which she had tagged along on since middle school. A track star, 10k events were her preference, but she won many first place ribbons and trophies for sprints, hurdles, and relays. Always on the move, she didn't slow down often, and when she did, martial arts, cooking, and ballet were her hobbies.

"It'll be okay." Cece patted him on the cheek, pulling him back to the present.

"I love you."

Cece's smiling eyes darted from him to her desk. Two crystal vases were on each corner, where he always placed her flowers. He gave them to her for every special occasion. She'd be his sweet pea and baby, forever.

"Knock, knock."

They spun around to find Maggie with her hands on her hips, shaking her head. "I guess my daughter has left me in the dust again."

Laughing the entire way to the entrance, Cece tucked an arm around her mama's waist and strolled toward her desk. "Since Miss Sally was gonna tell you how bad River was being again, I figured I'd get out of there before she gave you a report about me too."

He sat riveted to the edge of the leather trim between the two vases and secured his wife and daughter's hand in each of his. "Why? Should we prepare for something you haven't told us yet?"

With an innocent blink, Cece stuck out her tongue and sucked it back in, announcing with sugary sweetness, "I'm the stay out of trouble, good child. Just remember that when you're bailing River out. And as the older sister I feel obliged to warn you, Katarina and Max are the sneaky ones and instigators."

"Lying again, cupcake."

The boisterous, take-charge claim wrenched their attention from each other to the street- smart Don Juan in the doorway.

Rick scooted off the desk and extended his hand to the new associate. At that exact moment Cece grumbled an f-bomb under her breath. "Carter, welcome to Gateway. Eight on the nose. A good start." A firm and confident handshake gripped Rick's and spoke volumes about the tenacious, top-of-his-class Harvard graduate. Yet no one would ever suspect Carter lived on the streets for three years before volunteers at Kensington House unearthed his stabbed and bleeding remains, buried under boxes at the foot of the Manhattan Bridge, saving him at age fifteen.

"You can depend on me, sir." Carter launched another greeting directed over Rick's shoulder. "Mrs. Stone, a pleasure to see you again."

"You too. I trust my husband and daughter will keep you busy, but make sure you have fun. Take time to enjoy other things."

Carter's eyes flicked to Cece and narrowed. "Oh, don't worry, I plan to." Then switched to his boss. "Mr. Stone, where do you want me to start?"

Rick wanted to begin by knocking the smug smirk off Carter's face and throwing him out, far away from his fit-to-be-tied daughter. But Cece banished her daddy and his overprotective instincts years ago after he showed up unannounced at her apartment, let himself in with his emergency key, and got the wind knocked out of him when he found a boxer-clad jock flipping pancakes in her kitchen. His daughter strolled in a few seconds later, wearing a crotch-skimming towel with tangled, wet locks dripping over her bare shoulders.

Not only did he have to bite his tongue, but he had to swear on a stack of bibles he wouldn't interfere in her love life. Not that she had boyfriends. No, his daughter embraced college freedom and took after his one-night stand escapades. Payback and punishment for his wild and no-commitments attitude—his adult daughter's choices came back to haunt him.

"Oh, I'll take care of him all right. He'll be tossed out with the trash in three . . . two . . ." As Cece spit out her threat and before her fire-breathing temper sparked, Carter wandered around Rick and drifted to a stop at her stilettos, taking her on toe to toe.

Since the two of them began as Gateway interns together, Rick had watched them butt heads. Carter's dogged strength and savviness gave him a supreme advantage. His uncanny knack for reading people made him an excellent hire, and regardless of their differences, when Carter and Cece collaborated on accounts, they closed deals better than anyone else.

Wider than a linebacker, Carter's shoulders blocked Rick's view. Maggie huddled up next to him. She looped her arm through his and linked their fingers together. Laying her head on his shoulder, she prepared to watch the fireworks. With his hands tied, he rocked back on his heels and waited for the explosive show. Reduced to mere spectators, but not too old to get their kicks, Maggie aligned her lips along his ear and whispered, "Fifty bucks she has him on his knees in less than ten seconds."

Not willing to make a wager, or picture Carter in that position at the foot of his daughter, he swallowed his grumbling protest and took the sucker bet. Hard to resist his wife, he upped the ante. "I want it noted I'm throwing down a hundred under duress. My man card and his are about to go down in flames."

Maggie patted his chest and pinched his chin, pulling it toward her and away from the head-on collision and catastrophe. The teeny gap and her deliriously happy smile appeared as she pronounced, "Thou shall submit to the mighty Wonder Woman."

And he did—they did, in two-point-five seconds.

Dear Readers

Thank you for reading UNLIKELY ALLIES. If you enjoyed it, I would appreciate a shout out.

Review it: Please consider writing a review, either at the retailer site where you purchased UNLIKELY ALLIES, or on your blog.

Recommend it: Know other romance readers? Please let them know about UNLIKELY ALLIES. Recommend it to friends, family, book clubs, and others via social media. I'm always looking for the next great read too. Do you have a suggestion? Let me know about it.

Visit my website: *www.cckoen.com*. Future stories and information about my debut novel, INTENSITY, and the sequel, SERENITY, can be found there.

About the Author

C.C. Koen writes contemporary romance with a twist. An avid reader who enjoys mystery and suspense, her stories will never be what you expect. Determined to find adventure in her dreams and life, she enjoys skydiving, sailing and any activity that challenges her. Teacher by day, romance writer at night produce an active imagination that comes to life in her writing.

Chit-chat with me:

Facebook: *www.facebook.com/cckoenbooks*

Twitter: *http://twitter.com/authorcckoen* @authorcckoen

Goodreads: *www.goodreads.com/authorcckoen*

Visit my website: *www.cckoen.com.*

Other Books by
C.C. Koen

The Path to Serenity Series
Book 1: INTENSITY
Book 2: SERENITY, release date: October 2015
Book 3: BRANDED, release date: 2016

www.ingramcontent.com/pod-product-compliance
Lightning Source LLC
Chambersburg PA
CBHW060515180626
46817CB00002B/366